Gary Gottes with
degrees in Theater and Education from New York
University. After working as a probation officer in
New York jails and elsewhere, he moved to Los
Angeles and became chief copywriter in a large
advertising agency, creating dozens of TV and radio
commercials. Subsequently a journalist specialising
in the entertainment industry, he has written two
previous novels: *The Violet Closet* and *Blood
Harvest*.

Married, with a young son, Gary Gottesfeld now
lives in Encino, California.

Also by Gary Gottesfeld

The Violet Closet
Blood Harvest

Ill Wind

Gary Gottesfeld

Copyright ©1993 Gary Gottesfeld
The right of Gary Gottesfeld to be identified as the Author of
the Work has been asserted by him in accordance with the
Copyright, Designs and Patents Act 1988.

First published in Great Britain in 1993
by HEADLINE BOOK PUBLISHING PLC

First published in paperback in 1993
by HEADLINE BOOK PUBLISHING PLC

A HEADLINE FEATURE PAPERBACK

This edition published by arrangement with
Ballantine Books, A Division of Random House, Inc.

10 9 8 7 6 5 4 3 2

ISBN 0 7472 4168 6

Typeset by Avon Dataset Ltd, Bidford-on-Avon
Printed and bound in Great Britain by
HarperCollins Manufacturing, Glasgow

HEADLINE BOOK PUBLISHING PLC
Headline House
79 Great Titchfield Street
London W1P 7FN

For Marie Harris and Jim Hill

I would like to thank forensic anthropologist
Dr Judy Suchy for the hours she spent in introducing
me to the living world of bones. Without
her help this book could never have been written.

FURTHER ACKNOWLEDGEMENTS

He discovereth deep things out of darkness;
and bringeth out to light the shadow of death.
Job 12:22

The sleeping and the dead
Are but as pictures; 'tis the eye of childhood
That fears the painted devil.
Shakespeare: *Macbeth*

Prologue

Hugo Frye stood on the wooden balcony and sipped his breakfast coffee like he always did on the days he had to be in Northern California. His puffy basset-hound eyes looked out past the lush Madrone and Redwood trees, focusing on the endless span of cobalt ocean. Except there was a sense of uneasiness about this morning and it bothered him. The water, he realized, was unusually calm, and the air too heavy for this mountainous terrain. Normally, the waves would shatter against the high cliffs below and the wind would feel like cold needles jabbing at his skin.

His small, lithesome body suddenly tensed up when he heard the sounds of the coyotes howling up in the mountains. They were night animals. What were they doing up at this hour?

There was something wrong out there; he could feel it.

Hugo was starting to become irritated by all of this. He put his cup and saucer down on the table, reached into his pocket and took out his old Buck knife that he had had since he was a boy. Unfurling the blade, he began to carve the figure of a large centipede on the column of the balcony. The image took its place alongside the hundreds he had already cleaved in the guard-rail over the years.

When he finished, he slowly traced his finger over the perfectly detailed insect and counted its multitude of legs. This simple, almost unconscious act had always helped ease the apprehension he felt when he was away from home.

But not today.

Yes, something was definitely wrong. The restlessness inside him did not leave – it was growing stronger.

The coyotes were his dream helper. They were howling louder now, warning him that something bad was going to happen.

His mood suddenly began to turn foul. He plunged the blade deep into the railing, splitting the engraved centipede in two.

BOOK ONE

The Unearthing

1

The three white finger-bones jutting out of the makeshift grave were curved inward, as if patiently waiting to clutch some unsuspecting soul by the ankle and drag him down into the pit with the other remains.

Dutch squatted down by the mound, opened his worn black leather forensics case and took out a small brush. As he leaned over to get a closer look at the arched fingers, they suddenly reminded him of the frozen white jumbo shrimps he had stored away in his freezer a couple of months ago and had completely forgotten about.

There was also a skull next to the phalangeal bones. The Dutchman gently removed some of the dirt away from it with the brush. Its hollow eye-sockets were staring up at him, and the mouth was drawn open like it was pleading for its life back.

Pat Segata, the coroner, walked over and knelt down next to him. 'It could be a hit. You tell me, OK?'

'As soon as I get it all uncovered, Pat.'

'We found a shovel next to the grave.' He pointed his finger at the rust-coated spade leaning up against a boulder. 'Half the body is buried, and the other half isn't. Weird. Maybe the killer just got tired of digging and quit.'

'And just left his shovel lying around, huh? Not too smart,' he said dubiously. Looking down at the body, Dutch could see why Pat thought the person was murdered. The skeleton was buried in a pit that only came as high as the victim's chest. The rest of the bones were exposed. That bothered him. Why dig a vertical grave and not a horizontal one? Was this some kind of a ritual killing? Hits were usually done with a bullet to the back of the head. He arched his neck around to view the base of the skull. There was no hole in the cranium. No, not a hit, he thought. *Uh uh . . . something else.*

Suddenly the ground started to move, followed by a roar like the sound of distant thunder.

White-hot panic shot through the Dutchman, making the blood pound in his temples. Black spots began to dart past his eyes. He frantically reached out and grabbed Pat's arm and held it tightly.

The rumbling lasted for almost twenty seconds, then it stopped as suddenly as it began.

'Jesus, you OK, Dutchman? You're white as a sheet. I didn't know quakes got to you like that. The sonofabitch nearly knocked me on my ass,' Pat said. His lips were stretched across his teeth; he was trying hard not to laugh at the anthropologist's frenzied state.

'I'm all right.' Dutch released his grip on Pat's arm. His hands were shaking uncontrollably. He quickly glanced over at the sheriffs up on the hill. They were leaning up against their black and white four-by-fours, holding their stomachs, hooting, not bothering to hide their laughter. Two rookies were chortling the hardest.

Fuck them! They don't understand, Dutch thought. *Nobody did.*

6

He regained control of himself and looked down at the body. The quake had caused the fingers and the skull to break lose from the rest of the remains.

When he had first arrived in this desolate area of the Cucumonga Wilderness, he found those cops traipsing all over the grave. Their footprints were imbedded everywhere, infuriating the Dutchman. 'Why did you let them get this close, Pat? You know better than that,' he said, shaking his head.

The coroner shrugged, giving a tired, irritated smile. There was a sheen of sweat on his face. 'The quake put you in a bad mood, Dutch?'

He didn't answer Pat.

'Hell, we've been here almost two hours waiting for you in this damn heat. Forensics already scoured every inch of the area. So did your assistant. They couldn't find anything. If this was a fresh body and not just bones, we'd have been out of here a long time ago. The only reason we're here now is because the law says we need your Rabbinical blessing to tell us that they're human remains and not a goddamned sabre-toothed tiger in that ditch. I'm a doctor; you think I don't know what human bones look like? That's a Cartier watch dangling on the victim's left wrist-bone. I bet that means this guy's not Cro-Magnon, right? See, I'm not so dumb.'

Dutch stretched his neck from side to side, trying to rid himself of the small residue of fear that still clung stubbornly to his muscles. 'What else do you know, Pat?'

'I know somebody killed him, then did a half-assed job of burying the body. Simple as that. *Uno*, *dos*, *tres*.' He slapped his hands together with each number he called out.

Dutch nodded. '*Uno*, *dos*, *tres*, huh?' He normally liked the little coroner. Sometimes when he was in the city, they'd even go out for a few drinks and eat Italian. But right now he wasn't in the mood. He looked down at Pat, frowning. His weathered face was turning red through his two-day beard stubble. 'Keep those cops the fuck away, Pat. I didn't travel sixty miles on a gridlocked freeway for this entry-level shit.'

Pat saw his face, held up his hands and backed off. He had worked with this forensic anthropologist for too many years not to know his disposition. He'd seen first-hand what the Dutchman was capable of when provoked.

The coroner stood up, wiping the brown dirt off the knees of his navy 'wash and wear' suit. He then nervously ran his fingers through his thick black Asian hair that had streaks of grey woven through it. Standing, Pat was almost the same height as the Dutchman who was kneeling. The Japanese pathologist was five-four and weighed one hundred and thirty-three pounds. The Dutchman was six-five and weighed close to two hundred and twenty.

Pat walked up the hill, went over to the deputies, and said something to them. Their laughter began to fade.

Tara Malachi, Dutch's assistant, made her way past the officers carrying a black metal suitcase filled with her tools. She was a tall, attractive woman in her late twenties, and wore an over-sized, white T-shirt, khaki Bermuda shorts and dust-covered Reeboks. Her dark hair was short, spiked on top and duck-tailed at the back. Several studs and rings adorned the rims of her ears. Tara was a lesbian, never hiding that fact from Dutch or from the Anthropology Department at Point

Dume University, where they both taught. Dutch respected that, and kept her on staff despite grumbling from several faculty members. She knew bones better than anyone else — anyone except maybe him.

When she came to the grave, she bent down next to Dutch, opened the case and took out the trowels. 'I tried to keep these assholes away,' she said, as if reading his mind.

'I know that.' He trusted Tara more than anyone else. 'Have you photographed everything?'

She nodded. 'Two hours ago,' she said, referring to his lateness.

Pat came back and knelt next to them. 'What do you think, Dutch?'

'Patience . . . patience.' Dutch glanced over to a boulder jutting out of the ground a couple of feet away. Barely distinguishable capital letters, covered with dust, were scratched into it. He wiped the dirt from the rock with his hand and shaded his eyes from the sun so as to see better. The only letters he could recognize were H — A — R. The rest were illegible. At the bottom were some numbers. He could just read a 7 and a 92. Dates, Dutch thought. This was a makeshift tombstone, he suddenly realized. H — A — R was part of a name; 7 — 92 was the day and year.

'Who found the body?' he asked, turning to the coroner.

Pat pointed to the three people sitting up on the bluff, watching them. 'Hikers. They go to some Baptist college in Covina.'

The Dutchman turned and looked at them. They were lying against an incline, next to a dust-covered, expensive BMW, their eyes closed and their faces angled toward the sun. One was a girl — real pretty, with long, tan legs. She was wearing hiking boots and faded, cut-off jeans rolled up to the cheeks of her behind. He took his round, steel-rimmed glasses from the pocket of his denim work shirt and put them on. Nice legs, he thought. Sun freckles around the rim of her turned-up nose. He didn't remember Baptists looking like that when he was growing up in Ohio.

'That one's alive. Try concentrating on this dead one, OK?' Tara said scornfully.

Using the trowels, they carefully dug around the sternum, making a deeper hole. There were pieces of a pink-coloured T-shirt covering the rib cage. Digging further down, they uncovered strands of blond hair along with broken tortoiseshell glasses.

'How long do you think it's been here?' Pat asked. He didn't refer to the skeletal remains as *he* or *she*, because at this point he wasn't sure of the sex.

The Dutchman lowered his head and sniffed the skull. He could smell a dank aroma, which meant the body hadn't been here all that long. He then put his fingertips on the head, stroking it lightly. It felt porous. Shading his eyes with his other hand, he stared up at the sun.

'The bones aren't bleached yet. I'd say maybe three, four weeks – that's it,' Dutch said. He looked at the 7-92 on the stone slab once again. That date was probably accurate for the time of death, he thought.

Dutch glanced down at the ground. 'Lots of footprints. No way of telling whose now. Especially after you let those yahoos run around here like a herd of wild elephants,' he said, pointing his thumb toward the cops.

Dutch looked at the skull. The head was pulled back and the mouth agape. Had the victim been screaming

10

in pain when he or she died? Where there weren't footprints, he could see markings on the ground from animals and insects that had got to the corpse. Several metacarpal and phalangeal bones from the hands were missing. Probably carried away by carnivores.

Next to the skull were two pieces of opaque plastic tubing buried in the ground. He tried to pull them out, but they held firm. He wondered what they were attached to.

Dutch looked at Pat, as if to ask him the same question. The pathologist shrugged. Then he looked at Tara. She shook her head.

'It's time to get our friend out of here,' Dutch said. He stood up and walked up the hill, heading toward the deputies.

The older veterans, knowing what to expect, backed away from him.

Dutch didn't bother with them. Instead he went over to the two rookies who had been laughing the loudest at him before. They were wearing newly pressed uniforms and sported perfectly trimmed moustaches. One, looking like Erik Estrada, wore Porsche sunglasses and had a toothpick dangling from the side of his mouth.

'Need some help, guys,' Dutch said to them impassively, as he scratched the stubble on his chin.

The deputies looked over to their sergeant, standing with the other officers, to see if it was OK. Their commander nodded, the back of his hand now covering the grin that was spreading over his face.

Dutch brought them over to the grave and knelt beside it.

The tenderfoots, looking eager, also bent down and waited for instructions.

The Dutchman said to them, 'Start digging.'

The one with the Porsche sunglasses asked, 'With what?'

Dutch looked at Pat, then back at the rookie. He pointed to the deputy's clean, soft hands. 'Those.'

'What about that shovel?' The man motioned to the rusty implement leaning up against the boulder.

Dutch shook his head. 'Can't. It's evidence.'

There was chuckling from the older officers up on the hill. Sensing something was up, the rookies glanced over at their sergeant once again. Seeing the resolute look on his face, they began to dig.

A few minutes later the rookies saw what the other officers had been laughing about: skin attached to the bones of the lower skeletal area. With these bones came maggots − thousands of them − slithering in and out of the pelvic canal. The sheriff with the Porsche glasses stood up, clawing at his hands and arms, trying to remove the soft-bodied, legless creatures that had attached themselves to him.

'Don't worry. They don't like eating anything that's still alive,' the Dutchman said.

Pat snickered, so did the sheriffs up on the bluff. Only Tara remained serious, frowning at Dutch's antics.

The young officer ran over to the creek and threw his whole body into it, frantically trying to wash the vermin off himself.

'What about you?' Dutch said, turning to the other deputy, a Latino. 'You want to take a dip with your friend?'

Looking pale, the police officer forced his dry lips to crack into a slight grin, 'Nah, I seen bigger varmints in East LA − with hair and four legs.'

Dutch nodded, smiling. At least *his* sunglasses were police-issue, not like pretty boy's. Turning to Pat, he said, 'Our skeleton is definitely a man.' He pointed to the pelvic bone.

Pat acknowledged his comment. He knew a woman's pelvis would be wider, so she could bear children.

When they had dug past the rotted pants and down to the ankle-bones, Pat, Tara and the Latino officer helped Dutch carefully pull the remains out of the opening. After laying the skeleton and the loose pieces of bones on a stretcher, Dutch went back to the hole and peered into it.

At the bottom of the pit was a liquor bottle. Next to it was a blue-coloured container and a partially decomposed brown leather wallet. The two plastic tubes were inserted into the openings of the bottle and the container. Ignoring the maggots, Dutch jumped in, grabbed these objects, then quickly leaped back out. The deputies and the detectives up on the hill were already coming down to see what he had found.

Dutch first examined the liquor bottle. He flicked a maggot off its lip and scrubbed the dirt from the label. Smiling, he said, 'This guy had good taste in scotch. Scarpa single malt. Distilled in 1960. Stuff like this sells for fifty, maybe sixty dollars a bottle.' He then bent down and lifted the plastic container, pulling out the tube. When he looked at the blue lettering on the side, his smile disappeared.

'What is it?' Pat asked.

'Liquid Draino.' Dutch looked over towards the gurney, and at the skeleton's open mouth.

'Oh, Christ! You mean the guy drank that!' Pat

said, shaking his head and wiping his sweaty face with the sleeve of his jacket.

The Dutchman picked up the wallet, carefully pulled out the fragile driver's licence and looked at the photograph. A young man, Caucasian, around thirty years old with blond wavy hair, smiled back at him. He had the clean-cut face of a go-getter, a man who knew what he wanted. The name and address next to the picture were still readable. Harry Steiner was the man's name. That accounted for the HAR on the boulder. Most of the licence number was intact — at least enough for an ID to be made. The coiled edge of a business card stuck partially out from one of the pockets in the wallet. Dutch removed it. HARRY STEINER, CPA, was stencilled on it in raised italic lettering. He looked up to the top of the hill, toward the 740 BMW covered with dust. It belonged to the victim, he realized. He handed the wallet to one of the detectives, then went over to the gurney and peered down at the remains. He could almost visualize the flesh on the skull, the mouth twisted in agony, the screams as the acid worked its way down his trachea to his stomach, eroding his intestines.

'Suicide?' Pat asked.

'Yeah, I think so,' Dutch said, placing the bottle of Draino next to the gurney. 'He must have dug his own grave with that shovel you found. Then he got in, covered himself with dirt, and proceeded to drink half a bottle of scotch through the plastic straw. With the amount he drank, and with the sun beating down on his head, I'd say he was pretty wasted by the time he got to the second tube, the one that was connected to the Draino.'

'Then it's not a murder?' Pat mumbled, sounding somewhat disappointed.

'Sorry, Pat. Just a creative kind of guy who decided to give himself a goodbye party and a funeral before he killed himself. Even made a tombstone out of that rock, with his name and date of death on it. It's hara-kiri, LA style.'

As he walked up the hill back to his truck, a sadness began to overwhelm the Dutchman. He shouldn't have looked at the picture of the guy on the licence. Now the man was real to him: flesh and blood. Working with bones was different: there was no face, no name on them.

He was pretty sure Harry Steiner had a family that was still frantically looking for him. Probably an over-achiever who cracked up from the pressure of trying to keep everything afloat.

As Dutch got into his Bronco, he began to believe that there was something almost righteous about what this man had done. Harry Steiner wanted to feel the agony of the acid eating through his stomach. That way he would know that he was still alive, right up to the very end. Pain and consciousness – life's two inseparable partners.

As he started to drive away, he saw Pat leaning against the coroner's van and talking into the car phone. Looking in Dutch's direction, the small Japanese coroner put up his hand and waved for him to stop. He dropped the phone on the front seat of the vehicle, then trotted over to Dutch's truck. His face was glowing with excitement.

'What is it?' Dutch asked.

'I don't know yet,' Pat said, breathing heavily. 'That was the Beverly Hills PD on the phone. They said the quake uncovered some skeletons there.'

'Old or new?'

'They don't know. It's too soon to tell. They want to know where you're going to be, in case they need you.'

Dutch leaned his head against the cloth seat and rubbed his eyes. The thought of a drink sounded good. It would help calm his juggled nerves. 'Papa Padakos,' he said to Pat, popping the clutch into first and driving off.

It took Dutch almost two hours to get back to Malibu. Traffic was heavy on the 10 Freeway, going in both directions. The earthquake had closed a lot of offices, sending hordes of people home early. He turned the radio on and scanned the dial until he came to the all-news station:

6.01 on the Richter. Moderate damage downtown. The 405 at Sepulveda Pass closed due to rock slides. The eastern wing of Calabasas Hospital collapsed. Mass destruction in many areas of Beverly Hills. Rodeo Drive closed because of rock, glass and marble littering the heavily cracked street. Wide fissures in the pavements of Santa Monica Boulevard and other streets of Beverly Hills. Thirty-three people injured so far. No reports as yet of fatalities.

The heaviest devastation seemed to be in Beverly Hills. That was likely. He knew there was a huge fault under the area. Bones had been unearthed there. That was also possible. Ancient Indians' bones were always turning up in Beverly Hills.

The thought of quakes terrified him. *No, nobody could understand.*

His neck dampened with sweat as he began remembering that cold night back in the hills of Xenia, Ohio, when he was seven years old. The smell of Shalimar perfume seemed to permeate the air around him whenever he thought about it. Then the other odour came, the one he dreaded, the sickening, sweet one. Both smells were connected like Siamese twins. His mind just wouldn't let them go.

Couldn't let them go.

Sometimes he wouldn't think about what had happened then for months at a time. Then the images would come lunging back, haunting the halls of his mind like old lovers.

The Dutchman despised the forces of nature — despised their indifference and the pain they inflicted.

The walls of his windpipe suddenly felt as if they were closing up, making it hard for him to breathe. Dutch gasped for air.

Don't let the panic start again!

With trembling hands, he grabbed a cassette from the glove compartment and pushed it into the tape-player. Billie Holiday. That beautiful, drug-coated voice came up and began doing things to his head, clearing it of bad feelings. *Nobody could do it like her! Nobody!* He turned it up loud, making the car speakers rattle.

> *Mamma may have,*
> *Papa may have,*
> *But God bless the child that has its own . . .*

He fell again under her spell. Air began to enter his

17

lungs once more, and the smell finally went away.

At the beach, the Dutchman went north on Highway
1. Here, the traffic was also backed up. One of the
lanes was closed because of slides. He slowly snaked
past the expensive, pastel-coloured Santa Fe style
houses on the sand, with the ocean waves licking at
their huge bay windows.

Several miles further up, he came to the Malibu pier
and turned left into its parking lot. He knew Tara
would be waiting for him.

Dutch gave his Bronco to the valet to park. As he
walked towards the pier, he could feel his shirt sticking
to his back from sitting so long in the car. The salt air
coming from the ocean felt good against his face, and
he couldn't imagine how people would want to live in
that hot, desert wilderness that he had just come from.

Unlike the trendy restaurant one door down, the bar
the Dutchman walked into catered mostly to locals and
fishermen. No celebrities, no men with ponytails, no
peach-coloured walls and bleached oak floors. The bar
was shellacked mahogany and smelled of freshly
caught fish. Photographs of fishermen holding up
their catches and boats of all kinds covered every inch
of space on the panelled walls. The men, with jagged
fingernails and calloused hands, sat at the bar and at
tables covered with checkered oil cloth. They drank
boilermakers and talked about the run of rockfish and
sand sharks. A TV set hung over the counter, showing
a special news report on the massive earthquake.
Several of the locals were hunched over in their seats,
watching.

Papa Padakos was behind the bar. He was a short
Greek with faded tattoos running down his hairy arms.

18

When he saw the Dutchman walk past him, he held up a shot glass and smiled in greeting. The Dutchman nodded back.

Tara was already there, sitting at a table near the window, her foot up on the sill. She was staring out at the ocean, smoking a cigarette, deep in thought. A bottle of Anchor Steam dangled from her dirt-caked hand.

Dutch sat down at the table, reached for her packet of Marlboros, took one out and lit up.

'Buy your own,' she said, continuing to look out the window, her mind still on something.

Smoking his cigarette, he sat silently and watched the late afternoon light playing on her cream-coloured face and violet eyes. The Dutchman liked her face, liked her skin, liked the fuzzy hairs on her arms, liked the sharp angles of her thin, hard body. He even liked watching her now while she was thinking. Her eyes seemed depthless, sparkling with brilliance. There was a sadness there, too, he realized. It was always there with Tara, something unreachable underlying her whole being. Hell of a lady, though, he thought. *Too bad we have different tastes.* They had made love once, a couple of years ago, when her girlfriend left her for another woman. They had come to this bar, had a few drinks, talked about how their lives were fucked up, cried, got shit-faced. Eventually their hands touched under the table and their fingers entwined. They stayed that way for a long time, with their eyes locked on to each other's. The Dutchman finally took her back to his place. He was pretty drunk that night, but he remembered her as being a warm, tender lover. He also remembered the tattoo of a small butterfly under her left breast. Looking at her across

19

the table now, he wished he could see its blue wings one more time.

A buxom waitress came with the Dutchman's boilermaker. He took the jigger of whiskey, swallowed it down, then quickly took a gulp of the draft beer.

'Early for that, isn't it?' Tara said, finally looking at him.

'Early is relative,' he said, arching his bushy brows. 'By this time, in Ohio, kids are humping their girlfriends in the back seats of their daddy's car under the moonlight.'

'Pat looked disappointed about today's find,' she said with a wry smile.

'Pat's always disappointed when unearthed bones aren't the remnants of a serial killer's joyride. He works for Orville Priest and wants to please him. And the only way to please that sociopathic Chief Medical Examiner is to produce him a corpse that could get him media coverage. His biggest kick is getting up in front of the cameras and giving nicknames to the killers. ''The LA Basin Strangler'', ''The Calabasas Slicer''. The man's an asshole.'

Outside, a seagull with a piece of bread in its beak perched itself on the beam of the pier and stared at the Dutchman through the window. He stared back at it, drinking his beer, wondering which would be the first to give in and look away.

'How's Therese?' Tara asked hesitantly.

A streak of pain shot through the Dutchman's stomach, as if he had just swallowed a jigger of that Draino. He sighed and looked away from the bird. Squeezing the beer glass tightly, he said, 'The same. Hates my guts. Nothing's changed on that front.' He clasped his eyes shut, letting the pain take over his

20

body. He had discovered a long time ago that if he didn't fight the hurt, it would eventually ease to a dull throbbing. He could live with that. When the ache finally subsided, he said quietly, 'I'm seeing her on Sunday. I have to sign some final papers for the divorce.'

'I hear she's with someone else.'

Dutch put down the glass, rubbed his eyes, and ran his fingers through his thick blond hair. 'You know about that, huh?'

Tara nodded. 'She's an archaeologist. We're a small group. Everybody knows what the other is doing.'

A bruised laugh shot out of his throat. 'Hey, that's terrific! I'm a soap-opera star.' He let out a deep groan, then said softly, 'It had to happen, I guess. This guy coming on the scene makes it official between us.'

'Not always'.

'Shit. It was me that killed Max. I should have been more careful. I should have checked the weather. I should have been watching closer! I . . .'

She put a finger on his lips to silence him. 'It's OK, Dutch,' she whispered. She could see his pain over the loss of his son, and wanted to say something to ease it. Except there were no words to minimize this kind of hurt; she knew that.

He took her finger in his hand and kissed it. She was a friend, a good one. Nodding to the waitress, he ordered one more boilermaker. Tara shook her head, no, to another beer.

'Stay in the department,' he said to her, clearing his throat, wanting to change the subject.

'Uh uh, and we've been through *this* before, so don't start,' she said smiling.

21

Dutch leaned into the table. 'Come on, Tara, listen . . .'

'Forget it, Dutch. This is my last year. I don't need department heads with sticks up their asses telling me who I should bed down with.'

'Screw them! You love bones, same as me,' he said.

'I love old ones, not like that fruitcake we found today. I don't want to see another bone that isn't at least fifty thousand years old.' Her voice suddenly filled with exhilaration. 'There's that new dig going on in Tanzania. Bones have been found that may pre-date your Maybellene by two or three hundred thousand years. I've been invited to go. Why don't you come, Dutch? They'd love it if you did. There's nobody better than you. What the hell is here in California? The university hasn't even renewed your contract to teach next year. You'll be out of a job. You can't say this is bad timing!'

Yes, he was going to be out of a job soon; he knew that. The Anthropology Department had told him that they didn't like the way he did things. He wasn't scholarly enough, they said. They also didn't like the way he put off publishing his findings. That bothered them more than anything; because the more the department published, the more funds it received. Dutch had nothing against cut-and-dried articles; he just hated writing them. He already knew about the dig that was gearing up in Tanzania. Skeletal remains that could possibly be older than Maybellene. Damn! While heading an expedition several years ago, he had discovered Maybellene's bones in an Ethiopian gorge.

That was also where he first met Therese. She was the chief archaeologist on the dig. He had named the *A. afarensis* skeleton 'Maybellene' because Therese

22

loved Chuck Berry. The discovery caused a great stir in anthropological circles. She was the oldest remains ever found. Three million years old! Would he like to go back to Africa again and work on an even more remarkable unearthing? Hell, yes! He then cleared his head of the idea. No, it was impossible! He couldn't even afford the luxury of such thoughts. Letting out a breath, he looked at Tara and slowly shook his head.

'Wrong timing.'

Closing her eyes, she nodded in understanding. She suddenly leaned over and kissed Dutch on the cheek, then got up to leave.

'I have a date,' she said with a false, nervous laugh.

Dutch picked up on it. 'With Monica?' There was contempt in his voice. 'Why are you going back to her again? That woman's about as faithful as a Black Widow.'

'I guess I like my women unpredictable,' she said, shrugging uncomfortably. She blew him a kiss on her way out.

No, you like them to hurt you, he thought as he stared at the back of her thin tan legs racing out the door. *That's the only way you can feel safe to show your love. You need your bed to be made out of thorns – like me.* They both were in pain, Dutch realized, but for different reasons. Most times Tara would keep her pain inside. Occasionally, when the suffering got too much for her to bear, she would come to him like the night they slept together. There was so much that Dutch didn't understand about his assistant. As hard as he tried, he could never pinpoint her. She was as tenuous as the butterfly tattooed on her breast.

He finished his boilermaker and ordered another one. The sun was beginning to set, turning the sky into

23

a pale, blood-red haze. For the next two hours he sat there thinking about Therese and his son, Max. The familiar grief he had been living with since the day of the accident overtook him once again.

My son! My sweet boy!

Feeling the need for company, he turned his eyes toward the window, hoping to see the seagull.

It was gone.

Dutch's trailer home bordered on Trancus and Malibu. By the time he arrived there, the sky was the colour of black silk. As he got out of the Bronco, he could hear the whirring of a helicopter directly overhead. A searchlight from its cockpit was scouring the area. It was the police. A robbery must have taken place – probably at one of the mansions owned by a movie star up on the bluff, he thought.

When he opened the screen door and turned on the light, he found the mess he had left that morning waiting for him: books and papers piled so high on his desk that they formed a pyramid; jazz CDs stacked on the floor and on top of the big Bose speakers in the corners of the room; a trail of dry dog-food leading into the kitchen; empty bottles of Corona on the coffee table.

Therese would never have approved. She always kept their house squeaky clean when they were married. 'No one can function in a disorderly world,' she'd tell him, while organizing Dutch's desk with neat piles of his research papers on one side and his books lined up like the guards at Buckingham Palace on the other. Everything had its rightful place in her world. He used to open up his closet in the morning to be greeted by a methodical array of colours. His pants were queued exactly one inch apart from each other: first came the blue ones; navy, cobalt, azure − on up to powder. Then the browns: deep tans, beige, light chestnut, faded khaki. Blacks and whites had their own section. The same thing with his shirts.

'She'd throw a fucking fit if she could see this place now,' he said out loud. Except that would never happen. She hated him too much to ever come here.

He thought of Max again. All those nights of changing diapers. How many all together? He once figured it out to be around three thousand. Somewhere, a twenty-foot mound of non-biodegradable, shit-covered plastic lay buried underground with Max's name on it. It was the only thing left showing that his son had cast his shadow on this planet.

Dutch walked over to a gurney with a sheet covering it, at the end of the trailer. He removed the sheet and looked down at the assembled bones of Maybellene. The reason Dutch had the remains here was because the Ethiopian government wanted her back and the US State Department said no. Since Dutch was the one that discovered her, he was allowed babysitting duties until both countries worked out their problem. He knew he should keep the bones in a safer place than here, like the LA County museum, except he wanted them near him. Her skeleton was like the court jester from the dark side of his soul. Instead of a son, he had a pretend doll, except without skin and organs.

Looking down at her now, an ironic thought struck him: Maybellene was four feet tall − the same height Max would be today if he was alive.

He put the sheet over the remains, went into the kitchen and opened the refrigerator for a Corona.

Bitch, his sixteen-year-old black Lab, was lying on a blanket next to the stove. She picked up her tired head, whimpered, wagged her tail slightly, then put her wet, slobbering jowls back down on the quilt. He bent down and scratched her in her favourite place, under the ear. The old dog stuck out her tongue, trying to lick his fingers. He let her get in a couple of laps, then moved his hand away. Dutchman wondered when she would die. *Bones. Everything he loves turns to bones.*

Then he heard the phone in the living-room ring.

Dutch picked up the receiver. It was attached to an answering machine. Looking at the digital counter, he saw that he had received several calls while he was out.

'Hello,' Dutch said loudly into the phone, trying to talk over the sound of the helicopter up above. The whirring noise was stronger now and seemed to be hovering right over his house. Outside his window, he could see the beam of its searchlight frantically darting across his patch of beach.

'Where the hell have you been? I tried calling you at that bar you hang out in, the one that stinks of fish, but you'd already left.' It was Pat Sagata. His voice was cracking with excitement.

'What's up?' the Dutchman said in a deep throat, putting his legs up on the coffee table. He stuck the phone under his chin for support, freeing his hands to remove the cap of the beer bottle.

'What's up!' Pat said astonished. 'Don't you know? Where have you been for the last five hours?' Pat said something else, but Dutch couldn't hear. The noise of the chopper was getting louder.

'I can't hear you!' Dutch screamed into the phone.

'The earthquake ripped open Beverly Hills like a can of sardines, my friend! There are more bones scattered about than you can count,' Pat screamed back.

The noise outside was becoming deafening. All Dutch could hear were fragments of what Pat was saying. Something about bones . . .artifacts . . . another civilization.

'What? I can't hear you. This goddamn helicopter is breaking my eardrums!' the Dutchman yelled. Then he looked out his window and saw a blinding sight. The chopper was now hovering inches above the beach just outside his door. Sand was swirling around like a crazed whirlwind. Dutch read what was stencilled on its metal side: BEVERLY HILLS POLICE DEPARTMENT. 'You're not going to believe what I'm seeing, Pat.'

'I know what you're seeing. Just get the hell in it!' Pat bellowed.

The cockpit was illuminated and Dutch could make out the pilot. Sitting next to him was Tara. She was wearing a shit-faced grin and was waving frantically for him to get in. He had never seen her this euphoric – not even when she was talking about that dig in Tanzania. Whatever happened in Beverly Hills this afternoon must have been big. Without saying goodbye, he hung up on Pat. He stared at the phone for several seconds, smiling, thinking. The Dutchman hadn't felt this alive in a long time. Then he raised a fist in the air and let out a raucous yell, like he imagined Harry Steiner might have done right before he guzzled down the Draino.

2

'It's like a goddamn war zone down there!' the pilot shouted to Dutch and Tara over the engine noise of the helicopter. They were circling several hundred feet above the northern section of Beverly Hills.

More than a war zone. Much more! the Dutchman thought. Through the globular cockpit he could see the fancy boulevards and curving drives lined with palm trees. In all the years he had worked on digs he had never seen anything like this; nothing came even close. The entire area from where Santa Monica Boulevard crossed Wilshire, all the way east to where it met Doheny, was closed off to traffic. Sunset, as far south as Olympic, was also cordoned off.

Dutch had a good view of the section from this height: cars resembling thousands of ants were slowly making their way around the richest real estate in the country. Hundreds of police vehicles and fire trucks from LA County, West Hollywood and Beverly Hills were being used to reroute the rush-hour traffic; their blinking red and blue lights made the city hundreds of feet below look like Disneyland on the Fourth of July.

But it was the black asphalt streets that really caught Dutch's attention. Fissures, ranging from one inch up to several feet wide, zigzagged in all directions down

29

the length of the boulevards. From this elevation, it looked as if a giant feline had dug her sharp claws into thick strips of tar and scratched furiously in all directions. There were pockets of flames leaping from crevices. On some streets, cracked pipes shot water hundreds of feet into the air. As the 'copter passed over Rodeo Drive, Dutch could see deep chasms splitting the high-class stores of Hermes, Bijan and Gucci.

The helicopter abruptly veered to the right and descended on the lawn of a large estate at the corner of Rexford Drive and Sunset.

Outside, the odour of natural gas was strong. Dutch and Tara grabbed gasmasks that hung on a hook next to the door and strapped them on their faces. When the pilot opened the portal, several people, with their heads lowered to avoid the swirling blades, were waiting for them on the lawn. Though they all wore similar masks, Dutch knew who they were: the coroner, Pat Sagata; Beverly Hills homicide detective, Lieutenant Vince Falcone; Sergeant Jimmy Ciazo; and Chief Medical Examiner of LA, Orville Priest.

'We've been waiting for you!' Priest said gruffly. The mask made his voice sound hollow, as if it were coming through a deep tunnel.

Dutch couldn't see Priest's expression because it was covered by his mask, but he could see his eyes; they were filled with hate for him. Dutch knew the reason for that. It stemmed from an incident that happened a couple of years back. Dutch had come into the pathology lab one evening to examine bones that were found in Griffith Park. Orville, dressed in black-tie, was hurriedly locking the door to the laboratory. With undisguised arrogance he told the anthropologist that he was late for a party and to come back tomorrow to see the remains. Dutch, who had buried his son only a few weeks before, was in a bad mood. He didn't say a word to the coroner. Instead, he picked up a metal chair in the hallway and flung it through the frosted window of the lab. He then hoisted himself over the windowsill and broken glass, turned on the lab lights, went over to the gurney, removed the sheet and began to examine the remains. The next day the outraged ME went before the commission and demanded that he be fired. A hearing was held. Dutch was made to pay for the broken equipment, but never dismissed. He was too good at what he did, and they knew that. Orville, who was used to getting what he wanted, stormed out of the hearing room. No one had ever humiliated him like that before and got away with it. No one! The seeds of his hate for the Dutchman were firmly planted. One of Orville's chief virtues was his patience. He knew that this brazen anthropologist would fall one day, and he would make damn sure he was there when it happened.

Standing before the Dutchman today, with the few strands of hair remaining on his balding head whipping across his face from the wind currents of the chopper's blades, the old anger began to surface once again.

They walked away from the helicopter and over to the entrance to the mansion's wrought-iron fence. Falcone slapped Dutch on the back and held out his hand to him. 'It's been a while, Dutch.'

The Dutchman shook his hand, even though he disliked touching him. He felt his fingers were too soft and his nails too polished. Falcone, with his premature grey hair and movie-star looks, was tall and lanky, and walked with a stoop like a young Henry Fonda. Dutch could never figure out his age, because there were no wrinkles on his face. His Italian blue pinstriped suit and red paisley tie, like everything else about him, was coordinated right down to his shoe laces. Dutch always thought that Falcone and Dutch's wife, Therese, would have made the perfect couple; they could both skip happily along through life colour-coordinating the world. In the past, Falcone and the Dutchman had worked together on several cases where bones were found in Beverly Hills; most of them, however, turned out to be nothing more than skeletal remains of primitive Indians.

'Hey, *gumba*, how's it going?' Ciazo said to Dutch. His voice sounded like a file rubbing against rusty metal.

They shook hands. Dutch felt like steel bars had just wrapped themselves around his fingers. Unlike Falcone's, Ciazo's hands were vast and rough. He was almost as tall as the Dutchman, but he was broader. People seeing him for the first time, with his thick waist and neck, might mistakenly assume him to be out of shape. In reality, his stomach was as solid as granite and he was as strong as a bull elephant. Also, unlike Falcone, he bought his clothes from a Korean jobber who worked out of a basement in downtown Los Angeles. The cheap jacket he wore stretched tightly across his broad shoulders, and looked like the rust-coated side of an old battle ship.

Dutch had heard the rumours about Ciazo: that he was hard and brutal and wouldn't think twice about pulling the trigger on a suspect; that he loved his bourbon; that his wife had left him a note, took his three kids and went to live in Orlando with her sister;

32

that while drunk one night he had shot and killed a twelve-year-old Mexican boy in Pico Rivera by mistake.

Dutch respected Ciazo the way a zebra respected a lion sharing the same water-hole. There were no subtleties or shades in his voice when he talked, and when he looked at people, his black Sicilian eyes were as indifferent and dormant as a shark's.

'Did Pat fill you in?' Priest asked the Dutchman, pushing the loose hairs back over his head.

'Yes. He said you found bones and Indian relics in some of the fissures.'

'A few. It's still early yet,' Pat said enthusiastically.

'Artifacts are not Van Deer's concern,' Priest said coldly to the Japanese coroner.

Dutch was startled at hearing his last name. Ever since he could remember, people had always referred to him as 'Dutch' or 'the Dutchman'. Never Van Deer, or his first name Wilhelm.

'Archaeological crews will look into the find later,' Priest continued. Turning his dark eyes back to Dutch, he said, 'A graveyard was uncovered on someone's property − most of the remains lay buried underneath a tennis court. Probably one of those tribes that lived here before the Spaniards. Go over there and look at them, tell me they're of no use to the coroner's office, then go home.'

With his mask on and his thick, dark eyebrows meeting in the middle of his forehead, Priest reminded Dutch of a timber wolf. Never should have thrown a chair through his laboratory, Dutch thought. 'You sound like you're in a hurry to tidy things up, Orville.'

'You're damn right. This goddamn find is going to cost the city millions. Beverly Hills has to be sectioned

33

off until the bones and the artifacts are removed. They're all over the damn place! Every fissure you look down, you see bones, beads, shells, arrowheads − all kinds of crap. You know what traffic problems this is going to cause?'

'I don't live in Beverly Hills. Can't afford it,' Dutch said, grinning.

Falcone put his manicured fingers on Priest's thick, rounded shoulder. 'We'll work it out, Orville. The community will think of it as an adventure.'

'An adventure! Oh Christ, Falcone, you got to be kidding,' the ME snapped. He brushed the detective's hand off his shoulder as if it were an insect. 'No cars can come in or out of here. Without cars the shops and restaurants will die. Camel jockeys who live in multimillion-dollar homes around here will have to walk miles to bus-stops because they can't drive their friggin' Rolls Royces on the streets. These rich people don't know how to take buses, Falcone. Shit! They've never been in one! You think they're going to understand that they're out on an adventure, like Tom Sawyer? Because if that's what you think, then maybe you should be the one to tell them.'

Falcone's eyes hardened. He was about to say something when Tara cut in. 'Where are the bones?' she said impatiently.

Falcone turned abruptly away from the ME and pointed diagonally across Sunset towards Crest Drive. 'I'll show you.' Looking at Priest, he said, 'Are you coming, Orville?'

'No. The mayor will be holding a news conference in a few minutes on the corner of Beverly Drive and Charlieville. I want to be there.'

Falcone glared at Priest. Clearing his throat, he

said, 'Look, I think I should be there, too. I'm the homicide detective . . .'

Orville quickly cut him off. 'Homicide detectives look for dead bodies. Go and look for them. It shouldn't be too hard. There are hundreds of them under that tennis court.'

'And you're a coroner. Dead bodies are in your territory, too,' Falcone shot back.

'That's why I have assistants,' he said, giving Pat a quick glance. Without another word he turned and walked towards Beverly Drive.

'I hate that guy!' Falcone hissed, staring at Priest's back.

Dutch smiled under his mask. The ME wasn't taking any chances. He was an unattractive, barrel-chested man, and he wasn't about to let a stud like Falcone upstage him in front of the cameras, especially with the mayor present.

They made their way across Sunset Boulevard, carefully walking around large chunks of asphalt and gaping chasms filled with hot, rising steam. Firemen were everywhere, pouring water from hoses into the deep crevices, trying to extinguish the gas flames. Helicopters from the police and news media hung suspended over the scene, their searchlights criss-crossing each other.

Most of the homes seemed to be in good condition, Dutch noticed. Broken glass and blocks of stucco littered the gardens and streets. Some of the houses had fractures in them, but that was all. The stores and restaurants south of Santa Monica Boulevard were another story: many had literally been split in half. The sounds of ambulances coming from that direction filled the night air, adding to the malevolent atmosphere.

35

'How many casualties?' Dutch asked Pat as he climbed over a large slab of sidewalk that had buckled up from the ground.

'Seven known dead in Beverly Hills. I don't know how many were injured. It could have been worse. They think there are some survivors trapped under rubble in the Rodeo Collection.'

Dutch's belly tensed.

When they got to Crest Drive, they turned on to the cul-de-sac. To the right lay the excavation site for a five-star hotel that was being built. Overhead, a sleek black helicopter hovered twenty feet above them. Dutch looked up. It reminded him of a hungry crow looking for prey. He could see the initials JP in blazing red letters on its side. The chopper circled them for a few seconds, as if scrutinizing them, then quickly rose up and flew towards the ocean.

'Who's that?' Dutch asked, his eyes following the black machine.

Pat pursed his lips nervously. 'John Payne. The man who's building that hotel across the street.'

Dutch knew who he was. Payne was one of the wealthiest men in the country. He was also running for governor of California. The Dutchman didn't look away until the helicopter disappeared into the night clouds.

When they came upon the remains of the big Mediterranean house at the end of the block, Dutch and Tara let out deep breaths. Part of the building had caved in. The other half had divided itself clean down the middle, as if a crazed Goliath had taken an axe to it.

'What the hell happened?' Dutch said, noticing that

36

all the other homes on the streets had suffered little or no damage.

Falcone said, 'It's owned by a Lenny and Marsha Garowitz. Turns out Lenny thought he could save a few bucks by hiring an unlicensed contractor to do the work. This guy built him a home and a tennis court all right, but nothing that even came close to passing code. He bilked on everything, especially the concrete. Wait till you see the tennis court and you'll know what I mean. We found Mrs Garowitz at the bottom of one of the fissures in the front lawn.'

'How'd she get there?'

'Panicked when the earthquake hit. She was taking a bath at the time. Ran out of the house stone naked and fell into one of the cracks that opened up.'

'Was she still alive?' Tara asked.

'Yes, she was alive,' Falcone said, nodding. 'The earth closed up on her again after she fell in. It was weird. My officers were standing in her garden, when suddenly her hand pops up from under the ground and grabs hold of one of my men's leg.' Falcone laughed. 'The guy peed in his pants, he was so scared. We dug her out. Her collarbone was broken. She was half crazed, screaming that she was in a tunnel and that someone was down there with her. Said he tried to drag her away by her feet. She thought she was going to be killed. Then she started carrying on about some fucking Indian running wildly through the streets of Beverly Hills right before the quake. The paramedics had to shoot her up with a stiff shot of Valium to calm her down. I want you to see the tennis court first, then I want you to take a look at the fissure the woman fell into. You're not going to believe any of this.'

They climbed over the fallen debris from the house

37

that covered the front lawn, opened up the gate and went around to the back.

Big searchlights illuminated the property. Pat was right. They couldn't believe it. The garden was littered with fragments of human bones. It was as if the bowels of the earth had suddenly erupted and spewed out its dead. At the end of the yard were the broken remains of the tennis court. The green clay had hundreds of large cracks on the surface, and the middle had caved in to give the shape of a giant V.

Dutch and Tara climbed on top of the crumpled clay blocks, turned on their flashlights, and looked down into one of the enormous cracks.

More bones. These weren't fragmented. They were entire skeletons lying in foetal positions, approximately three feet apart from each other. Beads and other artifacts were intermingled with the bodies. Dutch stuck his head and upper torso further into the gap and moved the beam of his light around. He was able to count seven bodies. He had a feeling that there were a lot more of them down there, obscured by the earth and the broken slabs of concrete.

'You think this is an Indian burial ground?' Pat asked, kneeling down next to him.

'It has to be. I've just never seen one this big,' Dutch responded, moving his body away so that Tara could take a look at the bodies.

'What kind of Indians were they?' Falcone asked, standing on tiptoe, his masked face peering over Tara's shoulder.

Dutch shook the powdery green clay from his jeans as he got up. 'I'm not an archaeologist. My guess would be either Chumash, Fernandeño or Gabrieleño. They lived in this area for thousands of years. Then the missionaries came with their blond-haired Jesus. They also came with their diseases which the Indians had no defence against, and wiped them out.'

Tara took her head out of the crevice and looked up at Dutch. Her eyes were animated.

'Glad you gave up your date tonight, huh?' Dutch said.

'Screw you, Dutchman.' She grabbed his outstretched hand for support and lifted herself up.

'We need a crane,' Dutch said, turning to Falcone.

'A crane? What the hell for?'

'Maybe two cranes. We have to remove these broken slabs of concrete. There are bodies down here. Lots of them.'

Falcone sighed and scratched his perfect blow-dried hair with his manicured index finger. 'Hell, Dutch, what are we talking about here? Grab the bones you can see, tell me they're Choo Choos or . . .'

'Chumash,' Tara said coldly.

'OK, fine. Chumash. We'll take the bones to another location. Then we'll bring in one of those Indian witchdoctors like we've done in the past. He'll do his little dance and wave his magic wand around, and then we'll bury them again. Bid-a-boom, bid-a-bang! It's done. Opening up this entire tennis court would be like opening up a can of worms. Who knows how big this graveyard is? It could cut into other people's property.'

'We're not talking about other people's property, Vincent. Legally I don't have the right to exhume. That's the coroner's job. But when the ground opens up and spits out human remains, then I do have the right to examine those remains to determine their age and to see if they died of natural causes.'

'Oh, hell, Dutch, you know as well as I do that these goddamn fossils are useless to the coroner's office. You heard Orville. Nobody wants this shit.'

'Fuck Orville. This could be an incredible find,' Tara shouted, her face inches from the detective's.

'You can't dig up people's backyards and houses.' The upper part of Falcone's face was turning scarlet.

Standing at the back, next to the fence, Ciazo placidly watched all of this. His hands were calmly crossed in front of him, pushing the sleeves of his jacket up to his forearms.

The Dutchman moved in front of Tara. Looking Falcone firmly in the eye he said with a deadly softness in his voice, 'I want a crane here by tomorrow morning to remove this concrete. I also want ten or twelve men with shovels to start digging up the backyard. I want them to dig very carefully. For every bone they disturb, I will personally disturb one of theirs.'

'They're goddamn ancient bones, for God's sake! There's no meaning to them!' Falcone's hands flailed wildly in the air.

'Only I can determine that, Vincent. Either you get me the crane and the men, or I get a court order telling you to get them. Now let's see the fissure where they found the woman.'

Falcone was breathing furiously inside his mask, making the nylon material expand in and out like a balloon. Brushing past Ciazo's rigid body, he kicked open the gate and trampled out over the bushes and on to the lawn. Pat, Tara and Dutch followed. Ciazo stayed by the gate.

'We found her over here,' Falcone said, pointing to a large rectangular hole made with shovels.

'What do you want me to see?' Dutch asked.

'Hey, you like bones so much – you go down there and tell me.'

Dutch turned on his flashlight and pointed it down into the hole. He could see several human bones on the earth below. The floor of the fissure was wider than the sides, and rounded. He handed his light to Tara and slowly inched his way down, digging his hands into the dirt walls to steady himself. His fingers began to touch other bones that were still buried in the sides. Christ! How many bodies were there? he wondered. He didn't like going down into crevices, not right after an earthquake. When he reached the bottom, he could feel bones crunch beneath his feet. He knelt down and touched the rounded portion of the wall. This didn't make sense; it wasn't made of earth or rock. He scraped at it with his fingers. The curved section was smooth. He then tapped it with his knuckles. A dim, hollow thud echoed over and over again through the crevice, until it faded away.

This is man-made, Dutch thought. He shone the light into the tunnel extending away from him.

'What's down there, Dutch?' Tara asked from above.

'I'm not sure. Get down here.' Dutch moved into the tunnel to make room for her. Retreating farther into the darkness, his heart began pulsating in his chest and sweat dripped down into his eyes. He couldn't stand being in small openings, not since . . . *Again the smell of Shalimar*. Shaking his head, he brushed the thought from his mind and gulped down air.

Tara crawled over to him and saw his pale skin and frightened eyes. 'Are you OK?'

His breathing was heavy but he managed to nod. The feeling of claustrophobia was becoming unbear-

41

able. He wanted desperately to get out. Don't think about it, he said to himself. *Don't think about it!*

She moved in front of him, shining her light into the blackness. The beam bounced off the walls catching traces of red, white and black markings. Some were circular, others triangular with straight bold lines crossing over them. From the curved roof of the tunnel, skeletal hands and feet resembling wind-chimes dangled out of the cracks, reflecting in the flare of her light like expensive French crystal.

Suddenly there was a movement behind them. Dutch jerked around, shining his light at the direction of the sound. It was Pat.

'What the hell . . .' Pat's words faded when he saw the colourful graffiti on the walls and the bones hanging down. 'Is this an Indian cave or something?'

After wiping the sweat from his brow, Dutch banged on the tunnel wall and said, 'This thing's made out of brick or clay. The Chumash didn't use that kind of material. Even if they did, they didn't have the tools to make it this smooth.'

'Why Chumash?' Tara asked, lightly stroking the wall, being careful not to touch the drawings.

'For a couple of reasons.' Sweat broke loose on the Dutchman's forehead once again. He took a deep breath, trying to fight off his fear of enclosure. 'White, red and black were the basic colours the Chumash used in their murals.' He picked up one of the skulls from the earthen floor and flashed his light on it. 'This is the real giveaway. The head is brachycranic or round-shaped. That's a Chumash trait. The other tribes had narrower skulls.'

'At least we now know the name of the tribe,' Pat replied.

'Interesting,' Dutch said. 'The Chumash inhabited coastal areas. I don't understand why these markings and bones are this far south, unless these graves are ancient. Some archaeologists believe the Chumash lived here first, and the Shoshone tribe came in and pushed them towards the north thousands of years ago.'

'This *would* be a find then,' Pat whispered, his voice filled with excitement.

A scraping, crunching sound echoed abruptly against the clay walls. It was coming from somewhere close by in the darkness of the tunnel.

Pat shone his light in the direction of the noise, but after twenty feet the beam faded into the blackness of the passageway. 'It's rats!' he whispered, afraid that if he said it any louder they'd hear him.

Every part of Dutch's body told him to run, but he held fast. Detesting rats was also up there along with the forces of nature. He listened to the scraping noises for a moment to make sure, then said, 'No, it isn't rats. Rats make a different sound. Someone is sliding his body over the ground.' Then he remembered what Falcone had said about the lady who was trapped in here; she was screaming that someone or something was down here with her.

Dutch made a path by pushing away the bones from the walls and ceiling. They began moving towards the noise, crawling on their hands and knees.

The sweet, corrosive smell hit them as soon as they got twenty feet further into the tunnel. They started to gag.

'It's something dead,' Tara said, turning her face away.

Pat started to cough.

Dutch clenched his fists against both sides of the walls, pushing at it with all his strength, trying to make the terror go away. He couldn't go on, he needed to get out of this tunnel, needed to get out now! That smell, that awful smell! Then the intimate aroma of Shalimar rose up and brushed by his senses.

A familiar voice from deep within the caverns of his mind began to call to him. '*Dutchboy . . . my little Dutchboy.*'

The Dutchman moaned in sorrow. It had been so long since he had heard those words.

Suddenly an aftershock shook the ground. The top of the tunnel cracked open, dropping large fragments of human bones down on them like a winter hailstorm.

The sounds and smells evaporated and the old fears took over. Crawling on his hands and knees, he headed back to the fissure opening as fast as he could. All reason left him; pure terror was all he knew now. He had to get out! In the distance he could vaguely hear Tara calling him. He tore the mask from his face. Slithering on the ground, clawing at the floor with his fingers for traction, all he could think of was the cool night air. Clean air, with the smell of grass and dew! It filled his mind to the point where it wanted to explode. His face and body were covered with the white powdery dust of bones; he looked as if he had been rolling around in ashes.

In front of him he could see a beam of moving light coming from up above. Then he saw the hole. Pushing himself harder with his fingers, grunting, Dutch made it to the opening. He frantically grabbed on to the soft soil, dug his feet and hands into the side of the earth and lifted himself out.

A hand clutched on to his wrist, helping him. Dutch looked up; it was Ciazo.

He dropped on to the grass, head down, gasping for breath, trying desperately to fill his lungs with air. The smell of gas infiltrated his nostrils, burning them, making him dizzy, but he didn't care. He was out of the hole; that was all that mattered. Turning over and looking up, he could see the night sky saturated with the brilliant lights of helicopters. Tara and Pat were kneeling next to him now, a look of concern in their eyes. Falcone also bent down to look at him, *his* eyes expressing only humour.

'You OK, pal? The aftershock scare you? I hope you didn't wet yourself.' The detective's cheeks filled the sides of his mask as he grinned.

Though the Dutchman's head was aching and his eyes were blurry from the gas, he desperately wanted to grab this jerk-off by his Armani silk tie and stuff it down his throat. He was just about to do that, when suddenly he saw something across the street about twenty yards away. From where he lay he could see a figure running full speed towards them. It looked like a man, and he was holding a stick above his head. His mouth was open and his dark eyes were fiery. The others around Dutch hadn't noticed yet, because they had their backs turned. The man looked Indian; he wasn't wearing a shirt, and there were black, red and white painted stripes covering his face and upper body.

He was almost upon them now. His curled lips exposed stained, crooked teeth; the front one gold. His coarse, shoulder-length mane was flying in all directions, like the hair of a black angel.

Dutch could now make out what he was holding above his head. No, it wasn't a stick; it was an axe.

45

Then a scream erupted from the man's throat, filled with a rage that chilled the bile in Dutch's stomach. Everything happened in slow motion: the Indian running; the heads of Tara, Falcone and Pat turning in the directon of his shrieking.

The Indian was only a few feet away now; his maniacal cry was deafening. Foam massed around his angry, snarling mouth gave him the look of a rabid animal. He stopped abruptly in front of Pat, balanced himself on the toes of his dirty sneakers, and raised the axe directly over his head.

There was no thought in what Dutch did; if there had, it would have been too late. He leaped up, lowered his head, and aimed his two hundred and twenty pound frame directly at the Indian. Dutch's head shot into the little man's stomach like a battering ram going into a crack house door. A heavy grunt echoed from the Indian's lips as the air blew out of his lungs. His body lifted off the ground and fell into a clump of azalea bushes ten feet away. The momentum carried Dutch along with him. He landed on top of the Indian, then rolled over several times before he could stop. The rancid smell coming from the man was the same as that in the tunnel. The Dutchman choked. From the corner of his eye he could see Falcone pulling out his service revolver from the holster clip on his belt. Dutch sat up, looked over towards the Indian, and saw that he was also trying to get up. Then he turned to Falcone again, who was now aiming the S&W snub-nose, held in the police position, and cocking the hammer.

Dutch waved his hands wildly, shaking his head, screaming, '*Nooo*, goddamn it, Vincent!'

Then he saw Ciazo with his hands outstretched,

moving as quick as a leopard toward Falcone's gun. Dutch looked up and spotted a small, dark blur coming down in front of him. He realized what it was, but was too late to move his head away. At the same moment as the axe came down, he heard the crack of gunfire ripping through the warm air.

3

'Sewing always came naturally to me,' a man's high-pitched voice rang out. 'My mother was a seamstress. She taught me all kinds of stitches. I could do a double loop before I was seven.'

Dutch felt something tugging at his ear, pulling his head over to one side as he became conscious. Was this guy talking to him? He slowly opened his eyelids. A bright light from above glared down on him, burning his eyes. He quickly closed them.

The voice continued, 'Many of my colleagues prefer linen and silk. Personally, my favourite is catgut. It's made from sheep's intestines. That's what I'm using now. Also it's a *natural* material. Too many foreign objects in our bodies as it is.'

Every time Dutch's head was jerked sideways, a blast of unbearable pain shot through his brain. He groaned and opened his eyes again; this time looking away from the light. His vision was cloudy, as if he were swimming under water without goggles. He saw a patch of blue moving above him.

'He's awake,' Tara's voice said from his right side. She came into his view. Looking down at him, she touched his hand, holding it tightly. 'How are you, Dutch?'

He tried to speak but his lips felt like wet eels smacking together; he couldn't pronounce even the simplest words.

'Don't you move. This is very tricky,' said the voice wearing something blue.

He didn't have to tell Dutch that; but his head, like his lips, had a mind of its own. The man above him was holding a piece of string and moving his hand up and down like a puppeteer. Dutch's head jerked in rhythm to his motions.

Tara came back into his sight. She was hanging over him now. Her hand was on his cheek and she was stroking it. From where he was lying he could see straight into the top of her loose T-shirt. She never wore a bra, and she didn't have one on now. Dutch saw the butterfly — blurry, but there it was. He cursed himself for not being able to see clearly. Maybe if he lifted his head his eyes would focus better.

When he moved, there was a sudden tearing sound by his ear, followed by a stinging sensation; it was like a bandage being ripped from a hairy chest. A hot spasm shot through his skull, making his eyes water.

'Oh, now you've done it!' the man above him said irritably. 'I spent three hours sewing your ear back on. Now I have to start all over again.' Dutch could see him looking down at the floor. 'Ah, there it is! Don't move, miss. One wrong step and we'll be making him one out of rubber. I'm not a fan of those; the colour fades.'

Closing his eyes again, the Dutchman saw a vision of a man whom he took to be God standing next to a garage work-bench filled with babies. Cubby holes containing nuts, screws and small human limbs lined the wall next to him. He picked one of the tots up, grabbed an ear from a compartment, and began screwing it in to the side of the baby's head. As he twisted, the newborn screamed in agony.

'Tut . . . tut . . . tut. *Wat heel lief kinje,*' he said softly, smiling.

The sleeves of God's checkered flannel shirt were rolled up over his hairy arms, and a beer belly hung down over the first three buttons of his Levi's. When the ear was on tight, he tossed the tot on to a pink pile of crying infants that were writhing on an aluminium tray by his side. He then took the next baby, who didn't have any fingers, reached up into a bin filled with appendages, grabbed several digits and began popping them on.

Dutch smiled at this image of God, with his ruddy complexion and his rust-coloured crewcut. '*Wat heel lief kinje,*' he uttered. The Dutchman's lips moved while saying the words. 'What a good little baby,' he repeated in English. *Shit! God's my dad.* What a trip! Just before he passed out, he wondered if his father had ever said those words to him when he was a baby.

When he opened his eyes again, he found himself in a stiff bed with the mattress propped up. An IV was stuck in the vein of his right hand. He looked up and noticed a metal ring with a cloth curtain encircling his bed. Sunlight filtered through from some open window and he saw the spike-haired silhouette of Tara on the other side of the curtain. She was speaking to someone; her voice low and solemn. He felt feverish, and his mouth tasted like stale blood. The room was imbued with the stark odour of antiseptic.

He weakly lifted his hand and grabbed on to the

edge of the curtain, but Tara was already sliding it open on the other side.

She was standing next to the night-table, whispering on the phone. She raised a finger to Dutch, saying that she'd be right there. A few more unintelligible words, then she hung up. 'You look like Van Gogh,' she said to him.

Dutch touched his right ear. It was covered with gauze and it was throbbing.

'You're lucky you had a surgeon who sewed his own prom dress when he was in high school. He said there won't be much of a scar.' Her face was pale; dark shadows circled her eyes. It was obvious that she hadn't been to sleep yet. She poured water from a plastic container into a glass, sat next to him on the bed and held the cup to his mouth.

His lips still had a mind of their own and at least half the contents spilled on to his hospital night-gown. The water that managed to find his parched throat was cool and refreshing. 'How long have I been here?' he was finally able to ask after several false starts. His vocal chords felt like they were frozen in ice.

'Since last night. It's now three-thirty in the afternoon of the next day. You slept for both of us.'

Then he remembered the Indian. 'What happened to that guy?'

'The crazy one?'

He nodded slowly.

'In the Beverly Hills lock-up. He also nicked your scalp when he creamed your ear. You have a concussion.'

'At least he's not dead.'

'You're a prince of a guy, Dutch. Obviously he

52

didn't share the same feelings. He tried to slice your head open.'

'What was he doing there? I want to talk to him. How bad was he hurt?' His ear was screaming now.

'His left index finger was blown off by Falcone. If Ciazo hadn't pushed his gun away, that Indian would be dead now. It's been a hell of a night for missing limbs. While I was on my hands and knees in the grass searching for your ear, Pat was on his knees searching for the guy's finger. *You* came up lucky. From now on the Indian's going to have to stop counting when he reaches nine.'

Dutch said, 'He just better have a good reason for doing what he did.' He touched his ear again; the gauze felt wet and sticky. His pillow was covered with brown-coloured antiseptic and blood. He suddenly felt tired and wanted to sleep.

Sensing this, Tara stood up. 'Get some rest, Dutchman. Try leaving your ear alone, OK? A lot of good sheep gave up their intestines for you.' She patted his arm.

'The grave-site,' he whispered, his eyelids fluttering.

'I'm way ahead of you. I've been on the phone all morning while you were goldbricking. The concrete blocks on the tennis court have been extricated. I called the students that we can trust from the university to help us remove the bones. I've also made arrangements with the coroner's office to allocate us some space. We're going to need lots of it.' She threw him a kiss and turned toward the door.

'Tara,' he muttered.

She turned to him; her red eyes begging for some rest.

'Take pictures, OK?' he said.

She pulled a 35mm Nikon from her leather bag. 'This isn't my first dig, you know. Go to sleep.'

Before he passed out, the Indian came back into his mind. At the exact same moment last night, both of them had had a part of their body taken from them. How cosmic, he thought.

The Percodan the nurses gave him later in the afternoon deadened the pain, but it awakened old memories. As he drifted in and out of consciousness, a faded black and white movie played in his head.

Summertime in Ohio. The steel-grey, early morning light was turning pale as the sun came up. The humidity was thick, and the smell of dew rushed through the Dutchboy's veins, making him feel alive.

He was sitting on the wooden steps of the porch, intently watching an army of ants climbing up the banister, trying to get away from the wet lawn. It had rained hard last night and the ground was saturated.

Inside the house he could hear the box springs groaning from the weight of the man on top of his mother, and the headboard banging against the wall. Occasionally he would hear her quick, high-pitched gasps. The man would then say something to her, making her moan even louder.

The Dutchboy put his hands over his ears to block out the sounds. He did not like this man. His greasy, stiff overalls were covered with oil, and his stained white T-shirt smelled of stale sweat and chewing tobacco.

Twenty minutes later, Dutch heard heavy footsteps coming down the stairs and walking into the kitchen. It was followed by a deep cigarette cough. Not too long after that, there was the smell of bacon and coffee. The aroma floated through the screen door, making the boy's mouth water. But, as hungry as he was, he would not eat with the man.

The sounds of plates clattering and the whispering of his mother and that man were interspersed with sporadic laughter. Then more footsteps and the door opened. The man came out of the house and on to the porch, carrying a metal lunch-box and wearing a tool belt around his waist. The skin on the inside parts of his arms was freckled and soft. He patted the boy's head and took out a crushed Milky Way from his pants pocket.

'Here, kid,' he said, tossing the candy bar into his lap.

Dutch continued to stare at the ants, refusing to say anything or look up at him.

The man let out a laugh filled with phlegm, then coughed. He went down the steps towards his banged-up, rust-coloured Chevy parked by the kerb and drove off in the direction of Dayton, where he worked in a mill.

Just as he had all the other times the man had given him candy, Dutch dropped it down through a broken floorboard next to the steps. Three Musketeers, Juicy Fruits, Snickers and Almond Joys littered the ground beneath his house. While lying in his bed at night he could hear the fieldmice under his floor, tearing at the wrappings, trying to get at the candy.

His mother, wearing a flowered dressing gown and holding a cup of coffee, came over to the screen door. The scent of Shalimar from her skin filled the Dutchboy's nostrils with its sweet smell. Her golden wavy hair hung down over her right eye, like Veronica Lake's. She leaned against the jamb, pushed away the blonde strands from her face, and looked down at him.

'Wilhelm,' she said softly.

He didn't answer. His eyes remained locked on the ants. He didn't want to see the red blotches on her skin from the man's heavy beard.

Sighing, she turned and walked back into the house, softly closing the door behind her.

He shut his eyes tightly and thought of his father, whom he had never known. One time, when his mother was drunk, she showed him a photograph of a tall, heavy-set man with red hair. 'That's your old man,' she said, slurring the words. Her eyes, red from cheap gin, glowed when she mentioned him.

He wanted to ask her why she never wore a wedding ring, but something inside told him not to.

'What happened to him?' he would constantly ask her.

She would never answer him. She'd just stare out the window with a faraway look, then shrug her shoulders and walk off.

One day, when he wouldn't stop hounding her about it, she finally gave in. 'He's from the Netherlands. Hardly spoke any English when I met him. I doubt if the bastard speaks any now.' A hint of a smile played on her lips as the memories were evoked.

'Did I ever meet him?'

'When you were just a baby. He would hold you in his arms and sing songs to you in Dutch.'

The Dutchboy's eyes burned from the tears that were forming, and he fought hard to hold them back. 'Where is he now, Mamma?'

'Where? Probably on an oil rig somewhere – either

56

in the Middle East or the North Sea. That's all I know. He never said much.' She nervously lit up a cigarette. 'He don't write that often anymore,' she muttered sadly. There was an edge of hardness in her voice.

That was all Dutch knew of him – that he worked on things that resembled big erector sets. How brave and strong he must be, he thought. For months afterwards, he'd fantasize about being trapped on a runaway stagecoach, or being shot at by men whose faces were covered with bandanas, and how his father would come and save him. Then he would pick the Dutchboy up over his head, place him on his broad shoulders, and they'd go to the oilfields to live together. Once he saw pictures of the Dutch city, Utrecht, in the Sunday magazine section of the newspaper. It was springtime and the streets were alive with coloured tulips. Sometimes he'd imagine that his father took him to Holland, and that he bought him wooden shoes.

One morning, about two weeks after the man with the freckles on his arms gave him the Milky Way, he saw his mother sitting at the kitchen table with a letter crumpled in her hand. She was crying. He went over and put his fingers on her shoulder. She turned to him; her eyes the colour of raw meat.

'He's dead, baby,' she said. 'It turns out he was working in an oilfield in Venezuela all this time. A cable snapped . . . he was crushed.' That was all she could say. She put her head down on the table and sobbed. After several minutes, she stopped crying and looked at the letter again. 'It's from his company. He had an insurance policy for you that I didn't know about. It's for your education. He always told me he wanted you to make something out of yourself, that he didn't want you to end up like him.' She stared at the wall, biting her bottom lip and shaking her head in disbelief. 'Oh, God! That bastard,' she cried. Then she picked up the glass sugar server from the table and flung it at the sink, shattering it into thousands of pieces.

The man with the greasy overalls still came by and spent the night. Dutch continued to hear the box springs squeak and the headboard hit the wall in his mother's bedroom, but he never again heard her cry out in pleasure. Soon afterwards the man stopped coming around. Eventually, the mice under the house also went away, because there were no more Milky Ways being dropped down for them.

He heard the sound of a latch opening, then the overhead light went on.

Dutch opened his eyes and saw Tara. He wanted to close them again, drift back to Ohio to be with his mother, but Tara was now sitting on the edge of his bed and shaking his arm.

'Get up', she said.

Reluctantly he opened his eyes once more. 'What is it?' he mumbled. He reached over to get a glass of water from the night-table.

'The shit's hitting the fan out there.'

He quickly gulped the water down, then put the glass back. 'What fan?' The painkillers were fogging his brain.

'Jesus! Will you wake the hell up!' She grabbed him under his armpits and lifted him to a sitting position.

She was strong for a small-boned woman. Clearing the sleep from his throat, he asked, 'Did you get the pictures?'

'Oh, I've got your pictures, all right.' She held up a large brown envelope. 'I think you should take a look at them, then we've got to get you out of here.'

'What time is it?'

'Nine at night. They wouldn't let me up to see you, so I came through the back way.' She went to the closet, took out his clothes, and tossed then on to the chair next to him. 'Get dressed,' she commanded.

He wanted to tell her to go away, so he could go back to his mother, but he knew something was wrong or she wouldn't be here. He sat up and ripped the IV tube out of his vein, flinching at the sharp sting.

She was sitting next to him again, undoing his nightgown.

'I'm not wearing underwear,' he said groggily.

'Don't worry, there's nothing down there that I want.' She handed him his briefs. Dutch tried unsuccessfully to put them on, and she had to help. She also had to assist him with his pants and shirt.

He then went into the bathroom and splashed water on his face, being careful not to touch his ear. His teeth felt filmy when he rubbed his tongue against them. He looked in the medicine cabinet for a toothbrush. The shelves were empty except for a travelling size tube of Colgate. He put a wad of toothpaste on his index finger and brushed as best as he could. 'What's happened at the site?' he asked, putting his mouth under the tap and rinsing.

'Everything is happening at the site. That's why I want you out of here.'

Dutch looked up from the sink, his eyebrows arching in wariness. 'What about the bones? Have you seen them?'

'Only from the rooftop of a twenty-storey office

building on Santa Monica Boulevard. I can't get near the bones. The Chumash and the Fernandeños have formed a ring around the grave-site, and they won't let anyone near it. The Gabrieleños are also at the site. It's about to explode down there.'

Dutch groaned. Every damn time bones were found, those three tribes tried claiming them as their own.

Wiping his mouth with a towel, Dutch walked out of the bathroom. Tara had removed the photos from the manilla envelope and laid them out on the bed. She took a magnifying glass and handed it to him. 'I want you to take a look at these pictures, Dutch, and tell me what you see wrong with them.'

They were 11 × 14 black-and-whites. Dutch twisted the spiral neck of the lamp on the headboard so that the light flowed directly on to the pictures. Tara had taken several of the graves at different angles. The remains were laid out in several straight rows, with approximately twenty bodies to a row. Dutch held the glass up to his eye and tried counting the bodies. It was hard to tell the exact number because of the distance she had taken the pictures from, but he guessed it to be around one hundred and fifty. That didn't include the hundreds, even thousands more that were still buried under the earth. It was rare for a find to be this large.

He realized from first glance that there was something strange about the site: most of the bodies were in a foetal position with their heads facing towards the west. Others had their legs parted like frogs. Why at that angle? Then he remembered. The bodies found in many of the more ancient Chumash graves dating back over a thousand years were also buried in that way. These bones had to be *ancient*,

Dutch thought to himself This just might be one hell of a find.

'Losing an ear shouldn't slow your brain, Dutchman. Do you see something odd yet?' Tara was standing over him with her arms folded.

'Patience,' he said. He looked again. She wasn't talking about the way the bodies were laid out. It was something else. Then he saw it. No, they were not all in the same alignment. He brought the magnifying glass higher to his face in order to enlarge the middle of the photo. In the centre of the grave-site were two bodies, right next to each other, that lay at different angles from the rest: they were not in the foetal or frog position, and they seemed to be face-down.

'You talking about these two?' he asked, pointing to them with the glass.

'Yes,' she answered.

He looked at the photos again. They weren't very clear; a fuzzy whiteness surrounded the two bodies. He wished the pictures had been taken at a closer range.

There was something vaguely disturbing about these black and whites. But what? It wasn't rare for Indian burial sites to be found in California. He had worked on many of them. Just a few years ago, a lost village was uncovered in Encino with over two million bones and artifacts. Dutch had also been involved in that dig, but *he* had never experienced the feeling he had now. He needed to go the the grave-site and see what was there for himself. Before that could happen, however, he had to make sure there wasn't going to be a goddamn Indian uprising in Beverly Hills.

4

Pushing through a barrage of sightseers, policemen and reporters, Dutch and Tara made their way to the front of the wooden barricade on Wilshire and Santa Monica Boulevard. They showed their IDs from the university. One of the officers began speaking on a portable phone, and after several seconds of talking to someone at the other end, waved them through.

Electrical power was still out in most of West Hollywood and Beverly Hills. In the distance, tiny lights coming from windows of office buildings in Century City and West LA gave the blackness around them the look of a New England harbour at night.

Leaks from gas pipes had already been sealed up, but the buckled sidewalks and deep gashes in the pavement made their progress slow and treacherous. After several blocks, they finally approached Crest Drive, then the cul-de-sac. Large spotlights, angled on the burial ground, lit up the night sky. About one hundred and fifty people − cops, news personnel and Native Americans − were crowded on to Lenny and Marsha Garowitz's backyard. Pensive-faced Indians, some of them children and old women, had their arms linked tightly together, to block off the depression in the ground where the tennis court had been. Police wearing riot gear stood shoulder to shoulder, forming a circle around them. Some of the Chumash and Fernandeño teenagers openly taunted the troopers by screaming 'Pig!' and 'Fascist'. With their plastic visors down over their faces, the police patiently tapped their nightsticks against the palms of their hands in a single menacing motion, waiting for a sign from their captain to move in.

Dutch made his way through the crowd, holding one hand over his bad ear to protect it. The pain had returned but he didn't want to risk clouding his mind by taking another Percodan. When he reached the front of the line, he lifted his six-foot-five frame up on his toes to look over the heads of the mass of people.

Standing on the edge of the caved-in tennis court were two men. One was tall and lean and he was waving his hands in the air, trying to quieten the crowd. He was dressed in a wrinkled tan suit, with a striped tie loosened around his neck. The Indians had him surrounded, and were shaking their fists at him.

'John Payne,' Dutch said to himself. He had seen his photograph on the cover of *Time*. He was odious-looking, with thick white scars etched into his face. His mouth was slightly off centre, as if it had been torn from his jaw and later sewn back on. Dutch involuntarily touched his own ear in sympathy. Somewhere in his life, Payne must have been involved in a horrible accident, Dutch thought.

Next to him, staring down at the crowd with concern, was a good-looking bearded man in his mid-thirties. He was wearing a black double-breasted sports jacket, jeans and topsiders, without socks.

The Indians began to move in on Payne. Several officers and the man in topsiders stepped in front of him to act as a buffer. Waving their nightsticks in the air, the policemen used their bodies to cut a wedge through the flock of agitated people, and quickly moved the industrialist towards his black helicopter that was banked on the back lawn. But the crowd became too much for them, and many of the Indians broke through. One of them grabbed Payne by his jacket and flung him to the ground, beating him with his fists. The man with the beard also fell under a barrage of blows. With the swiftness of a panther, the pilot, wearing a helmet and visor, jumped out of the machine and hit the Indian who was on top of Payne with a wrench.

Yelling in pain, the Chumash grabbed at his head and went down.

The pilot began swinging the steel tool in all directions, trying to clear a space for Payne and the other man, so they could get up.

The swarm of people began to surge forward again, this time carrying Dutch along with them. They were now trying to get to the pilot. Looking over their heads, Dutch could see that the police were now on the other side of the crowd, attempting to get through. There wouldn't be enough time; nor were there enough of them. The pilot was barely holding off the attack, as it was.

Dutch grabbed a young Indian in front of him, and pushed him aside. Then, squeezing between several more bodies, he forced his way to the front of the line. The pilot turned and saw him. He stopped swinging the wrench long enough for Dutch to pass through. They stood back to back and turned in a circle. The pilot was wielding his wrench again. Together they managed to keep the Indians back, but several punches landed on Dutch, one of them hitting him on the ear. He almost went down from the pain of it. Blood began to trickle down his cheek.

With a space now cleared, John Payne managed to rise from the ground, then he leaped up into the chopper. Once inside, he turned to grab the arm of the other man and helped him in.

Still swinging the implement, the pilot backed up to the side opening, manoeuvred his body around, and leaped inside. The police finally broke through and began pushing back the crowd, using their truncheons on some.

Several officers escorted Dutch to the rear of the yard. When he reached the fence, he turned back towards the helicopter.

The deafening roar of its engine drowned out the cries of the crowd, then the chopper blades cut through the night air, sending people scurrying out of its way. The pilot looked down at Dutch and gave him a thumbs-up sign. Within seconds, the helicopter disappeared into the blackness.

The airman handled himself real well, Dutch thought. He had to be more than just a chauffeur. More likely he was Payne's professional protector.

Dutch turned around and saw old man Pete Johnson, a Gabrieleño, at the other end of the yard, standing near the ivy and Bougainvillaea. He was talking to some of the elders of the tribes. Pete was leaning against the white brick fence, calmly watching the action with both elbows up on the top of the wall. He wore baggy old jeans and a faded Lakers T-shirt that failed to cover his bulging stomach. His long hair, the colour and sparkle of steel wool, was parted in the middle and ran down his shoulders. He was known to everyone as 'Smokey Pete'. He got that nickname when Pete's father took him, as a child, to the turkey farm in Northridge where he worked as a plucker. Young Pete had got locked in the smoke oven by accident and the fire department had to be called in to resuscitate him. The elders in the tribe said that if you were around Pete on a hot day, your mouth began to water when he sweated, because he smelt so good. Today, Pete was Shaman to the Gabrieleños; he also had a doctorate and taught Indian lore at UCLA.

Dutch had met Pete a few times before, while working on other digs. He liked the old man; he could be crusty and ornery if pushed, but he never gave Dutch or the coroner's office a hard time when bones were uncovered.

'Hey, Smokey, how's it going?' Dutch said, walking over to him.

Without moving his body from the fence, Pete lifted his fingers in a greeting gesture. 'You're not too bad of a fighter for a college teacher.'

'I thought I was better than that,' Dutch said.

'What happened to your ear? You look like that crazy Dutch painter,' Smokey said. There was laughter in his eyes.

The Dutchman ignored Pete's humour. His ear was on fire again. He wiped some of the blood away with the back of his hand. 'They're getting ready to play Little Big Horn over there.' He pointed to where the ruckus was taking place. 'Why aren't you with them?'

'I'm a modern man, Dutch. If some crazy white people want to look at a bunch of dried-up old bones, I say let them. I'm not going to get my head cracked open over that kind of shit.'

'What if the bones were Gabrieleño?'

67

'Bones are bones, Dutchman,' the Indian said.

'Except they're not Gabrieleño. They're Chumash. Why do I think you already know that?'

Smokey Pete turned his eyes away from the gravesite and looked at him. Breaking out into a full-fledged grin, he said, 'You're one smart motherfucker, you know that?'

'I know that.'

'The Chumash know it's their bones, too,' the Indian said. 'You want to know a secret, Dutch? The ancient Chumash didn't give a damn about their bones. They were into reincarnation. It was their soul that mattered to them, not their bodies.' Pete moved away from the fence, put his hands in his pockets, and stared out at the crowd. The screaming was getting louder now.

'I need to see those bones, Pete,' the Dutchman said.

'Good luck,' Pete said.

'I just need to take a quick look at them to make sure they're Indian.'

'I said good luck.'

Dutch leaned against the fence, next to Pete. 'I can't do it without you.'

'Hey, talk to the Chumash. It's their bones, man.'

'You're respected in the Tribal Council. They'll listen to you.'

Pete took a packet of Clorets from his pants pocket and popped one into his mouth. Winking, he said, 'Don't try and massage my ego, Dutch. They're not going to listen to me. This is sacred shit you're tampering with.' He pointed to the other Indians by the site. 'Now, my brothers over there aren't as worldly as me. They hate anyone who fucks with their consecrated grounds, especially anthropologists. To them, you guys with your little PhDs are the devil.'

Dutch was used to this kind of frustration, and he knew it wouldn't do any good to push it with Pete. Smokey was right; Dutch was known as the 'vulture' to many of the tribesmen – the man who picked their bones clean. He'd have to wait until the fracas cleared up before he would be able to see the bones in the graveyard.

'How much do you know about Chumash culture, Pete?' he asked casually.

Pete turned to the three Gabrieleños standing next to him. They looked at each other, then laughed. The oldest one, with skin as wrinkled as beef jerky, laughed the loudest. He had no teeth and his mouth looked like a fathomless, black cavern.

Dutch had seen their secret glances and heard their strange laughter before. A tribe was like a private club. Outsiders could never gain entrance to the heart of their culture, not even on a guest pass. Dutch waited until the laughter died down, then said to Pete, 'I suppose that means you understand Chumash rituals.'

'I even know the Koran. You want me to quote it?'

Dutch believed him. He looked over to the front lawn where the tunnel was. Already guessing the answer, he asked him anyway, 'You know anything about Indian cave paintings?'

Looking as if he had just been challenged, Smokey straightened his back and replied, 'Hell, yes. I teach this stuff. You know that.'

'I got some great wall paintings to show you twenty feet away. Interested?' Dutch asked innocently.

Pete didn't answer for a couple of minutes. He just scratched his chin and looked deep in thought. Dutch waited. A grin slowly came over the Indian. How the hell could he say no to that? The Dutchman had him, and he knew it.

'You *are* one smart motherfucker,' Pete said finally, nodding in appreciation.

They went through the gate to the front lawn. When they came to the hole, Dutch looked down into it. Sweat broke out on his forehead. He glanced up and saw Tara looking at him quizzically. He let out a deep breath, trying to ease the fear, then climbed down the embankment.

When they reached the tunnel, they began crawling on their hands and knees; the beams from their flashlights rebounded off the smooth surface of the walls, exposing pieces of bone pushing through the cracks.

'How the hell did these get way over here?' Pete asked, pushing the bones out of his way.

The Dutchman smiled at the thought that Smokey didn't know everything. 'The earth's crust moves, especially during tremors. Over hundreds of years, relics that are buried deep in the ground can eventually rise to the surface. That's how we find prehistoric bones.'

When they reached the wall paintings, they stopped and turned their lanterns on them. Unlike before, there was no odour of rotting flesh.

'Jesus,' Pete whispered. He was staring wide-eyed at the coloured walls. He moved in closer, rubbed the paint with his hand, then licked his fingers. 'Chumash, all right,' he said nodding.

'Because of the colours?' Tara asked. She moved next to the wall, to see better.

'No. Any five-year-old could paint the colours red,

70

black and white.' Smokey leaned against the other side of the curved wall and crossed his legs to get comfortable. 'It's not the colours but what's in the paint. The red is a derivative from iron oxide, known as '*ilil* to the Chumash. The white is formed from a clay called '*ushtaqaq*. Black's nothing but pure charcoal. They mixed these colours with animal fat to bind them. You're welcome to taste it if you want.'

'I'll take your word for it,' Dutch said. The claustrophobic feeling was beginning to set in. He took a couple of quick breaths, making sure he could breathe.

'You're lucky you didn't ask the Chumash to see this. If they did, they would have hauled ass out of here.'

Tara perked up. 'Why?'

'Because only an '*antap* is allowed in the painted caves.' The first letter in the word '*antap* sounded like oh oh. 'That's a Shaman. They had supernatural powers. The ancient Chumash believed that if these symbols were misused, the world could be destroyed.'

'What kind of cave is this? You're talking ancient; this can't be that old,' Dutch said confused.

'It ain't. That's what's strange about what you're showing me. The walls feel like clay. It's hard to tell because it's so dirty in here, but it looks more like some kind of large pipe than a cave. The paintings are legit, but I don't think they're ancient. If they were, I wouldn't be able to taste the red ochre and the animal grease.' He pointed to some white and black triangles. 'The Chumash believed these markings symbolized funeral boats taking the dead to nearby islands.' He moved his finger over to an entire section covered with circles. 'They were also pretty good astronomers. The

71

large circle over here is probably the sun. This smaller one next to it, the moon; and the rest of them stars.'

Smokey suddenly noticed the large red circle with the curving black line going through it. 'That black thing's a centipede,' he said sombrely.

There was something vaguely familiar about that image, but Dutch couldn't remember what. Had he seen it before? Yes, he was sure of it. But where?

Dutch looked over at the Indian. 'Your voice just got serious, Smokey,' he said. 'What's so important about it?'

'Some of your bookworm colleagues believe that the centipede is the symbol of death in Chumash mythology. This just may be heavy shit you're dealing with here,' he said slowly.

Pete suddenly looked down to where the circle of light from Tara's lantern touched the clay floor. He crawled over to the lit area, picked something up and rolled it around in his fingers. He seemed disturbed. 'Jimsonweed. The *'antap* used it as an hallucinogenic.'

'Are there any *'antaps* left?'

'No. The Spanish brought Christianity to this area and destroyed the cult. A few survived, but by 1880 the *'antap* were as dead as a doornail.'

Dutch reached over and took the root from him. He put it up to his nose and sniffed. 'This weed can't be that old. It still has an odour.'

'I agree,' Pete said, looking disturbed. 'And I'm telling you, this isn't a cave.'

Dutch looked again at the black line through the circle. *Why was it so damn familiar?* He dipped into Tara's bag, pulled out a Polaroid camera, and took two shots of the design. Perhaps it would come to him

72

later. Meanwhile, the air was getting heavy in there, and he knew he couldn't stay much longer without panicking.

He was debating whether to go further into the tunnel when he heard Tara call out to them. She was about twelve feet deeper into the bowels of the cavern. Dutch and Pete crawled over towards her. Tara's flashlight shone on a fire circle of stones. Inside the circle lay charcoal remnants of wood and ash. The floor was littered with empty potato-chip and cookie bags. There were also dozens of old plastic meat wrappers, with yellowed Vons and Ralph's stickers on them. Some were newer than others.

'Somebody was living down here. Whoever it was, was no vegetarian,' Pete said, examining the names of the meat companies on the stickers.

Dutch noticed a mildewed army blanket by the side of the wall, and picked it up. It was infested with worms and he quickly dropped it.

Someone had used this place in the not so distant past, Dutch realized. Pete was right about the drawings; they weren't that old. Scanning his light over the area, he saw that the tunnel branched out into several different, smaller shafts. He wondered where they led to. Noticing that Tara was thinking along the same lines, he quickly said, 'Let's get an OK from the city's structural engineers before we try it.'

Tara nodded in agreement.

They turned around and made their way back.

When they regained the open hole, they could hear screaming coming from the tennis area, and the sound of wood hitting flesh and bones. Little Big Horn had begun. They looked up to see the riot police forcibly removing the Indians from the property. There was not much of a struggle; most went peacefully. Several of the teenage boys who had been yelling obscenities at the troopers now had bloodied heads and were handcuffed. They were led away to waiting police cars. The older men, women and children were being pushed back to the surrounding streets and away from the site by a line of police holding truncheons in both hands.

'The Nazis didn't go to Argentina after the war – they moved to Beverly Hills,' Pete said, his voice filled with anger.

'Then maybe you shouldn't hang out in this part of town, old man,' Falcone said, squatting next to the hole, and looking down at them. A toothpick hung from the corner of his mouth. He wore a white linen suit and a blue silk tie that matched the handkerchief in his breast pocket. The sleeves of his jacket were rolled up in a style that was popular several years ago. His head turned toward Tara and his eyes dropped down into her T-shirt.

Probably looking at the blue butterfly, Dutch thought with a flush of anger. He moved in front of her, blocking the man's view. Vince's smile faded when he saw the look on Dutch's face.

'I'm coming up. Move out of the way, Falcone,' the Dutchman said between clenched teeth.

Vincent Falcone did as he was told.

'I hear this is going to be a real family excavation,' the detective said, watching Dutch climb out. He was wiggling the toothpick between his teeth, digging at a piece of meat stuck in his side molars. When he dislodged the matter, he casually spat it on to the grass.

Dutch waited until Vince broke the toothpick in half

74

and dropped it on the ground Then he asked, 'Whose family are you talking about?'

'Yours.'

Falcone gave that snakelike smile again, and Dutch fought down an urge to smack him.

'I guess you didn't hear,' Falcone said. 'The earthquake uncovered a few Indian relics down the street where they're putting that new hotel up. The property's owned by Jonathan Payne. *The* Jonathan Payne,' he reiterated, wanting the importance of it to sink in.

Dutch thought about that black helicopter circling overhead. He turned and offered his hand first to Tara, then to Pete, and helped them out of the hole.

Falcone continued. 'California law says they have to excavate the remnants before the construction can continue.'

'I know what Californian law says,' Dutch said, brushing the dust from his shirt and pants, in the direction of the detective's Italian leather shoes.

With a look of disgust, Vince moved out of the way. He took the blue handkerchief out of his breast pocket and wiped off his loafers. 'Mr Payne isn't too thrilled with the prospect of having to wait to build his hotel just because of a few goddamn shells,' he said.

Dutch cocked his head to one side and smiled. 'Gee, that's tough. *The* Mr Payne must be worth over a billion dollars. He owns a movie studio, oilwells, restaurants, and satellite TV stations all over the world. In fact, he probably *owns* the world. Now he wants to become governor, probably because it's the only thing he hasn't done. A hotel is just pocket-money to the guy. Let him wait until the dig is completed.' He could see a glow in Vince's eyes, like

75

he had a secret that was trying to burst loose. His stomach knotting up, Dutch asked, 'Now, what did you mean, my family, Falcone?'

Smiling, Vince unbuttoned his baggy linen, designer jacket and put his hands in the side pockets. After a long pause just to make Dutch wait, he said, 'Mr Payne's hired your ex-wife as the contract archaeologist on the dig. I thought you should know.'

The air went out of the Dutchman's body. Aw, shit! Not Therese, he groaned to himself. Not Therese! *Goddammit, not Therese*! They hadn't worked together since Max's death. He looked at the detective and saw that he was still grinning; enjoying the pain he was causing. A rage overtook him. He closed his fists and locked his eyes on the detective's like radar zeroing in on an enemy plane.

The smile on Falcone's face froze in alarm.

'Dutch!' Tara yelled over to him, waving. She was standing with Pete by the excavated tennis court.

The anger drained from Dutch's body and he unfurled his fists. He brushed past Falcone, bumping against his shoulder, and went over to the site that had now been cleared of protesters.

Standing on the rim of the chasm, Dutch glanced down at the skeletal bodies lying in their foetal and frog positions. The full moon cast a yellow glaze over the bones. Looking down at the unearthing reminded Dutch of an ancient holocaust. According to Chumash mythology, the sun sets where the afterlife begins. That's why the heads were angled in that direction.

Tara took out the photos from her bag. They positioned them in the same degree as the graveyard, looking for the two skeletons that were distinct from the rest.

'There, Dutch,' Tara said, pointing to the centre left of the site.

He followed her finger and saw the two bodies. Yes, they were there all right. He sat down on the edge of the chasm, and twisted his body to the graves. Pete and Tara held his hands as he carefully let himself down the ten-foot wall. He didn't need a flashlight, because the area was lit up by floods. Putting one foot slowly in front of the other, he carefully walked between the bodies, sliding his feet forward, making sure he didn't disturb any artifacts or bones. He knew a scaffold should have been built first, reaching across the site to protect what was down there from being accidently destroyed. But there was no time for scaffolds; Dutch needed to see those bodies now.

When he reached the two skeletons, he kneeled down and studied them. Something was wrong here. *Very wrong*!

He glanced over at the other bones, and it suddenly dawned on him: the colouring and texture of these two were different. Dutch knew instinctively that the two bodies were not as old as all the others; in fact, not old at all.

His heart began to race. This was impossible! The graveyard had to be hundreds — parts of it even thousands — of years old. The remains in front of him couldn't be more than fifty at most. How the hell could that be? There was a noise behind him and he quickly turned around. Tara made her way over to Dutch and bent down next to him.

'What are you looking at?' she asked.

'These two guys don't belong here. They haven't been dead long enough,' he said, standing up. He scrutinized the area. The remains immediately surrounding the two bodies were in a closer proximity to one another than the rest of the skeletons in the grave-site. The fuzzy whiteness in Tara's photographs came from these compressed bones. Gesturing with his hands towards the dislodged remains, he said, 'They've been moved to make room for our two friends here. That's why they're all crowded together.' Instinctively he grabbed at his ear. It was throbbing and he wondered if it was infected.

Tara stood up to see. Her body stiffened as she realized that Dutch was right.

'I need to take a look at these bones,' he said.

'I'll get these remains to the pathology lab as soon as possible,' Tara said. 'Go home, Dutch. You look like shit.' She turned and headed back to call for the coroner's truck.

The Dutchman already knew he looked like shit. He rubbed his eyes, then took two Percodan tablets from his pocket and swallowed them. He figured he had just twenty minutes to get back to his trailer before the pills sent his head into orbit. Tara could handle everything here. She would wait for the truck and take the bodies to the lab. Right now he needed several hours of sleep before he could think straight.

Walking back to the perimeter of the chasm, he remembered that tomorrow would be Sunday and that he had to see Therese. More than anything, he needed sleep for that.

Pete was waiting for him at the rim, and offered the Dutchman a hand to help him out. 'This is not good what's happening here. A lot of centipedes running around in this place,' the Indian said bleakly.

A picture of that thin, multi-legged insect crawling over the side of a painted Indian cave quickly rushed through the Dutchman's mind. As he leaped up on the grass, he suddenly remembered where he had seen that symbol of death before. No, he was not one smart motherfucker like Pete had said. Smart motherfuckers don't take painkillers and then suddenly remember something as important as this. Now it was too late to do anything about it. Now he'd have to wait until morning to see if he was right.

5

Early the next morning, the Dutchman drove up to
Mulholland Drive and made his way east. When he
reached Encino, the sun was just beginning to show its
crown over the San Fernando Valley. He glanced at
the clock on the Bronco's dashboard; it was 6.45 a.m.
He had wanted to get up here earlier, but the pain pills
had made him oversleep. All the way here his mind
was on the thing he'd seen next to a grave by the
Encino reservoir three years ago. It was a long drive
from Malibu to the valley, and he was beginning to
wonder if he hadn't made a mistake in coming here.
The elements in this rugged, deserted area could efface
a lot of things after that period of time. Would it still
be there? Would it be recognizable? He had to find
out.

He parked his car by the side of the large reservoir
that supplied water to most of the Valley, and climbed
twenty yards down the mountain until he came to a
small ravine where the bones of a Caucasian male had
been unearthed three years ago.

After several minutes of poking through the brush,
he found the spot. Luckily, the grave had not been
filled in after the remains were removed.

A very bizarre case, he remembered. A lost

mountain-biker, who was a medical student, had come upon a human leg-bone protruding out of the ground. The heavy rains from the previous week had eroded the grave, exposing it. The police had been lucky. Someone unfamiliar with human anatomy would not have stopped, assuming it was an animal bone.

When a pit was dug and the bones became more visible, Dutch and his assistants discovered that most of the skeleton in the ground had been splintered into hundreds of pieces, which were then placed neatly on top of each other, almost in the form of a complex geometric pattern. The skull was not connected to the rest of the frame, nor was it anywhere in the grave. Police officers and bloodhounds searched the area for two days but couldn't find it.

The results of a coroner's inquiry, led by Orville Priest, determined that a cutting tool, probably a saw, had been used to dismember the victim in order to fit him into the small grave. The man's spinal column was cut cleanly through where the head would normally have been.

Microscopic pieces of powdered tooth enamel and dentine, a hard substance that covered the pulp of teeth, were found in the soil by the grave. DNA tests proved that they belonged to the dead man. This suggested to Orville and Dutch that the teeth had been deliberately knocked out of the mouth. The powdered substance also trailed away from the pit. This meant that the head had been taken somewhere else after it was hacked off. This troubled Orville.

'Why knock out the man's teeth if you're going to remove the head? What's the point in that?'

Dutch believed there may have been a point. It must have taken the killer a long time to methodically place the fragmented bones on top of each other like that. A lot of thought, and maybe even love, had to have gone into the execution. Perhaps the killer shattered the teeth in order to avoid having the victim identified by dental records, in case he was found later on. He assumed the killer was a man, because of the strength it would take to dig a grave in the hard earth and then cut up the body. The killer's first instinct may have been to remove the teeth. Then he realized that, with the skull still intact, the dead man could still be identified by head X-rays. If that was true, then it showed that the murderer was a cautious man who took no chances.

Carbon testing showed that the victim had been buried in that grave for almost twenty years. Facial reconstruction was only in its infancy at that time. Not many people knew about it. Perhaps the killer did, because he clearly had an understanding of forensics and anatomy. That meant that the murderer was bright and educated. The worst kind. They were calculating and prudent, the hardest to catch.

Dutch put what was left of the bones back together as best he could. Most of them had been destroyed beyond repair. Hairs found next to the body determined that the victim was blond. The length of the femur and tibia bones showed that he was at least six feet tall, and the ridges on the pelvic bones suggested that he was in his late twenties or early thirties. Since the killing had taken place twenty years ago, and there was no skull to make a true identification, there wasn't much hope of finding out who he was unless someone came forward.

The police scoured missing-persons files that were between twenty and thirty years old. A blurb was put into the newspaper about the find. When no one identified the victim, Dutch had requested the bones for his own collection. The coroner and the police were more than happy to give them to him.

What had jogged Dutch's memory last night was not the way the man was murdered, but what was painted on a flat granite slope next to the grave. It was a design: probably made by some kids who had climbed down there, Dutch had thought back then. Now he wasn't so sure. He remembered that the pattern formed a coloured circle around something black, resembling a curved snake with many legs.

Dutch climbed down an incline and immediately saw the rock with the markings next to the empty grave. The colours of black, red and white were faded from sun and rain, but he could still make out the design. A current of excitement swept through him. Taking his steel-rimmed glasses out of his shirt pocket and putting them on, he bent down next to the stone slab and traced his finger along the painted curves. He removed the two Polaroid shots of the centipede he had taken in the tunnel, and a small roll of masking tape from his shirt pocket. Tearing off two pieces of tape, he attached both photos to the rock-face next to the markings, and stepped back to get a better look.

No, he hadn't made a mistake. The curved lines on the rock arched the same way as the cave paintings in the Polaroids. He then counted the smaller lines in the photos, the ones representing the centipede's feet. There were forty. Using a pencil to help him keep place, he then totalled up the feet that were painted on the rock. Forty!

Removing his glasses, he stuck them back in his pocket and lit up a cigarette. He sat down on the dust-covered ground, pulled up his knees and rested his arms on top of them. There was now no question in his mind that whoever had painted the centipede on the side of the mountain also painted the one in the tubular tunnel. Dutch began to wonder how old the two skeletons found in the burial ground were. Was there a connection between all three of them? He leaned over and licked the paint on the rock to see if he could taste animal fat. No, he couldn't. Unlike in the damp tunnel, any flavour or odour that may have been here originally had been destroyed years ago by the dry climate.

The Dutchman crushed his cigarette into the parched earth and stood up. A mass of thoughts bombarded his head. Nothing felt right about this. He needed to tell the police, but what was he going to say? That a cave painting in Beverly Hills vaguely resembled a few coloured markings on the side of a mountain ten miles away? Falcone and the rest of the department would laugh at him.

Then the Dutchman thought about Jimmy Ciazo. Jimmy wouldn't laugh, he thought. No, he wouldn't do that. Instead, the gargantuan Italian would listen silently to what he had to say, not showing any emotion. His thick lips would be sealed tight, and his eyes would have the same unmoving gaze as a dead carp. Jimmy would form his own opinion on whether or not there was something strange about all this. If he agreed with Dutch, then he would look into it, no matter what the rest of the department said. Jimmy was never a team player. When Ciazo decided to look into a case, Falcone usually stayed out of the way because he was frightened to death of Jimmy. Most cops were.

Dutch got back into his truck and drove down the hill. At the first gas station he came to, he called the Beverly Hills Police Department and left his name, number and a message for Jimmy to phone him. He then dialled Tara's number and woke her up.

'Get the two bodies carbon-dated. I need to know how long they've been dead,' he said. In the background he could hear a female voice whispering. Dutch grimaced; he knew Tara was with Monica.

'What two bodies are we talking about here?' Her throaty voice was thick with sleep.

'The two from the burial site.'

More whispering on the other end of the line.

'I need the information as soon as possible,' he said, losing patience.

'Be nice, Dutch. What's the rush?'

'I'm not sure, but I think that headless body found up by the Encino reservoir three years ago is involved.'

'You're losing me. What does he have to do with the two skeletons in Beverly Hills?'

'Maybe everything, maybe nothing.' He told her about the rock paintings at the grave-site, and the similarity in the photos, then he hung up.

Getting back to the car, he once again looked at the clock. Shit, it was almost nine. He was supposed to be at Therese's at nine. Again his stomach tightened. Therese hated lateness, almost as much as she hated colours that didn't match.

He drove back down Mulholland Drive, then east on Ventura Boulevard. Turning south on Sepulveda, he went several miles into the hills to Stone Canyon. It was an area of winding roads and trees. Nineteen-sixties stucco houses with aluminium windows and sliding doors were mixed in with beautiful modern homes.

Dutch pulled his truck into the driveway of a house that was neither modern nor beautiful. It was hidden under overgrown trees and bushes that desperately needed pruning. The stucco on the walls needed new paint, and the mesh on the screen door was sliced open in several places.The front yard, except for a few patches of grass, was nothing but caked earth with sun-dried cracks in it. The house, like Max's body, was rotting away, he thought.

In the corner of the property a splintered wooden swing held by two rusted chain links, hung on the limb of a tree. The Dutchman remembered putting up that swing for Max when he was four years old.

After the accident, they had separated, and Therese left the university to work as an archaeological consultant for private corporations. Unfortunately, as Therese soon learned, jobs were few and far between. She found herself up against other qualified experts who also needed the work.

What he couldn't understand was why John Payne – *the* John Payne – had hired Therese to do the archaeological excavation on his property. She was small-time. There were many bigger firms that were better equipped to do this kind of job.

He thought about the first time he had seen Therese, in that godforsaken African gorge.

Dutch, with his large duffel-bag slung over his shoulder, had spotted her the second he climbed to the top of the ravine. Therese was down in the flats, bending over a table that held three-million-year-old canine bone fragments and patiently scraping the layers of dirt off them. She wore khaki shorts, and her long, shapely legs were stark white in contrast to the dark limbs of the Ethiopians working next to her. The straight hair down her back looked as fragile to touch as cocoon fibres. Round wire-rimmed glasses hung on the bridge of her nose.

Mesmerized, he had stood there for several minutes in the hot sun and watched her work. His loins began to ache. He couldn't remember the last time he had been this attracted to anybody. One minute she didn't exist, the next her presence filled every nook in his body.

Perhaps she could feel his heat, or maybe her back was tired from bending over − whatever the reason, she stopped what she was doing and turned around. She saw Wilhelm Van Deer on top of the chasm, looking down at her. He seemed out of place in this ancient gorge with his ponytail, big walrus moustache, cowboy boots, and T-shirt that said *It's Fun Doing It In Lahaina*.

'You're Wilhelm Van Deer,' she shouted up to him, smiling.

Dutch's heart felt like it was about to break out of his chest. 'You know me?'

'Yep.' She took a rag from the table and wiped her hands. 'I've read every paper you ever wrote in the field of palaeoanthropology. I'm a big fan of yours. I've been waiting for you ever since I heard you were going to be on this dig.' She climbed up the fissure, went over to him and shook his hand. Her fingers felt to him like smooth silk. 'You like three-million-year-old dogs?' she asked.

'My favourite,' Dutch said.

Her smile was wider now. 'Mine too.'

They had made love in his tent for a long time that

night, Dutch found her to be insatiable. When he was inside her, she would thrust her hips hard into his body, biting his neck, nipping at his cheek, her fingernails carving deep scratches in his back. When she finally came, she screamed unashamedly into the hot desert night, not caring what her colleagues or the Ethiopian aides in the other tents thought.

Afterwards, they wiped the sweat off their bodies with a wet cloth, then lay next to each other on the small cot and smoked a joint. She talked enthusiastically about the latest anthropological discoveries in Tanzania.

Dutch was impressed by her knowledge. While lightly stroking her damp buttocks with his fingertips, he asked what her favourite song was.

Turning around and glancing up at his smiling face, she asked, 'Why?'

'Maybe I'll sing it to you.'

She laughed. 'My favourite all-time song is "Maybellene". If you sing it, you better be able to duck-walk like Chuck Berry.'

He leaped up off the cot. Making believe he was strumming an imaginary guitar, he sang the entire song and did Berry's duck-walk, naked.

Therese laughed until the tears rolled down her cheeks.

Three days later Dutch had found the remains of an *A. afarensis* that pre-dated the oldest skeleton ever discovered. He named her Maybellene.

When they returned to the States, Therese moved to California to be with him. She got a teaching job at UCLA. They lived together for two years until they were married. A year and a half later, Max was born.

That was a lifetime ago, Dutch thought, turning

89

off the ignition of his Bronco.

He reluctantly got out of the truck, walked up the driveway and rang the bell. While waiting, he again turned to look at the swing dangling from the tree. For a brief second he saw a vision of his son sitting on it. Max was flying through the air . . . grabbing at the leaves . . . his small throat filled with laughter.

Then Therese answered the door. *Therese, with the milk-white skin.*

She was wearing a light-blue silk blouse tucked into faded, tight 501 button-down jeans.

Dutch loved Therese in jeans. Her long legs seemed endless in them.

Her fine, straight auburn hair was pulled back and held in place by a copper barrette. There was no make-up on her face. Dutch always liked the fact that she never wore any. It would have covered up her remarkable white skin. Her exquisite facial bones, like her small nose, seemed as if chiselled from English porcelain. Sometimes, when he looked at her, he felt that those delicate features belonged on a cameo, hidden away in someone's long-forgotten jewel-box.

Therese didn't look at Dutch through her round, steel-rimmed glasses. Instead, her eyes were focused deliberately on a fly climbing up the screen. She held the door open and stepped aside so he could enter.

'Hi,' he said in a low voice. Jesus, but she looked good in light blue, he thought. Light blue was her best colour. He struggled to fight down the all too familiar aching feeling of lost love that was rising up in his chest.

'You're an hour late,' was all she said in reply. Still avoiding eye contact with him, she moved out of the hallway and into the kitchen. He followed.

'I was doing some work up in the hills around Mulholland. I forgot the time.'

'It has *nothing* to do with work. You just don't want to sign those papers.'

'Not true,' he lied.

She took a cigarette from the packet on the tiled counter top and lit it. The morning sun filtering through the window illuminated her face. Though still beautiful, her skin was pale and drawn. There were faint dark circles around her eyes.

Max's death had taken its toll on her, he realized with a deep sense of guilt.

Therese sat down on a stool next to the counter and nervously took a sip of cold coffee from a half-filled mug. There was a fresh pot of it by the toaster oven, but she didn't offer him any.

Looking around, he could see that the kitchen, like the outside of the house, needed repairs. The dial on the oven was broken, and there was a leak in the kitchen tap that left a brown stain in the sink. Pieces of tile were missing from the counter, and sections of the linoleum on the floor were worn away, exposing older linoleum underneath. Again that flush of guilt. She had always taken pride in her things and what people thought of them. What the hell had he done to her?

'I hear John Payne hired you,' he said, trying to break the awkwardness.

'Yes, he did. Work is scarce in my field. As you can see, things need to be taken care of.' She gestured around the room.

'I've offered to help. You won't take any money from me.'

She smiled bitterly at him. 'What money are we talking about, Dutch? You're a week away from being out of a job yourself. Besides, I don't want your damn money.' She deeply inhaled on the cigarette, and stubbed it out in a chipped glass ashtray.

'I'm also working on the Chumash dig,' he said in a voice as steady as he could make it.

'Yes, I know. I was up at the hotel site yesterday. We didn't find any bones there; only some Indian artifacts. That means we won't have to see each other on this job.'

'Archaeologists and physical anthropologists always work together. That's like separating Ozzie and Harriet.'

She rolled her eyes. 'Oh, Christ, Dutch. What a dumb metaphor. Stop kicking a dead horse. The papers are on the table. Sign them, will you. I need to get them back to my attorney by tomorrow.'

'How about a cup of coffee first?'

'There's no time for coffee. Someone's coming over in a few minutes, and I'd like these papers signed and you out of here before then.'

He forced a lopsided jack-o'-lantern grin. 'Oh, is it the guy you've been seeing? He's coming over, huh?'

Her brow furrowed as she folded her arms across her chest and glared at him. 'It's none of your business who's coming over.'

I *am* kicking a dead horse, he thought. Nodding at the realization of it, Dutch stuck his hands in the back pockets of his jeans and walked over to the pine parson's table in the breakfast nook. Sliding his knuckles over its rough surface, he remembered how they had come across it. When Therese was six months pregnant with Max, she had spotted it on the sidewalk next to a row of filled garbage cans outside an apartment building. Someone had thrown it out. She rushed home to tell Dutch about it, saying that she needed it because it reminded her of the table in her Kansas home, where she had grown up. 'Get it for me, Dutch. Please go get it.' She was glowing, like only pregnant women can glow. His heart had shivered from her radiance. He drove to the spot that night, found the table, and put it into the back of his truck. She had spent the next several weeks contentedly rubbing the paint off it with steel wool and thinner, until the natural wood surfaced.

A lifetime ago.

He picked up the documents and pretended to scan them. All that was left to do now was sign. A simple signature and, presto, years of love and closeness automatically disappeared into some black hole. Only a dying house would be left to show that it ever existed.

Dutch slapped his pockets, searching for a pen.

'There's one on the table. If that doesn't work I have a hundred others around the house that will.'

He put on his glasses, sat down at the table and began signing several pages of documents, without reading them. If there were any surprises hidden in this jungle of technical claptrap, then so be it. Therese's signature and date were already on them. By the time he reached the last page, his hand was trembling so much that he had to steady it with the other one. After he signed the final document, he pushed the papers away from him. 'Done,' he muttered.

'Good,' she replied. She cleared her throat, trying to cover up the flimsiness in her own voice.

He attempted to rise, but his legs felt rubbery and he had to sit down again. After regaining composure, he grabbed the edge of the table and pushed up, forcing himself to stand. Then he went over to Therese and touched her gently on the arm.

She jerked her body away as if a snake had just touched her.

'Therese,' he said quietly.

She looked away from him.

Dutch dropped his hand. 'I loved him, too,' he whispered.

Her eyes, as if against her will, filled with tears. She looked up at him, her mouth beginning to tremble. She nodded her head. 'I know,' she barely uttered.

Dutch could feel her confusion, right down to his marrow, and it hurt. 'The marriage is over, and I'm going to try and live with that. It's your hatred that I can't live with. It's eating me up alive. You think I don't know what I did? I think about what happened every damn day.'

The hardness around her eyes softened, and for a moment she looked helpless and lost.

He slid his hands over her arms. This time she did not cringe. Instead, her eyes closed and her body arched in his direction. Just as her head was about to rest on his chest, a car's horn outside the house resounded, breaking the stillness.

Therese opened her eyes and pulled back from Dutch. 'Shit, you *had* to be late today, didn't you?'

A car door opened. Then they heard the crunch of footsteps walking through the fallen seeds from the pear trees that lined the driveway.

Dutch turned and saw the shape of a tall, slender man coming towards the house. When he reached the entrance, the figure shaded his eyes with his hands, leaned over and looked through the screen door.

Seeing Therese in the kitchen, he smiled and rang the bell.

'I think your friend is here,' Dutch said.

Therese pushed Dutch away and went into the foyer, towards the front door. The man opened it himself, and walked in. He put his hands on Therese's shoulders, said a few words in her ear, then made a movement to kiss her on the mouth. Embarrassed, she shifted her head to the side and his lips brushed against her cheek.

The Dutchman had never seen another man touch Therese before. The urge to run over and punch this intruder in the mouth was almost uncontrollable.

The man then looked up and saw Dutch. A look of momentary confusion crossed his face, then he relaxed. He grinned. It was an easy smile, the kind that said, *I know you.*

Dutch felt he had seen this man before, too. Where? He was good-looking with olive skin, white even teeth and curly black hair that was slightly long and sculptured around the neck. A meticulously groomed dark beard, with identical white splotches on both sides of his chin, wrapped around his angular features. His dusky, almost charcoal eyes were set deep into his skull. He had a lean, athletic body that said he spent considerable time in the gym. An expensive, dark green silk shirt hung loosely on his torso and was complemented perfectly by pleated khaki pants.

Then the Dutchman remembered where he had seen him. At the grave-site in Beverly Hills. He was the guy that had been thrown to the ground alongside John Payne when that fight broke out on the edge of the tennis court. Dutch was willing to bet that Therese had secured her job with Payne through this man.

'Wilhelm Van Deer, isn't it? What a lucky coincidence that we meet again,' the man said, walking over. He was almost, but not quite, the same height as Dutch. Again he smiled, and offered his hand. 'Miles Scone,' he said pleasantly.

At first Dutch didn't want to take it, but the man's smile seemed genuine, almost disarmingly boyish. Dutch relented and shook his hand. A faint odour of expensive European cologne emanated from his skin.

'I've been watching your work closely for many years. Too bad we had to meet in the middle of a fist fight.'

'You know me?' Dutch said.

'Yes. What you've accomplished in the field of identifying different tribal remains by the deviations in their crania is truly amazing,' he said.

'Are you an anthropologist?' Dutch asked.

'Nothing as interesting as that. I'm a lawyer up in San Francisco. Cooperate stuff. Dry as hell.'

'How do you know about my research?'

'Californian Indians are a hobby of mine.'

'Is that how you know John Payne?'

'John and I have been close friends since our freshman days at Stanford. In fact, I'm his campaign manager for the governorship. He's always been a Native American aficionado. I guess his enthusiasm wore off on me.'

'You were lucky in Beverly Hills yesterday,' Dutch said. 'Those Indians were one step away from ripping out your liver.'

Scone laughed. 'I know. Normally, John and the Indians have a terrific relationship.'

'Could have fooled me.'

'They're angry right now about a hotel John is

constructing on what they consider to be sacred grounds. They'll get over it.'

'I saw those grounds. They look pretty sacred to me.'

The warmth left Scone's eyes. 'Those skeletons were found a couple of blocks from the hotel. There have been no bones uncovered near the excavation itself. Besides, the grave-site is an old one. Hasn't been used in hundreds of years.'

'I didn't know consecrated ground lost its power with age. Ask John Payne to level Masada and erect his hotel there - then see what happens. The Israelis would have his balls on a platter.'

Scone cackled, then quickly flicked his hand in the air, as if to say, I'm not laughing at you. 'Sorry. The image of John's privates being paraded around on a saucer would be quite a whimsical sight, especially if you knew him. Meanwhile, you're the one that's removing the sacrosanct remains from those holy grounds and dissecting them on steel tables, not John Payne. The Chumash may only be annoyed with him, but they sure as hell have to be crazed with you.'

Scone talked like a lawyer; most of them did. But he had a point, and Dutch knew it. The Chumash would love to see Dutch skinned and quartered.

'When can work be resumed on the hotel and the streets be re-paved?' Scone asked.

'Everybody seems to be inquiring about that lately. After I sift through the bodies and determine which ones are ancient and which ones aren't,' Dutch said.

Scone looked surprised. 'Which ones *aren't*? What does that mean?'

'Some of the bones don't seem to be hundreds of years old.'

'How old are they then?' Therese broke in quickly. Her voice had taken on a professional tone, her eyes become clear and curious. Her scholarly look was back – something Dutch hadn't seen in a long time. He suddenly realized how much he missed it.

Leaning against the counter and folding his arms, he said, 'I can't tell how old they are yet. We have to do carbon tests to determine their age.'

'I've seen you determine age by sight, Dutch, and you were usually right on. How old?'

'Maybe twenty . . . maybe fifty years old. I'll know better after the tests.'

'That's hard to believe,' Scone said. 'The ones I saw were practically prehistoric.'

'Not all.'

'How many new ones did you find?'

'Right now, just two skeletons.'

Scone nodded as something suddenly dawned on him. 'Probably some of the elders in the tribe who knew about the ancient grave and found a way of getting into it so they could bury their own relatives.'

'Perhaps,' Dutch said. 'Until they're examined, I can't close the site. Neither can Therese.'

'That's for me to say, Dutch. Not you.' Her eyes were cemented threateningly on to his, and she was angrily biting down on her bottom lip.

He had just blown it with her. You didn't assume anything *for* Therese. She made her own decisions.

'I thought you were leaving,' she added. She put her hand on his arm, trying to nudge him towards the door.

'Was I? And I was just getting started.'

'I know all this is a bit awkward between us,' Scone said, trying to break the tension.

Dutch knew what he meant. His eyes narrowed at the man's frankness.

'This is a first for me, too.' Scone laughed nervously. 'I mean, this is the first time I've ever been face to face with the ex-husband before. I assume it's the same for you.'

This man was so damn civilized. He reminded Dutch of Leslie Howard in *Gone With the Wind*.

'Goodbye, Dutch,' Therese said, sensing his mood. She was scowling at him now.

'Sorry you have to leave,' Miles said. 'I love talking about bones, especially old ones. So does John Payne. Maybe all of us can get together. You'd like John. You two have a lot in common.'

Dutch scanned his face to see if he was really serious. He couldn't tell. His words carried all the right inflections, but that easy smile on his face was still there, clouding everything. The guy reminded Dutch of Tara's butterfly – a paradox.

Miles Scone held out his hand to him, a look of sincerity engraved deeply into his face. A feeling of resignation came upon Dutch, and he shook it.

'Sorry about your ear. Did they find all of it?' Scone asked. The corners of his mouth turned downwards in concern.

At the mention of his ear, Dutch hand automatically went up to the side of his head and touched the sticky gauze. It felt hot, and the stitches were making his skin itch. Dutch thought that maybe Scone was laughing at him, but again he couldn't be absolutely sure.

Without saying goodbye to Therese, he walked out of the house.

Dutch climbed into the truck and pulled out of the driveway. Looking in the rearview mirror, he could see

Therese's shadow through the screen door. She was leaning against Scone's chest, and he held his arms around her. The Dutchman waited until he was well down the street before he slammed his fist on the wheel.

He drove down Ventura Boulevard towards Encino, past the park where he used to take Max. In the middle of the greenery was a duck pond. It had been the boy's favourite place. When they arrived there, Dutch would usually do a magic trick for him. He'd show Max his empty hands, then he'd rub them together while reciting some unintelligible words. When he turned them over, two small paper bags of duck food would have miraculously appeared in them. Max always giggled and searched his father's jacket, then his shirt, for a secret compartment, but he could never find one. He would call Dutch the 'magic man' whenever he did that trick. Then the boy would grab the bags and hold out pieces of bread, to let the ducks and the ganders peck at his fingers. His voice would shake with laughter as they converged around him, hawking and nipping at the food.

Had two years gone by already? The memories and the pain were so sharp that it seemed as if it were only yesterday that Max had died. He began to curse the forces of nature again. The bastards had taken his son. Throughout his entire life they had taken everything that mattered to him.

That awful day once again engulfed him.

He and Max were together on a father-and-son vacation, sailing the British Virgin Islands – when the storm hit. One-hundred-mph gusts lashed out at the Dutchman, slapping him hard in the face as he frantically turned the winch to bring down the main sail. The sloop was rolling like a toy boat on top of fifteen-foot crests. Dutch knew Culebra was only several miles to the west. If he could keep the boat at an even keel, he would make it. Max was in the galley, strapped in his seat, attempting to draw in a colouring book with crayons.

The rain was coming down harder now, stinging his eyes. He rubbed at them with the sleeve of his yellow slicker.

This was not supposed to happen. He had checked the weather report before he left St Thomas and it said that the hurricane converging on the Venezuelan coastline and the Grenadines would miss the northerly islands. The sonofabitch had changed direction.

From the corner of his eye he saw Max coming up on the deck. He was wearing the red life-jacket Dutch had put on him before they set sail. When the boy spotted his father by the wheel, he smiled and went towards him.

The Dutchman screamed, but the sound of the raging wind drowned out his voice. Leaving the wheel, he rushed towards him and grabbed his arm. The boy laughed.

Dutch picked him up in his arms. Holding on to the safety rope, he carried him towards the steps leading down to the cabins.

'Daddy?' Max said, clutching on to his father's neck. 'When it rains like this, is God taking a shower or peeing?' His lips were pursed by the seriousness of his question.

Suddenly, a giant whitecap hit the bow, sending the fore-section of the sloop up out of the water at a ninety-degree angle. Dutch fell on his back and slid

101

down the deck towards the stern. Max slipped from his arms. The Dutchman desperately tried grabbing him but the safety rope pulled tight, keeping him from sliding any further. For a second, he saw Max's red jacket near the rudder, then it went over the side.

'MAX! MAX!!' Dutch screamed over the gale winds, but the boy was gone.

'Is God peeing, Daddy?' That was the last question Max ever asked him.

Forty minutes later, when Dutch opened the door to his trailer, he could see the red light blinking on his answering machine. First, he went into the kitchen to see if Bitch was all right. She was lying on her blanket wagging her tail, happy to see him. There was water and dry dog-food left over from that morning. He emptied the water dish in to the sink and refilled it. Tara had a key and also took care of Bitch when he wasn't at home.

He walked back into the living-room and took his messages: two from Tara, three from the UCLA Medical Centre demanding to know why he had snuck out of his hospital room in the middle of the night and one from Jimmy Ciazo leaving Dutch his home number.

The second call from Tara said: 'We're at a makeshift lab in a hanger at Burbank Airport. Right now I'm beginning to examine the two bodies. Get your ass over here. You're not going to believe this.'

Dutch called Jimmy first. The phone rang several times. 'Yeah,' Jimmy said, when he finally picked up. The 'Yeah' was like a hollow grunt.

'It's Dutch.' He told Jimmy about the centipede

102

painting in the cave resembling the one on the stone surface in the Encino hills.

The voice on the other end remained silent. Dutch listened for breathing, but heard none. He wondered if Ciazo sported gills instead of lungs.

'Centipedes? What do you want me to do about it?' the big Italian finally said.

'If the two skeletons in the grave-site haven't been there very long, then I think somebody should look into it. That's for starters. Then I'd want to know why there was a similar centipede painting on a stone next to a body several miles away. Even your interest has to be perked, Jimmy.'

Ciazo laughed. It sounded like the same grunt as before, only at a higher pitch. 'This just might hold everything up,' he said. 'Orville Priest and John Payne won't like that. If somebody killed these people like you may be suggesting, then everything is going to be put on hold for a while.'

There was a long silence, one that told Dutch that Jimmy was making up his mind about what he wanted to do. Finally he said, 'Let me know what you dig up. If something don't smell right, you call me. I'll work with you.' He hung up before the Dutchman could say anything more.

Dutch went into the bathroom and removed the bandages from his ear. The skin was a deep red surrounded by blue bruises. The stitches resembled little mosquitoes stuck on flypaper. He put some antiseptic over it, then wrapped it up again with a clean dressing.

He left the house and got back in his car. Sometimes he wished he didn't live so far from the rest of the human race. Burbank Airport was over an hour away.

He shifted into reverse and backed out of the driveway. Tara had found something big, he could tell by her voice. As he drove south, past the beach traffic on Pacific Coast Highway, he wondered just how big it was.

6

Dutch pulled into the parking lot adjacent to the airport. A hundred yards away, a jet with the blue and white Federal Express logo began taxiing down the runway, its engine screaming in his ears. He got out of the Bronco, grabbed his knapsack, and walked across the street towards the hangar.

Several coroner's trucks were parked next to its large open portal. A line of workers were taking the covered remains from the burial site out of the trucks, and bringing them inside the building. Police vehicles surrounded the airplane enclosure. Next to the structure, young Indian men in army fatigues were holding placards and walking single-file in a circle. The signs, painted in the black and red colours of the Chumash, read: INDIANS DON'T BELONG IN MUSEUMS and REPATRIATION − NOT OBSERVATION.

Repatriation, Dutch knew, was the word the Indians used for reburial. Most of the four hundred Native American tribes shared a common belief that the souls of the departed could not rest if the graves were disrupted. More and more Federal and State laws were being passed which sided with the Indians on this matter, making it harder for the anthropologists like Dutch to do their work. He suddenly remembered what Smokey had told him at the tunnel site about the ancient Chumash: they didn't care about their bones, since they were into reincarnation. Looking at their modern descendants holding up signs, Dutch couldn't fail to see the irony in all of this.

Trying to avoid a confrontation, he slipped in through the back door. What he saw in the huge hangar, which normally housed 767s, nearly took his breath away: hundreds of skeletons, wrapped in tinfoil like frozen TV dinners, were laid out on top of army blankets across a floor as big as a football field.

Many of his students were already opening the foils and cataloguing the bones in their notebooks. The place resembled an impromptu medical facility after some cataclysmic upheaval. At the other end of the building, Dutch saw Tara standing next to two gurneys. She was bending over one of the bodies on the table, and measuring its pelvic bone.

He threaded his way past the skeletons lying on the floor. She looked up and smiled when he approached. Her spiked hair was frazzled and her eyes were red from lack of sleep.

'Hey, Dutch. Are we planning on working today?' she said, grinning.

He ignored her and stared down at the bones. 'Are these the two from the site?'

'These over here.' Stepping back, she motioned to the two gurneys, acting like a merchant proudly displaying her wares.

Dutch moved in closer to take a better look. 'I couldn't see their features last night. It was dark and the heads were face-down.' He took a pair of plastic gloves from the medical table, put them on, and picked up one of the skulls. He ran his hand over it, sniffed it for age, then turned it upside-down to examine the teeth. Looking at Tara, he said, 'There's little wear in the incisors and molars. That doesn't make sense. Indians in this area had lots of tooth deterioration because of abrasive elements in their diets.'

He looked at the upper incisors and saw that they weren't shovel-shaped at the back. That doesn't fit, either, he thought. Variations of the Asian race, including Native Americans, had scooped configurations at the backs of their front teeth. This one didn't. He felt the top part of the facial structure. 'Indians have prominent cheekbones. I don't see that here. These cheeks don't protrude.' Pointing to the nasal area, he said, 'This is a projecting nasal bone instead of a flat one.' He put it back on the gurney. 'What does the other skull look like?'

'The same as this one,' she said, smiling. 'Which leads you to believe what, Dutch?'

Dutch shook his head in amazement. 'These aren't Mongoloid characteristics. So what I'm looking at are two Caucasoid remains.'

'It gets better,' Tara whispered. She moved in between the gurneys and pointed at the pelvic bones on the two bodies. 'Both pelves are shallow and broad.' She moved her hands to the front parts of both hips. 'Here's the pubic symphysis. Look how pliable they are on each of them.'

'They're women.'

'Right,' she said.

Dutch's eyes went to the iliac crest on one of the pelvic bones; it was a flat plate on the top, with a curved ridge. This one had deep grooves on the edges. 'It's not united,' he said, tracing the ridges with his fingers. That meant the girl had to have been fifteen years old, or younger, when she died. After fifteen, the crest meshes together. He saw the non-union of the iliac crest on the other body. He immediately looked down at the hip-bones: the femur sockets *were* joined together. The three parts in the hip-bone unite at about fourteen years of age. 'Both girls were between the ages of fourteen and fifteen when they died. Anything found next to the bodies?'

Tara reached over and took a labelled plastic bag from the table. She opened it up and carefully removed some fine strands of blond human hair. She pointed to the other bag that was next to it. 'It also contains blond hair, from the other body.'

'What the hell?' he uttered, confused. Two young Caucasian women with the same colour hair, who died at the same age, were found right next to each other in an ancient burial site. Were they captured by Indians a couple of hundred years ago and made to live with them? he wondered. He doubted that: the Mission tribes, which the Chumash were part of, didn't seize white women. Also the bones didn't appear to be that old. He'd have to have them bomb carbon-14 tested to determine the exact date of death. He looked at Tara. She was wearing that secret grin again. 'There's something else, isn't there?'

'Absolutely.' She gestured to the skeletons. 'The one on the left is Minnie, and the other one is Daisy.' Tara always named her bodies after Disney characters. She picked up a Ziplock bag from the table and opened it. Taking a small object out of it, she said, 'This was found next to Daisy's head.'

Dutch took it from her. It was a bobby-pin. 'No fucking way!' he said, shaking his head in disbelief.

'Ancient Indians didn't wear bobby-pins, Dutch. Read the small printing on it. It says Taiwan.'

'What about Minnie?'

She picked up the left shin-bone from the gurney. 'There's an old crack in the lower portion of the fibula. There are no traces of healing, so I have to deduce that the break occurred right after she was killed. There's also a gold cap on her left mandibular second bicuspid.'

Tara was good, Dutch thought. He had known that from the first day she walked into one of his classes. He thought about the remains found by the reservoir again. Was there some connection between the twins and the other victim? He had a hunch there was.

'Dutch,' Pat Sagata called out. He was standing behind him.

The anthropologist turned around. 'What are you doing here, Pat? I don't see any bloody spleens — just bones.'

Grinning at the Dutchman, he said, 'You're a funny man. I just hope you can make it as a comedian on David Letterman when your teaching contract runs out.' The Japanese pathologist had his suit jacket slung over his shoulder. He was wearing a short-sleeved shirt. A large ink-stain covered part of the pocket, from the pens he carried in it. Around his neck hung a loose, narrow black tie. 'How long do you think this is going to take? I'm getting pressure from Orville. He needs to know if these bones are forensic or archaeological.'

'What's the rush?'

'An entire city's being held up by its balls, waiting for some word from you. You like wielding this kind of power, Dutch?'

'Fuck Orville,' Dutch said, turning back to Daisy and Minnie.

'I have relayed him that message from you on many occasions and normally he would thank you for your suggestion. This time, however, he wants an answer.'

'What's so different about this time?'

The air-conditioning wasn't turned on in the hangar, and the sweat was pouring lavishly down Pat's face. He shrugged. 'You know Orville, Dutchman.'

'Christ, how do you work for that guy?'

Pat shrugged again. 'I got to make a living.'

'Let me show you something,' the Dutchman said. He took the bobby-pin from the bag and held it up. 'This was found in a graveyard that probably predates Columbus by several thousand years. How the hell did it get there?'

'Maybe the Indians found a way to get into the grave and they buried . . .'

' . . . their own dead.' Dutch finished the sentence for him. 'You're the second person today to tell me that.' He wondered if Pat had been talking to Miles Scone. 'The girls are Caucasian, Pat, not Indians.'

'Well . . . then, hell, maybe the hairpin floated in through the sewer,' Pat said.

'What sewer?' Tara asked, confused.

'That tunnel with the Indian paintings. The police checked with city planning. It's an old drainpipe built over three-quarters of a century ago when Beverly Hills was being transformed from a cow pasture. It hasn't been in use for the last fifty years.'

'And the blanket and foodstuff we found in it?' Tara asked sceptically.

He looked uncomfortable. 'A drifter. The sewer systems in LA are home to hundreds of them.'

110

'This particular sewer was a good twenty yards away from the grave-site. This pin was found fifteen feet beneath the earth, next to a white woman's head,' Dutch said. 'Bit of a coincidence, hey?'

'Maybe not. This bobby-pin was the same kind my mother used to wear. It probably made its way into the sewer years ago. Maybe it was left by a female transient. There were hundreds of cracks in that pipe. Rain probably washed it out of the drain and flushed it down the incline towards the graves.'

'Have I mentioned that there were white females found in the burial site, Pat? You seem to be ignoring that part. Did the rains also flush these women through the three-inch cracks and into the grave-site?' He was confused by Pat's reaction. Normally his mouth would be watering when Dutch showed him physical evidence of a possible crime. Had Orville and the illustrious city fathers of Beverly Hills got to him?

'Are these women of forensic value?'

'I don't know, yet,' Dutch said. 'I'm sending them out for testing.'

'How long is all this going to take?' Pat asked irritably.

Dutch put his hand on the coroner's shoulder. 'I said *white* women, Pat.'

The coroner didn't reply. Yes, they had got to him, Dutch conceded. There was no sense in telling him about the figure of a centipede found next to the body in the hills around the reservoir. Pat didn't really want to hear it. His grandfather died in the internment camp at Manzaner, and his father was killed in 1944 fighting the Germans in the 442nd Regimental Combat Team. Those tragedies coloured his life. Pat Sagata may be second-generation Nisei, but he had never felt a part of this country. Being a Japanese-American meant living with insecurity, and the biggest thing Pat was insecure about was his job.

Dutch said calmly, 'Carbon dating usually takes a few weeks. I'll put a rush on it. I wouldn't want Orville to bust a blood vessel.'

Pat avoided the Dutchman's eyes. He was uneasy. 'It's not me, Dutch. You understand that?'

'I know that, Pat. I just hope I'm wrong and these remains are over two hundred years old. I could live with being wrong on this one.'

'I'll tell that to Orville,' Pat said. He put on his jacket and left the hangar.

Dutch watched him disappear through the large doors. He hated to see that sonofabitch Orville turn the screws on Pat like that. The poor guy was caught in the middle.

He turned to Tara. 'Take photographs. Take pictures of every goddamn bone in this place, from every goddamn angle. Don't get chintzy on the amount of film you're using; it's Beverly Hills money we're spending. I don't want any surprises.'

She saw the ardent look on his face and understood. Wiping the sweat off her forehead with the back of her hand, she said pensively, 'You think they'd fuck with this?'

'Orville would fuck with anything.'

'Why? Because of the loss of some tourist trade, and a giant hotel that will have to wait a few extra days before construction can start again?'

Dutch shook his head, confused. 'I don't know why. We're dealing with bureaucrats. Take pictures. Use the Nikon, not the Polaroid.'

'Do you want to do a facial reconstruction?'

Dutch hated that. Restoration of facial features, to get a better idea of what they looked like, was the same to him as knowing their names or seeing their passports; it made them too human. 'Let's wait and see what the lab comes back with on the dating. If I find out the two girls are of forensic calibre, and not archaeological, then we'll start the process. What about the other remains? Has anyone found anything out of the ordinary?'

'No, not yet. Except for these two, everything, so far, looks ancient,' Tara said. She picked up her cigarette pack from the table and started to take one out. Then, remembering where she was, she put it back. If nicotine got on the remains, it would alter the accuracy of the carbon-dating process.

Dutch picked up her cigarettes and handed them to her. 'Take a break,' he said.

He pulled his knapsack over one arm and walked out of the complex, with Tara. Once outside in the bright sunlight, they lit up cigarettes. Tara took a deep drag, then sat down on the tarmac and leaned her back against the corrugated metal wall of the hangar. Dutch squatted next to her.

'These are recent deaths, Dutch,' she said softly. Her eyes were clouded with that faraway look again.

He knew *recent* didn't necessarily mean last week or last year. It meant the date of death in relation to the rest of the bodies found in the area. From his knapsack he pulled out the photos Tara had taken of the grave-site. He pointed to the section around the remains of the two girls. 'The surrounding soil and some of the other skeletons were disturbed to make room for these girls. There's no question but that they were put there later on. I don't understand *why* it was done. Pat's theory about the Indians burying their recent dead in that site is way off base. Burial grounds are sacred to Indians. They'd never tamper with one, and they certainly wouldn't move bodies around just to put new ones in. I also can't figure out how the hell it was physically done without anybody seeing it. Those bodies were buried deep beneath the ground; heavy machinery would have been needed to do that. Who would know about this ancient site?'

'Some of the medicine men, I'll bet,' she said. 'They always do. They just don't let us know about them — until one's uncovered.'

He tapped his finger on the glossy photo. 'When are the bones going out for carbon dating?'

'The truck from the lab should be here any moment. I'm sending the left femur bones from the two girls.'

She flipped her cigarette, and it landed in the street several yards away.

Dutch stood up and crushed his butt under his cowboy boot. He grabbed some change out of his pocket. 'I need to call Jimmy Ciazo,' he said to her.

Stretching from fatigue, Tara went back into the hanger.

Dutch walked over to the phone-booth at the side of the building. He dropped the change into the slots and called the direct work number that Ciazo had given him. After a few rings, Jimmy picked it up. Dutch explained that both skeletons were those of white girls. Ciazo didn't say anything. Dutch waited about thirty seconds. 'You breathing, Jimmy?' More of a pause. Dutch wanted to slam the phone down on him.

'When did the girls die?' Ciazo said finally.

'I'll know later on tonight. While I have you in a

talking mood, I need to ask you something. Remember what Falcone told me about that woman who owns the property where the bodies were buried?'

Again no answer.

Dutch continued. 'He said that she fell into the drainpipe, and that somebody was trying to drag her through it. Remember?' Another deep pause. Dutch sighed. 'This is long-distance and I'm running out of change, Jimmy.'

'So, what about her?' Ciazo said.

'Who do you think was down there with her? You think maybe it was the Indian who cut off my ear?' He heard a crunch on the other end of the line; Jimmy was biting into a sandwich.

With a full mouth, Ciazo said, 'This rich bitch was buried underground with a bunch of skeletons for more than half the day. After all that time, even *I'd* imagine some fucking ghoul was down there with me. Nobody took it seriously. This is some super-kike queen we're talking about here. She's the kind of broad who would put on a mink coat just to go the supermarket to buy a carton of milk.'

If everybody spoke like Jimmy, Webster's dictionary would be no larger than a three-page foldout, Dutch thought. 'What else did the woman say?'

'That this creature grabbed her by the ankle. She said his nails dug into her skin.'

'Did it?'

'She had some scratches there. She also had similar ones over most of her body. That was a big fall she took, and she landed on top of sharp bone slivers.'

Dutch suddenly thought back to the dragging sound he had heard in front of them when he, Pat and Tara were in the tunnel. 'Did she say what this person or thing looked like?'

'Uh-uh. It was too dark, and that part of the tunnel she was in was too narrow for her to turn around.'

'I bet it was the Indian, Jimmy.'

'The bitch was hallucinating.' Again the crunch on his sandwich.

Dutch was just about to hang up, when Jimmy said, 'She did say one weird thing.'

'What weird thing was that?'

'She said there was a terrible stink down there.'

The Dutchman's fingers clutched tightly around the receiver. 'Did she define that stink?'

'Yeah. She said it smelled like someone had fuckin' died and was rotting.'

Dutch also remembered that smell. 'Which hospital is she in?'

'UCLA Medical. The right wing on the fifth floor. The name's Garowitz. You going to see her?'

'Maybe. I'll keep in touch, Jimmy.' Dutch hung up on Ciazo.

Marsha and Lenny Garowitz; he remembered the names. He touched his bandaged ear; UCLA Medical was where he had it sewn back on. He had also been in a room on the fifth floor. Marsha Garowitz was right down the hall from him all the time. 'Ain't that something!' he said out loud. He would drop in on her tomorrow.

'It smelled like something had fuckin' died down there,' Jimmy had said to him. The man's a bloody poet, Dutch thought.

7

'Oh, Mr Van Deer,' a woman's singsong voice cried out.

Dutch looked towards the reception area. The fifth-floor head nurse was fiercely waving at him from behind the desk. She picked up a stack of files, tucked them under her arms, and walked over towards him.

'We've been very naughty,' she said, shaking a finger at him. 'You had no business leaving the hospital without authorization. That was a major operation Dr Marshfield performed on you.'

Dutch peered down at her. She was a short, squat woman in her mid-fifties.

'My ear's doing fine,' he said, moving backwards down the hallway, trying to get away from her.

She kept pace with him. 'That's not for you to say. It's Dr Marshfield's decision.'

'And how is the good doctor?' He hated walking backwards. His boots were sliding over the polished linoleum floor.

'The good doctor misses you. What are my chances of getting you back into bed so he can take a look at your ear? We haven't given your room away yet.'

Dutch mumbled something unintelligible to her as he looked down at the crumpled piece of paper in his hand. Marsha Garowitz's room number was on it.

Her lips tightened. 'There's a good likelihood that your ear is infected, Mr Van Deer.'

Dutch shrugged at her. When he came to Marsha's room, he found the door closed. He turned to the nurse, who had now placed herself between him and the door. Her legs were spread apart and her arms were solidly crossed. She reminded him of the Mother Superior who once blocked the boys' bathroom at his elementary school like this, refusing to let him use it because he had looked up the dress of one of the girls in the gymnasium. By the time the sixth period came along, his bladder had let loose and he peed in his pants in front of the entire classroom.

'Give me twenty minutes and I'll go back to my room,' he said to her.

Again she shook her finger at him. 'Is that a promise, Mr Van Deer?'

Dutch fluttered his eyelashes and crossed his heart. He waited until the nurse was safely back behind the reception desk, then knocked on the door. After several seconds, a sombre man in his late fifties answered it. He wore an expensive grey sports shirt with charcoal-coloured pants; a heavy gold piece, perhaps a coin, hung on a chain around his neck and lay submerged in a field of white chest-fur. His henna-dyed hair was placed strategically across his head to camouflage his spreading baldness.

'Lenny Garowitz?' Dutch asked, even though he already knew the answer.

'That's right,' Lenny said. He looked scornfully at the tall man in front of him, with the bandaged ear and wearing a Venice Art Festival T-shirt. 'What is it?'

'My name is Van Deer. I'm the anthropologist

118

who's looking into the bones found on your property.'

'There are no bones here,' Garowitz said. His round, bulging eyes, small chin and sharp nasal structure gave him the appearance of an owl.

Dutch leaned his body further into the door-frame, in case Lenny felt like closing it. 'I know that. I want to talk to your wife.'

Lenny was scowling openly now. 'Can't you see what a trying experience this has been for her? She's in no position to talk to anybody.'

'Who is it, Lenny?' A nasal New York voice came from behind the door.

Lenny looked back into the room. 'No one, dear. Just another one of those pesky archaeologists.'

'Physical anthropologist,' Dutch said, smiling.

His face turning red, Lenny pointed his finger at Dutch's chest. 'I don't care what you call yourself. Those damn kids from the university have been tearing up my property all morning, scavenging for bones. What kind of business is that for a kid to go into?'

Dutch laughed silently to himself. Good question, Lenny. 'I want to talk to your wife about the person who was with her when she was trapped in the tunnel.' Dutch's voice was calm, the smile frozen on his face.

'Let him in, Lenny,' the twangy voice demanded.

Lenny moved out of the way and Dutch entered.

Marsha was a good-looking woman in her late forties, with blonde weaved hair. Well-built. Probably does aerobics every chance she gets, Dutch thought. Her left arm was in a full cast that hung suspended on a pulley above the bed.

Sitting on a chair next to her was a tanned, healthy-looking girl in her mid-teens. The daughter, Dutch assumed. She was meaty, but her body was solid and

119

hard. The girl wore breeches and a pair of dirt-caked English riding boots. Her hair spread out in all directions, and there was a sheen on her forehead. Must have just come from a riding lesson. The girl's hair was also frosted the same shade as her mother's. Probably went to the same hair salon. Maybe they even went together. Standing in the corner, staring blank-eyed at *Days Of Our Lives* on the TV set, was a teenage boy. The son. He wore teeth braces, and had that gawky adolescent look.

'Are you the one they call Dutch?' Marsha asked him.

'That's me,' he said, walking over to her bed.

'Mr Falcone mentioned you,' she said disapprovingly.

'I bet he did. Except Mr Falcone doesn't believe there was someone else at the bottom of that chasm with you. He also doesn't believe that this someone stunk of something dead. I *do* believe it.'

Marsha's face softened. 'Sit down, Mr Van Deer.' She gestured with her good hand towards the chair that her daughter Sharon was sitting on. 'Move, Shassy,' she said, then patting her bed, motioning for the girl to sit there instead.

'That really isn't necessary. I can stand,' Dutch said.

'Sit down.' It was more of a command than an offer.

Rolling her eyes, Sharon stood up, went over to the window and plopped herself down on the sill instead. She folded her arms and pouted.

Dutch sat in the chair.

'Why do you believe me and not the police?' Marsha said, her head cocked suspiciously.

Every hair of her head was in place, and her lipstick

and eye make-up was perfect. Dutch wondered how she could do all of that with just one good hand. 'Because I went down into the crevice right after you were rescued. I could hear someone about twenty feet ahead of me, crawling through the tunnel. Also the smell was pretty bad.'

A satisfied smile played on Marsha's face. 'Those bastards were laughing at me. I knew I was right. They didn't believe me!'

Lenny came over to sit on the corner of her bed. He stroked her foot under the cover. 'Now, sweetheart, don't get excited . . .'

She brushed the air with her good hand, cutting him short. 'There *was* someone down there. Not only could I smell him, I could feel his breath on me.'

'What the hell is the reason for all of this? What difference does it make?' Lenny growled at Dutch. 'You're upsetting my wife.'

'Knock it off, Lenny!' Marsha snorted. She moved her foot away from his touch. 'I'll talk to this man if I want to. The only reason I'm in the hospital is because you thought you could save some money by hiring that goddamn Iranian contractor!'

Dutch looked Lenny over. He seemed tired and old for his age. His shoulders were slumped, and there was a slight bulge in his mid-section that hung over his belt. Probably works sixty or seventy hours a week in order to keep Marsha looking young and Shassy in designer riding clothes, he thought.

'Maybe it was one of those dirty homeless people that sleep in Roxbury Park,' Sharon popped in. 'Maybe he found the tunnel and decided to make his home there.'

Dutch smiled patiently. Shassy knew as much about

121

the homeless as he knew about horses. 'I think Roxbury Park is a lot nicer to sleep in than that musty, dark ol' tunnel, don't you?'

Shassy shrugged. Without being too tactful, she began studying Dutch's body, her half-closed eyes lingering on his crotch. Feeling uncomfortable, he folded his leg over his thigh and put his hands on his lap to block her view. He was beginning to believe she had a lot more hobbies than horses. Dutch turned back to Marsha.

'I hate earthquakes,' she said, shuddering.

Dutch nodded at that. So did he.

She patted her lips with a tissue. 'I was in the bathtub that morning. I take lots of baths. Baths help calm my nerves, even better than Xanax. It was Shassy's sweet-sixteen party that night. We were throwing it for her at the Hard Rock. That's where she wanted it. Personally, I would have preferred the Hillcrest Country Club. We had bought her a new 325 BMW convertible, and were going to give it to her there.'

'Red with tan leather seats. The dealer didn't have black ones,' Sharon said, disappointed.

'They were out of black. We would have had to wait six weeks for the new shipment from Germany,' Lenny said defensively.

Sharon pouted. 'You could have planned further ahead.'

No matter what this poor bastard did for his family, it would never be right, Dutch thought.

Marsha said sadly, 'We were going to blindfold her at the party, then take her outside to see it. Lenny even got a specially-made giant red bow from one of his friends who owns a gift-wrapping company downtown, to put on top of it. That damn quake spoiled everything. The bathroom suddenly started shaking and the walls ripped open. I couldn't believe it! It was like that Charlton Heston and Ava Gardner movie about earthquakes. I should have known it was going to happen. All morning long, you could hear the coyotes up in the hills, howling. They say that animals can tell before humans.' She glared at her husband. 'The goddamn house broke apart like it was made out of papier-mâché. Always trying to save a nickel every chance you get, even at the expense of your own family, aren't you, Lenny?' She looked at Dutch. 'Lenny manufactures men's underwear. May Company returned the entire spring order last year because Lenny tried to save a few bucks by inserting cheap elastic in the waists. They fell apart – just like my house.'

Lenny studied the nap in the carpet, his face turning the colour of an over-ripe apricot.

'The marble in the bathroom and in the foyer was all buckled in like an accordian. It *was* marble, wasn't it, Lenny? Not cardboard painted to look like it, right?'

He bobbed his head nervously. 'Venetian. The best you can buy, Marsha.' His voice was cracking, like the sound of a long-distance ham radio operator.

'Sure it was, Lenny. Great construction.' She turned to Dutch. 'I found there was a gap in the walls as big as a football field, and I made it outside to the front lawn. There I was, naked as a newborn baby, running over the impatiens like a maniac, screaming. Thank God nobody saw me.'

'What happened?' Dutch asked.

'The ground opened up between my legs, like a cracked eggshell. Before I knew it, I was falling. When

I hit the ground, I broke my collarbone. Before the aftershock came and closed up the ground, I got a glimpse of the skeletons. There must have been hundreds of them.'

'There were,' Dutch said. 'When did you know someone was there?'

'Right after the earth closed. You couldn't see him, but you could smell him.'

'Was he with you the entire time you were underground?'

'No, just a few minutes.' Tensing up, Marsha reached over to the night-table, took another tissue out of the box and wiped the perspiration off the upper part of her mouth, being careful not to smudge her lipstick. She then tossed it on to the mountainous pile already on the night-stand. 'I couldn't see his face, it was too dark down there. All I remember was that he grabbed my ankle and started dragging me deeper into the tunnel. I could feel his sharp nails digging into my skin. See?' She poked her right foot out from under the covers, and showed Dutch her ankle.

Dutch leaned over. Her foot was small and well shaped, and her toes were painted the same colour as a Tequila Sunrise cocktail. He moved his eyes to the scratches. He was not a forensic skin expert but he was fairly certain that they were made by claws or nails — probably human ones. 'Who saw these?' he asked.

'What do you mean who?' Lenny bellowed. Marsha shot him a look and he backed away.

'Other than the staff at this hospital, who else saw these scratches?' Dutch asked again.

'Some coroner with a strange name.'

'Was he Japanese, or did he wear a dark suit and looked like he'd forgotten to shave?'

'Yes!' she blurted out. 'That's the one!'

'Which?'

She stroked her face, emulating which one. 'The one who looked like a gorilla.'

'Orville Priest,' Dutch muttered.

'That's the name he used. How could I forget a *goyishe* name like that! I was hysterical when they pulled me from the hole.' Again she glared at Lenny, as if blaming him for her ordeal.

'Christ, I'm charged with everything that happens in your life!' Lenny shouted. He got up from the bed, threw open the door and sauntered out into the hallway.

Marsha turned to Dutch and said, 'When I showed that coroner my foot, he just patted my shoulder like I was a goddamn kid, and said, "There, there." Can you imagine? "There, there!" To me he said that?'

'Orville always had a great bedside manner,' Dutch said.

Marsha's bottom lip popped out in a sulk, and a tear raced down her face.

Sharon got up from the radiator and sat down on the bed next to her distraught mother. She put her arm around her shoulder, stroking it, and leaned her head against hers.

'That damn Indian,' Marsha muttered, barely audible. She rubbed the tears in her eyes with another tissue, causing the wet mascara to blacken her cheeks.

'I heard you talked to the police about him. Tell me about that Indian,' Dutch said, slowly standing up.

'He used to hang around our house when it was being built,' Shassy scoffed. 'That was six months ago. We had him arrested.'

Marsha blew her nose into the tissue, threw it on to

the pile, then said, 'He came back again. I saw him right before the earthquake. What an ugly man!' She let out a small grunt as the vision of the Indian began to take shape in her mind.

'Where did you see him?'

'At the excavation site where they're building the hotel. I was just coming back from getting my hair done for Sharon's party when I noticed him. He was acting crazy, like the last time. Punching himself in the face, jumping up and down on one foot. Screaming at the construction workers.'

Shassy quickly chimed in, 'He did exactly the same thing in front of our house. He scared us half to death. We were afraid to go out in the street. The neighbours were calling us and complaining. They thought we knew who he was. I was outraged! Why would we want to know anyone like him? That's when we called the cops. The judge said he would be put in jail if he ever came back. Six months later, there he was again.'

'This Indian,' he said in a hushed voice. 'What did he look like?'

Shassy answered him by putting two fingers down her throat, and made a face as if she was going to throw up.

Dutch waited for a fuller description. When it didn't come, he said, 'You think you can punch it up with some words, Sharon?'

'Short and wiry,' Marsha cut in. 'His teeth were terribly rotted. Long matted hair. He was filthy and he wore dirty tennis shoes with no laces and no socks.'

The Dutchman sighed. He remembered the man all too well. 'Did he have a gold tooth?'

'Yes!' both women said together.

'The front lower canine,' Marsha said.

Dutch angled his head at her.

Marsha shrugged. 'I know teeth. I was a dental hygienist. That's how I met Lenny. The first time he came in for an appointment it took me almost two hours to get the tartar off his teeth. By the time he left, we had already made plans for the weekend.'

'You've been very helpful,' Dutch said, backing out towards the door. As he reached for the knob he could feel the heat of Shassy's eyes honing in on his crotch again.

Outside in the hallway, Dutch turned and walked in the opposite direction to the head nurse and the reception desk. There was no way he was going to get back into one of those hospital nightgowns with his ass hanging out. After walking through several corridors, he came to the left wing of the hospital and found the elevator. Lenny was standing next to the ashtray, smoking a cigarette. Dutch nodded to him as he pushed the *down* button.

'It's safe to go back in the room now, Lenny,' the Dutchman said.

The underwear manufacturer looked tired, and his skin was the colour of mustard. 'You work like a *schvartze* all your life and for what? The county wants to press criminal charges against me. Marsha doesn't know yet.'

'Because of the house?' Dutch asked.

He closed his eyes and nodded.

'You shouldn't have cut corners, Lenny.'

'Who the hell could afford construction today? You know what my family costs me to keep them happy? Every time Sharon buys a horse, it's twenty or thirty thousand dollars a pop. You can't insure those dumb animals. If it breaks a leg or tears a tendon — bang! —

127

another thirty thou. And Marsha!' He slapped his forehead. 'She thinks she's the cream of Beverly Hills society. Suddenly she wants a huge house on the most primo property in the city. Nothing else would make her happy. I couldn't afford that. I *had* to cut a few corners. Now everybody hates me.'

'A few? That's more than a few, Lenny. The house was held together by spit.' Dutch's ear was burning and he knew he'd better get some aspirins in the lobby pharmacy. 'But look at it this way,' he continued. 'If everything was up to code on your property, then the burial site would never have been uncovered. The county may want your ass, but my colleagues owe you a debt of gratitude.'

Then Dutch glanced down and took a good look at the gold piece around Lenny's neck. It *was* a coin. 'Nice,' Dutch said, pointing to it.

Lenny lifted it off his curly white chest hair. 'Like it? It's a Spanish coin. I found it near my house, and had it appraised. It's worth a few bucks. Real old. The only piece of luck that fucking house ever brought me.'

'Found any more?'

Lenny tapped the side of his head with his index finger. 'Smart men don't talk about these things.'

No, smart men don't, Dutch thought. A few of those sold to the right people could hold off bankruptcy for a while.

The elevator opened and Dutch walked in. As it closed again, he caught a glimpse of Lenny's pitiable face, staring out the bay windows overlooking the university. His fingers were still clutching the gold coin around his neck. Probably the only security he had left.

There was no reason for him to be so facetious with that poor guy. He wondered why he felt so angry. What did that man do to him? By the time Dutch reached the lobby he knew the answer; Lenny had a wife and children. They were far from ideal but they were his. Dutch had no one. As he opened the door to the pharmacy, he found himself not hating but envying that careworn bastard.

8

The desk sergeant cupped one ear and looked up with friendly eyes at the man with the walrus moustache and the bandaged ear. 'Tell me one more time what you're asking for?'

'An Indian,' Dutch said loudly putting his hands around his mouth like a funnel and punctuating the vowels. *Inde-e-a-a-n*. The sounds of workmen scraping ladders on the floor and painters climbing up on scaffolds to hang plastic covers on the walls filled the hallway of the building. The police station, like the courthouse next door, was getting a face-lift. Odours of turpentine and paint permeated the dusty air, making Dutch's throat constrict.

The sergeant, oblivious of the smell, brushed his fingers through his closely cropped white hair and slowly licked his bottom lip. 'What do you want with this Indian?'

'I need to talk with him.' He was shouting to be heard over the noises.

Using some file folders as a fan, the sergeant said, 'After a while you get used to it.' He was referring to the stench. A paint-splotched tarp covered his metal desk. 'You his attorney?'

'No.'

'A relative?'

Dutch touched his ear. 'You might say we're related by blood.'

'Then you should be very happy to know that he made bail about two hours ago.'

Astonished, Dutch leaned over the desk and yelled, 'How the hell could he make bail? He had no money!'

The sergeant's friendly steel-coloured eyes hardened at Dutch's tone.

Clutching the ends of the desk in his hands, Dutch asked, 'Where's Falcone?'

The officer seemed surprised that he knew him. 'Detective Falcone is in the field.'

'Ah, shit!' Dutch groaned, banging his palms loudly on the desk.

The alcohol-induced capillaries in the sergeant's nose turned bright red. He stood up, his face inches from the Dutchman's. 'Watch your mouth, son.'

'What about Ciazo?'

The officer slowly sat down. His eyes broke away from the Dutchman's. 'He's here,' he muttered.

Dutch wanted to laugh, but he was too angry. Ciazo could instil fear in more people than anyone else he knew.

The sergeant picked up the phone and dialled Ciazo's extension. He whispered something into the receiver, then hung up. 'He'll be right out,' he said.

The Dutchman looked up and saw Jimmy's big, burly figure coming out of a cubicle at the end of the hall. He made no effort to sidestep the workmen and the other police officers standing in his path. Instead, they seemed eager to make room for him. Ciazo reminded Dutch of a great white shark: he was indifferent to anything around him that couldn't be eaten. He came over to the sergeant's desk. When he saw the anger in Dutch's ruddy face, he said in his raspy voice, 'Come with me.' Without further acknowledgment, he turned back the way he had come. Dutch pushed open the metal gate and followed him down the hall with detective cubicles on both sides.

Ciazo's office was exactly like Dutch had imagined it to be: spartan. There were few papers on his desk. No paintings adorned the walls, not even a calendar or photographs of his children. A clean coffee mug with THE BRONX SUCKS stencilled on it sat alone on a metal stand in the corner of the room. There were no surprises here; it was the office of someone who was uncommitted to life.

Jimmy went behind his desk and sat down. He didn't bother to offer the Dutchman a chair. He shuffled a couple of papers around until they were back in the same place they started from, then said, 'What do you want, Dutchman?'

Dutch stood by the door and folded his arms. 'What the fuck happened to the Indian?'

As usual, Ciazo didn't say anything for several seconds. He just stared at Dutch with his black, dull eyes. Then, 'What Indian?' A vague light lit up somewhere inside his head as it suddenly began to dawn on him. 'Oh, you mean the one who fitted your ear for a zipper. What about him?'

'He's gone. He made bail.' Dutch went over to the water fountain in the corner, put a cup under the nozzle and pushed the button. It was empty.

Ciazo didn't offer to get him a drink. He lifted his massive shoulders in a shrug. 'So he made bail. So what?'

133

'The sonofabitch tried to kill me! Bail's got to be pretty high on attempted murder!'

Jimmy laughed and Dutch was stunned. He had never seen the big man so much as crack a smile, let alone laugh. The noise coming out of his throat sounded like a car driving over broken bottles.

'Maybe the court didn't think you were worth much.' Surprised at his own humour, Ciazo laughed again.

Dutch waited for some kind of punch line to the joke, but there wasn't one. Ciazo was finished.

'What's the Indian's name, Jimmy?'

'How the hell do I know? He was Falcone's collar.' Ciazo leaned back in his chair and locked his thick, sausage-like fingers around the back of his head.

'I want to see the release forms.'

Ciazo grunted as he got out of the chair. Without looking at Dutch, he walked past him and out into the hall, his rubber-soled shoes squeaking on the linoleum floor. Dutch followed.

Ciazo opened up a heavy steel door and went down corrugated metal steps to the holding cell. It was humid down there. Naked light bulbs, protected by wire mesh, ran in a straight line down the ceiling.

As they walked through the narrow hallway, Dutch flinched at the harsh screams bouncing off the concrete walls and the shrill pitch of metal doors clanging shut. Jimmy, his eyes fixed straight ahead, never twitched or looked around. Nothing affected this man. Dutch wondered if Jimmy made sounds when he was having sex with a woman. He doubted it. He then wondered how the woman knew when Jimmy was finished? Maybe he gave her a hand signal.

Ciazo stopped next to a metal cabinet and took

down one of the loose-leaf logbooks on the top shelf. He opened it up, wet his thumb and turned the pages until he came to today's date. Moving his finger down the list of releases, he stopped at two names. 'It's got to be one of these two guys, except the names don't sound Indian,' he said, showing the book to Dutch.

Dutch looked at the names: Monroe Washington and Bobby Santiago. Dutch glanced wryly at Ciazo. 'My money's on Santiago, Jimmy.'

'Santiago sounds like a Mex.'

'Right. There are no pure-blooded Chumash still living. Most of them intermarried with the Mexicans. That's why I say Santiago.'

'Oh, is that right?' Ciazo scratched his head. 'You're sure this Monroe Washington can't be the Indian?' His voice became thick and whiny, a bad imitation of Stepin Fetchit.

Dutch ignored him. Ciazo, like most cops he dealt with, was a bigot. He was used to it. The Dutchman looked at the right-hand corner of the page to see how much bail was set for.

Fifteen thousand dollars. Hell, that wasn't enough! The Indian had maimed him. He could have been killed. Fifteen thousand! A goddamn pickpocket's bail is higher than that! Dutch looked to see who set it. The name on the bottom was Judge Robin Diaz.

A knowing smile stretched across the Dutchman's face. He slowly closed the log and put it back on the shelf. Robin Diaz. He hadn't seen her in almost two years. Except she wasn't a judge then; she was an Assistant DA. He had met her right after Therese had left him. They had dated a few times, then drifted apart. *Wrong timing*.

Dutch looked at his watch. Four forty-five. Court

ended in fifteen minutes. He told Ciazo he would talk to him later. Leaving him there, he made his way back up to the lobby of the police station, took the elevator to the third floor and walked through the overpass to the courthouse. Looking outside, he could see deserted streets where there had once been traffic jams. That meant the traffic was now doubly snarled in other areas of the city to make up for the emptiness here. Dutch knew that time was running out. The city was going to blame him and Therese for this mess if they didn't give the OK to start re-paving the streets pretty soon.

Dutch went into the building and took the marble stairs up to the second floor. An officer in the hallway told him Judge Diaz was in session and directed him to the courtroom at the end of the corridor. He went over to it, looked through the glass frame and saw Robin up on the bench.

She was more beautiful than when he had dated her, he thought. It was a natural beauty: little make-up, clear Latin skin, and dark, dazzling eyes that always seemed to be laughing.

He opened the oak door and walked in. The room was almost empty, except for the court groupies: bored retirees, who came with their brown-bag lunches every day by bus to listen to the trials.

Robin was looking down at a fidgety, overweight lawyer in a wrinkled blue suit standing in front of her bench. His puffy face was milk-coloured and covered with a coat of sweat. It was a face that said, *I'm hungover*. The lawyer was holding his thumb and index finger up to her and sliding them quickly over an imaginary object. Dutch wondered what it was.

Over by the table, a small man, hunched, late

twenties, wearing a cheap checkered sports coat and an unmatching striped tie with a double Windsor knot, was picking at his nails. His curly hair was greased back and he sported long, thin sideburns.

'It's impossible to do it with two fingers, your honour. The entire hand is needed,' the fat lawyer said with conviction.

'My, my. You've taught me something today, Mr Epstein. I never knew it took so many appendages to complete the act of masturbation,' Robin said. Her eyes were laughing at him.

'Takes all five fingers, your honour,' he said, nodding.

'You know this for a fact, do you?'

Snickering from the groupies at the back.

The fat man, looking assured, turned to the crowd, then back to Robin. He also laughed. 'If you had let me bring in a urologist as an expert witness like I asked, I would have proved it.'

'You know better. This is only an arraignment, Mr Epstein, not a trial. Your client was discovered by an undercover officer in a men's bathroom at Dodger Stadium.' Robin pointed to a young policeman in the back row. 'The officer testified that when he walked in he saw Mr Pyke alone in a stall, peeking over the top and watching a teenager urinating. He said that Mr Pyke was in the process of committing a lewd and indecent act.'

'The officer is mistaken. My client was standing over the toilet, holding his penis with only the thumb and index finger. That's not a lewd act. It's the way men hold themselves while urinating. As I said, you can't masturbate with just two fingers. It's a physical impossibility.' He emphasized his point by once again

137

holding his two fingers in the air and frantically pumping them up and down.

'So you told me, Mr Epstein.'

'It's a known fact. I don't mean to be disrespectful, your honour, but you're a woman. Men know more about these things.' He looked patronizingly up at her.

Her eyes stopped laughing. She stared silently down at him. A frozen smile slowly washed over her face, causing his to vanish.

She didn't say anything for a while, letting him squirm. Finally she said, 'Thank you for clarifying my gender for me, Mr Epstein. I feel a great weight has been lifted off my shoulders. What I don't understand is why a man needs five fingers when a woman can do it with only one? Perhaps we are more advanced than the male species. What do you think, Mr Epstein?'

More snickering. The groupies were leaning forward in their chairs now, their knees knocking together in anticipation. Judge Diaz was their favourite.

'Mr Pyke looks like a healthy man, with two strong fingers,' she said. 'I don't see why he couldn't do it with them, if he had the urge.'

'Your honour . . .'

She looked down at him, like a hawk looking over a frightened field mouse. 'Would you like to waste more of the city's time and plead your client innocent? Perhaps you can have him whip it out in front of a jury to convince them of how many fingers it takes.'

The fat man didn't answer. He brushed a hand uneasily through his thinning hair.

'Do I take that to be "No, I won't waste the city's time", Mr Epstein?'

He glanced over at his client. Pyke, gnawing at the cuticle on his thumb, looked at him helplessly.

Epstein turned to Robin, sighed and threw up his hands. 'Guilty, your honour. But no jail time.'

'Oh, I should say not. Obtaining orgasm with just two fingers. It may start a new rage. Replace Nintendo.' Robin checked her calendar. 'Tuesday, November second, at nine o'clock. Have your client in my courtroom then. If he's not here, your derrière is mine, counsellor.'

She banged her gavel and dismissed the court. Then she stepped down and went into her chambers.

The room emptied. Dutch waited. During the time she was up on the bench, Robin had never once looked directly at him, but he knew she had seen him.

Five minutes later, her young male bailiff walked out of her chambers and motioned for him to go in.

Dutch went over to the door and looked inside. Judge Robin Diaz was sitting behind her desk, with her knees propped up against the edge and her hands crossed behind her head. She was wearing slacks. Her black judge's robe hung across the arm of the couch. When she saw the Dutchman, she broke out into laughter. 'Get your ass in here, Mr *morsa grande*,' she said, stressing the *grande*.

'I wasn't sure you'd remember that name,' he said, grinning.

'Oh, I remember everything about you, Wilhelm Van Deer. I remember very well.' Her eyes were still laughing, but her lips quivered slightly, betraying her nervousness.

Dutch also remembered. *Morsa grande* meant 'big walrus'. She used to call him that because of his giant moustache. When they pounded the sheets together, she'd stroke his giant moustache with the tips of her fingers and moan, over and over again, *'Mi morsa grande, mi morsa grande,*' until she climaxed. My big walrus. He missed hearing that. It was good, what they had. Short-lived but good.

When he first met Robin, she was also licking her wounds; coming out of a bad affair with a married State Supreme Court judge. She and Dutch discovered they were the perfect solution for each other's needs. Once, after a heated session of love-making, they had lain in each other's arms and watched a video of *Last Tango in Paris.* Except for the 'butter' scene in the movie, there was very little in the movie that Dutch and Robin hadn't already done, and when the film was over that was soon rectified. They had laughed, saying how much Brando and the young Maria Schneider were like themselves — two lovers who were physically drawn together but who knew nothing about each other. It was the perfect arrangement.

What had happened to kill it?

The sticky talons of feelings. That was the culprit, Dutch thought. Trying to keep feelings out of what they had was like trying to keep a swarm of locusts out of a wheatfield with a can of Raid. Affection was allowed; passion was not. As soon as she discovered that a form of caring was beginning to rear its ugly head, she had stopped seeing him.

Dutch understood and didn't pursue her. *Wrong timing.*

'You put on a great show today,' he said.

'I try. It's been a while, Dutch.' She gestured for him to sit in the leather chair next to the desk.

He sat down, his eyes entranced by her face. He didn't remember her looking this good. Probably because he had been too busy mourning his own losses.

140

Her eyes also remained locked on to his. She said, 'So, how's my *morsa grande*?'

'In pain,' he said, motioning to his ear.

'I heard.' The smile dropped from her mouth.

Dutch glanced down at Robin's hands folded together on the desk, and saw a gold wedding band on her finger. 'You hitched?' he asked, surprised.

'Yes,' she said.

'When?'

'About a year and a half ago.'

'To who?'

'The judge.'

'The one that was already married?'

Robin nodded. 'He found out about you and decided that I was the one he'd wanted all along and not his wife. You know how the story goes. It's as old as your Maybellene. As long as I was available, he was in a constant state of befuddlement. The second he realized that I was capable of parting my legs for another man, the fog miraculously lifted from his tortured soul and his infinite love gushed forth.'

'You happy?'

'I think so, Dutch. He pisses me off sometimes with his hunting trips and his Polo clothes and his other male bullshit, but, yeah, I love him.'

She looked content, and he believed her. He felt a twinge of disappointment.

'So, to what do I owe the pleasure, Dutchman?' Her eyes playfully scanned his face.

'It's about Bobby Santiago.'

'What about him?'

'He got off pretty easily. Was I not *grande* enough for you?' A shade of anger coloured his voice.

Her eyes flared. 'That's cheap, Dutch.'

141

'No, Santiago's bail was cheap. The sonofabitch tried to kill me. Why so low?'

Her mouth was tight, annoyed by Dutch's remark. 'Because I'm a criminal court judge, and I have a job to do in spite of the fact that it was you who got hurt.'

Dutch looked confused. 'You want to run this one by me? I said he tried to kill me.'

'Not really. If he wanted to kill you he would have.'

'He tried to slice my head open.'

'Sorry, Dutch. He was aiming for your ear. He told me that he didn't think you were worth killing. Santiago is a Chumash Indian. You were desecrating his land. He was just trying to protect it. Chopping an ear off, according to him, is the way you deal with pillagers. I know the man. He's appeared before me in this court several times. He may be an itinerant, and he may be crazy from too much alcohol and drugs, but he's not a murderer. Since he's only a pest and not a danger to society, I couldn't go higher than fifteen thousand on the bail.'

'The guy's got soft hands with an axe,' he muttered.

'Lucky for you,' she said.

'How does an itinerant come up with money like that?'

'Through a bail bondsman, obviously.'

Dutch shook his head. 'He still has to come up with ten per cent of that. Fifteen hundred dollars. Itinerants also don't have friends with that kind of money.'

Robin's face darkened and she began to bite her lower lip.

Damn, she looks good doing that, Dutch thought. She used to do that thing with her lip right after they made love.

Robin suddenly picked up the phone on her desk and pushed a button. After several seconds, someone answered at the other end. 'Mary – good, you're still here. Look at today's calendar and find me Bobby Santiago.' While waiting, Robin leafed through several files on her desk and pulled out the one with the Indian's name on it. She delved through it. When Mary came back on the line, Robin asked, 'What was the name of the bail bondsman?' Whatever Mary said made Robin's eyes widen in disbelief. 'How was the bail paid, then?' she asked in a low tone. When she got her answer, she wrote it down on a yellow scratch pad, then hung up.

Dutch saw the confusion on her face and he moved his body closer to the desk. 'No bail bondsman, right?'

She said slowly, 'Someone paid the entire amount in cash.'

Dutch was stunned. 'Someone threw fifteen thousand dollars away thinking that this Indian nutcase would come back to court?'

She shrugged and nodded. 'It is a little odd.'

'Who?' he asked, standing up. This didn't make any sense.

She looked down at her notation. 'His bail was paid in cash by a Mr Hugo Frye. Santiago was then released into this man's custody.'

'Do you know who he is?'

'If he wanted to be known, he wouldn't have paid in cash, now would he?' Snapping her fingers, she said, 'Wait a minute!'

She got on the phone again. She called the cashier's office of the BH Police Department across the way. When someone answered, Robin identified herself and asked about the fifteen thousand dollar payment.

Excited, she gave a few huh huhs, then hung up. She looked up at Dutch and said, smiling, 'The girl remembered the transaction because the payment was in cash. She also remembered the bills as being new and crisp. The amount was paid in fifteen one-thousand-dollar stacks. Each stack contained brand new twenty-dollar bills. The clerk said there was a paper band around each one with an imprint on it.'

'What kind of imprint?'

'I don't know. She's taking them out of the vault so we can see them. Let's go, she's waiting for us.' She quickly got up, grabbed her black judge's robe from the couch and hung it on the back of the door. They left.

Even in the cashier's office, the smell of paint and turpentine filled the air. Dutch wondered how anyone could work in here without their brain cells being altered.

'Love the colour, Heidi,' Robin said to the black cashier behind the desk.

Heidi turned round and looked at the freshly painted pastel walls. She had a deadpan face. 'It's something, ain't it, judge? Big manly cops strutting through pink and turquoise hallways. Only in Beverly Hills could this happen.'

Robin laughed. 'You have the money?'

'Yep, here it is.' Heidi went over to a shelf, took down a box and dropped it on the counter. She said, 'This man, Hugo Frye, he was bland-looking. Someone you wouldn't notice if you passed him on the street a thousand times. Not a hunk, but not a geek either. Blond. Slightly built, but tight. Know the kind I'm talking about? If he was a woman, a man would

144

call her a spinner. Had real sad looking eyes. You think the name's real?'

'Who would make up a name like that?' Dutch said.

Robin picked up one of the stacks. 'Smokey Valley Savings and Loan,' she said, reading from the inscription on the paper band wrapped around it. She looked at the other piles; the same name was on all of them. She turned to Dutch. 'Mr Hugo Frye must have an account there.'

'I never heard of the bank,' he said.

'Probably a small S&L. It shouldn't be too hard to find. I'll make a few calls in the morning and find out who Hugo Frye is, and what Smokey Valley Savings and Loan is all about. Why do you care who bailed Bobby out? You're not out for vengeance, are you, Dutch?'

'Ears don't grow back,' he said.

'Are you?' she insisted.

Dutch grinned. 'No. I'm concerned for another reason. Have you eaten dinner yet, or do you have to go home to your husband?'

Her face softened. 'No, *mi morsa grande*, I haven't eaten dinner yet. And, no, I don't have to go home to my husband. He's a secure man. He understands old friends.'

'As long as he doesn't hunt them.'

'This will be a great test. Because if anyone can shake his self-assurance, it's you.' She looked him up and down, staring at his T-shirt, jeans and cowboy boots. 'Your attire is going to limit us. Don't you own a suit? No, I guess not,' she said, answering her own question. 'In fact, I don't remember much about you wearing clothes at all.'

They both laughed.

She took him to a small, family owned Italian trattoria across the street from the courthouse on Little Santa Monica Boulevard. Most of the formica tables were empty. The owner was a friendly Tuscan with silver hair and a waxed moustache that twisted up to a point. He knew Robin from the other times she had eaten here and welcomed them warmly. He told them that the earthquake and the excavation were killing businesses all over the neighbourhood. He sat them at the back, away from the street. 'Some college professors are holding everything up,' he said disgustedly. He gave them menus and walked away.

'He's right, you know,' Dutch said to Robin. 'We like to give the impression that we can look at broken pottery and tell everything there is to know about a civilization. That's a lot of horse crap. If some of us so-called scientists went to a dump a thousand years from now and dug up layers of beer cans and soda bottles, we'd probably surmise that a sect called Budweiser rose up and cast out Dr Pepper and his following. We actually get paid for doing this.'

Robin's eyes searched his face. 'You're a needed man, Dutch.'

He couldn't argue with her. Instead, he ordered the most expensive bottle of Barolo to help make up for the restaurant owner's losses.

While waiting for the wine to be uncorked, she said, 'I missed you.' The simplicity of her statement startled him.

Wrong timing. 'Too many ghosts stood between us then. Now a marriage,' he said, with a pathetic attempt at a smile. She nodded and looked away. Dutch suddenly realized that Robin may have cared for him more than she let on. As his fingers reached out across the table to touch her hand, the waiter came between them and poured some wine for him to taste. Wrong timing again, he thought.

Dutch ordered the osso bucco and Robin the rosemary chicken. When the waiter left, she said, 'Why so interested in the Indian, Dutch?'

He took a deep swallow of the rich red wine, then said, 'You know anything about centipedes?'

Robin looked at him strangely. 'You sure Santiago only whacked you on the ear?'

Dutch explained about the drawing of the centipede in the tunnel matching the one on the stone wall near the reservoir.

Her face turned serious. She'd seen too much as a criminal court judge to shrug anything off as coincidence. 'You think the two girls in the grave-site were put there recently?'

'Positive. I'll find out how recent when the carbon tests come back from the laboratory.'

She ran her finger around the rim of the glass. 'How could someone get into the site without disturbing the land over it?'

'Through the tunnel. That's the only way I can figure it. Smaller passageways led into the main one with the paintings. One of the shafts had to have gone through the Garowitz's backyard where the bodies were found.'

'So, assuming the girls didn't put themselves in the grave, someone very slight had to have done it.'

Dutch hadn't thought about the person's size. Robin was right. The passageways were only two feet in diameter. Whoever pushed the girls through had to have been exceptionally small.

'The man found at the reservoir was murdered. The

147

remains of the two girls are being tested to find out whether they were also killed.' He stood up. 'Let me call Tara to see if any of the reports on them have come back.'

Dutch went over to the phone booth at the back of the restaurant. He called her house. There was no answer. Searching through his pockets, he found the number of the makeshift lab in the hangar and called there. Tara picked up.

'Don't you ever check your messages, Dutch?' Her voice was glum.

'What's the matter?' He could feel his stomach tightening.

'Get over here,' she said quietly.

'Has the carbon dating come back yet?'

'You were right. Somebody wanted to fuck with the remains. Get over here.' She hung up.

Dutch slowly put the receiver back down in the cradle. Tara didn't say what had happened, but he knew her well enough to know it was bad.

'Dutch?' Robin said. She had got up and was next to him now, apprehensively studying his troubled face.

'I have to go. Something just came down.'

'With the bones?'

'Yes.'

'Do you want me to go with you?' She put her hand on his arm.

He turned towards her. Her dark hazel eyes were wide open with concern. 'No,' he said. He touched her silky cheeks with his fingers, then walked out the door.

Always wrong timing with her, he thought, as he made his way along the cracked pavement of the deserted street.

148

9

Dutch saw it as soon as he opened the door of the massive hangar. A groan started slowly in his throat and erupted into a volcanic flurry of four-letter words.

He watched helplessly as thousands of cotton fibres glided gently through the air like fresh snow. They landed softly on him, blanketing his hair, his clothes. The skeletal remains strewn across the floor were also covered with the white filaments, making them almost unrecognizable.

Tara, her hair completely white, sat cross-legged on top of one of the examining tables smoking a cigarette. Her shoulders sagged; she looked haggard and distraught. Several of Dutch's students were on their knees hopelessly trying to brush away the fibres from the hundreds of bodies; every time they removed some of the lint, twice as much would land on the same spot.

Dutch put his hand over his nose and mouth to protect his throat and walked over to Tara. If she was allowing the nicotine from her cigarette to contaminate the remains, then Dutch knew it was all over.

'How did it happen?' he asked.

Tara didn't speak. She took a deep drag from her cigarette and pointed to the air-conditioning ducts on the ceiling. He looked up and saw the small fibres flowing out of them.

'Couldn't you have got the unit turned off?' he asked in disbelief.

Tara shrugged. 'It wasn't turned on when we left. We took a break for dinner. When we got back, the entire hangar was covered with cotton. It was already too late.'

'Wasn't anyone here?'

'A couple of security guards and some of the help. They tried to get to the air-conditioning unit in the basement but the door was bolted from the other side. By the time they could break the lock, it was all over.'

Dutch's mouth was quivering with rage. Whoever did this had to have known about forensic science. In order to do a carbon test for accurate dating, the remains have to be free of natural fibres. Dropping cotton on them contaminated the bones. 'We'll never know how old they are now,' he said bitterly.

'Or how *new*!' Tara grunted.

'Somebody doesn't want us to know too much about these remains. What about the leg-bones you sent to the lab? Have they come back yet?'

'Yep,' she said with a caustic grin. Hopping off the table she dropped the cigarette on the floor that was covered with white fluff and crushed it with her foot. She walked over to the desk and unwrapped the large thigh-bone from the tinfoil. It was covered in a cotton fabric. 'Magic, isn't it? Somehow, between here and the laboratory, a fairy queen came down from heaven and covered this specimen in cotton.' Her voice was angry as she tossed the sample back on the table. 'I personally wrapped the bone and watched it go into the truck.'

'What about the one from the other girl?' he asked, even though he knew the answer.

Shaking her head, she unwrapped the other package of tinfoil. The bone was also bundled in cotton. 'Marty, the lab technician, said he doesn't know how this happened. He said that's the way he received it. I believe him.'

'That leaves the messenger,' Dutch said.

'I know,' she said harshly. 'He was the only one between here and the lab.'

'Why?' His voice was hard. 'What the hell don't they want us to find?'

'Who's *they*, Dutch? This can't be happening over an ancient dig,' Tara said, confused.

Dutch's eyes went up to the ducts. He walked across the large hangar, over to the door that said MAINTENANCE. He could see where the side of the door had been jimmied by security trying to break it open. Looking in, he saw the small passageway that led to the basement. There was another door at the end. This one had also had its lock broken by security. As soon as Dutch opened it, a white sheet of cotton particles rushed out of the cellar like a hailstorm, smashing into him and driving him back. He took his T-shirt off, tied it around his head like a bandana, and slowly made his way down the steps to the basement.

The air-conditioning unit was off now, but visibility was almost nil. Flying shreds of material whipped at his eyes.

Flicking at the lint on his face, Dutch knelt down and looked at the air-conditioning unit. The filter was lying on its side on the floor. Empty sacks that had contained the filaments also lay on the floor. He picked up the rectangular screen. Someone had removed the filter and loaded the blower with debris.

Dutch noticed a slightly open window that looked on to the tarmac. Whoever did this used that window to get away.

That person also knew about bones and how to prevent testing for age.

Orville and Pat Sagata popped up in his mind. They were pathologists and had an understanding of forensic anthropology. Both of them wanted this unearthing to go away: Orville for political reasons; Pat in order to keep his job. Did this have anything to do with the white girls found in the grave-site? Why should it cause such an adverse reaction in the coroner's office? Disgusted, Dutch dropped the screen on the floor and went upstairs.

Walking back into the hangar, he put his shirt on and tucked it into his jeans. He saw Orville, Falcone and several uniformed officers coming through the main entrance. The fibres were still hanging in the air, and the newcomers were thrashing wildly at them. They looked like bears being attacked by a swarm of bees. 'Pillow fight, Dutch?' Falcone asked.

Dutch had to suppress the urge to hit him. 'Who the hell did this?'

Frowning, Orville looked up into Dutch's angry face. 'What?' Then he understood and he turned red with fury. 'You think we did this?'

'Somebody doesn't want these bones tested. Very few people know what can ruin a test for carbon dating. Pathologists are some of them.' Dutch's voice was hard.

Priest put his finger on Dutch's arm and moved his barrel-chested frame close to his. 'Listen to me, you sonofabitch! I want these bones out of here by tomorrow morning. At six o'clock this evening the governor signed a law stating that anthropologists, colleges and museums have to turn over ancient bones and artifacts to the original tribes. The tribal council for the Chumash, as you goddamn well know, are demanding the return of *these* bones.' He pointed at the remains littering the floor.

Dutch had heard that such a law was pending. Like most of his colleagues, he had closed his eyes to it, hoping it wouldn't get passed. If bones couldn't be studied without the permission of the tribes, it would shake the foundations of anthropology. It was science versus religion once again. This time the latter had got the upper hand.

'I want these bones to disappear! I want the streets to be paved again!' Priest ranted. 'I want everything to look like nothing ever happened. You've milked your two minutes of glory in the sun, Dutchman. Find some obscure college that will have you and let us go about our business.'

'There are two bodies that don't belong in that graveyard, you baboon!' Dutch screamed back.

Falcone tried to step between them, but Dutch stopped him with his arm.

'Pat Segata told me that you were carrying on about some bodies. What are you talking about?' Priest hissed.

Dutch went over to the two gurneys and pointed to the skeletons. 'Take a look, Orville. Even a hack doctor like yourself can see that they're not Indian and they're nowhere near as old as the rest of the bones here.'

Orville walked halfway over to the tables, then stopped. 'How old are they?' he asked the Dutchman.

'They've been dead between twenty and fifty years. I can't say for sure.'

'I'll look into it,' Falcone said, sneaking a glance at Orville.

Dutch sneered. 'I bet you will.'

'You can't close down a city over this,' Orville snapped back.

'I told you, somebody tampered with the bones,' the Dutchman said.

Orville nodded in disbelief. 'And that somebody is me, huh?'

'I didn't say that, Orville.'

'I heard it. Didn't you hear it?' he said to Falcone.

'It sure as hell sounded like an accusation to me,' Falcone said, shoving a wad of Wrigley's Spearmint into his mouth.

'I'm calling Ben Lassen up in Marin County. Hopefully he's not busy and he can come on down to LA to sweep up this mess. You have until tomorrow morning to finish everything, then I want you out of here.'

Lassen was Dutch's counterpart up north, who was also a bone expert.

'Lassen is an ass-kisser, but even he'd have to reach the same conclusion,' Dutch said, trying to hide his disappointment. 'What about the hotel site? The excavation hasn't even begun there yet! You seem to be forgetting another law that's been on the books for quite a while: no digs can be covered up or building resumed until all artifacts are removed from the site.'

'Is that a fact?' Orville said, scowling back. His lips were pulled back into a grin. 'Ask your ex-wife about that one.' He pointed over towards the entrance.

Dutch turned and looked. Therese, along with Miles

Scone, had just walked in through the back door. A leather bag filled with archaeological tools hung from her shoulder. They were carefully stepping over the skeletal bodies as they came towards them. At one point she took Miles's hand for leverage in order to jump over one of the open bags of tinfoil.

Dutch's flesh tingled when he saw them touch.

Therese nodded to them. She dropped the heavy bag on the floor, causing cotton flakes to explode into the air, covering her legs in a cloud of whiteness.

Miles shook hands with Orville. The familiar smiles that lit up their faces told Dutch that they already knew each other.

Therese's boyfriend then turned to the Dutchman, and his smile grew even wider. 'Good to see you again, Wilhelm. What happened here?'

'You have an accident?' Therese said, looking at the white flakes.

'A bad one. Why are you here, Therese?' Dutch asked.

'Artifacts, Dutch. The ones that were found with the bodies.' She bent down and went through her bag, taking out several small scraping tools and a hammer.

'I thought there would be enough beads and shells at the site to keep you busy for a while.'

She shook her head. 'Not so.'

'We didn't find any important artifacts in the grave,' the Dutchman said.

'I'll be the judge of what's important.'

'Tell him, Therese,' Orville said.

'Tell me what?' Dutch asked.

Therese looked frustrated. Turning to Dutch, she said, 'My crew spent two days digging through every piece of dirt on that goddamn hotel site. There wasn't very much to examine. Anything of value was probably destroyed by the tractors when they broke the ground for the hotel.'

'We're closing the investigation down in a couple of days,' Orville said. 'It's out of your hands now, Dutchman.'

Dutch turned away from them and slowly walked back to the table that held the remains of one of the young girls. He leaned against it and lit a cigarette. How could Therese give up on a dig like that? Two days were not enough to tell what was down there. Had all the spunk gone out of her after Max died?

Therese walked over to him. He watched Scone and Orville talking to each other. They were in a heated discussion, unaware that she had left them.

As if reading Dutch's mind, she said, 'A good anthropologist knows enough to walk away when there's nothing there.'

'Are you talking about us or artifacts?' he asked her.

'Both.'

'I could never do that.'

'I know. You always had an insatiable need to kick dead horses to see if they could be brought back to life.'

Kicking dead horses again. It was one of her favourite expressions, Dutch thought.

She went over to the table containing Indian artifacts and picked up what appeared to be a one-foot piece of rusted metal covered with a hard mould-like substance. Holding it up to the light, she began to look at it closely. 'You were smart not to throw this piece away,' she said. 'A lot of anthropologists would have.'

156

'One of my assistants found it at the grave-site. At first she thought it was an old discarded lug wrench.'

'It still might be,' Therese said. She laid it back on the table, took the scraping tool and carefully began to scratch at the surface. 'It's terribly oxidized. I'll need acid to remove this corrosion.'

'For what it's worth, the guy who owned that bogus house in Beverly Hills is wearing an old Spanish coin around his neck. Says he found it near his property. There may be others. He's being coy.'

Therese's eyes widened. 'Interesting,' she said.

Tara made her way over to them. 'I just got the word we're being closed down tomorrow. I better tell the kids to go home,' she said to Dutch, her voice dragging.

'Why? We have tonight, don't we?' Dutch said.

'Look around, Dutch. We're beaten. What can we do with one night? They're coming in the morning to collect the bones.' She sounded defeated.

'Right now,' Dutch said, 'all I can produce are two skeletons that are non-Indian, and a simple drawing of a centipede that turned up in two places where dead people were. That's not enough to battle Orville and the rest of the city. The only thing we can do now is find out how these two girls died. Then maybe we'll have a shot.'

Dutch walked away from Therese and went over to his students, who were cleaning the lint off the bodies on the floor. He divided them into pairs. Each pair was responsible for inspecting the bones in a section of the room where it hadn't already been done. They all knew what to look for. If any of the bones in their estimation were not Indian, they were to tell Tara or Dutch. There were hundreds of bones, and it was

157

going to be a big, if not impossible, job to do in that short time.

After everyone got to work, Dutch picked up the phone and called a friend of his, an Armenian pathologist, Benny Benjamin. He worked the night shift, part-time, at the Medical Examiner's office. 'Busy, Benny?' he asked when he answered.

'Always, Dutch. Right now I'm looking at three dead teenagers on my tables. A drive-by shooting from a rival gang in Compton. What do you need?'

'I need tests done on bone samples of two teenage girls.'

'Always teenagers,' Benny said angrily. 'They're dying like flies, today.'

'I'll see you in an hour,' Dutch said.

'Dutch, please, I got three here already. Bring them over Thursday . . .'

Dutch hung up. He felt a hand on his arm and turned around. It was Therese.

'You won't give this up, will you, Dutch?'

'Not yet.' He could feel the heat of her body next to his. It was searing his skin. 'Will you?'

She brushed her fine hair from her face. 'I don't look at things that way. I'm a professional. I'll do my job . . . sift through the remnants. That's all I can do. But I'm not Lazarus. I certainly have no illusions about raising the dead. That's your role in life. I can walk away.'

Her intelligent eyes were sparkling. He touched her lightly on the shoulder, tracing his fingers down her arm. She shuddered. 'I don't believe that,' he said.

She shook her head in amazement and pushed his hand away. 'You don't stop, do you? Rejection must be your drug of choice. I have work to do. Good luck.

Find something to stop them. I know you; you won't be able to live with yourself if these bones are taken away.'

Dutch watched her walk back to Scone and Orville. She was right; he had to think of something to stop them from taking the bones away. But what? Whatever it was, he had eight hours to find it.

He left the hangar with the remains of the two girls, put them into the back of his truck and started to drive towards the 405 South. Changing his mind, he took the Pacific Coast Highway back to Point Dume University. He thought about the skeleton found by the reservoir. Maybe Dr Benny Benjamin should take a look at it, too. Was this a mistake? Was he so desperate now that he was grasping at all straws and wasting precious time doing it? No. His back was against the wall, and he had to cover all angles.

Forty-five minutes later Dutch approached the university. The main building was deserted except for the night watchman. He showed the guard his pass and was let through.

He took the elevator to the fifth floor. The heels of his boots cracked like shots from a .22 rifle as he walked down the corridor. Turning the corner, he heard a shuffling noise, like someone moving boxes, coming from his lab at the end of the hall.

When Dutch stopped walking, the other sound also stopped. Whoever it was had heard him. There was a crawling sensation in the pit of his stomach. The laboratory was where he and Tara kept the bones they were working on.

Dutch ran towards the lab, grabbed the handle of the closed door and pulled. Locked! Again he could hear movement inside. Through the crack between the door and the jamb he could see the beam of a flashlight wildly darting over the room.

Whoever was in there was probably looking for a way out, he thought.

Then the light went out.

Dutch reached into his pocket, grabbing a ring of keys. When he found the one he wanted, he stuck it into the keyhole. The tumbler clicked, and he threw open the door.

The room was dark. He slowly scanned the blackness for a figure or a shadow, but he couldn't see anything. Putting his hand over to the wall, he fumbled for the lights. When he turned them on, he saw a flash of movement on the other side of the room. Someone dressed in red overalls was crouching next to the lectern. As soon as Dutch's eyes focused on him, the man's hand jerked upwards, hurling something at him. It was a Neanderthal skull that he kept on his desk. Dutch moved quickly. The skull crashed inches from his head and splintered against the wall.

Before Dutch could regain his balance, the intruder was on him, holding a Phillips screwdriver in his hand. The Dutchman took the brunt of the man's weight in his abdomen and found himself falling back against the blackboard.

He was cornered in this spot. His eyes stayed glued on the screwdriver. If he tried to sidestep either to the left or to the right, he would be killed. His attacker knew that, and was waiting for Dutch to make just that move. Dutch desperately wanted to see his face, but he couldn't look away from the tool, even for a split second. His only option was forward. With luck, it would not be what the guy expected him to do, and the surprise would take him off guard.

Using his substantial weight, Dutch sprung outward, leaping on top of his assailant. As they went down on the lab table, Dutch grabbed the wrist that held the screwdriver. The guy was big, almost as big as him, but the Dutchman was stronger. The man tried to get leverage so that he could bring the weapon up to his chest, but Dutch held it down with his huge hand. As they scuffled, bones flew off the table and went crashing to the hardwood floor.

Dutch was now sitting on his attacker's chest, pushing his weight down into his rib cage. His legs were pinning the man's arms against the table.

The guy's face was turning red from the pain, and a thick blue vein bulged out on the side of his head. Dutch pushed down harder and the man gritted his teeth. He now had a good look at his face: about thirty, with straight red hair worn in a ponytail. A fake diamond stud was attached to his right ear. Not bad features, but the eyes were sunken into the skull and he had unhealthy skin. Crack, Dutch thought.

The man's face was now turning a deep purple. 'Want to talk?' Dutch asked. He lifted his body a couple of inches off the man's rib cage so he could answer.

'Fuck you,' he grunted.

Dutch pressed down again. The man yelped in anguish. Dutch put his hand over his mouth to stifle his voice and looked at the imprint on the man's red overalls: FARGO EXPRESS. That was the name of the messenger service Tara had used to bring the remains of the girls to the lab for dating. 'You're the guy who fucked with the bones, aren't you?' Dutch said, applying more weight on his rib cage.

The man's eyes were bulging out of their sockets now. Dutch had to ease the pressure or he'd pass out. As soon as he did, the man sucked in as much air as his lungs would hold.

'What are you looking for in my lab?' Dutch asked him. 'Who are you? You don't look like an Indian or an Indian sympathizer.'

The man didn't say anything.

Dutch said, 'We could stay this way all night, if that's what you want.'

Another few seconds passed, then the man under him nodded, indicating that he'd had enough.

Dutch leaned over to remove the screwdriver that was still in the guy's hand. As soon as he was off balance, the man slid his arm from under Dutch's leg, grabbed his bandaged ear and yanked hard. Dutch let out a scream and fell off the table. His shoulder hit the wooden floor hard and he let out a grunt.

A terrible pain shot through the side of his head. Dutch put a hand over his ear and felt his own warm blood. Somewhere behind him he heard a door slam and footsteps running down the hall.

He lay on the floor, letting the ache ease up. After a few minutes he opened his eyes and looked around. The man had left.

Using the table, Dutch dragged his bruised body to his knees and on to his feet. He hobbled over to the mirror by the laboratory sink and looked at himself.

'Oh, Jesus!' he said out loud. The sonofabitch had ripped the stitches loose from his ear. His bandage was saturated with blood, and a thin red stream trickled down his cheek.

He scanned the room. What had the guy wanted? Dutch suddenly understood. He went over to the

162

industrial metal shelves in the corner that were filled with several cardboard boxes. The sides of the boxes were labelled with a black marker. They contained skeletal remains that were waiting to be put back together. Several of the boxes had been taken from the shelves and thrown on the floor. Fortunately, the carton containing the bones of the man buried next to the reservoir had not been disturbed.

Dutch lifted the cardboard container from the shelf and placed it on the table. He opened up the lid and looked inside; everything seemed to be still there. Dutch wiped the sweat from his brow. If he had come five minutes later the box would probably have gone.

He picked up the huge carton, kicked the door open with his boot and hauled it out of the lab.

Dr Benny Benjamin was leaning over the body of a teenage girl lying on his table. His large Armenian nose was so close to her face that he could feel the coldness coming from her dead, young skin.

The chest cavity was ripped wide open and he had his hand inside her, trying to catch hold of her slippery heart. Suddenly he heard a rattling noise behind him. It sounded like metal carts racing down a supermarket aisle. He turned round quickly.

Dutch was coming through the double doors dragging two gurneys behind him. Both had skeletons on them and one held the brown box. A security guard tried to block his way but Dutch went through him. 'Hello, Benny,' he said. He pushed the gurneys towards the little doctor with the bushy moustache and knit-black hair, then sank down into a metal chair by the cabinets.

'I said Thursday, Dutch,' Benny said, looking

down at the anthropologist. His jaw dropped open when he saw that the left side of the Dutchman's face was caked in blood. Benny turned and gestured to the guard that it was all right. The officer nodded and walked back down the hall.

'I don't have until Thursday,' Dutch said, leaning his head back against the climate-controlled cabinets that held the dead bodies waiting to be autopsied. He began to feel lightheaded and closed his eyes, but quickly opened them again when he felt himself passing out. 'Hey, Benny, you know how to sew?' he asked weakly.

'I can truss a turkey. Why?'

Dutch slowly removed the wet bandages. His blood-soaked ear, held on by a couple of stitches, was hanging upside down against the side of his face.

'What the fuck happened to you?'

'Long story.'

'Dutch, I'm a butcher, not a cosmetic surgeon.'

'I trust you, Benny. You always had sweet hands. Sew me up, then do a test on the bones, OK?' Dutch closed his eyes again. Too hungry and tired to care at this point, he crossed his legs, folded his arms and fell into a deep sleep.

He was awakened by someone shaking him. It was Benny. Dutch turned his head to look out of the small window jutting through the concrete block wall; he could see the dawn breaking over the downtown office buildings.

'Time to go, my friend. My shift's over,' the pathologist said.

Dutch sat up. He was lying on a stainless steel gurney covered with dried blood that wasn't his own.

Next to him were the three tables holding the teenagers killed in the drive-by shooting. Their organs were hanging in three scales directly above his head. Dutch put his hand up to his ear. It was freshly bandaged.

'Your ears are going to be a little uneven. It's the best I could do. Wear your hair over them and no one will notice. You were so tired I didn't even have to give you an anaesthetic.'

'Thanks, Benny. I'll have it done right when I have the time.' Dutch slowly got off the table. His feet were unsteady and his body felt like it had aged thirty years. 'What about the bones?'

Benny broke into a wide smile. 'I think you may have a winner here.'

Because of his full eyebrows, big nose and thick, bristly moustache, the pathologist always reminded Dutch of Groucho Marx, especially when he grinned. 'Talk to me,' Dutch said, also beginning to smile. 'Did you find something with all three bodies?'

'Just the two, Dutchman. The girls. I ran a DNA test on their bone cells. You've got twins. Congratulations.'

Interesting, Dutch thought. 'OK, what else?'

'I used a scanning electron microscope and came up with minute traces of triorthocresyl phosphate in their bone marrow. Most times it goes through the system and never reaches the bones. We were lucky to find the substance in them. For that to happen, the girls must have ingested a large quantity of it over a period of weeks.

Dutch began to laugh. It felt good; he hadn't laughed in a long time. He went over to the aluminium sink that was filled with bloodstained cutting instruments, moved them aside, and washed his face

165

and hands. 'Tell me about triorthocresyl phosphate, Benny.'

'Sure. Then I want you out of my lab before Priest finds you here. The word is already out on you. You must have pissed the ME off real bad.' Benny poured coffee from a Krups machine into a Styrofoam cup and handed it to Dutch.

Dripping wet, the Dutchman took the coffee and sipped it slowly while he listened to Benny.

The hangar at Burbank was surrounded by remote news trucks from several TV stations. Once again the Indians were there; this time they weren't picketing or screaming. Several hundred of them were lined up on the tarmac across the way, their eyes steadily focused on the hangar.

Dutch found a parking space next to Tara's car and went round to the back entrance.

Inside, Priest and Falcone were over by the bodies directing the uniformed officers who were putting the skeletal remains in body bags. Dozens of the plastic bags were stacked up on several forklifts waiting to be taken to the coroner's trucks outside. Smokey Pete, the liaison for the tribal councils, was with them. He was making sure that the bones weren't disturbed by rough handling.

Dutch walked in and saw Tara and his tired crew of students sitting on gurneys and on the floor. They watched in silence as the bones were driven out of the room. When they saw the Dutchman, their faces lit up with hope.

Tara stood up, 'Anything?' she asked in desperation, putting her hand on his arm.

'Everything,' he said, giving her hand a squeeze. He

jumped up on a table, cupped his hands to his mouth and yelled at the top of his lungs. 'Bring the bodies back, Orville! Not all of them are archaeological!'

The activity in the room came to an abrupt stop. Orville, Falcone and Pete turned their eyes up to the Dutchman on the table.

Orville walked halfway across the hangar and stopped. He also cupped his mouth and shouted. 'You seem to have a problem understanding the way life works with grown-ups, Van Deer. You were fired yesterday. Get off this property!' He said it loud enough for the reporters over by the forklifts to hear him.

'The two girls were murdered, Orville! Murdered! You can't bury those bones, not yet!'

Priest's face flushed with rage. He strutted over to Dutch's table and grabbed the edge of it in his beefy hands. 'Get out of here or I'll have you arrested!'

Dutch looked over to the newspeople. They were coming his way. He could feel the hot lights for their cameras being turned on him. 'Triorthocresyl phosphate, Orville. That's what the girls died from.' He took the coroner's print-out from the back pocket of his jeans, bent down, and handed it to the attractive woman standing next to Orville. She was the anchor for Channel Seven. Other newspeople began to gather around her. 'Make sure it gets on the evening news, darlin',' he said.

Priest, livid, grabbed Falcone by his shoulder and pushed him towards Dutch. 'Get rid of him, goddamnit!' The detective motioned to several uniforms to get over to the table.

The pretty newswoman yelled up to him. 'Is this some kind of poison?'

He knew he had to talk fast because the police were trying to get through the crowd to reach him. 'Yes. Triorthocresyl phosphate is used in fireproofing and in lubricants. It's also used in plastics.' The police reached the front of the table and brought Dutch down. As they twisted his arms around his back in order to handcuff him, Dutch screamed to Orville, 'If those bones are so goddamn old, how did a chemical used in plastics get into their systems? Maybe the ancient Chumash threw Tupperware parties! Those girls were murdered, Orville!'

Priest watched as the police dragged Dutch out of the hangar door. The pathologist's face was ashen and his lips were trembling. The silence in the room was deafening. From the corner of his eyes he could see everyone in the hangar staring at him, waiting to see what he would do.

That Dutch bastard! He had left him no choice. After a long pause, Orville slowly turned to Falcone and said in a grating, low voice, 'Bring the sonofabitch back.' An overwhelming depression descended over him. The Dutchman had won. There was no way he could have the bones buried, not now.

BOOK TWO

Centipedes

10

Hugo Frye, wearing red shorts and a matching sweat-soaked tank top with *Bijan's* logo engraved on the front, was running a 5½ mph clip on a Santa Monica jogging path adjacent to the ocean. The sweat dripped freely down his head, which was completely bald, including the rim. His usual daily run was six miles. He began at Ocean Avenue, at the tip of San Vincente, ran all the way to Wilshire, then back to the ocean.

But today they had found the skeletons of the girls he had killed eighteen years ago, and he needed to run the course twice. He thought the additional exercise would make the fear in his gut go away. Except it didn't work. His breath was on fire and his aching lungs felt like they were going to explode out of his chest, but the terror lingered inside him, refusing to budge. It lay at the bottom of his stomach like a piece of hot lead, searing his intestines.

Everything was happening at once.

The Dutchman entered his thoughts, and the fear escalated. This anthropologist, Van Deer, had found the bodies, dug them out of their grave for the whole world to see. It was all out in the open now.

Damn that man! Why couldn't he leave well enough alone? It happened eighteen years ago. The killings were done with. The *urge* that made him do those kinds of things had long disappeared. He had a new life now. He was a happy man. Damn that Dutch bastard for bringing it back!

At least he had had the foresight to put up bail for Santiago and get him out of jail before the police or Van Deer could talk to him. That dumb Indian! Lopping off the anthropologist's ear like that. The Indian was a loose cannon. He needed to be stopped. Always did. Bobby was the one bad angle on everything. He should have killed him years ago. Nobody would have cared. Except he hadn't killed anyone in a long time, and he couldn't without the *urge*. Unfortunately, the Indian had disappeared before he had the chance to really think about it. After he'd paid his bail this morning, they'd left the courthouse and driven away in his car. When Hugo turned his head on Rexford and Santa Monica during a traffic jam to see if the left lane was clear, Santiago jumped out and disappeared into the lunch-hour crowd of doctors and attorneys. The Indian must have sensed what was going through his mind. Hugo had searched the streets for almost an hour looking for him, then finally given up. The Indian was like a black shadow on a moonless night when he wanted to be. Just as well. It wasn't time yet.

Hugo's eyes were not on the running path this evening. They were turned inward, on his own rage fermenting within. It simmered and tore at the linings of his flesh. This feeling, this terrible, awful, frightening feeling was coming back.

Damn that anthropologist!

The homeless and the crack addicts who sat on the grass rim of the Santa Monica jogging path watched

Hugo's contorted face in fearful silence as he ran by. They had seen that kind of twisted hate in men's eyes too many times before. It almost always came before a violent act.

A bag lady, wearing three sweaters and pushing a supermarket basket filled with aluminium cans and bottles, shuffled along the path in the opposite direction. She had her head down, looking for more scraps, and didn't see Hugo coming. As he ran past, he knocked into her, propelling her to the ground. He continued to run, oblivious of the strollers and the other joggers yelling for him to stop.

When he reached the tip of San Vincente Boulevard, he turned on to its grassy centre divider that was a supplement to the jogging path and continued his breakneck pace. This was his favourite part of the run, and he knew every tree that lined the thin, indented artery. Normally, he would slow down here to eye the young, tanned girls in shorts racing past him towards the beach. He loved the way their moist thigh muscles rippled under their skin, and the way their uneven breathing sounded like the gasps of copulation. They aroused him, especially the heavy ones with their big breasts and thick, sweaty legs. When he saw one he particularly liked, one who reminded him of the twins, he would turn round and run behind her, careful not to overtake. He would fantasize about how she might look without clothes on, and what it would be like to have her fat legs wrapped around his waist as he pounded his hard penis inside her hairy furrow. Sometimes he would actually achieve ejaculation this way. It was magnificent. Like having sex in a public place and not getting caught. Every so often one of them would become aware that someone was behind her and turn round. Hugo would jog quickly past her, twisting his head so she couldn't see his face. He would never approach them. That would be dangerous. The *urge* may be dead, but he never for a moment forgot that once it had run through his body like a raging river. He was too smart to let down his guard, even for a moment. Besides, it really wasn't necessary to establish contact with them. This was only a game he was playing, not the real thing; not like what happened eighteen years ago.

When Hugo reached Wilshire, he turned at the corner bank and ran back to Ocean Avenue for the second time. The path sloped gently downhill, making the run easier.

At Colorado, a sharp stitch pierced his right side, forcing him to stop. It was a pain most runners experience when they go too fast. Doubling over, he grabbed a lamp-post for support and gasped for air. His side was throbbing unmercifully. After a couple of minutes, the ache eventually subsided and he was able to get his breath back. He slowly straightened up and crossed the street, going towards the old wooden stairs butting up against the seven-hundred-foot cliff that overlooked the Pacific Coast Highway. He raced down them, taking three steps at a time. When he reached the bottom, he slowed his pace and walked south on the rim of the highway. The breeze from the oncoming cars buzzing by felt good.

His small house was located next to a deserted amusement park half a mile from the Santa Monica Pier. The park was decimated several years ago by a fire that swept through it, killing nine people. The owners, relinquishing any ideas of rebuilding, hoped to sell the land off to developers. Unfortunately, the bedrock under the property had eroded since the park was built, causing the water level to rise. The city refused to issue construction permits. Eventually, all the homes in the area became affected by the topographical deterioration and abandoned. This was OK with Hugo. He could live with a little water infiltrating the foundations of his house because that made him the only living soul in a three block area.

It was hot today, and the sour smell of stale beer and carnival food coming from the stands on the pier drifted by him. He was used to the odours now and he no longer noticed them. The street was filthy, like it always was. Newspapers whipped around his feet in the wind, and he would kick an occasional beer can or an empty whiskey bottle with his running shoe, sending it to the other side of the gutter.

When he first bought the house ten years ago from an old woman who was dying from some kind of fungus on the lungs, the noises had bothered him. The music from the carousel on the pier and the screams and laughter of the crowds would keep him awake for hours. Sometimes there would be gunshots piercing the stillness of the night: rival Santa Monica gangs fighting for street corners to sell their crack. A few months after he moved in, he had the interior of his house soundproofed. Now when he closed his door, the world he despised went away.

The interior of his small house was deceptively simple. From the looks of it, nobody would ever suspect he had money, and lots of it. There was the cheap mildewed furniture – always damp from the constant humidity in the house – a threadbare carpet and unframed pictures tacked to the walls.

A collection of leather-bound books was stacked on

the shelves over the fireplace. Most of them were bought from specialized mail order clubs: volumes about the two world wars; tomes by the early Greek philosophers — Thales, Anaximander, Anaximenes, Socrates. There were also the works of Kant, Descartes, Hegel, Spinoza, Russell. Hugo loved the great thinkers, especially the empiricists. Periodically, after reading one of their treatises, he would stand in front of a mirror, pretending to be one of them, and break out into a full oration about love and dying. Sometimes these dramatizations lasted for several hours. The bulk of his books, however, were scientific and medical in nature. Human anatomy had intrigued him ever since he was a child.

When Hugo opened the door and stepped into the house, he took a clean towel from the coat rack and wiped his sweaty head. Inside, he had to keep himself dry at all times. The moisture in the house would cause the hairless skin around his neck to break out in red welts if he didn't.

A loud motorized hissing from the humidifier came from somewhere downstairs. It was almost deafening, like a loud chorus of rattlesnakes. After wiping the sweat from his face and neck, he grabbed an opened bag of dried apricots from the coffee table and turned on the TV, flipping the stations with the remote until he came to the five o'clock news which had just begun. He was planning to watch it for a couple of minutes, then take a shower, when a video tape appeared of the Dutchman being interviewed by the reporters in the hangar earlier that afternoon. Next to him was his assistant, that tall, thin girl with the spiked hair.

Hugo sat on the couch and compulsively shoved several pieces of fruit into his mouth at one time. He watched in dread, the pouches under his sad puppy eyes beginning to twitch. They were talking about what he had done all those years ago. This anthropologist was a smart man. It hadn't taken him long to discover how he had killed them. Listening to his description of the way the girls had died made him feel both excited and fearful. Given time, what else would this man find out about him? This was not good.

He had sent Frank to ruin it all, but it hadn't worked.

'Mother of Christ! Doesn't anything ever stay buried?' Hugo screamed, banging his fists into the couch, sending a blanket of dust into the air. He began rubbing his thighs together, causing a pleasant sensation in his groin. His penis became hard, but he was not in the mood to stroke it.

He felt as if his whole life was a mass of unearthings, like the one in Beverly Hills. All his ugly secrets would eventually dig themselves out of the ground and humiliate him in front of everybody. It would be just like the last time. No matter how many precautions he took in covering up the aftermath of those *urges* in his past, they always seemed to rise to the surface. Humiliation was his lot in life. He always felt that dark shadow hanging over him. It clung to his skin like wet cobwebs.

He crouched forward, putting his head between his legs, and swayed. It was the only thing left from his childhood that soothed him.

He had successfully managed to alter most things about himself. His face was different, and he switched wigs to suit his moods. Even his name had been changed. When the police or Van Deer discovered who paid Bobby's bail, let them try to find Hugo Frye in their bloody computer! They won't. Hugo Frye can never be found. *Will* never be found! He was too smart for all of them!

There were no regrets about those changes. He hated his past. Hated the Hugo of old. But he could never allow himself to forget the past. Not for an instant. Forget the past and it will turn around and bite you on the ass every time.

In his past was a deep secret. A terrible one concerning something that happened when he was very young. He had never told anyone. It would terrify even the most brazen of men. As frightening as it was, Hugo savoured the memories of it like a child savouring the last few seconds of a cartoon show before a parent turned the TV off. He had always known that the source of his murderous *urge* sprung from that secret, but he felt no remorse. The *urge* may have turned him into a killer, but it had also given him a great sense of power. Once you'd killed and got away with it, never regretting the act for a moment, you were on a higher plane than most men.

Hugo needed that leverage. Without it, he felt people would treat him with scorn and repulsion, the way they had when he was a child. The memory of his childhood evoked feelings of pain and anger. With those emotions always came the image of his father looming over his head, his bloated alcoholic face looking scornfully down at him. How he had feared that man! *Oh, the hate he had had for him when he was alive!*

Hugo turned off the TV and lay down on the couch, placing the bag of dried apricots on his stomach. After filling his mouth once more, he folded his hands behind his head and thought about the time his father found out about one of the bad things he had done.

Oh, dear God! He would never forget that! He was in his mid-teens when they dug up the animals he had buried on that farmer's property! They said it was the smell that gave the graves away.

The terrible beating in front of everyone! His pleading! His screams! 'I won't do it again! I won't! I swear!'

After that, whenever he walked past his neighbours, they would stare at him with repulsion and hug their children to their bodies, making sure their innocent eyes didn't look up at him. To them he was a cloven-hoofed monster. An outcast. A leper.

The humiliation!

Eating all those apricots made his stomach heavy. He moved the bag aside, stood up and went over to the credenza. Kneeling down, he took out a bottle of Remy Martin from the bottom shelf. Twisting the top off, he poured the golden cognac into a snifter, then proceeded to warm the sides of the glass with a match. Hugo took his time. This was a ritual he enjoyed. Cognac needed the proper temperature to bring out the flavour, and he was a stickler for doing it right. Drinking cold brandy was boorish, and Hugo never saw himself as a boor. He was a sophisticate in everything he did . . . including the ways in which he had killed.

When the cognac was sufficiently warm, he blew out the match and slowly sipped the liquor, washing the heavy taste of the dried fruit from his mouth.

He caught a glimpse of himself in the mirror over the TV and smiled. He was now a good-looking man, with straight lips and nice even teeth. A big difference from the old days. In the old days he was a freak, something that went out only at night in order to avoid the kids who liked beating him up. They did plenty of that at school. But he was smarter than all of them, and he had survived. Survived very well.

He ran his fingers over his smooth scalp. Too bad about the hair. There wasn't a wisp on his entire body. It was a disease and he had to live with it. No amount of money could change that.

Sitting down on the couch again, he crossed his legs and carefully conjured up the Dutchman in his head. How he envied him his beautiful hair. This man, with fine blond hair like talcum powder strung together, was his harbinger of humiliation. Maybe even his executioner, if he wasn't careful. The anthropologist was his adversary and Hugo knew very little about him. Not good. That will change, he thought. He would certainly make it his business to find out everything there was to know about the Dutchman.

When the twins were dug up, it was as if no time had passed at all. The memories came flooding back, making it seem like the murders only happened yesterday. Where did all that time go?

Then he remembered the man he killed and buried near the reservoir.

At the thought of him, he could feel the old, familiar *urge* starting up again. The *urge* was the name he had given to that curious, frenzied feeling that suddenly sprang up inside him, making him commit strange acts. He had been calling it that ever since he was a boy and it had awakened in his soul. That inactive spirit was now beginning to tingle slightly in his bowels. It was just a glimmer, enough to say that it was still alive. Hugo was confused and frightened. Hadn't this feeling died? Perhaps not. Maybe the *urge* was just lying dormant, waiting for the chance to come back to life. My God, how easy it was to tap into that vein again! Like bodies, even *urges* can become unearthed. His mood started to turn nasty as the fear in him spread.

A familiar woman's voice inside his head suddenly called out his name. He usually heard it when he was troubled or scared. Hugo never thought that he was going crazy. He knew the voice was only part of his imagination, and not some twisted synapse in his brain. And when it came, he never felt frightened. In fact, he looked forward to it because it helped calm him down. The voice wasn't something he could conjure up. It came on its own. It was his mother's beautiful voice, the one that was tucked in the dark shadows of his mind, waiting for him. He had clouded memories of that same voice from when he was a baby. He envisioned her dressed in a white robe, swaying back and forth in a rocking chair, softly singing his name as he hungrily sucked on her teat.

H-u-u-g-o. H-u-u-g-o.

She would say it over and over again.

Hearing it now made him silently lip-sync along with her. It made him feel tranquil.

The *u* in his name slithered cleanly out of her throat, reminding him of a long, curving centipede.

The vision of the centipede became dominant in his brain. He leaped off the couch, went into the dining-room and took down the covered fish tank from the top of the credenza. Putting the aquarium gently on the table, he removed the cloth. The glass sides were fogged with moisture. Inside, two foot-long Trinidadian centipedes were lying dormant on a bed of leaves. There was a third, but it had disappeared somewhere in the house when the recent earthquake caused the tank to topple off the cabinet and shatter. He had searched every room but only found these two. This upset him. He knew how dangerous they could be.

Hugo removed the wire mesh from the top and carefully turned the glass cage over on its side, allowing the insects to crawl out. Freed from captivity, the arthropods tentatively made their way over the slippery rosewood table. Their long, thin bodies angled in all directions.

He walked over to the wardrobe and withdrew an empty hanger covered by a cardboard sheath. After removing the cardboard, he placed its tip next to one of the arthropods' mouth. Hugo watched with fascination as the centipede grabbed the end of it with its powerful jaw. Using its legion of legs, the insect slowly climbed up the shaft, its poisonous mouth snapping from side to side. Hugo waited until its antennae brushed against his fingers before he brought the cardboard cover up to the rim of the glass aquarium and shook it until the centipede let go and dropped into the tank. Then he held it next to the other one and did the same thing, only this time he let the jaws get even closer to his hand. When he was through, he put the mesh top and the cover back on. His darlings needed the dark and the humidity to live.

He had been playing this game with all species of arthropods ever since he was a teenager. But it was this breed that gave him the real rush. They were the most dangerous. He had been bitten several times by them. Once when his immune system was low because he had the flu, it was almost fatal. But that was all part of the fun.

Hugo had first found out about these giant centipedes when he was sixteen years old from a book on insects at the public library. He called the insectarium at the zoo for more information. Later on, a snake dealer in San Francisco taught him how to order them from special illegal insect brokers.

He used to believe – and still did to an extent – that one day, with enough patience, he would have one of these lovelies tamed. He had already introduced new things into their diet. No one had ever done that before. That's because no other human being, except himself, had ever experienced a special kinship with them. They were alike in many ways. He had learned a lot from them. They were wondrous, primitive things of nature.

And like the centipede, he was a survivor. It had been around a lot longer than man, and would be around long after man's flimsy, self-righteous dreams had turned to dust. That was his one belief, his one happiness. His salvation.

11

Therese spotted the Dutchman as soon as she walked through the door of Papa Padakos's bar. He was sitting at his usual table, with his long legs propped up on a chair and holding a beer bottle precariously between his legs. The Dodger game was on the small TV that hung over the worn mahogany bar. Tara, her arm dangling over the back of her chair, was sitting next to him, also watching the game. Empty bottles were on the table, along with a half-filled pretzel bowl.

Tara saw Therese heading their way and nudged Dutch. When he looked up and saw Therese, his eyes opened in mild surprise, then he quickly moved his foot off the chair so she could sit down.

'Good to see you so hard at work, Dutch,' Therese said.

Dutch grinned and saluted her with his half-empty bottle.

She sat down and pushed the empty bottles on the table away from her. Therese smiled at Tara. Tara gave her a warm one back. All three had been friends when times were still good.

'Where's pretty boy?' Dutch asked Therese. He wasn't drunk yet, but he had a nice glow going.

'Miles? He's asleep. Where you should be.'

Dutch saw that she was wearing light blue again. This time it was a stone-washed denim jacket, powder blue tank top and those same tight 501s. 'What are you doing here at the beach?'

'I felt like slumming.'

He gestured around the bar. 'Be my guest. Of course, at one time it used to be *our* place, remember?'

'You don't stop, do you?'

Shrugging, he forced his jack-o'-lantern smile on her again. 'It's that horse. It just keeps asking to be kicked.'

Tara groaned, put her bottle down on the table and stood up. 'I've seen this movie before. I've got to get going. Big day tomorrow. Good seeing you, Therese.' She leaned over and hugged her, then turned to Dutch. 'Get some sleep.'

'What's happening tomorrow?' Therese asked her.

Tara grabbed her tote bag from the back of her chair and slung it over her shoulder. 'We're starting facial reconstruction on the dead twins. It's going to be a bitch.' She let out a tired sigh, fluttered her fingers at them, then turned and walked towards the door.

Therese watched her disappear out into the night. 'How's her love life?' she asked Dutch.

'Same as it was when *we* had one. The names of the women may change, but the way they dump on her remains constant.'

Therese's eyes furrowed in sadness. 'I like her. Always have. She deserves better.'

'She doesn't *want* better. Try and accept it. She has.' He stared at Therese's profile. Her white flawless skin stretched like taut silk over her cheekbones.

186

Suppressing a desire to brush his fingers over it, he asked, 'Why are you here?'

She turned to him. 'I saw you interviewed on TV this evening.' Her nose wrinkled as if a bad smell had drifted by.

'You're telling me not to give up my day job, huh?'

'Let's just say Tom Sellick has nothing to worry about. If you're going to be on TV somebody should teach you how to dress. Don't you own anything other than T-shirts?'

'Not much.' He glanced down at the faded Ohio State T-shirt he was wearing and brushed the pretzel crumbs off it. 'You always liked dressing me. Now you have Miles to do. He looks like somebody colour-coordinated him right down to the tassels on his Cole-haans.'

'You're drunk.'

'Just a buzz. It helps my ear. Want a beer?'

'No, thanks.'

He leaned over and touched her arm. 'I like you in blue, you know that?'

Her top lip curled slightly. 'Forget it, Dutch.'

'OK, I'll forget it. So why are you here? You missed me, or something?'

'Not exactly.' She leaned into the table, her eyes all business. 'How many bodies do you think are buried at the grave-site?'

'Ahhh,' he said, suddenly understanding. 'Which bodies are we talking about? The Indians or the twins? Sound like baseball teams, don't they?' He gave a quick laugh at his own joke.

'Stop playing games with me, OK? You know what I'm asking.'

Dutch did know. In fact, he also knew *why* she was

asking. No, she wasn't here because she missed him. She was here because she was being pressured by Payne, the whole goddamn city of Beverly Hills and the Governor of California to close down the excavation at the hotel site. Before she could do it, however, she needed to know everything that was going on. That wasn't really part of her job. It was part of her own compulsive behaviour, like the need to match colours. It was a personal thing. So was her honesty. Therese may have needed this job badly, but if there was even the slightest possibility of something being uncovered at the excavation, she'd keep the site open, no matter how much she was pushed or threatened.

'The twins are a definite,' he said. 'I don't think there are any more new bodies buried there, but I'm not telling that to Orville or Falcone, at least not yet. Those girls were murdered and I'm not going to let it be shovelled under the table. I needed to keep their deaths high profile. That's why I didn't want the bones to be repatriated. There's also a third killing. A man, but he wasn't buried with the girls. He was chopped up and thrown in a grave several miles away from the other site.'

Therese waved her hand. 'I know about that. I also know about the painting you found next to his body. Any idea who these dead people are?'

'Not yet. That's why we're starting facial reconstruction on the twins. All I know is that the girls were about fifteen years old when they were killed, and that they have blond hair. We don't know who the male is. That's about it. Not much, huh?'

'How are the Indians going to take this hold-up on the bones?'

Dutch looked thoughtful as he swilled the brew around in his glass. 'Right now I'd say they're not happy campers. After they learn the facts about the murders, hopefully they'll see the reason for the delay and not try to fight it.'

'You think like a true Calvinist, Dutch. You know diddly shit about these people. The Indians don't give a damn about serial murders. They think it's a white man's disease. To them, all serial killers look like Al Pacino. Now what about this poison?' Her eyes were excited. She knew him well enough to know he wouldn't make something like that up.

'It's called tricresyl phosphate,' he said.

'What proof do you have that it's murder? Couldn't the girls have ingested this toxin by accident?'

He shook his head. 'I don't think so. Remember Benny Benjamin over at the coroner's office?'

She nodded. 'The pathologist who looks like Groucho. He slept on our couch for a couple of weeks when his wife threw him out.'

'That's the one. He just sewed my ear back on. According to some preliminary tests he performed, the girls had to have swallowed large quantities of the noxious compound over a period of at least several weeks before it could show up in their bone marrow.' He moved his face closer to hers and said in a deep whisper, 'You drink it one time it's an accident. You drink it for six or seven weeks, it's murder. You don't acquire a palate for tricresyl phosphate. It's got a taste that would knock over a grizzly bear. Those girls didn't die painlessly. Muscular paralysis is usually the first sign: that means they couldn't move. Ultimately, respiratory paralysis sets in and they die.'

An involuntary shiver shot through Therese as she

pictured the slow, tortuous deaths in her mind. 'It sounds pretty grim,' she said.

'It is. Think of something stuck in your throat so you can't breathe. Since muscular impotence has already occurred, you can't even put your hands up to your mouth or run to get help. You just lie there in agony until you go into a seizure, pass out and finally die.'

'What about the paintings of the black centipedes found near the bodies? You think it's the killer's calling card?'

'That's a question for the police, not for a forensic anthropologist. But I think you're partially right. The tunnel painting and the one found on the boulder near the man were the killer's own personal calling cards. They were meant for himself, and not for anyone else's eyes. The bodies were not supposed to be discovered. It was just a fluke that they were. The reason the man was cut up and buried in a secluded area was so that nobody would find him. And if it wasn't for the earthquake, the girls would also have remained buried.'

'But why a centipede? What significance does that kind of insect have in these killings?'

He took a swig of his beer and leaned back in the chair. 'That's a tough question. It certainly plays a part in Chumash mythology. I'll tell you what I think, though. The centipede is an arthropod. In a way, so was our murderer. The centipede paralyses its victims before killing them. Our boy did the same thing. He acted like one of them.'

'Oh, dear, you've uncovered a crazy out there, haven't you?' She wrapped her arms around her body in disgust. Therese hated insects.

'I think he identified with those creatures. I'll even go a step further than that. I'll bet you he probably envied them, too, because they could produce their own toxin while he had to go to a store and buy his. This creep would make Dr Mengele look like Albert Schweitzer.' Dutch licked his dry lips and said, 'I don't think anything could match the horror of not being able to breathe.'

A sudden terror took hold of him. It grabbed him by his throat in a steel grip and held tight. His heart began to pound against his chest and a strong current passed through his skin, as if he had brushed up against a live wire.

That smell of Shalimar! It was drenching the bar in its sweet, choking stench.

'Are you all right?' Therese asked, staring at his chalky face and damp brow.

Dutch was trying to breathe but he couldn't get air to enter his windpipe. Where the hell was Billie? He needed her now. Dutch quickly got up from the chair and raced out of the door.

Therese grabbed his frayed coat from the back of his chair and followed him outside. At first she couldn't find him in the darkness. Squinting into the night, she looked round, finally spotting his large grey shadow over by the edge of the pier. He was doubled over, clutching tightly on to the wood railing, his mouth open as he desperately gasped for air. The colour of his face was now almost a pale blue.

She dropped his coat on the ground and ran over to him. Putting her hands on his shoulders, she shook him hard. 'Breathe, Dutch. It's in your head. It isn't real,' she said firmly. 'Breathe, goddamn it!'

During their marriage, Therese had seen this happen

to him several times. She had told Dutch to go and see a psychiatrist, since his own doctor could find nothing wrong with him, but he had refused. Once, after an unusually severe seizure, she had gone and talked to one herself. The specialist had told her that her husband may be experiencing severe panic attacks. Without an examination, it was hard to give an accurate diagnosis. He said that the root of these disorders usually had to do with something that had happened in early childhood.

Leaning against the rail, Dutch now fought with all his strength to breathe. Finally, his windpipe opened up and he sucked the cool night air greedily down into his lungs.

Therese watched silently as he inhaled over and over again. His face was cloaked in sweat, but his colour was returning.

'If you don't get help with this, it will kill you,' she said quietly, handing him his coat.

It was cool and damp. He put the coat on and buttoned it. 'I'm fine,' he eventually said, looking away from her and staring out into the black, fathomless night. He could hear the waves hitting the pilings under his feet.

'What happened when you were a boy, Dutch? These attacks have something to do with that, don't they?'

'When did you become a psychiatrist?' His tone had a hard edge.

'I know nothing about your childhood. It was something you never talked about,' she said.

'Then why start now?' She was beginning again, like she had when they were married, he thought. The pounding of his heart eased up as the oxygen

192

circulated through his veins.

'I had a history with you.' Her voice was rock solid, but a hint of pain underscored it.

'History means something that is past and can't be recaptured. Let's keep it that way. It was your idea and it was a damn good one.'

She put her hands up, as if in surrender. 'You got it, Dutch. Whatever you want.'

'Are we through now?' he said crisply.

'Not yet.' Her eyes stared coldly at him. 'I have something to show you.'

'Business?'

'Absolutely.'

The cold wet spray slapped them in the back as they walked away from the edge of the pier, towards the parking area.

Therese paid the attendant, took her keys from him and went over to her Toyota at the other end of the empty lot. She opened the boot and took out something wrapped in bubbled packing material.

'What is that?' he asked.

'The main reason I came to see you.' She unravelled the plastic until a dark metal object appeared.

Dutch took it from her. 'It looks like a cross,' he said, fingering the five-pound piece of metal.

'It *is* a cross, but it's not just any cross. Remember that encrusted thing your helper found near the hotel site? I had it cleaned with acid.' Therese opened the front door, slid inside and put on the interior light. 'Get in, Dutch, and bring it with you,' she said impatiently.

Dutch got in on the passenger side. In the light he could see the object more clearly. The cast was a dull copper colour, but the weight and feel of it said it was gold. It looked old. Probably belonged to a Spanish missionary, he thought. He glanced at Therese and saw the excited gleam in her eyes.

'Read the inscription,' she said.

He turned the gold piece round, searching for it. Then he saw some faint lettering in the centre where the sections of the cross came together. He took his glasses from his jacket pocket and put them on. Holding the icon at arm's length, he squinted as he tried to read it.

'You're getting old, Dutch.' Therese took it from him. Pointing to each letter, she slowly read, 'I – N – R – I'

'Even I remember that one,' Dutch said.

Then she moved her finger under the letters. 'This is what I want you to see. The date . . . 1768. Anything happen around that time that rings a bell?'

He shook his head. 'Uh-uh.'

'Hand in your anthropology degrees, Dutchman. Remember Juan Crespi? He was a missionary in the eighteenth century who kept a daily journal on the Chumash Indians.'

Dutch stared blankly at her.

'Don't you remember the unearthing we worked on in Encino a few years ago?'

Crespi! Of course, he thought. The lost Indian village. The duck pond where he used to take Max was part of that find. Scholars had known about it for years through Crespi's diary, but could never pinpoint the exact location. When the Encino site was uncovered, it was agreed by most archaeologists, Therese among them, that this was the location of the hidden village. Millions of artifacts had been dug up confirming this.

'Crespi discovered the tribe in 1769. A year after this was forged,' she said.

'You think the cross belonged to one of the priests?'

'Stylistic analysis says the age is legitimate.'

'What are you thinking, Therese?'

'That maybe there was another Indian village. A village that Crespi didn't write about in his diary, or if he did, it got lost somewhere.'

'That's a big maybe. It could be that Crespi or his cohorts just left their cross behind while making their way over the Santa Monica mountains into Encino. Have you found anything else?'

'Yes, and so have you.'

'You talking about Lenny Garowitz's gold coin?'

'Yep. And the ones he may be socking away.'

Dutch thought it over. Could be.

She took off her glasses and rubbed her eyes. Putting them back on again, she said, 'I also found fragments of old cloth and mahogany shavings.'

'What's so important about that?'

'Mahogany trees are not indigenous to California. But they are to Spain.'

'Are the fragments remnants of something?'

'Yes. Furniture. The Spanish have always used that type of wood. Even in the 1700s. The cloth I found is woven from the same material used by Jesuit priests back then.'

'Like Crespi.'

'Right.'

'What else have you found?'

'Nothing, yet.'

Dutch perked up. 'You want to keep the site open, don't you?'

'Yes, goddamn it. Who knows what's really down

there? What if there was another village? Payne's construction workers probably destroyed a lot of the articles while excavating the ground. That's why we haven't found much at this point. At first I thought we'd got everything that was down there. Now I'm not so sure. If I can sift through the site, dig deeper, I might come across another layer of artifacts.'

'And if the site is really ancient, you'll come across other layers after that,' he said.

'Right.'

Dutch could see the frustration etched on her face. 'Have you talked to Payne about this?'

'Yes. He's given me a week to find something to prove my theory. That's not enough time.'

'He can't just give you a week. The law says . . .'

'He doesn't need the law. He's John Payne, remember?'

'Talk to him again.'

'I will, but he doesn't like this. He's invited me to a party at his hunt club. I'll talk to him there.'

'You going with Miles?'

Glaring at him, she said, 'None of your buisness, Dutch.' She turned off the interior light in the car.

She was right. Dutch looked at her profile. Even in the darkness he could tell that her face looked tired. He suddenly felt exhausted himself. The beers had done their job. He opened the car door and stepped out into the night. The cold felt good and invigorating. He squatted down next to the driver's side window and said to her, 'Look, I'm sorry about before. It's just that my childhood was pretty uneventful.'

A smile, an almost caring one, brushed past her lips. 'You're a liar, Dutch. I could always tell when you were lying. Your eyes begin to flutter like a ham actor in a silent movie.'

That's exactly what they were doing now, he realized.

She closed the door, started the car and drove away.

He pulled the collar of his coat up over his neck and watched the Toyota dissolve into the darkness.

I could never tell you, Therese, he thought, walking to his Bronco. His stomach shrivelled up when he thought about what had happened to him in Ohio so long ago.

He got into the truck, opened the glove compartment, and took out a new Billie Holiday cassette he had bought that morning. When he had ripped the plastic off the casing, he started the truck and shoved the tape into the player. The rolling piano of Sonny Clark reverberated in the Bronco, then *she* started to sing:

> *I love my man,*
> *I'm alive, I say I don't*

Her voice sounded scratchy and tired. He could hear the drugs and despair chipping away at the doors of her soul. Dutch stayed in the parking lot and listened to two more tracks before he finally shifted into first and drove away.

Hugo lay on his weight bench in the bedroom, resting his head on a damp towel. He had just finished his third set of bench presses and his pectorals were all pumped up. Pockets of sweat trapped in the sculptured ridges of his stomach muscles dripped on to the floor as he breathed. Downstairs in the basement, the motor of the humidifier hummed, making the room feel like a steamy furnace on the bottom of a ship. The humidity didn't bother Hugo. He liked it. When the army sent him to Vietnam, he had loved going off into the wet jungles by himself, sitting on a rock, naked, letting the heat drain the salt from his body.

The TV was on, and they were replaying Dutch's interview on the eleven o'clock news. This man is all over the place, uprooting what should remain buried, Hugo thought. He was like a dentist poking into the raw nerves of his molars. Again the feeling of humiliation crept over him. No, he wouldn't let that happen again. He would never be beaten like that in front of people again. Never! Never! His body tensed up from the anger in him, making the cobra tattoo sway back and forth on the inside of his arm.

Now he had to take care of this other thing. He sighed. *One thing always leads to another.*

He got up from the bench, wiped his body with a towel, then showered and dressed. He put on a pair of chino pants and a Polo T-shirt. Opening the wardrobe door, he eyed the different coloured wigs in the humidity-controlled cabinet on the shelf. Each one was a different style. The blond toupee on the top shelf was the one he had worn when he went to the courthouse to pay Santiago's bail. This time, after a bit of thought, he selected the brown one, with the JFK parting on the right side. When he wore it, he looked like a lawyer or a Federal agent. Staring into the mirror over the dresser, he carefully fitted it on his head. The wigs were top of the line and had cost him a fortune. It was hard to tell them from the real thing.

Hugo grabbed his tweed jacket from the wardrobe,

took two envelopes from the nightstand and shoved them into the side pocket. He then turned off the lights and left the house. He wasn't concerned about break-ins. All the windows were barred and the door was made of thick oak and had special steel locks.

He drove north on the 405 Freeway and got off at Mulholland Drive and turned west. The snake-like road was dark and solitary, hugging the top of the Santa Monica mountains that divided LA from the San Fernando Valley.

Two miles further down, Hugo pulled off the road and on to a plateau high up over the bright lights of Sherman Oaks. He parked away from the one desolate street lamp that tried, but failed, to light up the area. A hundred feet away was a parked Ford pickup truck.

Frank was already here.

Hugo got out of the car and looked quickly round. Looming out of the darkness directly in front of him was the recently built Presbyterian church. The tar-covered section next to it was its mammoth parking lot.

Hugo walked towards the back of the church, where its wall ended on the edge of the cliff. That was where they had agreed to meet. Turning the corner of the massive building, he saw Frank standing there, the lights of the Valley below illuminating his shadow.

Frank was smoking a cigarette. Every time he sucked the smoke in, the burning tobacco lit up his face. He was the red-headed man with the diamond stud who had tried to steal the bones at the university.

Hugo had met Frank several months ago while having a drink at a gay hangout over in West Hollywood. Hugo didn't consider himself a homosexual, nor did he think he was straight. He had no strong feelings about that one way or the other. When the sexual craving came upon him, he didn't differentiate between men or women to satisfy it.

Frank had been sitting on the bar stool next to Hugo, and started to talk to him. At first Hugo was repulsed. There was something seedy about Frank, like a hustler who continued to stay on the streets though his time had passed.

Throughout the conversation, Frank's eyes were constantly shifting around the room. Hugo noticed that his hands were peeling from the dryness and were also shaking. The man was a crackhead. He must have been a looker when he was eighteen, but that had to be fifteen years ago, Hugo thought. His shirt was faded from too many washings and his cowboy boots were scuffed, which also meant that he didn't have much money.

Hugo smiled. Perhaps it was good they met.

The man was on the thin side from doing ice, but he was still big and somewhat muscular. The jock type: not too bright, and his talk never cut the surface of anything.

After a while, Frank got drunk and his conversation became filled with self-pity. He said he used to work as a bouncer at the discos on the Strip, but he had been unemployed now for several months. There were no jobs out there for him. Then he started talking about his financial problems.

Hugo knew the man was in a holding pattern, circling, getting ready to hit him up for money. Probably for sexual favours. Hugo didn't mind. Let the man do his number. He bought Frank several drinks, only half listening to him. While he was talking Frank's eyes kept darting all over the bar, as if he were unconsciously looking for the pipe. Tired of hearing him whine, Hugo finally suggested that he work for him on a part-time basis.

'Doing what?' Frank asked, his head bobbing up and down from too many drinks.

'You seem to know the streets.'

'I guess.'

'I'm a busy man, Frank. I don't have that luxury.'

Frank grinned as it dawned on him. 'You want me to find you men?'

'On occasion. Other times women. I don't have the time to search them out.'

Frank's lids started to sag over his watery green eyes. 'You want the type that does weirdo things, don't you?'

'Perhaps.'

He leaned over, his alcoholic breath in Hugo's ear. 'You want to hurt them or they you?'

'Them.'

'I know some. They're expensive.'

'They always are.'

That was several months ago.

Tonight, when he heard Hugo approaching in the dark, Frank turned round.

'Mr Frye. You scared the shit out of me.'

'A big man like you, Frank? Come on.'

Frank dropped his cigarette on the ground and stepped on it. 'You're the quietest guy I ever met.'

'I know. Gives you the creeps, doesn't it?'

'Nothing like that.' Frank forced a laugh. It sounded phony. He was wearing a fake leather bomber jacket. Taking his hands out of the pockets, he rubbed them and danced on his toes. 'Cold night, Mr Frye.'

'Very.' Hugo took one of the envelopes and gave it to him.

Frank's eyes lit up. His hands were shaking and he had difficulty opening it. When he did, he ran his thumb over the twenties and the one hundred dollar bill inside. It didn't feel right. His drawn eyes looked up questioningly.

'It's what we agreed upon, Frank,' Hugo said quietly.

Frank quickly closed the envelope and stuck it in his pocket. 'You know I trust you, Mr Frye. It just felt a little thin, that's all.' A nervous smile cut across his face. Again he banged his hands together and danced.'We had a slight problem getting the skeleton at the school.'

'*You* had the problem, not me.'

'You're right. Absolutely right. It's my problem . . . sorry about that. I didn't know that bone doctor would be coming back. The school was supposed to be deserted.'

'You feeling sore, Frank?'

His eyes turned bitter. He looked at Hugo. Was he laughing at him? 'Just my ribs. The fucker tried to crush me. I wasn't ready for him coming in like that.'

'You should have been. Maybe if you'd kept away from the pipe that day you would have fared better.'

'I made him hurt, though.' He nodded, grinning at what he had done. 'The guy's ear was all bandaged up. I grabbed hold of it and ripped it off. You should have heard it. Sounded like tearing a page out of a magazine. He screamed like a pig with its throat cut.'

Hugo was not impressed. 'I paid you to get bones, not an ear.'

'I did wreck their experiments with the cotton fibres

202

at the hangar. Just the way you told me. That was a great idea of yours Mr Frye. I also took care of the messenger.'

'That was part of the first job. Did you kill him?'

'No. Just gave him a headache.'

'Did he recognize you?'

'I wore a sailor's hat over my head. The knitted kind. It covered most of my face.'

The man was a fool, Hugo thought. 'It was eighty degrees out that day. You must have blended in pretty good with that hat on.'

'Nobody noticed me, Mr Frye.'

'I bet. You only completed one of the two jobs I gave you. You didn't get me the bones.'

'Yeah, I guess so,' he said sheepishly. 'What do you want them for, anyway?' Frank regretted it the second he's asked the question.

Hugo didn't answer. He stared at him with a face cut in stone, his eyes betraying nothing. After several seconds, he said, 'When you scavenge through the envelope after I leave, you will see that I have only paid you half the money.'

The redhead frowned.

'Fair is fair, Frank. You get paid for what you accomplished, not for your time. You have an opportunity to make up the other half.' He took the other envelope from his pocket. It had a US Air logo on the front. 'This is a Red Eye ticket to Cincinnati and a voucher for an Alamo rental car. A Honda Civic. Drive to a town called Xenia and find out everything you can about a Wilhelm Van Deer. He was born there.'

'That's the guy . . .'

'Who sat on you. Yes, I know. You have three days

203

to accomplish this. There's a reservation in your name for two nights at the Motel 6.'

Frank grunted his disapproval as he pocketed the envelopes. 'Jesus, Mr Frye. The Red Eye, Motel 6 . . . You really know how to send a guy first class.'

'Let's not have any illusions about ourselves, Frank. You are what you are. I want to know everything you can find out about this man.'

'Like what?'

'The man likes bones. That's a little strange, don't you think? Find out why, and you'll know something about him.' Hugo stared at him for several seconds, then moved closer, stopping only when his face was inches from Frank's.

Frank felt his breath on his neck, and the bile in his stomach curdled. 'What is it, Mr Frye?'

Hugo reached over and touched Frank's long coppery hair, running his hand slowly through it.

Frank's neck muscles contracted at the touch, but he didn't dare move. Hugo's fingers felt like living slippery *things* crawling over his scalp. This man scared him like no other.

'You have lovely hair, Frank, did you know that? A little ratty from the crack, but still lovely. So red and thick. It reminds me of a sea anemone, the way the wind blows through it.'

When Hugo came home, he removed the glass aquarium from the top of the credenza and placed it on the table. Then he walked into the living-room and opened the cupboard. He pushed aside several folded sweaters on the shelf and took out a two-foot-square cardboard box with small holes in its sides. Putting the sweaters back in place, he went into the dining-room

204

and removed the grid covering the top of the tank, then opened up the box.

As if knowing what Hugo was going to do, the enormous centipedes angled their flattened bodies upwards. In the box were dozens of live Asian cockroaches that he purchased illegally from an exterminating company in Miami. He received a fresh supply weekly. The smaller, local ones would have been just as tasty to his beautiful pets, but the larger creatures couldn't fly and it was more fun watching them. He grabbed several in his hand and tossed them into the tank. Then he looked on in fascination as the centipedes descended on the cockroaches, biting them with their powerful jaws. The roaches tried desperately to get away, some even climbing halfway up the tank. Then, as the paralysing toxin worked its way into their nervous systems, they dropped on to their backs, their hairy legs whipping frantically in the air. Still alive, the roaches could do nothing but watch helplessly as the centipedes began to devour them.

When the feeding was over, Hugo put the screen over the tank, covered it up again and placed it back on top of the cabinet. It always gave him a rush to watch his little friends eat. That was something he never grew bored with.

Later that night, Hugo lay in bed wide awake. He couldn't sleep. The face of the Dutchman wouldn't leave his mind. Angry passions suddenly started erupting inside him again. *Yes, he is the one that has been sent. I must be careful. I must prepare for him. He will not stop digging until it is me he has unearthed.*

He knew he had to stop the anthropologist; that was inevitable. The more he thought about it, the more he was beginning to look forward to it; like a brother who fantasizes about destroying a sibling before he gets a chance to tell daddy that he did something wrong.

Dutch screamed and sat up in the darkness. 'A nightmare,' he muttered to himself. *Always nightmares*. His breathing was heavy and his body clammy. He glanced over to the illuminated clock by the side of his bed: 2.20 in the morning.

Bitch heard his moans and hobbled over to the bed. She put her head on the blanket and whimpered.

There would be little sleep tonight. He got out of bed, took out a Heineken from the fridge, then opened the metal door of the trailer and let the chilly ocean breeze tickle his damp body.

Bitch came over to his side and tucked her head under his dangling hand to be petted. Dutch scratched her slowly and thought about the dream. It was not the first time he had had this nightmare. This time, though, was the most vivid.

His mouth being forced open by invisible hands . . . wet cement being poured down his throat. Hardening into concrete. Unable to gag, to breathe. Fear, like nothing he has ever known. Unbearable claustrophobia. Continous suffocation, with no merciful death to make it go away. Running down a long, endless tunnel. His mouth forged into a hideous, silent scream.

Then he would wake up, like now.

Except this time it was different; more realistic.

This time he could feel and taste the porous cement, and he could see the hands that were once invisible. They were strong and hairy.

He knew that the reason the dream was so graphic tonight had to do with the murdered girls. Those poor souls had experienced his worst nightmare. How could someone kill another human being in that way? What kind of anger could provoke a man into performing that kind of gruesome torture? It had to be an ugly and twisted anger of the worst kind.

Dutch looked out into the clear, black night. The sky was alive with stars. His heart was beating wildly and his breathing was heavy. Whoever committed the murders was still out there. He believed that as firmly as he had ever believed anything in his life.

He sat outside on the rim of the trailer and sipped his beer. As he listened to the ocean break against the beach, he wondered what the man who painted centipedes was doing now.

Was he asleep? Dutch doubted it. The killings were now in the open. This crazy bastard must be worried about that, or he wouldn't have gone to such lengths to bury them in an old Indian graveyard.

If he wasn't asleep, then he also had to be up and thinking. About what? Maybe right now the madman was looking up at the same stars as he was.

Maybe he's thinking of me, Dutch thought. That made sense. Dutch was certainly thinking about him.

Bitch, realizing her master was not going to go back to bed, limped into the kitchen, sipped some water, then lay down on her blanket and immediately fell asleep.

12

The ringing of the phone echoed through the metal trailer, causing the nomadic dogs that prowled the hills to howl.

Dutch opened his tired eyes to a curtain of blackness. His thoughts about the killer had given him little sleep last night. Dropping his hand to the floor, he groped for the phone that was buried under several volumes of books and magazines. When he finally found it, he put the receiver on the pillow and tucked his arms under the cover.

'Did I wake you, Dutchman?' Smokey Pete said on the other end.

Tired as he was, Dutch recognized the gravelly voice. 'What time is it?' he mumbled.

'Five. I need to talk with you. I'll bring breakfast, you make the coffee. Try and do a decent job of it. See you in an hour.'

He hung up before Dutch could say anything.

Six in the morning was the perfect time to be out on the beach, the Dutchman thought. He loved the foggy grey tint of the sky, the cool sea air with the smell of damp salt, and the harsh cries of seagulls as they circled the ocean looking for food.

Nothing else seemed to exist at six o'clock. No traffic jams above him on the Pacific Coast Highway, no loud radios and beer-drinking teenagers lying on the beach sizzling in the hot sun. This was his hour. This was the time land's end belonged to him alone.

He sat on the rocky sea wall, about a hundred feet out in the water, and slowly sipped coffee from his mug. The black boulders of the jetty, once ominous and pitted from being constantly bombarded by ocean spray, were now covered with the graffiti of love-smitten teenagers. Bitch was sitting by his side, frantically biting at the sand fleas that embedded themselves in her fur. Dutch's thermos bottle and an empty cup were propped up against one of the rocks.

There was no leeward side to the breaker, and the early morning wind cut into Dutch's skin. He turned up the collar on his frayed coat and blew warm breath into his hands. In the distance he could see the large, bow-legged figure of Smokey Pete coming his way. His long hair was braided and he was walking barefoot on the sand. The big Indian was wearing a yellow plaid flannel shirt and black sweatpants that were rolled up to his knees. He was holding a pair of tennis shoes in his hand and had a brown bag tucked under one arm. When he got to the quay, he slowly stepped up on the boulders and carefully made his way towards Dutch.

The Dutchman smiled at him. 'You're a man who knows how to be on time,' he said. He looked down at Pete's exposed legs. Thin red and blue veins, resembling a New York subway map, wrapped themselves around his ankles.

'I didn't wake you when I called this morning, did I?' Pete asked.

'Not really. I was going to get up.'

'I figured that. You're the only other motherfucker I know that's awake at this hour.' Pete let out a long breath of air as he sat down on a flat rock next to the Dutchman. He placed his sneakers between his meaty feet, handed Dutch the bag and wiped his sweaty face with a bandana he took from his shirt pocket. 'Long walk from the road to these rocks, Dutch. I'm not one for exercise.' He slapped his gut to emphasize his meaning. Leaning over, he picked up the thermos and poured himself half a cup of coffee. He then took out a flask from his pants pocket and filled the rest of the cup with whiskey. Pete offered the pint to Dutch, but the anthropologist waved a hand, refusing.

The Dutchman opened the bag Pete had brought, took out two bagels with cream cheese and handed one of them to the big Indian. They ate in silence, watching a flock of birds sitting on top of a garbage tow a couple of hundred yards out in the ocean.

'Thanks for the breakfast,' Dutch said, after finishing the bagel. He dug his hand into the bag for another one.

'You like living near the water, Dutch?' Pete asked, licking the cream cheese off his fingers.

'Yeah, I like it.'

'Not me. I like the desert. It's dry and hot. Too fuckin' damp by the ocean. My arthritis starts acting up whenever I get close to it.' Pete squinted into the grey light. 'Did you know that the Chumash used to fish right where we're sitting now? Their villages were all around here.' He pointed behind them, where multi-million-dollar homes clung precariously to the bluff overlooking the ocean. 'You don't see any Chumash here today. They couldn't afford the rent. When the Indians lived here, they called this patch of beach land — not property. Land is God-given and free; property isn't. That's where us dumb Indians made our mistake. We should have called it property and charged *you* heathens rent. Then, instead of collecting welfare, we'd be rich and watching the seagulls just like you do every morning.'

Dutch laughed. 'Hey, I'm a real fucking millionaire, Pete.'

'I thought all you blond gods had bucks,' Pete said, also taking another bagel from the bag.

'First of all, you didn't have a choice about this land. The heathens *took* it from you. And for all that noble savage bullshit of yours, you love the good life, same as me.'

Old Pete's face spread into a deep grin. 'I guess I'm part of both worlds, Dutch. That's the only way to survive when you're an Indian.'

Dutch nodded his head in understanding. He knew all about the tragic plight of the mission Indians. Before the Spanish sailed into the Santa Barbara Channel in the sixteenth century, the Chumash were a flourishing and affluent tribe. Some of their villages were big enough to be called towns. Eventually forced off their lands by the Spaniards, they went to live and work in the missions that were being built along the California coastline. There, they were converted to Christianity. Conditions in these religious stations were no better than slave labour. Many died of smallpox and measles. Utterly depressed, suicide and abortions became a way of life for them. When the United States finally took over California, the Chumash tribe was almost nonexistent.

'Since I'm half-infidel, half-Indian, that makes me the logical person to talk to you,' Smokey said.

'So there's a price to this breakfast, huh, Pete?' Dutch poured himself another cup of coffee.

'I like you, Dutch, you know that. But not enough to get up at the break of dawn just so I can eat bagels with you and watch the birds shitting over the ocean.'

'Were you sent?' The Dutchman wrapped his hands around the coffee mug to keep them warm.

'Yep.'

'The tribal council?'

'Partially.'

'They want their bones back, right?'

'They're real upset with you, Dutch.'

'I know,' he said sullenly. 'I can't give them back, not yet, anyway. We haven't dug up all the bones yet. If that maniac's buried other people in and around that grave, then it's my job to find them.' He looked at Pete. 'You said partially. Who else sent you?'

Smokey took in another deep breath, let it out slowly, then said, 'John Payne.'

'Oh, Christ!' Dutch said, standing up. He put a foot up on a boulder and looked out at the sea. 'I keep hearing that name. Why is that, Pete?'

'Payne is a big contributor to Native American causes.'

'Sure. It's all tax deductible.'

'It's more than that, Dutch. He's assembled factories right on the reservations so Indians can work. He's built hospitals and schools. Established scholarships for colleges. The man's an Indian freak, except he's richer than most of them. We like rich white men who want to share their wealth with us.'

Dutch looked sceptically at Pete. 'What about the delay on his hotel? Isn't that what Payne's worried about?'

Pete thought about it for a second, then said, 'Maybe, but that's only a small part of it. Payne's a strong believer in repatriation of Indian bones and artifacts. In fact, he was one of the leading supporters of the new bill giving the bones back to Native Americans for burial. Payne's an independent eccentric, one of the last of the great speculators. He and the council are sending me to Sacramento to talk to Governor Davis about all this.'

'Why the governor?'

'He and Payne are friends. This is his last term in office. When the governor steps down, Payne will be running in his place.'

'I heard.'

'Needless to say, *he's* also mad at you. I hate flying, so I thought I'd talk to you first. I don't want this to become a major issue, Dutch. There're more important things for Indians to deal with than this, like jobs and housing.'

Dutch shook his head. 'No can do, Pete. Sorry. The unearthing continues, and the bones stay where they are until every one of them is examined.' Quickly changing the subject, he asked, 'Do you know Bobby Santiago?'

Pete turned and stared up at him with blank, dark eyes. 'Who?'

Dutch knelt next to him. 'Bobby Santiago.'

Pete shrugged. 'Sounds like a Mexican busboy.'

Dutch knew he was lying. 'He's Indian, claims to be Chumash. I figured since there's only a few thousand of your kind left in LA you might know him.'

'Do all the Dutch people in LA know each other?' Pete suddenly grinned. 'Hey, is that the guy who cut off your ear?'

'Yeah. He's also the guy who may have done these killings.'

'Don't know him, Dutch. Sorry.' He began rubbing his bare feet to get some warmth in them.

'What about a man named Hugo Frye?'

Again, the Indian shook his head. 'Who's he?'

'He's the one who bailed Santiago out of jail. How about Smokey Valley Savings and Loan? Does that ring any bells?'

Pete scratched his chin and shook his head again. 'Nope. What happens if I get one? Do I win a cruise or something? Maybe a lawn mower from Sears?'

'It's important, Pete.'

'Lots of things are important. Mine is getting those bones and artifacts buried.' Pete stood up and wiped the sand and salt water off his sweatpants. 'I got to go. Looks like I'm going to be having panic attacks at thirty thousand feet because of you, motherfucker.' He picked up his tennis shoes and held them in his hands. He started walking away, then stopped and turned back to Dutch. Pointing a finger at him, he said, 'Better watch your back, Dutchman. You don't ever want to get an Indian pissed off at you.' Winking, he made a slicing motion next to his ear, then turned and walked down the jetty towards the beach.

No, Dutch thought, he didn't want to get an Indian pissed off at him. He only had one good ear left.

Dutch picked up the thermos, put the used bagel wrappers in the paper bag and went back to his trailer. Inside, he undressed and turned on the shower. Just as he was about to go into the stall, the phone rang. Groaning, he turned off the water, went over to the bed and picked up the receiver.

'Van Deer?' It was Jimmy Ciazo.

'Yeah, Jimmy.' It was cold in the trailer; he took a blanket from the bed and wrapped it around his naked body.

'I've been checking on the guy who attacked you at the university.'

Dutch stiffened, and his hand involuntarily went up to his bandaged ear. 'Did you find him?'

'Not yet. Turns out this guy was not the real driver for the messenger service. We found the real one lying in the men's bathroom at Zuma Beach. He was wrapped in one of those big garment bags that you put mink coats in to keep fresh. His head was split open and he was barely alive. Somebody wanted to screw with those bones of yours real bad.'

'You've scored on that one, Jimmy. Were you assigned this job, or are you doing this on your own?'

'Let's say, more on my own. Your name's been trickling down from the state capitol. Nobody here seems to want to break their ass over you.'

'There's a crazy out there who killed those girls, Jimmy.'

'Maybe. And maybe he's long dead. We don't know how old those bones are, do we? The murders took place years ago. Trust me, no one's interested. Beverly Hills is big buisness, and you're bankrupting it.' Jimmy cackled at his joke. 'Falcone wants you to come down and look at some shots that are similar to the creep you described to us. That's the best you're going to get from the LAPD and the Beverly Hills police.'

Dutch moaned. 'He may not be in any of your mug books.'

Jimmy said coolly, 'You're probably right. I'm only passing on Detective Falcone's orders.'

'Can you check on anyone who goes under the name of Hugo Frye? F−r−y−e.'

'What's he done?'

'Paid full pop for the Indian's bail.'

'You coming in?'

'I don't know. Maybe later. Thanks, Jimmy.' He hung up. Dutch was not going to waste his time going over smudged, coffee-stained photographs. The attacker wasn't going to be in any of them. Even if he was, the shots would be so grainy that the Dutchman probably wouldn't recognize him.

Everybody, from the governor down, wanted this just to go away.

The contamination of the bones meant he could not determine how long the girls had been dead. That didn't mean he couldn't find out what the girls looked like when they were alive, using the process of reconstruction. Somebody out there might recognize them.

Was sabotaging the identification of these two teenagers the reason somebody went to the trouble of robbing a messenger man and tainting thousands of bones? Probably, Dutch thought.

Who were those girls? he wondered as he got into the shower. Were they locals? Were they from another state? Christ, they could even have been from another country! There must have been a missing persons report out on both of them. Knowing when they were killed would have narrowed the time-frame and made the search somewhat easier. Without that, finding who they were was going to depend mostly on luck.

They were twins, and that should help. How many twins disappear every year? One of them had a cracked leg bone. Both had blond hair. That was about all he had. He knew there would be no dental records after all this time. Not much to give the police. With facial reconstruction, he would have more. He would know what they looked like. That's the part he dreaded the most, because then they would become humanized. He especially hated it when they were children or juveniles. Why did so many goddamn killers like them young?

Just as he stepped out of the shower, the phone rang again.

Dutch wrapped a large terrycloth towel around his dripping body and picked it up. It was Judge Robin Diaz. Her voice sounded cheerful, alert.

'I have a call in to the Federal Banking Commission in Washington. I should have something on Smokey Valley Savings and Loan in about half an hour,' she said.

'You're a judge. Is there any way of stopping them from taking the bones?'

'Not as the case stands now,' she said. 'An immediate injunction can be issued to put a moratorium on the collection of the bones if you can prove that more than just the twins have forensic value. Can you do that, Dutch?'

'I don't know.'

'Are you going to be home?'

'No. I have to be at the coroner's office downtown.'

'My courtroom is on the way. Come over. I should have something by then. I'll buy you a cup of coffee.'

'You got a deal,' he said, smiling. After he hung up, he quickly towel-dried his long hair and wrapped a rubber band round it so that a silken ponytail hung down between his shoulders. He didn't bother to shave. Instead of the T-shirt he normally wore, he opted for a light blue broadcloth. It was one of the few button-down shirts he owned, and the colour went well with his tanned body. He took a pair of khaki pants and brown loafers from his wardrobe and put them on. It was rare for him to get dressed up. Then again, it was rare for him to have coffee with someone like Robin.

The bailiff let him into her chambers. She was leaning over her desk, pouring herself a cup of coffee. Court wasn't in session yet.

'Hello, *mi morsa grande*,' she said, smiling at him.

He could smell the subtle fragrance of her perfume as she came over and handed him the styrofoam container filled with black coffee.

'The name, Smokey Valley, should have been the clue. I didn't even see it.'

'You know where it is?' he asked.

'I got the call from Washington. Smokey Valley is the name the ancient Indians gave the San Fernando Valley hundreds, maybe even thousands, of years ago. They named it that because of the smog. Inversion layers were here way before Exxon.' She ripped a piece of paper from her pad and handed it to him. 'I called them. Here's the address and the name of the man I talked to. The Savings and Loan company is located in the city of San Fernando. I spoke with their loan officer. A pleasant chap, until I mentioned the name Hugo Frye. That turned him into ice. It was like I had a twelve-gauge shotgun pointed at his head and was about to rob his bank.'

Dutch put his cup on the desk. His mind was beginning to race. 'Where's the main office?'

'There is no main office. There's only one bank. It's

a small S&L.' She smiled. 'Ready for this? Smokey Valley Bank is a cooperative, owned and run exclusively by the Chumash, Gabrieleño and Fernandeño tribes together. Ninety-nine per cent of their loans are given to their own people.'

He brushed away several fine strands of hair that hung down in his face. 'Did Frye or the bank actually put up the money? If it was the bank, why did they want to bail out this crazy Indian? You saw Bobby Santiago. He's a transient. His clothes are held together by wishful thinking. Why would a bank put up that kind of money for someone like him? We know that a lot of cretin-type thinking went into some of the investments made by S&Ls in the past, but putting fifteen thousand dollars into Bobby Santiago has got to head the all-time dumb list.'

A knock on the door. The bailiff's voice on the other side saying, 'Court is ready to convene, your honour.'

'Thank you, Joe,' she said. She turned back to Dutch. 'We don't know if it was the bank. Frye could just be a customer and it was his own money. She stood and zipped up her robe, then blew him a kiss. 'See you, Dutch.' Robin went into the courtroom, closing the door behind her.

Dutch sat there, thinking, staring at the oak-panelled door. A good woman. Bright. She came from a poor Mexican family; worked her way through college and law school. Nobody ever handed her anything; she earned it all, including the job she now had on the bench.

His mind quickly turned towards the Indian, Santiago. Why would anybody bail out an alcoholic and a drug user? What was so important about him?

Robin didn't think Bobby was capable of killing anyone. Dutch wasn't so sure. The Indian looked to be around forty; that could put him in the right age bracket for the murders. She said he only meant to cut off his ear. Maybe not.

He got up, put his half-empty cup down on the coffee tray and left through the back exit.

The colour on the walls of the coroner's office was a pale, institutionalized green. Several of the fluorescent lights on the water-stained ceiling were either out or blinking, emphasizing the morbid atmosphere on this floor where the dead were kept. Dutch walked towards the room containing the bones of the twins, his heels scraping softly against the grimy linoleum floor.

Gurneys holding bodies covered in plastic bags lined the hallway. Some were waiting to be autopsied, others were kept there until space opened up in the temperature-controlled steel cabinets.

He found Tara in the small lab that the coroner's office had set aside for the reconstruction. She was standing over a table gluing different size pencil erasers to the facial area of one of the skulls. The rubber tips indicated the average tissue thickness of the skin on the face of a white female. She looked up when she saw Dutch come into the room.

The sound of a toilet flushing. A second later an attractive girl of about eighteen, with greasy, unwashed hair come out of the bathroom wiping her hands with a paper towel. She was wearing an overly large black leather motorcycle jacket and skin-tight black leggings. Like Tara's, her ears were studded with rings and gold posts. Her hair, also like Tara's, was cut short and spiked. Dark purple lipstick spread across her mouth.

'Oh, my,' Tara said to Dutch, with an abashed giggle. 'Have you ever met Monica?'

Dutch stared at the girl. She grinned back at him, tossing the paper towel in the wastebasket. More of a smirk than a smile, he thought. A mole, like the one Madonna had, accented her upper lip. 'No, I've never met her,' he said in a tight voice.

Monica sauntered over to him and held out a hand. Her nails were painted black. 'Tara's told me *all* about you, Dutch.' The smirk remained on her face when she highlighted the *all*.

'All, huh?' This little shit knew that he had slept with Tara. He turned and glowered at his assistant.

Tara looked down, her white skin turning scarlet.

Monica put an arm around Tara's shoulder, looked Dutch straight in the eyes, then kissed his assistant hard on the corner of her mouth. Before Tara could react, Monica loosened her grip on her shoulder and headed towards the door. Opening it, she looked back at Dutch, slowly licked her dark violet lips, smirked once more, then left.

Dutch got her meaning: *don't fuck my woman again*. Turning to Tara, he said, 'You like them young, huh?'

'Kiss my ass, Dutch.' Her voice was flush with embarrassment. She went back to putting strips of rubber on the head of the skull.

'What does your lady do? You never told me.'

Tara looked up from the table. Her eyes were hard. 'She's a waitress at a Sizzlers restaurant. Any more questions?'

Dutch held up his hands and backed off. He knew he'd be treading in dangerous waters if he continued.

Tara's moods, when aggravated, could reach the murkiest of depths. For whatever reasons, she was very protective of that pimply-faced girl. Always had been. People, no matter how bright they were, had strange obsessions. Monica was hers.

He looked down at the job she was doing. The missing teeth had been moulded into place, and she had already attached the lower jaw to the rest of the skull. The pieces of rubber that she was working with were right where they were supposed to be on the structure. The next step would be to wrap strips of clay over them and mould in the facial features. Then add some skin colour paint, hair, a neck. In a few days, a fifteen-year-old girl would rise from the dead.

He could resurrect the dead. Even Houdini couldn't do that. Yes, he was the real magic man all right.

A couple of centuries ago they would have burned him at the stake for what he was doing now, he thought. He bent over to help Tara with one of the rubber pieces that had come loose.

13

The Dutchman sat in the driver's seat of his Bronco chewing on a cheeseburger while waiting for Jimmy Ciazo. Across the street, on the seedy end of Brand Boulevard, was the Smokey Valley S&L building. It was small and nondescript, hemmed in by a cheque-cashing place on one side and a Seven-Eleven on the other. Gang graffiti blotted out most of the colour on the brown stucco walls. A plain, unobtrusive sign with the bank's name printed in block letters hung over the aluminium doors.

When he finished eating, the Dutchman tossed the empty Burger King wrapper and the plastic Coke container into the back seat of the truck. He had worked on the beginning sections of the facial restoration with Tara all afternoon. When she had finished spreading the Plasticine material over the skull, he would go back and mould the features to conform to those of the dead girl. No other forensic anthropologist could touch him when it came to duplicating facial expressions. He was known worldwide for this ability, a distinction that made him uncomfortable.

Before he drove to San Fernando, he had called Jimmy and told him to meet him in front of the S&L.

They agreed upon four-thirty, half an hour before the bank closed.

A shadow suddenly fell over him, blocking out the sun on the left side of his four-wheeler. It was followed by tapping on the car's window. The Dutchman turned towards the sound. The detective was leaning into the glass, looking at him. He was actually smiling. His cheap copper-brown sports jacket hung over his big arm. Jimmy's neck, the size of a linebacker's, was popping out of his tight collar.

Dutch got out of the truck, took one look at the run-down neighbourhood, and decided to lock it.

'So why am I here?' Jimmy asked, as they crossed the intersection towards the bank.

'Because the loan officer at this institution doesn't want to talk about Hugo Frye and the amount of money that was put up for Bobby Santiago's bail. An anthropologist isn't going to make a dent in changing his mind. I hope you don't take this the wrong way, Jimmy, but I have a feeling that when he takes a look at you he's not going to hide behind the cliché that he'd be betraying his client's trust if he discussed the matter with us.'

'What the fuck do you want me to do with this guy? Whip him with my dick?'

'Just be your natural self, Jimmy. It seems to work with most people.' Dutch pushed open the glass door and they went inside.

The receptionist's desk was right by the entrance. A pretty, chestnut-skinned woman with straight black hair looked up from behind it, saw the two men and smiled.

Dutch looked round. It was a large room with a dozen or more desks stacked in rows. Men and women dressed in business clothes were working behind them. All of them had the same features as the receptionist: prominent cheek-bones, dark skin and black hair. Indians. The entire bank was run by Native Americans. There were cubicles surrounding the desks. These were the offices belonging to the upper echelon of the bank.

Next to the front door, an Indian in his late twenties, his wife and their young daughter, with short, straight hair, were sitting on an imitation leather couch. The man was wearing stiff new jeans, and the woman a flowery dress. Probably loan applicants, Dutch thought. The little girl saw the Dutchman staring at her. She giggled, then tucked her head under her father's jacket. A second later she peaked up at him, giggled some more, and hid her head once again.

'Can I help you?' the receptionist asked. Her smile was warm and her mahogany eyes sparkled.

Dutch took out the piece of paper Robin had given him with the name of the loan officer. 'I'd like to see Mr Roberto Gomez. My name's Wilhelm Van Deer.'

Her smile faded and the glimmer went out of her eyes like a gust of wind on a lit match. She picked up the phone and pushed an extension button. When someone answered, she quickly said, 'Martha, it's Jenny. A Mr Van Deer wants to see Mr Gomez.'

They knew who he was. Dutch looked over to the cubicles. He saw a woman in one of them pick up the phone. Next to her was a tan-skinned, middle-aged man wearing a dark blue blazer with copper buttons. The woman was obviously his secretary. She cupped her hand over the mouth piece and said something to him. The man turned and looked out at Dutch through the glass partition. He quickly turned back to his secretary and shook his head, no.

That's my man, Dutch thought.

Jenny nodded into the phone several times, gave a few, 'uh-huhs', then hung up. Looking up at Dutch, she said nervously, 'Sorry, Mr Gomez won't be in today.' Dismissing him, she began to peel some polish off one of her sculptured nails as she looked down at a copy of *People* magazine on her desk.

Dutch painted a frozen smile on his face, a big one. Putting one hand on the desk and the other on the magazine, he leaned over and whispered, 'I know he's here. I even know which office he's in. You want to make that call again, or do I just go right in and surprise him?'

Even with his smile, the big man looming over her desk had an unsettling presence. She rolled her chair away from him.

Dutch was about to pick up her phone and ring Gomez himself when he felt Ciazo's steel fingers wrap around his biceps.

'Thank you, we're going,' Jimmy said pleasantly to the girl. His grip tightened on Dutch's arm as he swung him towards the door with his massive strength.

Surprised, Dutch turned to Jimmy, then back to the receptionist. She was looking at the bank employees behind her. The male Indians had moved away from their desks and were slowly walking towards him and Jimmy. The detective pushed the door open with his foot and half-carried Dutch outside. He didn't let go of his arm until they had crossed the street and were back at the Bronco. With grim faces, the Indians walked out of the bank building and stood on the corner watching them.

'What the hell are you doing?' Dutch snapped pulling away from Jimmy.

The detective didn't answer. He stuck his hand in Dutch's pocket and pulled out his keys. Then he quickly opened the car door, got in and unlocked the passenger side. 'Get in, asshole,' he muttered.

Dutch looked over to where the Indians were congregating. They were talking among themselves, staring hard at Jimmy and him. One of them, who looked to be in his early thirties, with an expansive chest and big arms, started crossing the street. Several others followed, heading in their direction.

The Dutchman could see the ugly looks on their faces now and understood Jimmy's concern. He leaped over the fender of the Bronco to the other side and promptly got into the passenger's seat. Ciazo popped the clutch into first and sped away. The Indians, who were now in the middle of the street, quickly spread out in both directions, trying to avoid the car.

Jimmy made a quick left, causing the tyres to squeal on the asphalt. His face was taut with anger. 'Pete was right. You are one dumb motherfucker,' he said finally. He slowed down and made another left.

Dutch looked at him, confused. He was also angry. 'What the hell are you talking about? The girl was lying. He was there.'

'No shit,' Jimmy said.

'I saw him.'

'So?'

'What do you mean, so?'

'What were you going to do? You going to take on twelve guys just so you can talk to one guy? What the

229

hell kind of arithmetic is that? You fucking crazy, or what?'

'You're a cop!' Dutch shouted, his face turning scarlet.

'You think that's going to stop them? Being a cop never stopped anyone in Pico Rivera or Compton when I was working there.' His voice was grim. He slowed down even more, then made another left. Jimmy had now completed a circle around the block and was back on Brand Boulevard again. He found a spot across the street, half a block down from the bank's parking lot, turned off the motor and opened his window for air. The Indians had gone back into the bank. He leaned down in the seat, pulled a bag of peanuts out of his jacket pocket and ripped the top off. Without offering Dutch any, he turned the bag over in his mouth and dropped most of them into it. He chewed the salty peanuts slowly, his dead eyes fixed firmly on the back lot across the street. He looked at ease, as if he had done this kind of thing a thousand times before.

'We're waiting until we can get Gomez alone, right?'

'Good call, Dutchman. Maybe you ain't no dumb motherfucker after all.' Jimmy cackled, then finished off the peanuts and tossed the bag out of the window. 'The odds get better when you use a little fucking common sense.' He began removing bits of nut from his teeth with one of his business cards.

A grin crossed Dutch's face. Ciazo may not have much going in the humanitarian department, but he was good at what he did. Dutch slumped in his seat and waited with him.

Forty-five minutes later the employees started

leaving the bank. They went out through the back door to the parking lot, got into their cars and drove off. There was no sign of the man with the broad back wearing the navy blazer.

Fifteen minutes went by. No one else came out. A late model green Olds Sierra sat alone in the lot. Concerned, Dutch looked over at Jimmy. The detective's face was as expressionless as a slab of granite; his solid, unblinking eyes remained honed on to the door. Suddenly, he jabbed the Dutchman in the side with his elbow. 'There he is,' he said with that guttural voice.

Dutch turned and looked at the back door. The Indian with the blazer had just walked out. He locked the door with a key, then headed towards the Oldsmobile. He was a heavy man with large, round cheeks and dark skin. Dutch guessed his age to be somewhere in his forties. His hair was cut short and he was partially bald. He walked with a limp, his left hip swaying whenever he took a step. A prosthesis, the Dutchman thought. The man was missing a leg.

The loan officer got into the Olds and drove out of the parking lot. Jimmy turned the ignition on. When the man passed them going in the opposite direction, Ciazo waited several seconds before making a quick U-turn. He stayed a block behind the Olds, dropping even further back when the Indian got on the 118 Freeway going west.

Dutch leaned into the windshield, looking for the Olds. He scanned all the lanes in the clogged freeway. The green car wasn't there. 'You lost him,' he said, annoyed.

Jimmy didn't answer him. He moved into the slow lane and stayed there until the signs for the 405 came into view. He took the south exit. Cars were moving at a snail's pace.

Again Dutch poked his head up, looking out of the window. The Oldsmobile wasn't anywhere in sight. Sitting back in his seat, he said, 'How do you know he's here?'

Jimmy didn't say anything.

'You got sonar or something?'

Again the detective didn't answer.

Dutch sat back in the seat. If Jimmy said he knew where the Indian was, then he knew where he was.

Jimmy eventually turned on to the Hollywood Freeway going east. They had been driving for almost an hour now in the rush-hour traffic. Living and working at the beach, Dutch had forgotten what it was like at this end of Los Angeles. The city was so over-populated he wondered why more people who lived here hadn't killed each other.

Jimmy got off at the Glendale exit. He followed the parameters of Echo Park, with its ducks and giant lily pads, then went east on Sunset Boulevard. About two blocks in front of them, Dutch caught a glimpse of the Oldsmobile. He had it in his sight for only a few seconds, then it disappeared in a barrage of cars going towards Dodger Stadium. One of the reasons for this heavy traffic was that there was a game tonight. Just before the Elysian Park entrance to the ballpark, Ciazo turned left on a small side street that twisted and turned up into the hills. Every so often, Dutch would catch a flash of green metal, or a flare of light as the sun reflected off the chrome of the car in front of them. Then the Olds would turn on to another winding road, and disappear into a web of overhanging oak branches.

The Spanish-style houses were old and run down in this Mexican neighbourhood. Steel bars surrounded the windows, and the names of gang members were spray-painted on the stucco walls.

Dutch saw the green Oldsmobile parked in the driveway of one of the houses. The Indian, holding a briefcase, was getting out of the car.

Jimmy kept driving.

'Hey,' Dutch said to him.

'I saw him,' Jimmy replied. He drove about half a mile further, then parked the car by the side of the road. 'Give the guy a few minutes to settle in.' He got out of the car, stretched, then went behind a tree and peed. He then came back to the car, sat on the front fender and lit a cigarette.

Dutch also got out. At a window of one of the old houses with a terracotta roof, he could see the dark eyes of a child staring out at him from behind broken blinds. Dutch smiled at him.

The blinds snapped shut.

Dutch lit a cigarette. He walked a few feet, trying to get the circulation back into his legs.

'I didn't know Indians lived by the ballpark,' Jimmy said.

Dutch picked up the back of his leg, leaned against a tree, and stretched it as a runner would do.

Jimmy looked at his watch, then flipped his cigarette into the brush. 'The guy's had enough time,' he said. He and Dutch got back into the car. The detective made a U-turn, using someone's lawn to do it, and drove back to the Indian's house. He parked the car about twenty feet from the front porch.

They got out of the car and walked up the driveway. Toys were spread out on the asphalt, and a bicycle was

233

lying on the grass. The man had children. Jimmy didn't notice; his eyes were fixed on the living-room window and the door. They climbed the stairs leading up to the porch. Ignoring the bell, Jimmy curled his hand into a thick fist and banged hard on the wood.

A few seconds later, a small, pretty Latino woman with smooth skin opened the door a couple of inches; a thick chain lock was in place. Ciazo held his badge towards the crack for her to see. A glimmer of fear crossed her eyes. She muttered, '*Un momento*,' and then closed the door. A man and a woman whispered in Spanish on the other side, then the door opened again. It was the Indian. His blazer and tie were off and the top button of his shirt was loose.

Stepping in front of Dutch, Jimmy said to him, 'Gomez, right?' His voice was rigid.

The Indian nodded at his name. His dark eyes stared coldly at the detective. It was obvious that he did not like cops.

'Open up,' Ciazo said harshly. 'I want to talk to you.' He pushed hard on the door with the palm of his hand, demonstrating to Gomez how easily he could snap the chain if he wanted to.

The Indian, still glaring at him, unhooked the latch and opened the door part way. His body blocked the corridor. Jimmy pushed the door all the way open, backing Gomez against the wall, and walked into the house. Dutch followed.

Two small girls, their mouths covered with ketchup, ran from the dining-room table to their mother's side and hugged her legs. They looked suspiciously up at Jimmy.

'You have a warrant?' Gomez said to the cop, his

face inches from the detective's. His lips were trembling with rage.

'I don't need one. You invited me in, remember?'

'The hell I did!'

Dutch had had enough. Jimmy had done his job; now it was his turn. He got between the two men, smiled and held up his hands. 'I just need to talk to you for a few minutes. No police. No hassle.'

The Indian stared at him for a second, then nodded. 'He stays out of my face,' he said, motioning to Jimmy.

Looking over into the den, Dutch asked, 'You think we could sit down?'

'He keeps his mouth shut,' Gomez said adamantly, his eyes glued on the detective.

'You got it,' Dutch said, giving Jimmy a look that said, *Do it*.

After a beat, Jimmy pulled his eyes away from the Indian and nodded, OK.

Gomez looked from Jimmy to Dutch, thinking. A couple of seconds later he knelt next to his children. He put his hands on their backs, whispered something to them, then pointed to the dining-room. As they walked backwards to the dinner table, they continued to stare at the two pale men. Gomez stood up, nodding to his wife that it was OK. She went into the dining-room with her kids.

'You got two minutes. That's it,' Gomez snapped at them. He limped into the den, the metal joints on his prosthesis making a loud grinding noise. Dutch and Jimmy followed.

It was dark in the room because the heavy drapes were spread across the windows. Even in the dim light, Dutch could see that the den was pleasantly decorated in brown and sepia colours. Two matching floral couches faced one another across a marble coffee table. Framed photos of Gomez, his wife and his two girls were on the walls, and a reproduction of 'The Last Supper' hung over the fireplace.

Dutch and Jimmy sat on one couch, Gomez on the other.

'What do you want?' the loan officer asked, his face puffed out. 'You scared the hell out of my kids, pushing the door in like that.'

Dutch could feel Jimmy tensing. He quickly said, 'Who's Hugo Frye?'

'A client of the bank's. I don't have to talk . . .'

'He plopped down fifteen thousand dollars in cash taken from your bank to pay the bail of a derelict Chumash named Bobby Santiago.'

'Never heard of him,' Gomez said coldly.

'Sure you haven't.' Jimmy sneered.

Gomez scowled back at the detective. 'You scare my kids. You call me a liar. Fuck you, man.'

Jimmy started to move. Dutch put his arm in front of the detective, preventing him from getting up. When Ciazo's body eased up slightly, he said, 'You know about the bones of the girls that were found in Beverly Hills?'

'Sure I know about them. I also know who you are,' he said, with contempt. 'You're the scumbag who's been defiling those graves.'

Dutch ignored the Indian's remark. 'Those girls were murdered. They were only fifteen years old when they died. How old are your girls, Mr Gomez?'

'Five and seven,' he said. His eyes flickered for a split second as he thought about his own daughters and what Dutch was saying. Then he growled, 'Don't try to use scare techniques on me, man. Those murders happened years ago!' He was inching off the couch, getting ready to throw them out.

Dutch said, 'They were killed in a way that you wouldn't wish on your worst enemy. It took them weeks to die. They were transported to the grave-site through unused sewer pipes like pieces of garbage. Santiago knew about those pipes. I think he even lived in them at one time. That's why we need to talk to him.'

'I don't know who or where he is,' he said emphatically.

Dutch knew he was lying. He could smell it. 'There's no evidence that this maniac is dead, or that he even stopped killing young girls. He could still be out there. He might even be this Bobby Santiago.'

Gomez's face remained stoic, but he was squeezing his hands together real hard now. Dutch was willing to bet that they were good and clammy.

'I told you, I don't know where this guy is.'

'Sure you do.' Dutch leaned forward. 'Give him to me. Nobody will know it came from you.'

Gomez's face hardened. He slapped his good thigh with his heavy hand and leaped up. 'You've had more than two minutes. Let's go, friend. If you don't leave,' he said, looking away from Dutch to Jimmy, pointing his finger at his face, 'I'll call some *real* cops.'

A hoarse scream suddenly exploded from somewhere in the house, followed by a volley of curse words. The sound seemed to be coming from all directions.

The three men froze.

The noise was filtering out through the air vents. Dutch followed Gomez's gaze up towards the ceiling.

'What was that?' Jimmy asked, also looking up. 'You got a crazy aunt locked away in the attic?'

The screaming and cursing started again, followed by muffled sounds and several sets of footsteps scraping along a wooden floor.

Dutch knew that voice well. The crazy Indian, right before he cut off his ear, was screaming like that. He bolted for the stairs, taking them two at a time.

He ran down the brown-carpeted hallway on the top landing, pushing open bedroom doors. The master suite was empty, so were the girls' rooms. He kicked open the bathroom door. Nothing. At the end of the corridor was a closed door. Dutch turned the knob; it was locked. Jimmy was at his side now, so was Gomez. 'He's in there. Open the door,' Dutch said to the loan officer. He was breathing hard.

Gomez just stared back at him. The hate emanating from his eyes burned into Dutch's skin.

'Get out of the way,' Jimmy said, taking out his Beretta from the holster at his waist. He released the thumb safety and was moving closer to the door, getting ready to kick it in, when they heard the sound of a latch turning. Then the door opened slowly from the other side. At first, all that could be seen was a veil of darkness within. Then out of the murky shadows the figure of an old Latino man emerged. His body was bent and he shuffled. He looked from Dutch to Jimmy, then nodded to Gomez. '*Que paso*, Roberto?' he said.

Jimmy held the gun in two hands, pointing the barrel at the old man.

'Put it away, Jimmy,' Dutch said, seeing who it was. The man standing at the door, with the missing teeth and leathery skin, was the old Indian who was talking

238

to Smokey Pete at the mass grave-site in the Garowitz's backyard. Muddled sounds were coming from inside. The Dutchman walked past the man and into the darkness. He felt for the light switch on the wall, found it, and turned it on. The room lit up, exposing three men wearing suits and ties standing next to a bed, blocking his view of it.

Dutch recognized the young Indian men; they worked at Smokey Valley S&L. Their faces were rigid, determined, and their bodies, fists curled, were poised to strike. The muscular one, when he saw Jimmy with the gun, grabbed a lamp from the night table and held it threateningly over his head.

A gruff male voice coming from behind the Indians said, 'Put it down, Bernard. It isn't worth breaking a good lamp over the heads of those two assholes.'

Bernard, his eyes never leaving the gun, did what the man said. He slowly put the lamp back down on the table.

The Indians were blocking his view, but Dutch knew that voice. 'Hey, Pete, we seem to be seeing a lot of each other lately.' He walked towards the bed and the three Indians separated to make room for him.

Smokey Pete was sitting on the edge of the bed with his back propped against the headboard. He was holding a pint of whiskey in his hand. The Indian, Bobby Santiago, was lying in his arms, his head in Pete's lap. Bobby had on a pair of dirty jeans and was shirtless. His body was twitching uncontrollably, as if he had a live wire connected to him. His right arm suddenly jerked spasmodically into the air. Pete grabbed it, forcing it back down. The Indian, although he appeared to be unconscious, let out another stream of curses.

Pete took the bottle and held it up to Bobby's lips. He poured a few drops of whiskey into his mouth, most of it finding its way down his chin. The Indian's tremors eased a bit. Looking up at the anthropologist, Pete said, 'What's the matter, Dutchman, you never saw anyone going through the DTs before?'

As if to emphasize the point, Bobby started to gag. Pete rolled the Indian's head over to the edge of the bed, grabbed a basin from the nightstand, and held it under his face. Bobby tried vomiting, but nothing came out. His head dropped limply down on Pete's lap again.

Pete gently stroked Bobby's hair. Sick and helpless, the Indian moved his body into the foetal position. Looking up at Ciazo holding the gun, Pete said, 'If you're going to shoot him, you better do it now. As you can see, you got one dangerous motherfucker here, Jimmy.'

14

'You lied to me, Pete,' Dutch said.

'About Bobby here? Shit, that ain't no lie, Dutch.' He put his arms around the sick, semi-conscious Indian. 'Bobby never killed anyone that mattered. Maybe a few VCs in 'Nam, but that was it. He especially never killed any white girls. In fact, he never even *liked* white girls. He said he could never stand the way they smelled.'

Pete had more university degrees than most men, yet he intentionally put words together to sound as if he never got past the third grade.

'You lied to me, man,' Dutch said again. His voice was tight.

'Hey, you *gringos* never lie? Sell me that and I'll sell you thousands of acres of fertile, green reservation land that the US Government gave our people.'

Jimmy was only half listening to Pete; he was too busy sizing up the other three men. When he was satisfied that they wouldn't go macho on him, he stuck his gun back in the holster. He walked over to the bed and looked down at Bobby. 'Yeah, that's the sonofabitch who lopped off your ear, Dutch. This guy don't like the way white girls smell, huh? Take a whiff of him! He stinks worse than a black whore's pussy.'

241

He scrunched up his nose. Then he bent over and poked the limp Indian hard on his bandaged hand. Bobby suddenly opened his eyes and shrieked in pain.

'It's infected, you sadistic bastard,' Pete growled at him. 'Maybe you want to stick your teeth in it, too.'

Jimmy smirked. 'Don't get mad at me, Smokey. Falcone was the one that shot his finger off, not me.' Grinning, he motioned to the dressing on Dutch's ear. 'You guys look like twins.'

The groans and cursing started again. Bobby's entire body began jerking wildly all over the bed. The three young Indians grabbed Bobby's arms and held them to his side while Pete poured some more whiskey down his throat. When Bobby spit it up, Pete forced some more into him. Eventually, the spasms subsided and Bobby fell once more into a comatose state.

Pete carefully took Bobby's head from his lap and laid it down on the pillow. He slowly got up from the bed. Looking at the liquor bottle in his hand, he said angrily, 'Bobby's got the sickness bad this time. Can't cold turkey him. I have to shovel this shit down him or he'll die.' He put the pint on the dresser and walked to the door. Turning around, he said to Dutch and Jimmy, 'You guys coming, or you want to put shackles on Geronimo here, so he don't escape?'

Jimmy and Dutch glanced over at Bobby, saw he wasn't going anywhere in his condition, and followed Pete out of the door. Gomez trailed behind them, his squeaking prosthetic leg dragging on the carpet. The other men stayed in the room with the sick Indian.

In the entry way, Dutch put his hand on Smokey's shoulder and said, 'Pete, this thing about Bobby isn't going to go away, you know.'

Pete smiled. 'You holding a grudge about your ear, Dutch? The man's out on bail. It's all legit. You have no right harassing him.'

'It has nothing to do with my ear. It has to do with the killings of those girls.'

'Talk about this somewhere else, fellows,' Gomez said indignantly, shifting his eyes towards the table where his two children were sitting. Both kids were leaning forward in their chairs trying to hear what the men were saying.

'Sorry about that, Roberto. Mind if we use your backyard?'

'Go ahead, Pete. Just get these guys out of here, OK?' It was meant more for Jimmy than Dutch.

Pete went into the den and pulled back the sliding aluminium door that led to the yard. He walked outside on to the grass and sat down on a stone bench surrounded by pots of dwarfed orange trees. Dutch and Jimmy went with him. Gomez stayed inside, slamming the sliding door shut. He locked it and pulled the drapes closed. Dutch realized that Pete had deliberately led them outside so they couldn't get back into the house.

Hispanic sounds and warm smells of spicy food from the neighbourhood infiltrated the yard. Lemon and lime trees were lined up at one end to give a false semblance of privacy from the other houses.

Jimmy walked over to the toys lying on the grass, bent down and picked up a Barbie doll. The plastic figure seemed tiny in his big hand. His face turned sullen as he lightly stroked its reddish straw hair. Letting out a small, guttural groan, he gently put it back down on the ground.

Dutch watched him. He wondered if the doll

somehow reminded him of his own kids that his wife refused to let him see.

'Leave Bobby alone, Dutch. He didn't kill anyone,' Pete said sombrely.

Dutch leaned against the overhang, put one foot behind him on the bougainvillea-covered trellis, and hooked his thumbs through the loops of his jeans. 'What difference does he make to you? You and Bobby are not even from the same tribe. You're Gabrieleño, he's Chumash.'

'Bobby didn't kill anyone,' Pete said again.

'Who's this Gomez? Is he related to Bobby?' Dutch asked gesturing toward the bank officer's house.

'No. They were in the same regiment together in Vietnam.'

Dutch tapped his leg. 'Is that where he lost it?'

'He stepped on a Claymore,' Pete replied, nodding.

Jimmy emitted a quick laugh as he looked at Dutch. 'Everybody I meet lately seems to be missing body parts.'

Pete ignored the Italian. 'Bobby didn't kill those girls, Dutch.'

'You sure about that?' Jimmy said, going over to them.

Dutch looked at Jimmy. He was surprised by his sudden spurt of interest.

His response hit home with Pete, too. 'What are you talking about? Why would Bobby do something like that?'

Jimmy pulled up the slack in his trousers and put his size twelve foot on the bench next to Pete. 'Remember all those food wrappers and things that were found in the tunnel? The preliminary tests came back on them. Bobby's fingerprints were all over the more recent cartons and plastic bags. That means he's been hanging down in those tunnels. He could have been living there for a long time. Maybe he wasn't there alone. Maybe he had a friend with him, like the shithead who murdered those girls. Maybe they did it together. Lots of possibilities on this one, Pete. The older supermarket wrappers were too tainted to be of help forensically. But we have some idea of their age. One of the supermarket bags had its logo on it. That chain went out of business fifteen years ago.'

'You don't know if they belonged to Bobby,' Pete said pensively.

'Oh, I know. I just can't prove it, that's all. If we could have lifted prints from some of those old wrappers, and matched them up with the Indian's, then I'd say we'd have had us one hell of a case. It's too bad.'

Dutch was surprised by this. Why hadn't Ciazo told him about the fingerprints before?

Jimmy continued, 'Microscopic blond hairs were also lifted from the floor of the tunnel. All except one kind matched the hair follicles of the dead twins. The other kind is dark and thick, like an Indian's.' Smiling, he said, 'You think I could have a sample of Bobby's hair?'

Dutch stared at the big Italian in amazement. *The sonofabitch withheld all this from me!*

Pete stood up. 'Ask Bobby, it's his hair. You think you can get any information out of him? Well, you just go upstairs and talk to the man, Jimmy. Be my guest. Just don't stand too close to him, he may puke in your face. He already did that to me once today.'

Jimmy's beefy jaw moved in to meet Pete's. 'I bet

you knew all along that Bobby was living in those tunnels.'

Pete shrugged, then turned and walked towards the gated fence. 'If you think so, my friend, subpoena me at Bobby's trial. Until then, we're both free men.' He unbolted the lock, and stood there with one hand in his pocket and the other on the gate, waiting for one of them to leave.

Jimmy didn't want to go just yet. He slammed the metal gate closed and turned to the Indian, his lustreless eyes becoming alive for a moment. 'I want to know where that Chumash is at all times. Is that clear, Pete?' His finger was pointed directly at Smokey's nose. 'If he turns up missing, so will you.' The seed of life receded from his eyes once again. Without saying anything more, he opened the gate and made his way down the alley leading to the street, his massive shoulders scraping against the sides of the graffiti-covered walls.

Pete looked thoughtful as he stared at Ciazo's back. He said in a muted tone to Dutch, 'Keep a harness on that one. He's mean.'

A cold feeling swept over Dutch. 'What's so important about that drunken Indian? Why are you protecting him like this?'

'There are not many of us left, Dutch. If we didn't take care of our own, we'd be as extinct as the sabre-toothed tiger.' Without saying anything more, he snapped the gate closed and walked back to the house.

Dutch believed there was another reason Bobby was being protected. Looking up at the window above the overhang, he could see the curtains pulled apart and several cold, dark eyes staring down at him.

The aluminium sliding door opened again. Just as

Pete stepped in, Dutch yelled to him, 'Hey, Pete!'

The Indian stopped and turned.

'I need to talk to him,' the Dutchman said.

Pete just stared at him, not saying anything.

'Come on, Pete. Give me a break. I'm not Jimmy. I believe you. The guy didn't do it, OK.'

The old Indian stood up against the door, his probing eyes looking Dutch over as if he were doing a CAT scan of his soul. After a few seconds, he said in a low voice, 'I'll call you when he's functional.' Then he walked inside and slid the door shut.

Functional, Dutch thought. *Christ, that could take forever!* Right now, Bobby's status was only a step above a vegetable. He left the yard and went down the alley to the street.

Jimmy was leaning against the Bronco waiting for him. When he saw Dutch he tossed him the keys and got in the passenger seat. Dutch didn't say anything. If he tried, it would come out wrong, and Ciazo would probably kill him. He unlocked the driver door, entered, and furiously slammed it shut. Starting the engine, he pulled out on to the street.

Dutch kept quiet all the way to the bank. Jimmy stared impassively out of the window, also not saying anything. When they got back to the S&L in San Fernando, Dutch pulled into the parking spot next to Jimmy's brown Fairlane. The detective opened the door and got out of the Bronco. Not bothering to say goodbye, he started walking towards his car. Dutch locked the door to his four wheeler, rolled up the window almost to the top, leaving a few inches, then yelled to him, 'You used me, you sonofabitch.'

The huge Italian stopped, slowly turned and stared at Dutch through the glass. A diminutive smile cracked on Jimmy's impassive face. 'How's that, Dutchman?'

'You withheld information from me.'

Jimmy strolled back to the Bronco. With his stocky fingers, he gripped the edge of the driver's window through the slight opening. Squeezing it hard, he said, 'Would I do that to you? That's like calling me a liar, Dutch.'

Dutch shrugged. 'Yeah, well, I guess that's what you are, Jimmy. A liar.' Knowing that Jimmy couldn't get to him gave him courage.

Ciazo's fingers were turning white from pressing down on the glass. 'You want to get out and discuss this?' The smile remained on his face like acid etched in tempered steel.

Dutch knew better that that. 'Fuck you, Jimmy. I'm staying right here. I thought we were working together?'

'We are, Dutch.' The smile widened and his lips parted, exposing chunky, stained teeth with deep recesses between them.

'Why didn't you tell me about the fingerprints and the hairs found in the tunnel?'

'Had nothing to do with you.'

'Bullshit!'

Jimmy was turning red. His fingers were now subtly scratching on the window, itching to get at him.

Dutch put the car into first, getting ready to take off in case Jimmy decided to get violent. 'You needed me to get to Bobby. The Indians don't trust me, but they sure as hell trust you even less. Why do you care about these old murders, Jimmy? Nobody else does. Everyone in the police department is just going through the motions except you. For a minute I thought Falcone and the city council put you up to this. I was wrong. You're doing it all on your own, aren't you?'

Jimmy stared at him, his crimson face no longer stoic. 'Fuck you, Dutchman,' he hissed, sounding like a broken steam pipe.

'You want to be a hero, Jimmy? Is that it? You want to catch the bad guy and make Falcone look like shit?'

Dutch was answered by Ciazo's big foot kicking in the metal on the Bronco's door. 'Get the fuck out of the car, you Dutch bastard!' he screamed.

Conversation was over. Dutch hit the gas pedal and took off down the street. In the rear-view mirror he could see Ciazo standing in the middle of the boulevard glaring at him, his fists balled up like giant raw beef patties. Dutch's heart was pounding, thinking about what that big Italian could have done if he had got his hands on him. He suddenly remembered the Mexican boy Jimmy had killed. He wondered if the last thing the kid saw before he died was Jimmy's ugly, raging face. Dutch shuddered at the thought.

As he turned on to the 101 Freeway going downtown, the question jumped into his mind again: why was Jimmy so interested in this case? The Italian had had him believing that he was just bored with working for the Beverly Hills PD and that he needed more action. Not true. Jimmy wanted something else. Was Dutch right about his wanting to show up the Beverly Hills police force?

After he killed the kid, they put the nails into him. He was passed over for advancement and given all the shit jobs that nobody else wanted. He lost their respect. Jimmy ended up working clean-up detail under Vince Falcone. More humiliation.

That may have done it, Dutch thought. More than

anything, Jimmy needed respect. Without it, the drinking had become an even bigger problem. When his wife finally left him because of his continued violence and drunkenness, she took the kids with her.

Jimmy's innards may be pickled, but he wasn't stupid. When Dutch discovered the bones of the murdered girls, Ciazo saw his chance to get out from under the crap heap.

Jimmy wasn't interested in who really killed those girls. He was focusing in on Bobby because he was a likely suspect and would give him the least trouble. Forensic evidence, however slight, was against the Indian. Dutch wondered how long Bobby would remain alive if Jimmy ever got his hands on him. With him dead, the case would officially be closed. An embarrassed, passive police department would give Jimmy their respect again.

Another question took over: what did he himself want with all of this? Dutch had done his job, now it was up to the police to find the killer — if he was still alive. What difference should it make to the anthropologist if they didn't choose to pursue this case?

Forget the girls. They were becoming flesh and blood to him. *Bones. That's the only thing that counted. Bones!*

With a shaking hand, he quickly popped in the Billie Holiday tape. Would she do it for him again?

> *Southern trees bares strange fruit*
> *Blood on leaves*
> *and blood at the root.*

No, she didn't do it for him this time. The words of

the song sent a chill into the pit of Dutch's stomach.

Blood on the leaves.

Was Billie his herald of what was to come?

Again he thought about the killer. Fear of that nameless monster began to creep up the shafts of his vertebrae like wild growing ivy.

The bulging eyes and the twisted mouth . . .

Here is a fruit for the crows to pluck . . .

Oh, Billie . . . Those words!

The smell of Shalimar again.

Everything turns to bones in the end.

Dutch wiped the sweat of panic from his face, then ripped the cassette out of the player, breaking the tape, and tossed it on the back seat.

His ear was aching again. He opened the glove compartment with his free hand, felt around inside, and grabbed the bottle of extra-strength Excedrin. Snapping the top off with his thumb, he put the plastic bottle to his mouth, counted out three tabs with his tongue and chewed them up.

The day shift had gone home and the basement floor of the coroner's office was nearly deserted. An occasional light bled through the smoked glass partitions separating the offices, showing that some of the city's bureaucrats still worked late.

Dutch, with his knapsack strung on his shoulder, walked towards the room that contained the bones of the twins. His body hurt from fatigue and he wished he could lie down for a couple of hours. As he passed the Chief Medical Examiner's office, the door opened and Orville walked out. He was holding a tattered briefcase and looked as tired as Dutch. When he saw the anthropologist, the familiar frown came over his face like a well used curtain.

'Hello, Orville,' Dutch said, stretching his arms over his head, trying to get life back into his fatigued body.

'Van Deer. What are you doing here?' Orville muttered.

'I'm doing facial reconstruction on the girls.'

'So I heard.' His narrow, hateful eyes tore through Dutch.

'Those twins were murdered and noboby gives a shit. Why do you think that is, Orville?'

'You don't know for sure *when* they were killed,' the ME snapped back.

'No, not for sure. That's because someone screwed with their bones.' Dutch could see a slight flinch ripple across Orville's face. 'After I reconstruct the face, we'll show it on television and put it in the newspapers. Maybe there's somebody out there who remembers those twins. Maybe there's somebody out there who gives a damn.'

'You're going to do this all by yourself, huh?'

'All by myself, Orville. I'd ask the police, but they seem busy lately.'

'They will always be busy for you, Van Deer,' Orville sneered. He strode towards the elevator, his body flushed with anger.

Dutch could smell the scent of the ME's sickening sweet cologne as he brushed past him. He waited until Orville got in the elevator, then he opened the door to his makeshift office and walked in. Two of his undergraduate students, Kelly and Paula, were sitting by the skull of one of the twins. Their eyes were puffy from exhaustion.

'Go home,' Dutch said, taking off the knapsack and

putting it on the table next to the skeleton. 'You guys did good. Where's Tara?'

Kelly, the perkier of the two, said, 'Home asleep. She said she'll see you in the morning.'

Dutch watched them walk out of the door. He was glad that Tara was sleeping. She was going to need all the rest she could get; for the next several days she'd be working day and night in this room putting together a face. A job that normally took two weeks was going to be attempted in seventy-two hours.

The Dutchman stretched again, then opened his knapsack. Removing two changes of clothes and a Dob bag, he set them down on the desk next to a box of different coloured eyes. Then he took out a container of coffee and a tuna sandwich that he had got from an all-night diner. He was famished. As he took a bite, he turned to look at the remains of the twin lying on the table. A sudden current of fear began to play with the chords of his gut. He saw that the skull was now completely covered with clay. Plastic eyes clung to the face like blue snails. There was no expression etched on the face; just traces of lumps and crevices where a nose and cheek-bones should have been. It was as if a thousand caterpillars had shed their cocoons and placed them over the face of a sleeping child.

He dropped the sandwich on the table. The fear began to well up now, banging on his throat muscles to be let out. He tried to force it back down. No, there was no face now, he thought, but soon there will be. It was up to him to supply it. God, how he hated doing this! It was against nature, creating life from bones. Against God.

He put his hand on the clay, gently sliding his

fingers over the cold, soft surface. Closing his eyes, he felt the eye sockets, the nose, the mouth, the chin. Dutch could visualize the girl in his mind now; he almost didn't have to create her likeness. How beautiful she must have been, he thought. *How innocent*! Then his hands, as if they had minds of their own, began to mould. They pressed gently down on the curvature of the cheeks. His fingers began to glide and knead, rubbing the clay into a fine smoothness.

Be patient, my darling. You'll be alive in a very short while.

Two hours later, Dutch walked away from the skull, went over to the sink and washed the clay from his hands. He needed a break from his delicate work; his eyes were raw and his back ached from bending over the head. He rubbed his shoulders, lit a cigarette and strode over to the window and looked out. It was almost ten o'clock; the streets of downtown LA were deserted except for the derelicts and the homeless who now controlled the city at night. Across the street he saw a man sitting on a bus stop bench. He was slightly built, with his hair worn in the John Kennedy style.

Was he looking up here? Dutch watched with detached curiosity as a derelict in tattered clothes, holding out one hand for money, approached him. The man quickly got up off the bench, walked east, and turned the corner, disappearing from Dutch's view. The beggar followed him for twenty feet, then came upon a filled trash can. He bent over it and began sifting through its contents for a few seconds. Seeing that there was nothing there, he looked up in the direction the man had gone and began to follow him.

Dutch moved away from the window, rubbed his eyes and put out the cigarette. He went over to the skull lying on the table. It was now starting to acquire human characteristics: the brow was square, and the frontal lobes were beginning to take shape.

Dutch remembered Tara's name for this one. She called her Minnie. 'OK, Minnie,' he said, his throat filling with emotion as his fingers clawed at the supple clay where the mouth was going to be. 'Let's see your beautiful smile.'

Hugo felt the heat from the Dutchman's soul feeding into his as soon as their eyes met. His heart soared when he finally saw the beautiful blond man walk over to the window and peer down at him. He had been sitting there for almost two hours, staring up, hoping to see him. If it wasn't for that cretin asking for money he would have stayed longer. Hugo knew Dutch would be there because the news said that he would be working on the reconstructon of the twins' facial features. Somehow he had to stop that before it happened. The Dutchman must not find out who the girls were. Not that.

Hugo felt a strange kinship with this man who was determined to expose him. They were like brothers, in a way. Perhaps even twins. Hugo laughed at that. What was he picking up about this anthropologist? Maybe Frank would help fill in the pieces when he got back from Ohio.

Then he heard the shuffling footsteps behind him. They scraped against the pavement like sandpaper, ricocheting cleanly off the brick walls of the deserted buildings.

At first Hugo was annoyed. He knew it was that

vagrant following him. Then he smiled. Perhaps it was time to do a test.

Hugo walked faster, his bony shoulders tearing through the cool night like the bow of a ship ploughing through water. The dry Santa Ana winds were blowing fiercely tonight. He pulled up the collar on his wool sports jacket and thrust his fists deep inside his pockets. His fingers curled around the rattail file that he always carried with him for protection.

He passed under the Golden State Freeway and came to Brooklyn Avenue. The empty street was filled with dreary concrete warehouses. The only sounds were cars speeding thirty feet above him on the freeway.

Hugo stopped to listen. The footsteps were still heading his way. He turned into an alley that separated a machine shop and a loading dock. His pace slowed down.

Suddenly he heard movement coming from the crushed empty boxes that littered the passageway. Hugo pulled out the rattail file from his jacket and held his breath. A cat leaped out from the trash and on to an oil can. It stared at Hugo, hunched its back, snarled, then leaped through his legs and out of the alley towards the safety of a street lamp.

Only then did Hugo let the air escape from his lungs. Holding the file down by his leg, he leaned against the wall and waited.

Would he pass the test?

The vagrant, a small scraggy man, wearing somebody else's oversized shoes and jacket, peered into the alley. Total blackness inside. He listened for Hugo's footsteps.

Only silence.

He had started to turn back when Hugo's hand reached out, grabbed him by his matted hair and pulled him into the darkness.

The indigent let out a slight *oof* when his body slammed against the brick wall. Before he could move, Hugo's forearm, the one with the cobra tattoo, was against his throat, snuffing out all sound. Hugo tightened his grip, pinning him against the wall, then pushed upwards until the man's feet were barely touching the pavement. His eyes began to bulge and small white saliva bubbles appeared on his lips. An unwashed, foul odour emanated from the derelict, causing Hugo's lips to curl with revulsion. Hugo raised the pointed file up to the man's face, letting the street lamp illuminate its shadow. He wanted to make sure this man could see it. He needed to feel the fear in him.

He did.

Would he pass? It wasn't Hugo that would be doing this thing. It would be the *urge* doing it.

'This is a test,' he said to the derelict. 'You understand that?'

The man's eyes swelled even wider and he trembled. His bowels suddenly gave way. Hugo could smell the stench of fresh faeces as he pressed his arm tighter against the man's throat.

The *urge* that Hugo had thought was dead began to awaken and spread through his body. It pinched down on his heart, his liver, his lungs, eventually making its way up to his head and wrapping its talons around his brain. It had been so long! He could feel its awesome strength. Its power!

It had always been alive, waiting for him. It had never died!

Then it suddenly faded, like a lamp whose cord has

been pulled out of an electrical outlet. So fast. One minute it was raging with all its fury, then . . . nothing.

He could not do this thing without it. Hugo loosened his grip. The man dropped to the pavement, sobbing, coughing. Like a lizard, he began slithering on all fours towards the lamp-post. He grabbed the steel column with his arms, took a deep breath of air, then vomited.

So close, Hugo thought, watching him. The thing inside him was almost back. Then he turned into the darkness and quickly strode towards the other end of the alley.

Several minutes later, Hugo walked into a coffee shop on Brooklyn Avenue. Several vacant-eyed drifters were sitting at the grimy counter sipping coffee, trying to balance out their systems after bingeing all day on cheap wine.

Hugo sat at a table at the far end of the diner, his back to the other customers. He looked down at the greasy menu and ordered a steak extra rare from a waitress with bubble-gum-coloured hair. His need for meat was insatiable, especially after what had almost happened. It had been like that in the past, too. At the thought of it, the saliva rose burning up in his throat and dripped down the corners of his thin lips. He wiped his wet chin with his hand.

When the food came, he shovelled it ravenously into his mouth, shredding the tough beef with his sharp teeth like a chain saw tearing through pinewood.

When he had finished, he left money on the table and walked quickly out of the restaurant before anyone had a chance to study him.

Again his mind filled with thoughts of the

Dutchman. At first he wanted to hurt him badly, as he had been hurt as a child. Then the hate began to turn warm with love. Instead of killing the anthropologist, he had a great desire to hold him to his breast and kiss him.

Hugo began to smile.

He had failed the test. That was a good sign. He didn't yet know if he wanted to kill again. But the *urge* wasn't dead. That he did know. It was there, waiting. Like the voice of his mother, it would come when it was ready.

He quickly turned the corner and disappeared into the squalid night.

15

Downtown LA on weekends is a city frozen in time:
nothing moves, no voices ring out. The only sound is
the Santa Anas whipping through the alleys and
passageways of abandoned office buildings and
warehouses. As night descends, it becomes a different
story. Under the shroud of darkness, the homeless and
the insane come out and fight for a piece of the
pavement with knives and bottles. When the first light
falls, the unlucky ones can be seen lying face down in
the streets, having failed to survive the drugs, alcohol
or the blade that etched a smile on their throats. The
fortunate ones are curled up asleep in cardboard boxes
under the Golden State Freeway. They have made it
through another night.

On Sunday morning, Judge Robin Diaz, wearing a
light tan trouser-suit, entered the coroner's building
and showed her ID to the security guard. She then
proceeded down the main corridor.

At the end of the hallway, she spotted a tired-
looking East Indian with a turban wrapped around his
head. He was emptying wastebaskets into a big
container on wheels. She asked him where Dutch Van
Deer's lab was. He didn't speak any English.
Gesturing towards the elevator, he pointed down-

wards, then curved his long shaky finger to the left.

Robin smiled. She had grown up in a multi-national ghetto of LA, where the barriers of different voices eventually dissolved into the common language of pantomime.

Once downstairs, she found the right room without any trouble. When she opened the door, the rancid smell of unwashed bodies and stale take-out food poured out of the confined laboratory and into the hallway. Grimacing, she swept her hand like a fan across her face and went in.

Tara was sitting cross-legged on top of a steel medical table, a lit cigarette dangling from the corner of her mouth. She was studiously clipping out a black and white photograph of a teenage girl from an old *Life* magazine. Grabbing a pin from the plastic box near her, she pegged the picture to a cork board on the wall. Next to it were several other photos of young girls. She turned round when she heard Robin walk in. The anthropologist's face was haggard and tired. 'Hi. You're Robin, right?' Her voice was hoarse from too little sleep and too many cigarettes.

'You must be Tara. Dutch called me last night. Asked if I'd come by.'

'I know. He told me.'

They shook hands.

'Is he here?' Robin asked.

'Dutch? Yep.' Tara flicked her cigarette, the ash dropping to the floor, and motioned to the gurney over by the wall. The Dutchman was sleeping on top of it, his face covered by the sports section of the *LA Times*. Lying next to him was the skeleton of one of the twins. They were both in the foetal position, reminding Robin of two lovers in repose after sex.

Bitch was lying on the floor by the side of the gurney gnawing on a large fibular bone. She stopped when Robin approached, and moved her head forward to sniff her out. The old dog wagged her tail in remembrance from two years ago, then went back to her nibbling.

'Is that a human bone she's chewing?' Robin asked, her hand to her mouth.

Tara looked down at Bitch and shrugged. 'Yeah. She loves human bones. It's from a neighbourhood derelict. It keeps her out of the important stuff around here.'

Dutch turned his body towards the voices, pulled the newspaper from his face and slowly sat up. His clothes were wrinkled and stained with sweat and dried clay. He yawned, scratched his matted hair, and rubbed his heavy beard stubble with his dirty hands. When he saw Robin, he grinned.

'You look like every woman's worst nightmare,' Robin said. 'When was the last time you bathed?'

He jumped down off the gurney and once again scratched his head. 'I don't remember.' He looked at Tara for an answer.

Tara shrugged. 'Two . . . three days. Something like that.'

'Something like that,' Dutch repeated. He stepped over the slew of fast food chain wrappers and Dominos pizza boxes that littered the floor, went over to the trough-shaped sink, turned on the cold water and put his head under the tap to wake himself up.

Tara got up off the table, walked over to the desk and took out a blond wig from a box sitting on top of it.

The Dutchman wrung the water out of his hair with his fingers and wiped his face with a towel. 'She's been keeping me pretty busy,' he said to Robin, gesturing to the sculptured face of the twin on the chair by the cork board. The mould was now done. The only thing remaining was the hair.

The judge walked over to it, knelt down and looked at the reconstructed face. Without touching the clay, her hands slowly traced its fine features: the small, puckered nose; the cleft indenting the delicate chin; the high and defined cheekbones. 'How beautiful she must have been,' she whispered.

'Yes, she was,' Dutch said. 'I want to keep her that way. That's why I need you.'

'You think some one will destroy her.'

'They already tried with the bones.'

Robin nodded. 'I have a steel safe in my house. Nobody could break into it. Besides, it would be plain dumb to try and rob a criminal court judge.'

'That's how I see it, too. You didn't have to come all the way downtown. I could have dropped her off.'

Robin laughed. 'Great, Dutch. My husband already thinks I'm renewing my affair with you. What do you think he'll say when he sees you walking into my house holding a girl's head?'

'That a true gentleman would have brought flowers,' he answered.

Tara draped the shapeless blond wig over the bare clay head and stepped back. 'Here she is,' Tara said. She looked thoughtfully at the mould, then glanced up at the photos on the wall. Grabbing the scissors, she said, 'Pick it, Dutchman. The bubble look or the French twist. I was only a baby then, so I can't help you.'

He shrugged. 'I was into Roberto Clemente, not women's hairstyles.'

Robin looked confused.

Dutch said, 'We're going on the assumption that the girls were killed around twenty years ago and we're trying to figure out the type of hairstyle they may have worn.'

Robin walked over to the cork board and studied the photographs. After a minute, she said to Dutch, 'You're sure they were fifteen years old?'

'Positive.'

Again she looked at the photos, then at the sculpture. 'Go natural,' she said finally.

'Why?' Dutch asked.

Robin went back to the cast and bent down again. 'Something about her,' she said softly, studying the face. The blue glass eyes of the sculpture stared blankly back at her. 'She doesn't look like she would have been into trendy hairdos.'

'You just might be right,' Tara said with an awakening respect for Robin. She quickly bent down next to her. 'Dutch?'

Leaning against the gurney, he said, 'Go with it. Let's see what we get.'

Tara turned to Robin. 'Straight or the crown flip at the back?'

'Straight. Let's keep her classy.'

'Bangs?'

'Why not?' Robin said.

Let them fiddle with it, Dutch thought. Right now, he needed a shower and a shave. Glancing down at his watch, he saw that it was seven-thirty. He grabbed his Dob kit, a bath towel and a change of clothes from the top of the desk and left the room. The private bathroom used by the pathologists was across the hall. He undressed, got into the stall and took a long shower, scrubbing three days of grime from his weary body.

By the time he got back to the room, the hair was finished. He walked over to the cast, squatted down and stared at its face for several seconds. Strange, sad emotions intermingled within him. Yes, Robin was right. She was beautiful. How real she looked! *Flesh and blood*. No, there was no going back, not now.

'Who were they, I wonder?' Robin asked.

'I don't know. They have a right to their name and I'm going to make sure they get it,' Dutch said. He got up, went over to Tara's bag that was hanging on the back of the chair and grabbed the Nikon. He adjusted the flash, letting the light bounce off the wall, and took several shots of the head. When he was finished, he pulled out the roll of film from the casing and dropped it into his pocket. 'This goes to the media.'

Dutch and Tara then placed the head in a box, letting its crown protrude so it wouldn't get crushed, and stuffed newspapers around it for protection. He carried it carefully out of the building and put it into the boot of Robin's Mercedes, parked on the street.

'Don't tell too many people about this,' he said, as she got into the car.

She laughed, 'No one will know, *including* my husband.'

Hugo's mouth tightened as he watched Robin start her engine. Then he turned his head, focusing on the Dutchman walking up the steps and going back into the building.

He was sitting in the front seat of the rented Cadillac

El Dorado that was parked diagonally across the street from the lab. He was wearing a green Izod pullover, matching pants and large teardrop styled sunglasses. A garment bag was visible in the back seat. If a black and white cruised by and saw him sitting here, he would look like a clothing salesman who worked from this industrial area and came by on Sunday to pick up his samples.

It was a stroke of luck that he had decided to drive downtown this morning instead of in the afternoon. Otherwise, he would have missed seeing this pretty woman. He had been surveying the building for the last couple of days, hoping to find the Dutchman and that assistant of his out of the lab. It didn't happen that way. They hadn't left the building since Friday. Just as he pulled up today, he had spotted this Latino woman from the Mercedes going inside. He had a feeling about her and decided to wait. It had to be the Dutchman she was coming to see, he thought. There was no one else inside the building except the cleaning crew.

When they came out together, he knew he'd been right.

Who was she? he wondered. Nice car for a Mexican. Must be successful. Her clothes certainly said so.

Then Hugo saw the box the Dutchman was holding, and his stomach suddenly tied itself into knots. He knew immediately what was in it. The blond hair protruding from the top was familiar. Not an exact copy of the twins', but close enough.

He was too late!

He had spent the last forty-eight hours concocting a plan to steal the head out of the lab before it was finished. Even went as far as getting a detailed blueprint of the building from the city planning office Friday afternoon so he would know where everything was. It would have been so easy. No problems.

Just walk into the building holding an attaché case. Smile. Show the old man with the turban a false ID. It was one of several he had stolen from the interns at the Tacoma hospital when he had plastic surgery done on his face fifteen years ago. Never knew when it might be needed, he had thought back then. Last night he had peeled away the see-through cover and cut out the old photograph of the doctor. He replaced it with a recent one of himself, then patched a new piece of plastic over it. He had done such a good job that no one would be able to tell, even if the ID was held up to the light.

Once past the guard, he would patiently attempt to explain to the janitor who didn't speak any English that he was one of the pathologists who worked here, and that he had lost his key to the forensics lab. Pointing to the key ring attached to the janitor's belt, he'd ask to be let in. He'd help the old man understand by giving him a five-dollar bill for his time. Just smile through it all.

It would have been so damn easy.

Now it was too late. This Mexican woman had the cast. That must mean Dutch had finished the face. He now knew what she looked like. This was not good.

He turned his face away as the Mercedes made a U-turn and drove past him.

Who was this woman? he wondered. A friend of the Dutchman's? Perhaps his lover? Well . . . he'd find out soon enough. He pulled out and followed a short distance behind the Mercedes. She turned on to the freeway going west.

During the drive, he began to think of Frank. His plane was scheduled to land at LAX from Ohio in half an hour. They needed to talk.

Last night they had spoken on the phone. Frank, sounding frustrated, had told him that he'd searched for three days and couldn't find anything of interest on the Dutchman.

'The man exists. There has to be something,' Hugo said impatiently.

'There's nothing. I talked to his neighbours, his old teachers, some of his childhood friends. Nothing. I swear it, Mr Frye. The guy was an all-American bore. The Campbell's soup kind. Played football and basketball in high school. All that shit.'

'He also played with bones, Frank. All-Americans normally don't do that.'

A pause, as if Frank were thinking, then, 'There was one thing. A small article in the Dayton newspaper about something that happened to him when he was a kid. An accident.'

Hugo blinked twice in rapid succession. 'What kind?'

'A tornado. It killed his mother. But that was a long time ago.'

Hugo's wafer-thin lips cracked open, revealing white teeth like chips of ivory. 'Bring the article, Frank. You and I are going to talk.'

The man was a fool, he thought, hanging up on him. Frank had wasted three days looking for glaring facts about the Dutchman instead of concentrating on the ambiguous ones. The pieces that made up this man, like all people, lay hidden between the cracks, covered with dust and time. They are never out in the open for everyone to see and fondle. Frank had the key to the anthropologist, but didn't even know it. Now Hugo would have to burrow into Frank's soul to get at Wilhelm Van Deer. Oh, well, when you dance with fools . . .

He followed the woman into Beverly Hills and up into Benedict Canyon. She pulled off on to a small street and parked her car in the circular drive of a large colonial mansion. A realtor's *For Sale* placard hung on a pole in her lawn.

She'd done well for herself, he thought, driving slowly past. He had copied her licence number while behind her on the freeway; now he also had the address. When he came to the STOP sign at the corner, he took his time before moving on. He looked into the rearview mirror and watched her take the box out of the car and walk into the house. Only when the door closed did he step on the gas and turn the corner. Even if he didn't have the sculpture in his possession, at least he knew where it was. Now it was up to him to get it back.

He stuck the piece of paper containing the licence number and the address into his wallet. Today was Sunday. Nothing was open. Tomorrow he would find out her name.

The phone on the laboratory desk rang. Tara picked it up, listened to the voice on the other end, said a couple of words, laughed, then held the phone out to the Dutchman who was washing off his sculpturing tools. 'It's Therese.'

Dutch wiped his hands on a towel, then reached over and took the phone. 'We've spoken more times this week than we have in two years. What gives?'

'What are your plans for this afternoon?'

270

'Depends. Business or pleasure?'

Therese said coolly, 'Business. Always. Never forget that.'

'If I do, you'll remind me. Why?'

'John Payne asked me to invite you to that hunt party I told you about.'

Dutch looked confused. 'What for?'

'I don't know. The man probably wants to talk to you.'

'About what?'

'I'm sure he wants the bones from the Beverly Hills site to be repatriated. He sounded friendly. If you explain your position to him . . .'

'He already knows it.'

'Maybe he'll change his mind.'

'Doesn't sound like it,' Dutch said. He picked at some dried clay under his thumbnail.

There was a pause on the line. 'It would help me,' she said finally. 'I need more time on the dig. If we both speak to him . . .'

'You think it would make a difference?'

'Maybe.'

'What kind of party?' he asked.

Her voice lightened. 'It's supposed to be a variation of a fox hunt. Do you ride?'

Dutch grimaced. 'You mean horses? Not since I fell off a merry-go-round when I was five.'

'Doesn't matter. Will you come?'

'Does that mean we go together?'

'Yes. I'll pick you up at the helicopter pad on the roof of John Payne's office building around three o'clock. Know where that is?'

Payne's art deco office building was an historical landmark in mid-town. Everybody knew where it was.

They gave tours through it on Saturdays. 'That's several hours from now. How about lunch?' he asked.

Her voice became cold. 'Sorry, I'm busy.'

'Miles?'

'No, not Miles. I go to the cemetery on Sunday mornings. Try it some time.' She hung up.

Dutch sighed and placed the receiver back on the cradle. He had not been back to the grave since the day Max was buried.

'Go home, Dutchman. We're through here,' Tara said, seeing the dark shadow cross his eyes. It had to do with Max, she thought. The shadows always came when Therese brought up the subject of his son.

He nodded, rubbing his shoulders. They ached from two nights of sleeping on a steel gurney. 'You, too.'

'I intend to sleep for the next three days straight.' When she had finished packing the instruments into her worn black bag, she turned to him, her cigarette clasped between her teeth. 'You seeing Therese?'

'Yes. This afternoon.'

'Get it together with her, OK? You guys are tearing each other up.'

She was right, he thought, grabbing his knapsack from the back of the chair. Part of him wanted his feelings for her to disappear from his life. Yet, at the same time, he was also afraid of that happening. A big hole would be left. What would take its place? No, better to feel love than nothing. Without it, he would be one of the walking dead, like the outcasts that lived on the streets.

With Bitch following behind, Dutch left the lab and walked out into the bright sun he hadn't seen for two days.

16

The yellow cab let Frank out next to the Santa Monica pier. Grabbing his lightweight duffel bag from the boot, he paid the driver, leaving him only a fifty-cent tip.

He headed towards the underbelly of the pier. It was a warm day and the wharf was jammed with Mexicans and blacks playing arcade games and going on rides. Every inch of rail space was taken up by human bodies fishing off the pier. The thought of eating anything from these polluted waters made Frank queasy.

He headed towards the large boulders under the pier where Hugo had arranged to meet him. The sand was covered with debris and he had to weave his way past broken glass, fly-infested garbage and wooden beams. When he got to the rocks, he stopped and looked round. The rancid smell of the garbage was making him feel sick. Where the hell was the guy? He didn't like meeting him alone like this, especially after hearing stories about what Hugo did to the *chicken hawks* Frank procured for him. They said he put tape across their noses and mouths and forced them to hold their breath. If they could do it for three minutes without passing out, he paid them an extra fifty. Hugo also liked putting his fingers in corners of their bodies where fingers shouldn't go. He hurt them badly when he did that. The man was way too creative in his playtime. Word was out on the streets about him. It was becoming harder and harder to solicit tricks for this weirdo.

Frank was sweating profusely in his Naugahyde bomber jacket and cord pants. Ohio was cold and wet. He had come here straight from the plane and hadn't had time to change.

Then he looked up and saw Hugo. He was sitting on top of the boulder directly above him, staring down at him, grinning. His arms were wrapped around his legs, and his chin was resting on his knees, resembling an impish gargoyle perched on the cornerstone of a church. He was wearing running shoes, shorts and a tank top. This was the first time Frank had seen him so lightly clad. He was surprised by the sinewy muscles on the man's arms and thighs. Not an ounce of fat on him. His skin looked so colourless in the light leaking through the floorboards of the pier that it was almost transparent, exposing the veins and arteries in his body. It looked as if he had spent his entire life indoors. Something strange about the texture of his skin, too. What? Then Frank saw it. No hair on his arms and legs. Wait a minute. What had happened to the hair on his head? Had he shaved it off since Frank last saw him? Maybe he never had hair to begin with and always wore a wig. The guy gave him the creeps.

Hugo jumped down from the boulder and landed on his feet like a supple cat directly in front of him. He stared at Frank for a moment, an amused look filling his eyes, then said, 'Follow me.' He turned round and headed away from the boulders towards the main highway.

Frank picked up his bag and followed. Where the fuck's he going, he wondered. Hugo was walking fast and he had to double his pace to keep up.

Hugo stayed a good hundred yards in front of him. He turned right on Pacific Coast Highway, then left a couple of blocks away, heading towards the fire-swept amusement park.

When Frank reached the corner and saw the forsaken neighbourhood, a dour feeling came over him. This place was like a ghost town. Everything was boarded up. There were no people on the streets, yet he could hear laughter coming from the pier a couple of blocks away. He looked up at the blackened, twisted steel girders of a Ferris wheel in a weed-infested lot close by. The beams were reaching out towards the sky like gnarled fingers covered with third-degree burns. Frank suddenly had an impulse to run. Then he thought about the money Hugo owed him and changed his mind.

The sweat was pouring freely down his face now, and his breathing was coming in heavy gasps as he tried to keep up. Hugo was now about a hundred yards away. Frank saw the bald man turn into the gate of a house, then disappear into the doorway.

Frank slowed down. All the houses on the street had wooden planks over the windows, except the one Hugo went into.

'*Gawdamn*,' Frank muttered out loud. When he came to the gate, the front door swung open, as if beckoning him in. Was this where the turkey lived? They had met eight or nine times in the six months they had known each other and this was the first time he had been invited to Hugo's house. His head once again told him to get out of here, but he fought off the fear and walked inside.

The second he stepped into the house, the humidity hit him like a blast from an open furnace. And that stench! It smelled like a foetid, stagnant pond. No, not a pond. A jungle. A decaying, steaming jungle. It was the odour of wet earth and . . . and what? Frank felt he knew what it was, but he just couldn't put his finger on it.

It was dusky inside because the windows were covered with heavy drapes and closed shutters. Having come in from bright sunlight, Frank's eyes hadn't adjusted to the darkness. He squinted, trying to see clearly. 'Mr Frye?' he said, looking round.

'Over here, Frank.'

The red-headed man saw Hugo's silhouette coming towards him, holding a glass with some brown liquid.

'Iced tea. Drink it.' Hugo handed the glass to Frank, then closed the door, making the house even darker. 'Now sit down. We have to talk.' He motioned to an armless wooden chair on a worn Persian carpet in the middle of the room.

Frank looked at the couch, then at the padded armchair next to it, and started to head towards them.

Hugo moved in front of him, blocking his advance. 'No, Frank, I want you over there.' Hugo's voice was friendly, but non-negotiable. Once again he gestured to the hard chair.

Frank did as he was told. Beads of moisture covered the wooden seat. He brushed most of it off with his hand and sat down. He wished he had followed his instinct and not come in. Now it was too late. Hugo was paying him well for going to Ohio. If only he didn't need the money to support his habit he would have kissed this lunatic off. How could a guy live in this heat?

Hugo sat down in the pillowed chair. He crossed his legs, rested his elbows on the armrest and put his fingertips together, forming a pyramid. 'Tell me about Wilhelm Van Deer,' he said softly, like an adult talking to a child.

The heat was becoming unbearable. Frank placed the drink on the floor, then took his jacket off and put it on the back of the chair. He wished he had a tank top like Hugo's and not this damn sweater. 'You have a radiator broken or something?' he asked, hearing the hissing noise of the motor downstairs. 'How do you stand it? It's a sauna in here.'

'I like it this way. Talk to me.'

Frank wiped his face with the sleeve of his sweater. 'Like I told you. There was nothing. Just that small article in the paper.'

'When did you come across it?'

'Right before I called you. It was the last thing I found.'

'Then we'll come to that last. Where was he born?'

Frank took a small spiral pad from his back pocket and folded the cover over. 'He was born in the Netherlands.'

'Where?'

He traced his index finger down the page. 'Rotterdam. I got that from a copy of his birth certificate at city hall.'

Hugo slowly nodded his approval. 'Were both his parents from there?'

Frank shook his head. 'No. I talked to the older neighbours, the ones that were around when he was a kid. One of them . . . she must have been seventy-five . . .' He searched the page for her name. 'Polly Archer. She lived next door to the kid and his mother. Said his mother was born in Xenia, worked as a waitress in a bar. She met this big Dutch guy who was an oil rigger and moved to Rotterdam with him.'

'Did they ever marry?'

'No. But she had his child. That's Wilhelm Van Deer.'

Hugo narrowed his eyes at him. 'I could figure that one out, Frank. So the Dutchman was a bastard?'

'Yep. When he was two, his mother left Rotterdam with the boy and moved back to Xenia.'

'Why?'

'According to the neighbour, the oil rigger was a lady's man. Loved to fuck around. I guess she caught him dipping his pen in another inkwell.'

Hugo frowned. The man was so low class. 'Go on.'

'She got her old job back at the bar and raised the kid by herself.'

'And the father?'

'Died in an accident on an oil rig in Venezuela when Wilhelm was seven or eight.'

'Was he a happy child?'

Frank shook his head at these questions. What the hell was so important about all of this? He turned another page over in his book. 'I think he was happy. Nothing to say he wasn't. I spoke to his high school buddies. They said he was real popular but a loner, kept mostly to himself. One of them said he hated heights and cramped places, but that was his only weirdness.'

'Interesting,' Hugo said, his eyes lighting up.

'His basketball coach said he was over six feet tall by

the time he was in ninth grade and that he made a hell of a centre. Van Deer scored forty-two points by himself in one game. UCLA and a few other colleges offered him athletic scholarships. He turned them all down.'

Hugo's eyes widened further. 'Why was that?' he asked quietly.

'The schools didn't have the kind of classes he wanted.'

'Like what?'

Frank glanced down at the threadbare rug, slightly embarrassed. 'Something to do with science. I didn't really get into it with him.'

Hugo sighed. This man was a fool. 'Do you think the classes could have been in forensic anthropology?'

Frank smiled. 'Yeah. That makes sense. I should have thought of that.'

'Where did he eventually go to school?'

'Indiana University.'

Hugo nodded. 'Indiana U has a big anthropology department. That meant his interest in bones started before he went to college.'

Frank's sweater was now sticking to his body with the humidity. He bent down and lifted the glass of iced tea from the floor. The heat had made him terribly thirsty. It tasted like rusty water, but he finished it anyway. He looked at Hugo, hoping he would offer more. But the bald-headed man didn't.

'Let's retrace his life a bit,' Hugo said instead. 'He was an all-star in high school.'

'That's what his coach said.' He pulled at the collar of his sweater, quelling an urge to take it off. 'Honestly, Mr Frye, this heat . . .'

'Did he have a girlfriend in school?'

279

'You talking about high school?'

'That's where we are right now, Frank.'

Frank stared at Hugo. It was hard to see him very clearly because there were no lights on, but his eyes were now adjusted to the semi-darkness. He noticed that the man hadn't moved an inch. He sat in the same position he was in when they first started this. The crazy bastard was so fucking cool, he thought. Even in this oven he was cool. A sheet of sweat coated Hugo's muscular arms and legs, making them glisten. That was when Frank saw the cobra on the inside of his forearm, its flattened head ending at the tip of his palm. The perspiration made the scaly skin of the tattooed reptile sparkle as if it was real. Every time Hugo's muscle twitched, the snake came alive.

The bald man sat there, his fingers up to his chin, waiting for an answer.

Frank let out a deep breath and looked at his notes. 'There was a girl he was seeing. Went together all through high school. According to the teachers I talked to, she was brilliant. She won a statewide science contest and was a runner-up nationwide.'

'Her name, Frank.'

Again he scanned the wrinkled pages. 'Mary Francis Hoolahan.'

'What happened to her?'

'She became a nun. Lives in Africa now. Stitches the jigs back together after they get into one of their tribal fights.' He laughed. 'That dumb prick probably waited all those years to get into her pants, then she dumped him for the man on the cross.'

Hugo restrained his anger. The man was a cretin. 'You said she helps put the natives back together. Is she also a nurse?'

This time Frank did not look at his notebook. 'No, she's a doctor. Went to NYU medical school before she went into the convent. I forgot to tell you that.'

Go slow with him. 'What kind?'

'An orthopaedist.'

'That's a bone doctor, Frank,' Hugo said.

'Yeah. Hey, that's right! I never thought of that.'

Hugo leaned forward, his arms resting on his thighs now. 'This woman must have taught him about bones. But that doesn't explain why he was interested in them.' He stood up, causing the wet seat cushions under him to squish, and went over to the bookshelves above the fireplace.

'Mr Frye, I'm dying in this sweater.' Frank began to pull at the collar, as if to emphasize his point.

'Take it off,' Hugo said, staring at a framed photograph on the mantel of himself dressed in army fatigues. His mind was still on the Dutchman.

Frank began to pull off his sweater, then changed his mind. The thought of being topless in front of this man made him feel uncomfortable, vulnerable. He pushed the soaked sweater back over his stomach. 'What difference does it make that this nut likes bones so much?' Frank said irritably. 'Maybe it took the place of people.'

Hugo turned round and faced him. His thin lips spread apart in a slight smile. 'Maybe you're right.'

'I am?'

'Bones are the halfway point to life. The skeletal body resembles a human, but it's the meat on it that gives it life. Perhaps that's what Wilhelm Van Deer wanted to avoid.'

Frank's jaw dropped in confusion. What the fuck was this maniac talking about? Looking at the

281

madness in the eyes that were directed so forcefully on him, he wanted out of there. Drugs or no drugs. Fuck the money!

As if reading his mind, Hugo went over to the end table next to the couch, opened the drawer and pulled out a thick roll of one-hundred-dollar bills. He counted out six and dropped them on Frank's lap, then put the rest in his pocket.

'That's the other half of the money I owed you, Frank. Plus an extra hundred.'

Frank fingered the bills. They felt damp and mildewed, like everything else in this house. Again he looked up at Hugo, confused. 'What's the extra for?'

'For helping me understand the Dutchman's passion for bones.'

'I guess it's me that doesn't understand now.'

'I know that, Frank. Don't let it worry you.'

Anger rose up inside Frank. This sick bastard was putting him down.

'Now tell me about the newspaper article.'

Frank pulled out his wallet and removed a small, two-inch Xerox clipping. 'Here it is.' He handed it to Hugo. 'Like I told you on the phone, it doesn't say much. I don't know if you can read it in this light.'

Ignoring him, Hugo held the clipping in front of him. He was used to reading in darkness.

The devastating tornado that destroyed most of Xenia last Thursday has produced another miracle. Eight-year-old Wilhelm Van Deer has been found alive, trapped under his collapsed house, after spending four days with nothing to eat or drink. The fire and police department worked throughout most of the night trying to free him. His mother, Megan O'Rourke, did not survive.'

Hugo's eyes glistened with tears as he began to understand Wilhelm's phobias about heights and restricted spaces. The article he held in his hand explained that and more, but Frank couldn't see it. Why should he? Only people who knew could truly understand. He now saw that he and the Dutchman were more than equal adversaries. They were two sides of the same coin. Each other's twin; soulmates.

Look at him. He's starting to cry now, Frank said to himself. He turned away from this psychopath and tried to wipe his eyes that were stinging from sweat. His legs began to twitch from being in the same spot for so long. He needed to get out of here, needed a toke. *Shit*! Then he saw a sudden movement behind Hugo. It looked like something crawling on the plastic cover of the turntable over by the bookshelves. Nothing he could identify, just something dark. Frank blinked and rubbed his eyes so he could see better, but when he looked again it was gone.

Hugo saw Frank's eyes looking over his shoulder and turned round. 'What is it?'

'I don't know. I think maybe you got a snake in the house, Mr Frye.'

Hugo rushed over to the turntable and yanked it off the shelf, dislodging the wires. There it was! The giant centipede he had lost when the tank broke during the earthquake. It was trying to crawl into the air hole in the receiver. He picked it up by the tail and took it into the dining-room. Putting it gently on the table, he reached up and took the tank off the credenza.

'There, there. Nobody is going to hurt you, sweet

thing.' Hugo picked up the anthropod once again by the tail. The head curled around its body and the jaws opened, trying to bite his fingers. Before that could happen, Hugo had the centipede back in the tank.

'What the hell was that?' Frank said, his body cringeing in horror.

'A friend,' Hugo replied, his eyes filled with gratitude. 'I owe you, Frank.' He reached into his pocket and pulled out the wad of bills again. This time he counted out five, and put the rest back in his pocket. He went over to the ex-bouncer and knelt down next to him. 'These are for you,' he said, holding them close to his face.

Warm as it was, Frank could feel Hugo's body heat, making the room even hotter. When he put his hand out for the money, Hugo quickly withdrew it from his reach.

'It's yours, Frank. But you have to do something for me first,' Hugo said.

He knew he should say, 'No thanks,' get up and walk out. No, not walk out, back out. You never turn away from someone like him. The guy keeps giant bugs for pets. *Oh, sweet Jesus!* Except he couldn't take his eyes off the money. Staring at it, mesmerized, he said, 'What do you want me to do?'

'There's an Indian I want you to find for me.'

'What kind?'

'A drunken, crazy one. You don't have to do anything. Just find him and tell me where he is.'

'You can't do it yourself?'

'I'm a busy man. I have responsibilities. Before you leave, I'll give you all the information on the places he might be.' He put two of the bills on the chair between

Frank's legs. As he did it, his hand brushed slightly against his cord pants.

Frank flinched from Hugo's touch. He had to get out of here.

The bald man smiled, smelling the man's fear. 'Now let's go over everything one more time. Tell me all you know about Wilhelm Van Deer. I'm sure there are things you missed the first time around.'

Frank needed the pipe. His legs were shaking badly now. The last time he had a hit was in the bathroom of the Cincinnati airport. That was hours ago. He had to get out of here and find his dealer. 'I thought you said I could go.'

'Not quite yet.'

Frank groaned. He closed his eyes and clenched his teeth.

'Maybe you'd like another iced tea before we start?' Hugo said, holding his hand out for the empty glass.

17

'Oh my, a tie yet! Be still my heart!' the attractive bushy-headed anchor from Channel Seven said from behind her desk, shaking her head at Dutch's limp attempt at dressing up. He was wearing a wrinkled tweed sports jacket, a frayed, light blue shirt, an out-dated knit tie, faded jeans and scuffed cowboy boots with worn down heels. Smirking, she put her egg salad sandwich down on her paper-strewn desk and wiped her mouth with a napkin. Sounds of printers and UPI machines crackled like machine-gun fire throughout the large, busy office.

Dutch pulled at the tight collar of his shirt; it was pinching his neck something bad. A tie was a rarity in his life. It had taken him twenty minutes of fiddling in front of a mirror this afternoon to remember how to knot a Windsor. He took out the roll of film from his jacket pocket and dropped it on the desk next to her sandwich.

The anchorwoman pushed a half-eaten pickle away from the black plastic capsule and picked it up. 'What does she look like?'

'An angel. She and her sister deserved better than to die like that.'

'I appreciate the exclusive.' She put the film in her desk drawer.

'You got the lock on it because you promised to get it shown nationally. The local stations alone won't work.'

'Don't worry. I'm friends with Koppel. You'll see it on the evening news tonight.'

'One other thing. Can you phone me first if anyone calls claiming they know the identity of the girl or the twins?'

'Sure.'

Not able to stand it any more, he undid the first button of his shirt and pulled the knotted tie away from his neck. 'Get their names and numbers, OK?'

'Any reason?'

'Personal.'

Again she agreed.

He thanked her and started to walk away.

'Oh, Van Deer?'

Dutch turned back to the newswoman.

'Dump the tie. You're cuter in T-shirts.' Grinning, she shovelled another bite of egg salad sandwich into her mouth.

He drove down Wilshire. Traffic was light because it was Sunday. A couple of blocks west of La Brea, Dutch saw the famous pink granite building that Payne owned. It was now a landmark. *Architectural Digest* said that its strong symmetrical shape rivalled the Chrysler building in New York.

Dutch parked on the street and went inside. A geometric fountain stood in the centre of the lobby. Gustav Klimt's mosaic mural weaved its way over the walls and on to the ceiling. Paintings by Kandinsky,

Delaunay and Léger hung on the inlaid marble, looking down over the atrium.

Next to the elevators, a bored security guard sat behind a desk. Dutch gave his name and waited patiently for him to scan the list on his clipboard. Satisfied, the man pointed to the elevator at the end of the lobby. It went directly to Payne's private helicopter port on the roof.

The brass lift was circa 1920s, but the motor that ran it was modern. It took less than ten seconds to get to the forty-fifth floor.

When the copper doors opened, he saw Therese sitting in Payne's black helicopter parked on the tarp. She was talking to the pilot through headphones. They were laughing. Dutch ducked under the blades and got in. He took the headset from his seat and put it on.

'You're ten minutes late,' she said to him, her laughter fading. She was wearing a bare-shouldered, blue cocktail dress that brought out her dark eyes.

'You look good,' Dutch said, strapping himself in.

'Thanks. I love your tie.'

He flicked some lint off it. 'Be nice. The last time I wore this was the day we got married.'

'I thought it looked familiar.' She laughed in spite of herself.

The helicopter pilot turned to them, the large helmet and visor covering most of his face. 'Hi. I'm Kevin Rousette, the barnstormer of this heap. It's good to see you again, Mr Van Deer.'

Dutch smiled. He remembered the man well. 'It was a lot of fun that day.'

'Not many men would have done what you did. I told Jonathan. He was very grateful.'

Therese looked at Dutch, confused.

289

Dutch strapped the safety belt around him. 'Didn't your friend Miles tell you? There was a slight altercation with the Indians down at the grave-site, right after the bones were discovered.

'Mr Van Deer stepped in and helped out. Otherwise we could have all been badly hurt.'

'You looked like you were doing OK without me,' Dutch said, staring at his own reflection in the back of Kevin's glossy black helmet.

The pilot laughed. 'Just a few tricks I learned in the army.'

Dutch prodded. 'I bet you're a lot more than Mr Payne's chauffeur. His part-time bodyguard maybe, huh?'

The back of Kevin's helmet bobbed up and down in assent. 'I guess you can say that. Someone's got to do it. The man seems to attract trouble like fleas to a dog.' There was affection in his voice for his boss.

Therese cut in. 'Yes, Miles did tell me what happened. Thanks, Dutch,' she said, with a touch of embarrassment.

'I didn't do it for him. If I had known who he was at the time, I would have made a *U-eee*. Did you meet Lenny Garowitz?'

From Miles to Lenny Garowitz. Therese knew how Dutch's mind worked. If he didn't like the subject, he simply changed it. 'Yes, I met him. I went over to his rented condominium yesterday. Their house in Beverly Hills has to be re-built from the ground up. I surprised the man. The second I told him who I was, his hand shot up to the gold piece round his neck. He didn't let go of it until I left. I figured it would take the jaws of life to pry his fingers loose. But I got a glimpse of it. It was Spanish all right, circa eighteenth century. I asked him about it, but he said it was a family heirloom. I asked him if he had any more. He said no.'

'The man's lying.'

'I know that.' She was annoyed that Dutch didn't give her credit for figuring that one out for herself. 'I've got to get Payne to give me more time on the dig.'

The helicopter followed the 101 west, then turned north towards Bell Canyon. Looking down, Dutch could see white-fenced roads and exclusive Tudor and country-style homes with large stables behind them. Stately mansions jutted out of the hillside. The sun ricocheted off their windows, making them look like jewels encrusted in brown earth. The vegetation in the hills was sparse, the terrain composed mainly of brush and rocks.

Only one residence, almost hidden behind trees, stood directly on top of the mountain. By its majestic size, Dutch instinctively knew it belonged to *the* John Payne. He could see a wrought-iron gate cutting across the road barring access to the entrance of the estate.

'It's like a goddamn castle,' Dutch said in amazement, as the stone mansion, with its multitude of lookout towers, loomed up in front of him.

'It *is* a castle,' the pilot said. 'Payne's ancestors were English. They toiled in the fields of the lord who owned it. When Payne made his fortune, he bought the castle and had it taken apart piece by piece and transported here. It was put together exactly as it was in England. He claims the castle helps him stay close to the common folk because he remembers the poverty his ancestors endured.'

Dutch groaned. 'What a crock.'

Therese said, 'The common folk believe him, and that's all that matters. Payne is smart. He knows that

291

money alone can't buy the governor's mansion. He also needs the support of the people.'

'That's right,' the pilot said. 'He hangs out a lot with blue-collar workers. You know why?'

'Because there're more of them,' Dutch cracked back.

'Lots more. The man's a mover and a shaker, with the masses on his side. He finances huge environmental projects. He funds undertakings to find ways of saving the Amazon rain forest. He builds hospitals that specialize in treating killer diseases.'

Dutch asked him, 'How long have you been working for Jonathan Payne?'

'Seems like forever. I met him in Vietnam. We were in the same unit. When I got back to the States, I was lost. I had no idea what I wanted to do with my life. He gave me a job flying him around. I've been with him ever since.'

'Was he in combat?'

The pilot shook his head, indicating that this part of the conversation was over. 'No one who works for Mr Payne can discuss anything personal about him. It's a hard and fast rule. I've probably said too much already.'

'Let's get impersonal, then. He has a great interest in Native Americans.'

'A very unusual man,' the pilot said, refusing to go any further.

'You sound like you respect him a lot,' Dutch said.

'He's a great man. Loyal to people he likes. Treats me well,' the pilot replied.

Another convert for Mr Payne, Dutch thought. He turned to Therese. 'I forgot to ask you. Is Miles going to be there?'

'Yes.' Her eyes were hard, daring Dutch to say anything more about it.

He didn't.

As they flew over the estate, he could see droves of expensive cars and limos parked off to the side. One of them had the flag of the United States and the flag of California attached to its fenders. It belonged to the governor. Miles was here somewhere, too. Dutch began to feel an ache in his chest.

Well-built men in suits, holding walkie-talkies, were standing by the entrance of the house and around the lawn. Their heads moved slowly in a robotic motion as they scanned the grounds. Dutch could see other men like them on top of the tower. Were they the governor's men or Payne's? Dutch wondered. Probably both.

In the distance, he could see three fields of riders scattered over the hillside. The first two fields were in full gallop chasing after something. Several participants were dressed in traditional pink coats and carrying whips. The others wore black jackets. Hounds were barking and racing in front of the thoroughbreds. They were kept in line by several whippers-in.

The helicopter lit down on the lawn next to the circular driveway. The pilot opened the door for them. They lowered their heads and stepped out. Dutch cupped his hand over his eyes, shading them from the sun's glare, and looked around the well-trimmed green grounds. 'What are they hunting?' Dutch asked Therese.

'I don't know. I didn't ask.'

'Hello,' a voice said behind him.

Dutch turned. An old man was coming towards

them. He seemed to be the butler and was wearing black tails with striped pants. 'Are you here for the hunt, sir?' he asked Dutch, deliberately ignoring the way he was dressed.

'I'm Wilhelm Van Deer,' Dutch said quickly.

The stoic expression remaining glued to his face, the butler said, 'Yes, of course. Please come this way.'

Dutch and Therese followed him into the house.

The interior looked like a medieval movie set, except that Dutch knew everything in here was authentic: the stone blocks making up the walls were at least several hundred years old. Most of the large tapestries that decorated them were also pre-Renaissance. Next to the medieval hangings were several oversized thirteenth-century rococo mirrors. Native American art including rare Navajo rugs found their place alongside their European counterparts. Authentic Frederick Remington sculptures of the old west were displayed next to the intricate thirteenth-century mosaics of Cimabue and the Italian frescoes of Giotto. Dutch was amazed by the effect of it all; the rooms were filled with a cacophony of different styles of art and furniture that spanned centuries and cultures.

Two hundred-year-old baroque Italian chandeliers hung fifty feet in the air and looked down upon the black tie crowd that congregated in the hall. Like the array of art in the chateau, the guests also came in an arrangement of colours and styles: Africans in turbans mingled with the pale-skinned Pasadena elite; wealthy oil-soaked Iranians in Armani tuxedos whispered seductively in the ears of their tanned blond dates; over in the corner by an ice-sculptured fountain, a well-known movie actor was in deep conversation with a beautiful Pakistani woman covered in a silk sari.

In the main room, a large table stretching seventy feet in length was filled with a display of colourfully decorated food. To complement the hunting motif, most of the delicacies were freshly killed game. An entire barbecued boar, tusks and all, adorned the centre of the table. Next to it were plates containing thick slices of grilled venison. Encircling all of this were trays of pheasant and quail, complete with legs and heads.

Waiters weaved their way through the crowd. Some held trays of hors d'oeuvres, others poured red and white wine in the guests' empty glasses.

'Many of Mr Payne's visitors are up on the tower watching the hunt. Would you prefer to stay here or go on up?' the butler asked.

Feeling out of place in his rumpled jacket, Dutch opted to go upstairs.

They took the stone steps up to the tower and out on to the rectangular keep. A smaller group of people, also wearing black ties, were standing next to the lookout slots in the stone donjon and peering through field glasses.

In the distance, Dutch and Therese could see the hunters racing through the hills. They took binoculars from the table next to them, went over to an opening in the stone fortress and focused in on the riders.

The horses were now about twenty feet behind the hounds, whose eyes were steadily fixed on something in the brush. They were yelping and snarling, running at full speed.

Dutch moved his attention to the area of scrub and trees up in the jagged knoll. A yellowish shadow darted out of the shrubs and zigzagged down the hill.

He adjusted his binoculars, trying to see what the hounds were chasing.

Then he saw it. A coyote. By the condition of the animal, it had to have been running from the hunters for some time now. Its coat was lathered and its tongue was hanging out of its gasping, foam-covered mouth. It was limping as it ran. The foot must be broken, Dutch thought.

The coyote tripped and toppled down the hill. It let out a piercing, high-pitched yelp as the mangled paw scraped against the rocky ground. When it hit bottom, it tried desperately to get up but couldn't. The animal began crawling on its stomach, trying to get away from the frantic dogs. The hind legs dragged lifelessly behind its body.

'Its back is broken,' Dutch said to Therese.

Her face turned pale, but she continued to watch.

The hounds were barking wildly now. They raced down the hill towards the wounded animal. At first they circled the coyote, snarling and yapping. The coyote tried fighting back, its powerful mouth snapping at the dogs.

The hunters on the hill, reining in, sat on their sweat-soaked thoroughbreds and watched the attack.

Sensing that the coyote was exhausted, the dogs began to move in. Fangs bared, saliva dripping down their jaws, they inched forward. Knowing the end was coming, the coyote stopped trying to defend itself, laid its head down on the ground and exposed its neck.

Dutch watched quietly, his mouth clenched shut.

The hounds moved in, ripping and tearing at the animal's throat. One sharp howl from the coyote and it was over.

Up on the hill, the master of fox hounds dug into the

side of his horse with his spurs, forcing it to gallop down the incline towards the skirmish.

Dutch recognized him. It was John Payne.

Payne let out a loud *Ya-haaaa* as he rode his horse through the hounds. Leaning over, he quickly scooped up the mutilated coyote. He let the hounds snap at its pelt for a few seconds as a way of praising them, then dropped it in front of him over his saddle. Continuing to *Ya-haaa*, he raced down the hill towards his chateau, the head of the coyote bouncing lifelessly against the side of the horse.

There was applause from the guests up on the roof.

Dutch had had enough. If Therese wanted to be with these people, then let her; he just wanted to go home. 'Are you staying? I'm leaving.'

She was visibly shaken by what she had just seen. 'Dutch, please, you have to talk to Payne.'

He nodded in understanding. She had come with him so he could meet Payne, but she was really Scone's date. 'You in love with that guy?'

Her eyes flashed anger. 'You have no right to ask that.'

'I'm asking anyway.'

'Yes,' she said defiantly.

Enough was enough. He left her standing there and walked back down the winding tower steps. He heard her calling out his name once, but he didn't turn round. When he reached the main hall, he pushed through the throng of colourfully dressed people and made his way out of the front door. He felt like a damn fool. What had possessed him to think they could ever get back together?

As he began to walk towards the helicopter pad, he saw Payne leading the hunters through the open gates.

The horses were lathered and sweaty, and the riders looked tired and dishevelled. Their clothes and faces were covered with dirt. Further down the hill, the 'whips' were rounding up the excited hounds and taking them back to the compound.

What the hell am I doing here? Dutch wondered. More than anything right now he wanted to be sitting in his bar in Malibu, a boilermaker sliding down his throat.

There was nothing for him and Payne to talk about. Why had he let Therese prod him into coming? He had had enough pain for one day.

Dutch glanced up at the tower. He could see Therese standing with several of the black-tied guests up in the keep. She was staring down and waving, but not at him. Two men on horseback were looking up at her and smiling. One was the familiar strapping figure of the incumbent governor. The other was Miles Scone on a black lathered steed. His handsome face was shrouded with dust.

The guy would look good covered with horse shit. Damn! Watching him look at Therese made Dutch's stomach feel as if a serrated knife had ripped through it.

Therese turned and saw Dutch staring at her. She flared her nostrils, then moved her eyes back to Scone. Miles glanced around to see whom she was looking at. When he saw the Dutchman, he flicked the reins and walked his horse over to where he was standing. Scone arched his waist over the saddle and looked down at him. A smile cut through his bearded face.

He removed his black velvet helmet and said, 'I'm glad you came.' He leaned down, offering his gloved hand to Dutch. The Dutchman took it. Scone's grip was especially strong today. The relish of the kill must be still searing through his blood, Dutch thought.

'Too bad I can't stay,' he said.

Miles glanced down at him, his smile fading. 'That will disappoint Jonathan. He's expecting you. I told you, he has a great interest in old bones.'

There was something about Miles that was strangely appealing. His smile was warm and inviting. Dutch could see how Therese would be attracted to him. 'I'm more interested in *young* bones,' he said.

'So you told me.' Miles turned serious. 'Why don't you give it a rest? No one wants this, you know.'

'That's what I keep hearing. Bad for business, right?'

'Something like that. It's just a shame they weren't found in some unpopulated area or in the slums.'

'It would be OK to rip up houses in the barrio, but not in Beverly Hills, huh?'

'You're a grown man, Wilhelm. You know what I'm saying.'

He did know and he didn't like it. He looked away from Miles and over to the governor who was sitting on his red mare and talking to some of the other riders by the main entrance of the castle. He was laughing and conversing loudly, but his eyes were focused directly on the anthropologist. Turning again to Scone, Dutch asked, 'Is this just your advice, or is it also Payne's and the governor's?'

'It's everyone's advice,' he said pleasantly. Then he trotted back to the other riders.

Dutch estimated it would take him ten minutes to get to his bar if he could find the damn helicopter pilot.

'Where are you going, Wilhelm?' he heard someone behind him say.

Turning round, Dutch saw John Payne on his horse by the edge of the tennis courts. Wearing his pink coat and sitting on his midnight-coloured steed, he looked like someone out of an English pastoral painting. The man spurred the horse's flanks, sending it into a canter. When the animal was only a few feet away from Dutch, he pulled on the reins and walked the horse over to him.

'I hope you're not thinking of leaving,' Payne said. The man's voice was smooth and persuasive, like a salesman in the jewellery section of a high-class department store.

Dutch knew better than to fall for his appeal. Payne hadn't made millions by oozing charm. He took a good look at him. His hair was silver, but his scarred face was young, the kind that didn't flash its age. Maybe he was in his late thirties or even forties. Dutch couldn't tell. 'I'm leaving,' he replied.

Payne backed his horse up, blocking the path to the helicopter. The dead coyote dangling from the saddle brushed against Dutch's jacket, staining it with blood.

John Payne began to study him, as a boxer in the ring studies his opponent. 'Why don't you follow me to the stables? We can talk in quiet there.' He pointed to the old butler walking towards them. 'Maximilian will get you anything you need. Hell, you're a guest. Make yourself at home.' Payne broke into a grin, leaned down and whispered into Dutch's bandaged ear, 'You and me, we got to talk. Get an understanding going.'

Dutch moved away and looked up at Payne. Propped up on his horse, the billionaire looked

300

confident, like a man who was used to getting what he wanted.

Payne wiped the dirt from his face with his blood-stained glove. 'Walk my guest over to the barn,' he said to the butler. Then he dug in his spurs and cantered toward the stables.

'It's that way,' Maximilian said to Dutch, nodding towards the large barn over by the riding ring about a hundred yards down the hill.

Dutch thought about following him. He realized he didn't have much choice, since he didn't have transportation and his only way out of here was by the helicopter Payne owned. If the pilot wouldn't take him, then he'd have to walk.

Peering over Maximilian's shoulder, he watched Payne reach the stable and dismount. Dutch suddenly felt a desire to talk to him. Payne probably knew more about the lives of the mission Indians than the Indians knew about themselves. If the killer was Indian, then he might be a help in finding him. 'Let's do it,' he said.

The old man smiled and winked. 'Good idea, sir.' He seemed relieved.

As they walked down the hill towards the stables, Dutch said, 'He's crazy, isn't he?'

'He's a visionary, sir,' Maximilian said in a bored tone, his eyes fixed in front of him.

'I mean . . .'

'I know what you mean,' the butler said.

Dutch understood. Maximilian was equating crazy and visionary as the same thing.

Looking round, he caught a glimpse of several Indians from the S&L bank standing over by the main entrance. They were talking with the governor's security men. Strange. One minute they're loan

301

officers, the next they're Payne's guards, he thought.

When they reached the stables, Dutch followed Maximilian past several stalls containing champion Arabs. The horse Payne had ridden was being hosed down by a stable hand. Blood from the coyote ran down the steed's torso and intermingled with the water on the ground.

'He's in there, Mr Van Deer,' Maximilian said, pointing to the door of the large tack room. He then turned round and climbed slowly back up the hill. Dutch opened the door.

The first thing he saw when he entered was a roomful of stuffed heads and pelts of animals indigenous to the west. The snarling, ferocious mouth of boars, coyotes, bison, bears and lizards, their wild marble eyes frozen open, stared down at him from the walls.

Near the corner, Payne's long-legged body was leaning over a butcher's block table with the dead coyote laid out on top of it. The billionaire was holding a blood-soaked, pearl-handled Bowie knife and was slicing the coat from the animal's back. The coyote's partially severed head hung down off the edge of the table. Several impatient cats were sitting by Payne's feet, yowling, staring hungrily at it. His sleeves were rolled up and his hands and arms were covered with blood. The scarlet coat and gloves he had worn for the hunt were thrown across a bale of hay by the door. 'Glad you could make it,' he said to the anthropologist, not bothering to look up.

Dutch turned away. The smell of blood and manure was making him feel sick. 'You said we needed to talk.'

Payne gave a quick, deep laugh, like someone trying

302

to gulp in air. 'That I did. I love skinning animals,' he said, with childish excitement in his voice. 'Great hobby. It relaxes me. Learned it from my father. When I was a boy, we used to go hunting and fishing together.' The laughter in his eyes suddenly darkened for a second, as if he were reliving one of those times in his head. Then he shook it off.

Dutch picked up on it. He wondered how much fun he'd really had cutting up animals with his father.

Payne slit open the belly of the coyote and the intestines tumbled out, skating across the table like giant worms. The eager squeals of the cats became louder. With one motion, Payne quickly cut the head off. It dropped on to the straw-covered ground. Fresh blood from the exposed jugular of the coyote splattered across the industralist's tan riding breeches.

Payne laughed heartily, watching the head roll across the floor, and the cats chasing after it as if it were a soccer ball.

'They want the brains,' Payne said, winking at Dutch. 'Cats love brains.' He wiped the blood-stained Bowie knife on his pants, then put it back into a leather sheaf by his coat, all the time watching his guest from the corner of his eye to see his reaction. The anthropologist was pale and shaken. Payne smiled. 'You OK?'

Dutch lied and nodded yes.

'Sorry. I sometimes forget that this sport isn't for everyone. Perhaps we should go outside.'

Dutch didn't believe that Payne had made him watch the dismemberment without any forethought. Men like him knew what they were doing every minute of their lives. The Dutchman was unnerved by what he had just seen, which meant John Payne now had a

303

distinct advantage over him. He wondered how many business deals were made in this barn after a skinning.

The industrialist opened the wooden door and they walked outside. Payne stopped by the hose attached to the side of the stable, turned it on and washed the blood from his hands.

Dutch pulled a cigarette from his pocket and lit it, siphoning in the smoke, trying to calm down. His hands were shaking. 'You should take your act to Vegas. Those albino leopards wouldn't hold water next to you.'

Payne laughed, and turned off the hose. Wiping his hands on his stained white dress shirt, he said, 'Sit down. Sit down.' He gestured to the fence surrounding the training ring. Payne climbed up and sat on the top post.

Dutch lifted himself up and sidled next to him. In the middle of the ring, a stableman was training a horse on a lunge rope. The air smelled of new-mown hay and farm animals. It was quiet here. A far cry from the forced laughter and the odours of champagne and thick perfume that filled the main house.

'Nice, isn't it?' Payne said, as if reading Dutch's mind. 'It's even prettier at night. When I can't sleep because of the pressures in my life, I come down to the barn.' He laughed. 'For some reason, the second I lay my head down on a bale of hay and cover my body with a horse blanket, I'm out like a light. I envy men who can accept the simple things of life. That's the way God intended it to be.'

Dutch glanced at Payne's profile. His intense eyes, as they looked out upon his property, were like polished opals. There was a sadness etched deeply into his scarred face. For a second, the industrialist reminded Dutch of that child he wistfully talked about, the one who loved to hunt and fish. His Rosebud. Dutch wondered what had disturbed him when he mentioned his father back in the barn. Nothing was what it seemed. Not with a man like Payne. 'You're missing your party,' he said.

Payne inhaled deeply, taking in the fresh smells. 'The hell with them. They'll eat my food and drink my wine just as well without me there. In fact, they'll probably do a better job of it, knowing I'm not next to them counting the bottles.' He laughed loudly. After a pause, he said, 'Thanks for the help at the grave-site. I guess I owe you for that one.'

Dutch shook his head. 'You don't owe me for anything.'

Payne looked at him with amusement. 'Most men would have wet their pants after hearing that.'

'Maybe I will take you up on it. How about some extra time on the hotel dig?' Waiting for his answer, Dutch picked a piece of tobacco off his tongue and flipped it on to the soft earth in the ring.

'OK. That's what you came for, isn't it?'

Dutch looked at him, surprised.

Payne peered at him like a hawk. 'I know everything about you, Van Deer. When someone interests me, I make sure I find out about them. I know where you were born . . . who your favourite comic-book hero was. Even the name of the girl you first slept with. Mary Francis, wasn't it? It was in the back of her daddy's car.' Jonathan was smirking now.

Dutch nodded slowly, controlling his amazement. 'It was a Winnebego. Belonged to her uncle.' The man doesn't like to lose, Dutch thought. 'I'd rather you just understood the need for the unearthing.'

'You think I don't?'

Dutch watched the young Arab colt going round and round in a circle on the lunge rope. His gait was majestic.

'He'll make a fine endurance stallion when he matures,' Payne said.

Dutch turned back to him. 'Your hotel could be put on hold. I know it will cost you, but you can afford the wait.'

Payne mulled over what Dutch had said, then his eyes hardened. 'It has nothing to do with money. That hotel is a dream of mine. My dreams don't wait for anybody.'

'So I hear,' Dutch said. He could feel a vague sensation of fear rising inside him. The man was an egomaniac and he had to watch how he approached him. The simple life that Payne reminisced about, like Citizen Kane bemoaning his sled, was only the outside trimming of his persona. It was the part that made his package look attractive. Inside, there was a man of ice and no compromises.

'That property may be worth more than you know,' Dutch said, trying to turn it round.

Payne leaned closer to Dutch, his lips cracking into a shrewd smile. 'You think there's something down there, don't you?'

The Dutchman didn't answer him right away. Payne could be intimidating, but right now it was he who was holding the cards. Stroke him nice and easy, Dutch thought. He slowly took a last drag, then put the cigarette out on the fence and stripped it. 'Maybe,' he finally said. 'Therese thinks so. There could be an entire Indian village under those grounds. Maybe something else. We don't know yet. One week isn't enough time to find out. You're a leading expert in Indian artifacts. You know the importance of all this.'

'What do you mean something else?'

Payne's face was very close to Dutch's now and the anthropologist had to move his head back in order to see him clearly. 'We found a gold cross belonging to the Spanish missionaries. A gold coin also turned up. Who knows what's down there? Therese hasn't even touched the tip of the iceberg yet. It would be your find. You'd get credit for it.'

Payne began to smile. His mind was running on like a computer now. Then he looked at Dutch and slapped him on the leg. 'Maybe we could make a deal, you and me.'

He had the man. Dutch scratched his head, shrugged. 'Like what?'

'A trade-off. Do the dig, take your time doing it, but put the other baby to sleep?'

'What other baby are we talking about?' Dutch said.

'This talk about bones.' Payne made a face to show how frivolous it all was.

'Two girls died . . .'

'So what?'

Dutch stared at him, confused.

'They're dead. They've been dead for a long time. Nobody cares. What matters is today.' Again he slapped Dutch on the knee. 'What do you say?'

Dutch felt a weight in his throat. So that's Payne's beef. It wasn't the bones of the Indians. It was the bones of the twins. What did they have to do with him? Dutch took a good look at the man. Payne's white hair was thick and dry, reminding him of packing fibre. He was far from handsome. From this angle, his mouth seemed even more lopsided. Up close, the tiny scars covering his face looked like the aftermath of bone and skin reconstruction.

'I don't think I want to put that one to sleep,' Dutch said quietly.

Payne removed his hand from the Dutchman's leg. 'I hear that college of yours isn't renewing your contract.' His grey eyes were slyly turned on him.

Dutch had an idea where this was going. 'No, they haven't.'

'Any prospects for a job?'

'Not yet.'

'I'm on a thousand college boards across the country. Pick any one you like. I'll see that you get a position there. Hey, I got a better idea! I'm funding that dig in Tanzania. Why don't I send you to lead it? What do you think?'

The unearthing that Tara was going on. It was tempting. Dutch shook his head. 'No thanks. I'd rather know who killed those girls.'

'Why the hell are they so important to you?' Again that cold voice.

'I think I should be asking you the same question.' Dutch locked his eyes on Payne's. 'Why is this city so apathetic about the brutal death of two fifteen-year-old girls? I've seen more police action on a jay-walking ticket.'

Payne's face was turning red from frustration, making the white scars even more pronounced. 'Dollars and cents. You're trying to keep a prime piece of land like Beverly Hills paralysed because of a couple of murders that happened eighteen years ago.'

Dutch looked deeply at Payne. Then he said slowly, 'What makes you think that's when they died?'

Payne's eyes betrayed a glint of confusion for one brief second, then they faded to amusement. 'Must have read it somewhere. Maybe it was on TV.'

No. Dutch hadn't said anything to the media. He hadn't known the exact year the girls died. Dutch had only given the police and the coroner's office a vague estimation ranging from twenty to fifty years. He let it alone. 'Let me tell you what I think,' he said. 'I think the thing about Beverly Hills being a financial disaster because of this unearthing, and the uproar over the reburial of Indian bones, is all a bunch of shit. Somebody tampered with those bones so I wouldn't find out who they belonged to. That someone is also putting pressure on the city not to help in the investigation. That someone has to be pretty powerful.' Dutch raised his eyebrows at Payne and waited for an answer.

The industrialist moved his head close to Dutch's face. 'Drop this,' he said, his breath whipping across the anthropologist's cheek like a gust of arctic air.

'Why?'

'It's not your business.'

'I think it is. You have Indians acting like guards outside your property. Why is that? Those are the same guys who work behind a desk at a savings and loan company in the valley.'

'Times are tough. They need the money. I let them moonlight for me.'

Then it hit Dutch. 'Do you own Smokey Valley Savings and Loan?'

'What if I do?'

'Who's Hugo Frye?'

A shadow crossed Payne's face. 'Why are you asking?'

'He put up bail for an Indian named Bobby Santiago. He has an account at your bank.'

Payne's eyes shifted back and forth. 'I own the place, I don't run it. Ask the man who does.'

'I tried. But I think you already know that.' Dutch pulled his tie even further down his neck. He waited a bit, then had to ask it. 'Why are you trying to stop this murder investigation? Did you know those girls?'

Payne slowly got off the fence. He stretched his long legs, and, putting his hands on his thin waist, arched his back. 'I think we're done, bone man.'

Dutch also got down from the fence. 'Who are they?'

Payne didn't answer.

'You know who they were. Goddammit, they were just kids.'

Again Payne didn't answer.

'What about the man killed at the Encino reservoir? Do you know anything about that?'

This time Payne turned and glared at him, but still remained silent.

Dutch felt something touch his leg. Looking down, he saw one of the satiated cats rubbing against him, purring. He pushed it away with his foot. 'Whoever killed the girls also killed the man. Maybe it was someone who was Chumash, or at least knew about their culture. That's the only thing that makes sense.'

Payne looked contemptuously at him. 'You don't seem to understand, do you? Leave it alone.' He said it softly, but the words were like rivets piercing Dutch's body.

'I know what the girls look like now. I'm going to find out who they were,' Dutch said.

310

Payne looked surprised. 'You finished the reconstruction of the face?'

'Yes.' He didn't know Payne had been aware of what he was doing.

Payne moved closer to him. 'What did you do with it?'

Dutch almost told him that he could see a picture of one of the girls on the six o'clock news tonight. Then he caught himself. He wasn't sure how far this man's tentacles stretched. Payne could very well have the power to stop something like that from happening. Instead, he said, 'She's tucked away in a safe place.'

Payne noticeably winced. Then he said sombrely, 'I think we're at an impasse, bone man. I talked to Orville Priest this morning. He's going to tell you to turn all the bones over to him by tomorrow morning. That includes the skull of the girl you reconstructed.' He then turned round and walked away, heading towards the big house.

Dutch was stunned. But at least he had the photos to work with. 'OK, what about the dig? Are you going to give Therese more time?' he called after the man.

Payne didn't answer or turn back to look at him.

That man had fangs like a rattler, and could strike like one when provoked, Dutch thought. He was not someone Dutch wanted for an enemy. Therese's cause hadn't been helped much, either, by all of this. Well, he wasn't about to give the girls up. Not now. Not after he knew what they looked like. The twins were no longer bones to him.

The rest of the cats slinked out of the barn and stared up at the Dutchman. Seeing that he had no food to give them, they turned away and began licking the coyote's blood off each other's faces.

When Dutch reached the pad up on the lawn, the helicopter was gone. Near where it had stood was a beat-up taxi. The driver, who had a flat Slavic face, stuck his head out of the window. A cigarette dangled from his lips. 'You the guy that needs to go back to mid-Wilshire?'

Dutch nodded.

'Get in. Somebody from the house called and told me to come and get you.'

'Did they pay you?'

The driver looked suspiciously at Dutch. 'No, they said you were gonna pay. Any problem with that?'

'No problem.' Dutch got in and slammed the broken door shut. No helicopter, no limousine. When John Payne disposes of someone, he doesn't waste time in doing it, he thought.

The taxi pulled away on the gravel path, jerking Dutch's head back into the worn plastic seat.

18

'Take him home. Sober him up,' Papa Padakos said to Tara in disgust, pointing a thick, hairy finger at the Dutchman.

Tara looked over to the end of the saloon by the bay window. She spotted Dutch sitting there alone, with his legs in the usual position, propped up on a chair. His shoulders sagged and his chin arched downward, almost touching his chest. He was staring intently at the empty shot glasses and beer bottles on his table. He slowly laid the bottles on their sides and pointed the necks at Padakos like cannons.

Her eyes grew concerned. She could tell he had been drinking heavily. That was rare for him. Something must have happened. 'How long has he been here?' she asked.

Padakos shrugged. 'Since late this afternoon. It's Sunday. I want to close up early.' His gruff accent was from the Aegean side of Greece.

The place was empty. It was ten o'clock – late for Malibu. A few of the regulars were up at the bar watching Australian football on ESPN.

She walked over to Dutch, took a chair from another table and straddled it, leaning her chest into the back. Crossing her arms over the curved rim, she laid her chin on her hands and looked down at the table. She counted seven shot glasses and three beer bottles. The boy had a bad day, she thought. Then she noticed his ear. A brown rust colour was seeping through the bandages.

'It's infected again,' she said to him, pulling on her own earlobe.

'Fuck it.'

'If you don't take care of it, they'll amputate the damn thing. You can't afford to keep losing pieces of yourself, Dutch. There won't be anything left of you except that ugly tie.'

He pushed the bottles and glasses violently away, sending them rolling off the table and crashing down on to the floor. Padakos looked up from the bar, shook his head, and began to scrub the dirty glasses.

'I guess it didn't go well with Therese today,' Tara said.

'Fuck her,' he mumbled. His voice was thick.

He was very drunk, or he wouldn't have said that. 'Let's go home, Dutch.'

He looked at her with unclear eyes. 'Fuck you, too.'

She wasn't going to push it with him. Just play it gentle for now, wait until he finished off his drink, then grab him by his arm and drag him the hell out.

Dutch held the filled shot glass up to his face. Closing one eye, he began to study the caramel-coloured liquid inside it. 'Fuck this, too,' he muttered. He quickly gulped the whiskey down hard, then chased it with a couple of long swigs from his half-filled beer bottle. After wiping the foam off his walrus moustache with the back of his hand, he turned to her, smiled, and gave off a small belch. Eventually he asked her, 'How did you know I was here?'

314

'Padakos called me. He wants to go home.'

'Have a drink,' he said, waving to Padakos and pointing at Tara.

The Greek, ignoring him, started to wipe down the bar.

Tara reached over and took the beer bottle away from him. 'Come on, Dutch. Let's go.'

'Monica waiting for you? Hell, she'll be there when you get back. Relax. She's always there. Where else does she have to go?' Suddenly he slammed his fist on the table, sending the lonely jigger into the air and on to the floor. 'They fired me, goddamn it! The sonsofbitches fired me! They want to give the bones back to the Indians. Thousands of years of history . . . all that knowledge wasted. They'll all go right back into the ground again.'

Tara looked tired and drawn. 'Dutch . . .'

'We could have probed those bones . . . found out about their diseases. Maybe it would have helped find a cure for the same kinds of diseases in modern man. These assholes don't understand that.'

Tara didn't say anything, she just sighed. Getting up, she went over to the phone next to the bathrooms and called Monica, telling her she'd be late. Then she went over to Padakos behind the bar and ordered a couple of cheeseburgers, a pot of black coffee for Dutch and an Anchor Steam for herself.

Padakos groaned. 'Tara, I want to go home. *Pleease*!'

She grinned and said, 'You want to tell the man he got to go, then you do it.'

Padakos leaned over the bar and looked at the sour face on the big Dutchman. Throwing his hands in the air, he turned back to Tara. 'Not nice, what you do.'

'Also a side of fries. Don't burn them like you usually do.'

High waves lapped against the moorings, sending a spray of salt water across the large windows of the now empty bar.

The Dutchman downed his third cup of coffee and wiped his mouth on a napkin. The caffeine was beginning to kick in, diminishing the effects of the alcohol. 'The man doesn't make many mistakes or he wouldn't be as successful as he is,' he said, pouring more ketchup over his fries.

'How badly did you piss him off?' Tara asked.

'Plenty bad.'

'They showed the photos of Minnie on the six o'clock news tonight. Maybe we'll get some action.'

'Maybe.'

Hunching over the table, Tara sombrely sipped her Anchor Steam, thinking. 'Meanwhile, what do you want to do about the bones?'

Dutch stared glumly down into his plate. Pushing it aside, he said, 'What can I do about them? I can't hide a couple of thousand ancient skeletons in my closet by tomorrow and tell the police I misplaced them.' He shrugged. 'The bones go back to the Indians.'

'I keep coming back to Payne. He scares me. What does he want?'

He sipped his coffee. 'For one thing, he doesn't want me to find this guy.'

'*If* he's alive.'

'I think he is.'

'What's the great man afraid of?'

'I don't know. If I find out who the girls were, it's going to lead me to their killer. That's just what

Payne doesn't want to see happen. And if he doesn't want to see something, he knows how to make it go away.'

She crossed her arms, thinking about that. 'If it gets too rough, I suppose you can move in with me.'

Dutch grinned behind his cup. 'Only if I can get to see that butterfly flap its wings one more time.'

She grabbed a fry off his plate and flung it at him. 'Fuck you, Dutchman.'

'Let's talk about that option when I move in.'

Tara drove Dutch back to his trailer in time to see the replay of the photos of the dead girl on the eleven o'clock news. She then went on home to Monica.

When Dutch opened the door, Bitch came hobbling out of the kitchen to greet him. She was unusually hyper and her body was shaking. Dutch had seen this before and didn't pay much attention to it. He turned on the lights, then bent down to pat her head. When his hand drifted down to her back, he noticed a patch of hair missing near her shoulder. Puzzled, Dutch began to examine the area. Strange. The dog had never gnawed at herself before. He wondered if she had worms. Tomorrow he would find time to take her to the vet.

His stomach was sour. He went into the kitchen, took a box of Tums from one of the drawers and chewed a couple, then took a Coors out of the fridge. Taking the remote off the coffee table, he sunk into the couch and turned on the TV. The pretty face of the Channel Seven anchor grinned at him. He turned up the sound.

The image of the young girl he'd reconstructed came on right after the weather report. It was probably a repeat of the six o'clock story. What the station had done was show the same face twice by using a split screen process. This gave the impression of watching twins.

Looking at the young innocent faces, Dutch tried to force down those feelings of a human connection with them that was sprouting up once again.

Those eyes . . . those earthy lips. They were imploring him to find their killer.

Why had he done this? Why hadn't he let the dead remain dead! The Indians were right: Dutch was the devil. He had done the unthinkable; he had brought them back to life. All societies had a name for his kind: warlock, banshee, afreet, wyvern.

Those eyes! They were begging him now, reaching out and engulfing him in their unthinkable sorrow.

Dutch clicked off the TV and ran his fingers hard through his hair. What the fuck had he done? He lay back against the couch and sipped his beer, thinking. He had gone beyond the point of no return. He had seen their faces. Now he would have to find their killer. It didn't matter if the man was dead, his maggot-infested bones decaying in some unmarked grave. Dutch would scream this bloodsucker's name for the world to hear. Then he would yell out the names of the girls. Yell them out.

They deserved names!

No one should die without one. Not having their names to whisper in the killer's ear was like saying that the girls never existed.

They deserved to exist!

The phone rang, shattering his rage.

Dutch picked it up.

'I saw the girl on the TV. You're a real artist, Dutch.

318

Maybe you'd like to do my bust one day.' It was Smokey Pete.

'I only do dead people, Smokey.'

'I'll wait.'

'What do you want, Pete?'

'The girl caressed my Gabrieleño soul. Maybe it's time you guys got together for some serious conversation.'

Dutch sat up. 'Me and Bobby? Can he talk?'

'He's still floating around in the ozone level, but I can interpret for him.'

'When?'

'Tomorrow morning, about nine, OK? We'll meet on the breakwater. Don't bother with the bagels. Bobby will think they're flying saucers and run.'

Dutch hung up. 'All right! All right!' he yelled, slapping his thigh. The reconstruction of the face had got to Pete. That was good.

Dutch believed Bobby was the key to unlocking the door of the twins' deaths. Bobby knew those painted tunnels like the back of his hand. They cut right through the ancient cemetery. In his jumbled mind, the pathways must have suggested a religious place of sanctuary. If Bobby didn't commit the murders, then Dutch was sure he knew who did. With luck, tomorrow he would have an answer.

Dutch thought about the girls again. *You will have names, my darlings. I promise you.*

He finished his beer, then took a hot shower, letting the heat open the pores in his skin, so the alcohol could wash out of his system. His bones ached and he had a terrible headache.

Dutch stepped out of the stall, dried himself off and changed the bandage on his ear. The wound was red and pus-coloured. Tara was right. It was infected.

Walking over to his bed, he saw Bitch lying on top of the blanket. She was shivering, and her large frightened eyes looked up at him.

What was she doing here? She liked to sleep in the kitchen. A shadow of uneasiness crossed his gut.

He went over to the dog and put his hand on her head. Bitch moved into it and started to whimper. Dutch could feel her skin vibrating with terror.

A sense of dread came over him when he realized that there was something underneath the blanket and that she was protecting it. He shoved Bitch off the bed and saw that the cover was raised in the middle. Yes, there was something under there. He flung the blanket off the bed.

The skeletal remains of Maybellene stared up at him. Her leg bones were spread apart, revealing the patch of black hair taken from Bitch's coat. It was draped over the pubic area of the pelvic bone, making it appear as if she had a vagina. Lipstick was spread crookedly across the broken mouth of the skull. With her legs unfolded, Maybellene looked like a smiling whore, waiting for her customer.

A feeling of rage, then helplessness, came over Dutch. Someone had come into his house . . . touched his things! Hurt his dog! Violated Maybellene, the mother of all mankind!

Dutch began to think. Who knew he had the bones of Maybellene? The government, his department, the coroner's office. That was all. It was never advertised. No, there was also someone else who knew. John Payne. He had told Dutch this morning that he knew everything about him, including the first time he got laid. Was it Payne who did this?

Suddenly a strange, sickening feeling entered his body at the thought of who it really might have been.

It was *him*!

A vague smile spread across his face as he realized something. *He fucked up*!

The man fucked up!

The bastard had let him know he was alive. Maybe he did it on purpose, maybe not. It didn't matter. He was no longer intangible, a bodiless creature. He was a living, breathing entity. Being alive meant that he was vulnerable, that he was capable of mistakes. This bastard was in his trailer only a short while ago. He was so close now that Dutch could almost smell him.

The man had fucked up, all right! Yes, indeed!

And the next time, Dutch would be there waiting for him.

Hugo lay in bed, curled up in the foetal position, with the damp sheets covering his head. He had been sleeping this way ever since he could remember. It made him feel safe. The covers acted like a shield, not allowing the terrifying *haphap* in.

He had made a terrible mistake in going to Van Deer's home, he knew that. It was a stupid thing to do. Damn careless! But he couldn't resist. He had to make the Dutchman know that he was still alive.

He had had no choice. It was that *urge* again. The feeling was becoming more and more alive with each passing hour. This time it had come upon him like an army of angry red ants, tickling and nipping at his insides until he gave in. That horrible, wonderful *urge*!

The Dutchman was his soulmate . . . no doubt about it! They were like twins, with only one spirit between them. But it was he who dominated that spirit! It had to be him. The control centre could only be in his body, not in Van Deer's. He would make sure of that.

Hugo started to giggle at the thought of he and the Dutchman as siblings. Twins were his favourite things in the world. Hadn't he proved that years ago?

No longer able to contain himself, he laughed out loud, overshadowing the steady hissing noise that seemed to fill all the rooms. Embarrassed, he put his hand to his mouth. *Oh, my!* He giggled again.

The Dutchman was quite an artist, he suddenly thought, thinking about the sculpture that had appeared on the evening news. He had forged the girl exactly as Hugo remembered her. That was Natalie; the one with the sensuous cleft in her chin. The only thing missing was the mole on the right side next to her eye. And the eyes were brown, not blue. But how was the Dutchman to know that? What was the other one's name? Oh, yes, Beverly. It was all coming back to him now. So long ago, and it was coming back to him like raging waters returning to a dry river bed.

Then he thought of the man he had killed next to the reservoir. A blast of cold fear overtook him, and he began to exhale air in short, staccato puffs.

He suddenly began to find nothing humorous in his situation, and he cursed himself for having toyed with the Dutchman. Stupid! Stupid! he thought. A man like himself couldn't afford such deviations. If the world were to find out what he had done – *Oh, God!* It would be like the day they discovered what he'd done to the animals!

The *urge*, it was a curse from hell. He had controlled it for so many years. Now it was coming back; beginning to overtake his soul again – gnawing away at it until he gave in. He tightened the muscles in his stomach and held his body stiff, as he used to when he was a kid. Sometimes that helped in pushing these strange emotions away. Closing his eyes tightly now, he stayed that way, not daring to breathe, until the sensation left him. A moment later, he could feel it dissolving from his body like snowflakes melting in the sun. With sweat dripping down his face, he inhaled deeply. He was safe for now — but for how long? It will be back again, he knew that. Why was he so damned?

Then he thought about the Dutchman again. Unconsciously, he began to trace a wiggly line on the sheet under him with his finger. Then he made forty straight lines through it.

BOOK THREE

The *Haphap*

19

Dutch washed the lipstick off Maybellene's skull with a mild saline solution. It took over an hour until he was satisfied that all traces of the red pigment were gone. After wiping the skull dry, he carried the bones back to the corner of the room and covered them with the blanket.

He then ran his hands across the window frames in the trailer to see if there were any traces of forced entrance. There were none. The intruder either had a key or knew how to pick a lock, Dutch thought.

He walked over to his closet and opened the door. Inside, the entire area was congested with two-foot-square cardboard boxes piled on top of each other. The names of different kinds of bones were written on the sides of the cartons with a black marker. When he found the one inscribed PHALANGES, he removed the box, placed it on the floor and opened up the flaps. Inside, several hundred human finger-bones lay on top of each other. He pushed them aside, burrowing further down, stopping when he came to something wrapped in white cheesecloth. Pulling it from the box, he unwound the material until a nickel-plated, broken-handled Colt .45 lay exposed. He popped the clip from the grip. There were seven bullets in it, a full load.

Holding the gun in his hand after all this time, he thought about the day it was given to him.

'Take it, Wilhelm,' his mother said, handing him the gun outside the house. The Ohio wind blew her black veil against her face, outlining her features like a death mask.

He took it from her ebony-gloved fingers and inspected it, turning it over slowly in his hand. The sun bounced off the metal of the barrel, making his eyes burn.

'That's the only thing he left you, baby. That and the insurance. Put it in the house and let's go.' As she lifted her veil to wipe her nose with a lace handkerchief, the boy could see her swollen, watery eyes.

Instead of doing as he was told, the Dutchboy hid the gun in his coat pocket and took it with him to the cemetery.

The boyfriend who gave him the candy bars drove them. When they arrived, Wilhelm and his mother went over to the speckled granite stone of his father's newly dug grave. His mother had requested that the body be shipped here. It had snowed last night and the head of the stone was capped in white. Two blackbirds sat on top of it staring at him. He raised the gun, and caught one of them in the barrel sight.

'*Peuw, peuw.*'

The sandpaper voice of his mother's friend called out to them through a phlegmy cough: 'Hey, babe, come on. I'm freezin'!'

The boy looked past the rows of gravestones, towards the voice. He was sitting sideways in the driver's seat of his rust-coloured Chevy. The door was open and he was stamping his feet on the iced road to keep warm. A sheep-lined coat covered his bulging frame. He got out of the car, blew smoky frost into his hands and rubbed them vigorously. Looking at the boy, he smiled and said, 'Hey, Red Ryder, let's go. I'm going to be as stiff as your old man if I stay here any longer.'

Wilhelm slowly turned the gun in his direction, found him in the sight and cocked the hammer.

The smile froze on the man's face. His eyes widened with fear. He turned to the Dutchboy's mother. 'Hon, is it loaded?'

Eyes hidden somewhere behind the black see-through cloth, she stared back at him, not answering.

'Hon?'

The boy moved the sight up to the man's head, closed one eye and wondered the same thing as he pulled the trigger.

Peuw. Peuw.

No, it wasn't loaded. He discovered the bullet clip up in the attic several months later, in a chest filled with his father's clothes. That was twenty-five years ago. Dutch always wondered what would have happened if the Colt had had shells in it that day. There was no doubt in his mind that he would have killed that fat bastard. Maybe his mother would have been visiting him in prison when the tornado struck and she would still be alive today. The sweet odour started to return, and he forced it away by thinking of Billie — Billie with the brown cocoa skin.

Mamma may have . . . Papa may have
But God bless the child that's got his own . . .

* * *

Dutch spent an hour oiling the moving parts of the gun, then snapped the metal clip back into the grip. He slid the barrel towards him, forcing a shell up into the chamber. The old Colt still worked.

He was ready for the man.

Too tired to change, he dropped down on to his bed and tucked the gun under the pillow. Bitch jumped up on to the mattress and moved her arthritic body close to his for warmth. Dutch wrapped his arm around her thick coat. Within seconds, they were both asleep.

The phone rang.

Dutch jumped. He picked up the receiver. It was the Channel Seven anchor.

'Did I wake you?' she asked.

Dutch looked at the clock. It was ten to eight. He was supposed to meet Smokey Pete and Bobby in a few minutes. 'No,' he muttered.

'I told you I'd call you as soon as the inquiries on the twins started coming in.'

Dutch rubbed his eyes hard, cursing himself for not being more alert. 'How many did you receive?'

'Twenty-three.'

Dutch groaned.

'Hold on,' she said. 'Twenty-three for the entire country isn't so bad. You're lucky. The fact that they were fifteen-year-old twins narrowed them down. Besides, the majority of the calls were not reputable.'

'Were any of them valid?'

'Four. Two were about male twins. Is that a possibility?'

'No. There are differences between men and women, even at the skeletal level. What else?'

'Another inquiry concerned two five-year-old sisters.'

'What else?'

'The fourth was about two fifteen-year-old girls who disappeared about twenty years ago.'

Dutch sat further up in bed. 'Were they twins?'

'No. Just schoolmates.'

'The ones I'm looking for were twins, not friends.' He sank back down against the bedboard.

'It's still early for these kinds of calls. I'll keep you posted.'

'Thanks.' He hung up. Dutch wasn't under any illusion that someone watching television out there would recognize the reconstructed face. It rarely happened like that. He had to try it because it was the only quick, tangible way left open to him. The police weren't helping, and he didn't have permission to use their mainframe computers to cross-reference missing teenagers. It could take him months, perhaps years, of just going through files without that kind of access.

He looked out of the window and saw Smokey and Bobby Santiago walking on the sand towards the rocks of the sea wall. The younger Indian looked weak and frail. Pete was holding him by the arm, helping him over the boulders and driftwood. A Cherokee Jeep was close by, and Dutch could see two of the Indians from the S&L sitting in the front seat.

Dutch quickly put on a pair of jeans and an Ohio State sweatshirt. He went into the kitchenette and took a mug from the shelf. After filling it with hot tap water, he poured about three teaspoons of instant coffee into it. Grimacing, he quickly gulped it down.

Let them wait, he thought. If he was going to face that goddamn Indian who cut off his ear, then he wanted to be ready for him.

* * *

331

'Good morning, Dutchman. A little nippy today,' Smokey said. He was wearing an old, frayed cardigan. His hands were in his pockets. He was sitting on a sea-bleached wooden pillar that had washed up on the quay. Next to him, hunched over, sat Bobby Santiago, shaking from the DTs. His eyes were staring lifelessly at the rocks covered with sea salt. He was wearing a satin LA Dodgers warm-up jacket that was a couple of sizes too large for him.

Dutch nodded to Smokey, but he had his sights fixed on the Indian. 'Did you make sure he kept his hatchet at home, Pete?'

'Come on, Dutch. Let bygones be bygones. He's ready to make up. He wants to apologize.'

The Dutchman touched his bandaged ear. It felt hot and burning. He squatted down on the graffiti-covered rocks, squinting at Bobby. 'You cut my ear off, you sonofabitch!'

The Indian slowly glanced up at Dutch. A twinge of remembrance crossed his face. His parched lips cracked open in a grin, exposing his brown crooked tooth. He tapped his own ear and the smile broadened even further.

Smokey put his big hand on the Dutchman's shoulder. 'Leave it, Dutch. That's not what we came for.'

'The fucker cut off my ear!'

'What are you going to do? Cut his ear off to get even? Bobby probably wouldn't notice if you did.'

Pete was right. The anger began to wash off Dutch like the waves receding from the Malibu shoreline. He looked away from the sallow, shivering Indian and out towards the sea. The garbage barge was still there, and still covered by a blanket of crying seagulls. This time, though, the wind was blowing towards them and the smell was putrid. He sat down next to Bobby, on the other side of Pete, and stretched his legs. 'OK, let's forget about this,' he said finally, pointing to his ear. 'Tell the little shit I accept his apology.'

'You're a good man, Dutch,' Pete said, reaching his hand over Bobby and slapping him on the back.

Dutch turned to Santiago. 'So, Bobby, what have you been up to for the last twenty or so years?'

Bobby shrivelled back under his jacket and looked down again at the black rocks.

'You told me he could talk,' Dutch said to Pete.

'Now I didn't say that. I told you it's time you guys had a conversation, that's all.'

'How do you do that? The man's on Pluto. Has he said anything to you about the twins?'

Pete shook his head. 'No, he hasn't. If he knows anything, we're going to find out.' He moved his big frame off the wood pillar, knelt down next to Bobby and grabbed him by the arms. He then shook him hard, making his head jerk back and forth like a woodpecker's. 'I told you, this is the man you talk to. He's not the other one,' he patiently said to the dazed Indian, as if he were a child.

'Who's the other one?' Dutch asked.

'Ciazo.'

'Has he been around?'

'Oh, he's been around, all right. The guinea bastard tried to break my door yesterday. He came around when no one except me and Bobby was in the house.'

'Why?'

'He wants him. I don't know why. I held him off by threatening to break his head open with a crowbar I was holding. Bobby ran and hid under the bed.'

333

An uneasiness came over Dutch. He began to wonder again why this half-crazed Indian was so important to Ciazo.

'Keep him away from me, Smokey,' Bobby mumbled. His dark frightened eyes looked pleadingly up at the old Indian.

'He won't get near you. I promise you that,' Smokey said, stroking Bobby's back reassuringly. Turning to Dutch, he said, 'See, I told you he can converse.'

'Why are you scared of Jimmy Ciazo, Bobby?' Dutch asked.

Bobby looked confused. Shaking his dirty, matted hair, he said, 'What the fuck you talking about, man?' He turned to Smokey. 'What the fuck's this one-eared guy talking about?'

'I'm talking about the big mean-looking detective that wants to stretch your asshole.'

As Dutch's meaning dawned on him, Bobby began to scratch his cheek. 'I ain't scared of that piece of shit.'

Smokey shook his head, confused. 'This Indian's crazy, Dutch. I never saw a man run as fast as he did when Ciazo showed up at the door.'

Dutch heard something different coming from Bobby. Something that Smokey didn't catch. 'He thought we were talking about someone else. Maybe he thought that someone else was at the door instead of Ciazo.'

Pete looked at the Indian. Bobby was chewing nervously on a sleeve of the baseball jacket. 'Is that right, Bobby? You think we were talking about someone else?'

Bobby took the sleeve out of his mouth and

shrugged. He curled his legs up to his chest then wrapped his arms around them to protect himself from the wind.

Dutch studied Bobby's face. His skin colouring was a ruddy purple: a combination of too much sun, too much cold and too much alcohol. Scar tissue from past fights, like white ringworms, cut deep paths through his eyebrows. His hands also showed traces of living off the street: the knuckles were calloused and cracked, and the bloodied, jagged fingernails were bitten almost down to the cuticles.

'You like centipedes, Bobby?' Dutch asked suddenly.

The Indian's head shot up. His eyes swelled with terror. 'What?'

'You know what.' He wriggled his fingers in front of his face. 'Those leggy little creatures.'

The Indian looked away and fixed his frightened gaze on the garbage scow. The gulls, as if feeling his terror, flew up in the air, fluttering and cawing in all directions.

'What do those bugs have do with Bobby, Dutch?' Pete asked.

The Dutchman ignored him. 'You a painter, Bobby?'

No response.

'You like painting circles and squares and triangles? You like the colours red, white and black? The colours of the Chumash? They're your people, right?'

Again no answer. Bobby's eyes remained focused on the garbage and the seagulls.

'You were in Beverly Hills screaming at the construction workers building the hotel the day of the earthquake. Why? What was under the ground that you didn't want them to dig up? There were no bones found there.'

335

No answer. Bobby's eyes were becoming glassy, with a faraway look in them.

'Anything else under that ground? You had to have known about the Indian graveyard across the street because of the tunnels.'

Nothing from Bobby.

'During the earthquake, a woman fell into one of those tunnels. She said a man who smelled like rotting meat tried to drag her away. Was that you?' Dutch bent over to sniff him. 'You stink, Bobby, but not like that day.' Dutch shook his arm. 'Let's go back a few questions. You like insects with all those legs? Is that why you painted one of them in the tunnel?'

A long pause. Bobby then closed his eyes tightly and muttered something under his breath.

Dutch couldn't understand him. 'What did you say?' He moved closer to Bobby.

Pete grabbed Dutch's arm to keep him off the shaken Santiago. 'He said, "There were too many legs." '

Santiago drew his body deeper into himself and rocked back and forth. He began mumbling some kind of chant.

Dutch pried Pete's hand from his arm. 'What's he doing?'

'It's the Chumash prayer for the dead,' Pete said sombrely.

'I thought only a shaman could do that.'

Pete sighed. 'That's what he is.' He moved back on the pillar. 'He's from the *'antap* cult. So, now you know, OK?'

Dutch was surprised. 'Bobby?'

Pete nodded.

'I didn't know there were any left.'

Bobby began to sway, as if he were in a deep spell. Words, as old as the dawn of history, tumbled incoherently out of his mouth.

Dutch stared at the priest wearing the baseball jacket and torn sneakers. 'What happened to him, Pete?'

'War. He was taken prisoner in Da Nang and spent some time as a POW. He came back alive, if that's what you want to call it. Bobby was never the same.'

'He could have got out of the army. Why didn't he? Did he believe in fighting the Vietnamese?'

'Hell, no. He just wanted to get away.'

'From what? Didn't he like being a shaman?'

'You don't like it, Dutch. You're made into one. I don't know what happened.'

'Did he enlist?' Dutch asked.

Pete nodded. He closed his eyes, and moved his lips as he counted on his fingers. 'In seventy-four,' he said finally.

Dutch also did some arithmetic. 'That's eighteen years ago. The two sisters were killed right around that time.'

'You keep coming back to that. I told you, Bobby wouldn't kill anyone in that way.'

Dutch rubbed his eyes, they were burning from lack of sleep. 'I don't think he did, either. I think he knows who did, though. That's who he's scared of, not Ciazo. Where's he been living all these years?'

'Mostly in the street, or at the mission downtown when they have room for him. Sometimes he stayed at his uncle's farm.' Pete sat there on the piece of timber, studying his shoes, looking deep in thought. Then, after several seconds, he glanced up and said, 'You think he saw the guy?'

337

'I think so. He may even know him. That's what Ciazo was alluding to at Gomez's house. Bobby hung out in those tunnels in Beverly Hills. How long has he been doing that?'

'No one knows. His father was rough with him. He tried to teach him to be an *'antap* by smacking the prayers and traditions into his head. When Bobby was a boy, he used to run away for days at a time. We could never find him. He hid out in the tunnels.'

'Is that when you think he painted the walls?'

'You sure it was him that painted the walls, gringo?'

Dutch looked curiously at Smokey. 'You said yourself that only a shaman can create those paintings. They were sacred.'

Smokey put his hand on Santiago's swaying shoulder. 'The boy, here, said something to you. You weren't listening.'

Wishing he had worn a sweater to ward off the cold, Dutch wrapped his arms around his body for protection. 'What the hell are you talking about, Pete?'

'Too many legs.'

'What?'

'Bobby said there were too many legs. He was talking about the centipede on the wall. I don't think he drew it.'

'You mean he wouldn't have drawn one with that many legs?'

'I think that's what he meant.'

Dutch was shivering as hard as Bobby now. Looking over at him, he saw that the Indian was scrunched up, his head in his lap, chanting in a monotone. The Dutchman knew that he would not get through to him today. Whatever 'conversing' they had done was now

338

over. Turning to Pete, he said, 'If Bobby didn't make those drawings, then who did?'

Pete shrugged.

'Another Indian? It had to have been someone who was familiar with Chumash rituals.'

'You're right.' Pete shook his head, confused. 'The rituals and the meanings of the paintings were only known to *'antaps*. I may be an Indian historian, but even my knowledge of them is limited. As far as I can tell, those paintings were exact replicas of Chumash drawings found in caves around Santa Barbara.'

'Are there any more of these shamans around?'

'Not like Bobby. He was the last of them. He was taught to be an *'antap* by his father, who, in turn, was taught by his father. That kind of thing has been going on since the time your ancestors were banging coconuts on rocks to find food.' He put his hand on Bobby's shoulder and squeezed it gently. 'Something went wrong here. Maybe it was the war. Maybe it was before the war. I don't know. Ten thousand years of Chumash knowledge that was passed down to him is now scrambled and lost somewhere in his head.' He sighed and clucked his tongue several times. 'A fucking tragedy.' Pete stood up and took Bobby by the arm. 'Help me with him, Dutch.'

The Dutchman bent down, grabbed the Indian's other arm and lifted him up. They half carried, half dragged Bobby across the quay and on to the sand. The two Indians got out of the Jeep. One of them was a teenage boy with long hair and a bandana round his head. They took Bobby from them and gently put him in the back seat.

'I thought he was up to talking,' Pete said.

'He probably was until I mentioned the drawing of

the centipede. Did you see his face? He was terrified. I'm telling you, he knows who did it, Pete.'

Pete nodded. 'Maybe. We'll see.' He slapped Dutch on the arm. 'I'll call you when he comes round. We'll try again.'

He watched Smokey climb into the truck. The old Indian looked troubled. 'Too many legs,' Dutch whispered to himself. That seemed important to Bobby.

He went back into his trailer and made a call to a colleague of his, Jack Curphey, the chairman of the entomology department at Point Dune University.

'You interested in centipedes, Dutch?' Dr Curphey asked, after the anthropologist explained what he wanted.

'Yes, Jack.'

'Intriguing little creatures. Millions of years old. They belong to the phylum Arthropoda. Come on down. We'll talk.'

Curphey was in his small, overcrowded office filled with books and student's dissertations. Glass tanks containing different kinds of insects sat on the shelf by the unwashed window. The entomologist was peering into one that held large spiders when the Dutchman walked in. He was a tall, thin man, wearing a white smock that was too short for him. His bony, hairy wrists protruded several inches past the sleeves. The top part of his balding crown was shiny from the tonic that kept the hair on the sides of his head in place.

'Hello, Dutch,' he said without looking up.

Dutch went over to him and shook his wet, limp hand. Curphey was one of only a few forensic entomologists in the country. He and Dutch had worked on several cases together. The doctor was never called in on a murder case unless the body was in a state of decay. Several years ago he had shown the coroner's office how to determine the time and place of death by proving that the blowfly reaches the crime area way ahead of the police. Blowflies have a terrific olfactory sense, he told them. Within minutes of a death, they swarm over the carcass and deposit their eggs. The growth stages of the larvae are as predictable as the rotation of the planets. The police began using Curphey, especially when drugs were involved. He could pinpoint the exact geographical origin of a shipment by identifying the insects found in the seized contraband.

'Found a job yet?' His voice was soft and wet like his hands.

'No, Jack, I haven't.'

'Too bad. I'll miss you. You want to learn something about centipedes?'

'Right.'

Curphey pushed his glasses up on the ridge of his large nose. 'They're part of the Myriapoda class of arthropods.' He pointed to the spiders. 'Let me take care of my beauties first and I'll be right with you.' He opened up a wire cage next to him containing several live hummingbirds. Putting his hand inside, he snatched one and took it out. The frightened bird trembled in his clasped fingers. Curphey patted its head. 'There, there, my pretty little one.' The words were spoken with loving affection. Turning to Dutch, he gestured towards the tank containing the large spiders. 'These are Panamanian bird spiders. Hummingbirds are their favourite appetizers.' He opened the mesh top of the cage, tossed the bird in, then quickly closed it again.

'God's most wonderful creation,' Curphey said wistfully.

'The birds?'

'No, the spiders. If God favoured the humming-birds, they would be eating the spiders instead of the other way around. Now, what would you like to know about centipedes, Dutch?'

'How many different kinds are there?'

Curphey laughed in a high voice. 'How many? At the latest count, maybe three thousand. That doesn't include the millipedes which are very similar in looks. If you do include them, the count goes up to eleven thousand. Why?'

'If I showed you a drawing of one, do you think you can identify it?'

Curphey shrugged. 'It depends on how accurate and intricate the illustration is.'

'It's not an illustration.' Dutch took the Polaroids of the tunnel painting out of his pocket and showed them to the entomologist.

Looking at them, he once more began to laugh. 'Is this a joke? Who drew this? No, don't tell me. It was a kindergarten project, right?'

'It's an Indian painting.'

'I told you, there are eleven thousand species, most of them indistinguishable from the others. I need something specific to even begin to tell you what kind it is.'

'An Indian told me that there were too many legs on it. I counted forty.' He took out another photo, the one taken from the painting on the boulder at the reservoir. 'There are also forty on this one.'

342

Curphey looked at it, shrugged, and said, 'If you can see a centipede in this, you have an incredible imagination, Dutch. All I see is a few scribbles, probably made by a bored kid with a magic marker.'

Dutch felt frustrated. He didn't know where he was going with all this. Bobby saying that there were too many legs played in his mind like a stuck recording. 'How many legs does a centipede have?'

'The name, centipede, is a misnomer. Those cuties don't have a hundred legs. The *Scrutineer coleoptrata*, the normal centipede found in these parts, only has about fifteen pairs.'

This didn't make sense to Dutch. Indians, especially the ancient ones, only knew what was indigenous to the area they lived in. Why would the artist embellish the amount of legs? 'Do any of them have that many?' he asked.

Jack Curphey squinted his eyes, thinking. 'Yes, I believe there is one type that's large enough,' he finally answered. 'But it doesn't come from the southwest. In fact, it isn't even native to the United States. Come with me.'

They left his office and took the stairs down into the basement. Using a key, Curphey unlocked a door over in the corner and entered a large, rectangular room. It was dark and damp inside, with a pungent smell to it.

The annex was a concrete structure that housed rare insects and small reptiles. The sounds of living things crawling over wire mesh resonated subtly from all corners of the room. Curphey took a flashlight from the desk by the wall and turned it on. It emitted a small, yellow light.

'Centipedes are night creatures. They need humid

343

places to live or they'll dry up. They don't have a layer of waterproof wax on them like other insects and arachnids.'

They walked past tanks of strange, multi-legged creatures. As the beam from the flashlight touched their bodies, they shrank away from it and scurried quickly under rocks or shredded paper. The entomologist stopped when he came to a large cage.

Stooping down to look into the tank, Curphey said in a voice filled with loving emotion, '*Scolopendra gigantea*. That's probably your forty-legged arthropod.'

Dutch also knelt down. Inside was a huge centipede, almost a foot long. Its antennae started to move away from the light. 'Where's it from?' he asked.

'They're native only to Trinidad or Colombia.'

That was thousands of miles away. Why was this insect painted on a tunnel wall in Los Angeles? Dutch pointed to the centipede. 'How do you go about getting one of these things?'

'First of all, they're not *things*, Dutchman,' the entomologist said. 'Second, you just don't go about getting them. The Department of Agriculture is quite strict about letting insects into this country. The wrong ones getting loose could disrupt whole chains of species because there are no natural predators to keep them in bounds. What you do is contact a zoo in either Colombia or Trinidad and request them. Then you get an export document. When they arrive in this country, you show the papers to the authorities, proving that they were legally acquired.'

'That's it?'

'That's it. Except that *Scolopendra gigantea* is rare and zoos don't easily give rare species up.'

Dutch straightened. 'Is there anything special about them?'

'Their jaws. You wouldn't want to get bitten by one.' He stuck his finger into the tank, stroked the centipede's outer cuticle, then quickly withdrew when the sharp jaws moved his way. Turning to the anthropologist, he smiled and said, 'Care to try it, Dutch?'

When Dutch got back to Malibu, he found two messages on his answering machine. One was from the Channel Seven anchor and the other was from Kevin Rousette, the helicopter pilot who worked for John Payne. What did he want? He tried Marla first but her line was busy. He then called Rousette.

The man picked up on the first ring.

'This is Wilhelm Van Deer,' Dutch said.

'I had a feeling it was you,' Kevin replied. The voice was lively.

'I missed you yesterday. The cab ride back was a little long.' Dutch's voice was terse.

'Sorry about that. John Payne gives the orders. If he says to disappear, then I disappear.'

'What's up, Kevin?'

'I saw your sculpture of the dead girl on the news last night.'

'Yes?'

'Jonathan's real upset about this. You were on his mind yesterday when I flew him and Mr Scone out of Bell Canyon.'

'Too bad.'

A pause. Then, 'He's wrong, you know. If the girls were killed, then the guy who did it should be caught.'

'Did *the* Mr Payne say otherwise?'

'Maybe.'

'Why the sudden interest?'

'You helped me out at the grave-site. I like paying off my markers.'

'I thought you didn't like to talk about your employer.'

'Never on his turf.'

'What about now?'

'Try me.'

Dutch wanted to test the waters. 'I asked you yesterday: was John Payne in the army? You didn't answer.'

'Yes.'

'He was in the army?'

'Yes.'

So far so good, Dutch thought. 'How did he bang up his face?'

'You just asked that question.'

'In the army?'

'Yes.'

'In the war?'

Kevin clucked his tongue impatiently. 'Yes. Read *Time* magazine. It's all in there. Friendly fire. Napalm. Ask me something that wasn't in *Time*.'

OK, go for the big one. 'Did he know the twins?'

A longer pause this time. 'Perhaps.'

'Why perhaps?'

'I heard bits and pieces in the chopper yesterday. I can't be totally sure.'

'Who was he talking to? Miles Scone?'

'Yes.'

'Christ,' Dutch said out loud. 'What did you hear Payne say to him?'

'Something about how the girls weren't worth

346

anything when they were alive. Why the big stink about them now?'

'That doesn't necessarily mean he knew them.'

'I thought it did,' Kevin said. 'You have to have heard the way he said it.'

'You and I have to talk,' Dutch said.

There was a pause, then Kevin said, 'OK.'

'What's good for you?'

'Pick it.'

He suddenly remembered Marla. 'Let me get back to you.'

'One thing.'

'What?'

'What I say to you stays with you.'

'You got it.' Dutch hung up, then dialled Marla's number. This time it rang.

Her cheerful voice got on the line. 'We received one more call,' she said.

'From who?'

'A man. He said he knew the twins when they were alive. His voice sounded slow and flat, like he was high. It's probably nothing. Still, I'm passing it on to you because I told you I would pass on all the calls.'

'What did he say?'

'He said you forgot to put the mole on one of their faces.'

'That's it?'

'That, plus you screwed up on the eyes. He said they were brown, not blue.'

'Did he say anything else?'

'No.'

'What part of the country is he from? Did he mention that?'

There was a pause on the other line. Dutch could

tell she was scanning her notes.

'Here it is. Santa Alicia,' she said.

'Where the hell is that?'

'Inland a bit. Between Santa Barbara and San Luis Obispo. It's an agricultural area. The locals work in the orange groves and vegetable fields. Mostly Mexicans and Indians.'

Every reflex in his body became alert. 'Does this doper have a name?'

'James Ashton.'

'An address?'

'Yes. He didn't want to give it to us, or even his name. We had to put a tracer on the line to get it.'

'Is that legal?'

Marla laughed. 'We're in the news business, Dutch. You want it?'

'Yes. One other thing. I don't think you need to concern yourself with telling the police about this call.'

'They asked me to.'

'I know. It'll lead to nothing. Trust me on this one.'

Marla laughed again. 'You're lying to me, Dutch, but OK. That's it on the favours.'

'Thanks,' Dutch said. He copied down the address she gave him, then hung up.

He called Kevin Rousette back.

'Something came up,' he told the pilot. 'Let me call you tomorrow and we'll set a time.'

Dutch hung up the phone. He hated to put Kevin Rousette off. The man could change his mind and bow out by tomorrow. This, however, was more important and couldn't wait.

Marla said the man lived in Santa Alicia, and it was near Santa Barbara. Smokey Pete had told him today that the hills around Santa Barbara were filled with Chumash caves.

Before he left, he called Tara and told her to feed Bitch.

Dutch had a feeling about this one. His heart was pummelling. They had to be the girls. He was getting close, and he knew it.

20

Two hours outside Los Angeles, Dutch turned on to the 166 Highway. He drove for thirty more minutes, passing scores of pickers working in onion fields. The bitter aroma stung his eyes and he closed his windows. Eventually he came to the foothills of the Sierra Madres. The town of Santa Alicia next to the mountain's crest was nestled between the orange and lemon groves.

Ever since he left LA, Dutch had had the feeling that he was being followed. Nothing he noticed on the road, just an intuition. Each time he felt it, the back of his neck tingled. He found himself glancing every few seconds into the rearview mirror. Nervously licking his lips, he reached across the passenger seat and felt the cracked wooden grip of the Colt inside the pocket of his windbreaker.

He drove down Santa Alicia's main street. It was a town that had got lost between the cracks of time. A barber shop, a diner, a hardware store, Woolworth's and an art deco movie theatre with the name of a three-month-old film on the marquee lined the sleepy street. Men wearing straw hats and cowboy boots sat idly on chairs outside some of the stores. Most of them looked Indian or Mexican and were sipping bottled root beer. Two old Indians in serapes sat on the steps of the courthouse playing an ancient gambling game called peón.

Dutch pulled out a piece of yellow paper with James Ashton's address on it from his shirt pocket: One Vista Road. On the seat next to his bag was a Thomas Guide. He opened it up and scanned a map of the area but couldn't find the street he needed. He pulled the dusty Bronco into a Texaco station for gas and directions.

A teenage attendant, with stark Indian features and thick black hair, grinned at Dutch when he asked where Vista Road was. Sparse black fuzz covered his cheeks, like the hairs on a peach. 'You looking for Ashton?' he asked, putting the gas nozzle into the Bronco's tank.

'Yeah, James Ashton. How do you know?'

'You said you wanted Vista Road, right?'

'That's what I said.'

'Well, there's only one person livin' up there, man, and that's Ashton. One Vista Road. There ain't no Two or Three Vista.' The Mexican laughed, exposing three gold teeth. He took a greasy oil rag from his back pocket and wiped the sheen of sweat off his dirt-streaked face, then pointed a blackened finger in the direction of the mountain. 'You'll see an unpaved road behind the Vons parking lot a few streets down. That's Vista. You know Ashton?'

'No.'

'Be careful with that guy, man.' He pointed the same dirty finger to his temple. 'He ain't too right up here.'

'Is he crazy?' Dutch asked wearily. He had met enough lunatics this week to last a lifetime.

The Mexican shrugged and put his hands in the back pockets of his jeans. 'He blasted away at me an' my friends a couple of years back with the biggest damn gun I ever saw.'

'Why?'

Again he shrugged. He began shuffling his feet. 'I don't know, man. It was round two in the morning. All we was doin' was drinkin' beer and bourbon, and listenin' to some good heavy metal on the boom box. We was havin' a crazy ol' time. Ashton comes out of his house and starts firin' at us. *Bam! Bam!*' Holding an imaginary rifle in his hands, he began to mimic the man. '*Bam!* This fucker starts screaming an' cursing. Me an' my friends were so scared, we was shittin' in our pants, running in all directions.'

Ol' Ashton didn't sound so crazy to Dutch. A bunch of assholes rockin' 'n' rollin' at two in the morning would piss anyone off. Still, firing at a bunch of rowdy kids was a heavy thing to do, Dutch thought. He paid the Mexican, got in his car and drove several blocks to the back of the Vons parking lot. There was a road — more like a path — leading up the mountain. He put his vehicle into four wheel drive and slowly ascended the hill.

When he reached the top, the road divided. Dutch pulled over and got out. At first, all he could see was a dense forest composed of spruce, alder and laurel. He climbed up on the roof of his vehicle and looked in both directions, trying to see over the foliage. About a hundred yards to the right he could just make out the top segment of a red brick chimney poking out above the trees.

Suddenly remembering the story about Ashton and his big gun, Dutch leapt down from the top of the car,

crept around to the passenger door and took the Colt
from his jacket pocket. He tucked it under his jeans,
next to the crease of his back, then flipped his T-shirt
over it.

Just as he was about to get back into the truck, he
heard the sound of brush and leaves being pushed
aside. Crouching down low behind the door, his hand
reached around his back for the gun.

A tall stocky man, with a long, thick red beard came
out of the underbrush. He was wearing faded
Wranglers and an unbuttoned checkered flannel shirt
with a black T-shirt under it. Turquoise bracelets hung
from his wrists and a red bandana was tied round his
head. More turquoise adorned the thick belt encircling
his fat belly. A big game rifle rested over his meaty
arm. The back of his hand had a white poppy tattooed
on it.

Dutch slowly moved his hand away from the Colt
and stood up. The muzzle of the rifle was pointing in
his direction. It was a big bore Heym Express.
Expensive. The rifle could down an elephant at a
hundred yards.

The big man's eyes were hard and filled with
suspicion. A deep purple scar ran down the length of
his cheek and disappeared into the unwashed mass of
red beard. 'What do you want?' he asked. His voice
was surprisingly high for a man his size.

Dutch knew who he was by the size of the rifle that
the gas station attendant had described to him. 'I'm
looking for James Ashton. Would that be you?'

The man moved his thick index finger towards the
trigger. 'Why?'

A cold edge gripped Dutch at the thought of what
that gun could do. 'Because he knows the names of the

354

twin girls who were murdered twenty years ago.'

'They were killed eighteen years ago,' he said emphatically. The barrel of the gun was now pointed at Dutch's mid-section.

Again that abrupt sensation of fear tickled his stomach. That was the number Payne had thrown out at him. 'Eighteen years it is.' His mouth was dry and he swallowed hard.

'How'd you know where to find me?'

'The TV station. They know how to do things like that.'

Redbeard slapped his hand against a tree. 'Ah, fuck! I shouldn't have called them. I wouldn't have if I wasn't a little loaded.' He then looked dourly at Dutch. 'You a cop?'

'No,' Dutch quickly said.

'You that bone doctor they were talking about on the TV?'

Dutch nodded. His eyes were frozen on the big hole in the barrel of the rifle.

'You look more like a fuckin' hippie than a doctor. Cops know it was me that called?'

Dutch shook his head. 'Channel Seven is keeping it quiet. I'm the only one.'

Ashton studied him for several seconds, then said, 'You want to find out who killed them, don't you?' His eyes narrowed and his fat finger curled around the trigger.

Ashton expected an answer and Dutch wasn't sure what the right one was. He also wasn't sure what would happen if he happened to give the wrong one. He took a deep breath, and said, 'Yes, I'm looking for their killer.'

Ashton's face relaxed. 'Good,' he said quietly. He

pointed the muzzle to the ground. 'I knew they were killed. They couldn't just disappear like that. Nobody tried to find them. It was like they never existed.'

'You knew them?'

The heavy man nodded his head yes. 'Come on.' He turned and walked back into the woods. Dutch followed. The heavy branches engulfed Ashton and snapped at his body. He seemed indifferent to them, brushing them away with a flick of his fleshy hands.

A makeshift cabin came into view. Parked next to it was a black, shiny Harley Davidson 74 Shovelhead. The bike had to be worth a small fortune, Dutch calculated.

Ashton pushed open the crooked door that hung by one good hinge. Though it was noon and sunny, the thick trees blocked all light from infiltrating the house. Inside, Ashton turned on the lamp. He put the hunting rifle against the wall, stalked into the kitchen and opened up the small, grimy refrigerator. Grabbing two cans of Bud, he kicked the door shut with his black motorcycle boot and walked back into the main room.

Dutch was standing by the door scanning the place: newspapers cluttered the floor; large, big-based speakers filled both corners. Heavy metal CDs and cassettes were piled next to them. Ashton handed him a can and gestured for him to sit down on the velour couch by the wall, with the flattened stained pillows. A flag with a skull and crossbones hung over the sofa. Dutch sunk down into the deflated pillow. He wondered what Ashton did for a living. Something told him that he'd better not ask.

Ashton sat on a wooden chair across from him. He popped the tab on his beer can and took a deep swallow. The suds hung like white stalactites off his beard. He didn't bother to wipe them off. 'They were good kids,' he muttered.

'The girls?'

'Yeah.' Ashton stared into space, his eyes burning with hate. 'Beverly and Natalie.'

Dutch put his beer down on the coffee table and leaned towards Ashton. 'Beverly and Natalie? Were those their names?'

'Yep. Beverly and Natalie Stripling.' He took another long swill.

They now had names. The flesh was growing on their bones. 'How did you know them, James?'

Again the long, mournful look. 'They were in my history class in high school.'

'Where was that?'

Ashton looked confused. 'Where? Right here. Where do you think?'

Now it was Dutch's turn to look unclear. 'You mean they came from Santa Alicia?'

'No, they didn't *come* from here. They *moved* here. They originally came from Chicago. Say, you don't pick up on things too fast, do you?'

Dutch ignored his remark. 'Stripling doesn't sound Indian or Mexican.'

'No shit!' Ashton snickered, showing a mouth with several missing teeth. 'Everybody in this fuckin' town are either spics or redskins. Those girls were a welcome sight. Nice and white. You know the kind I mean? None of that Indian shit in them! Real beauties, too. Blondes. Their daddy moved here because of a job.'

'What kind of job?'

Ashton shrugged. 'I think he worked in the chemical

factory at the end of town.' He finished off his beer, got up and sauntered off towards the kitchen.

A moment later, he returned carrying two fresh brews, both of them for himself. He sat back down on the chair, put the cans next to his feet, bent over and began rifling through yellowed newspapers lying on the bottom shelf of the coffee table. His buttocks began to rise above the back of his jeans, exposing the crack of his ass. Ashton grabbed an old high school yearbook with a black eagle on the cover which he opened carefully. The pages were torn and discoloured. When he came to the middle of the book, his expression turned grim. He tapped the upper right-hand corner of the page with his finger. 'That's them,' he said.

Dutch took the book from him. The page contained about thirty black and white photos of smiling sophomores. He looked at the two photos Ashton had indicated. Natalie was the one with the mole on her face. He'd recognize the twins anywhere. *Hadn't he raised them from the dead?* Their faces in the pictures were glowing with health, wonderment and naivety.

Dutch looked up. 'You said they disappeared. Why didn't the authorities try to find them?'

Ashton ran his hand through his long greasy hair. 'They did for one night. Natalie was the first one reported missing. The next day it was Beverly and the father. The goddamn police came to my house and questioned me all night. A couple of days later the school got a letter from the father saying that Natalie was homesick and had gone back to Chicago by herself. He said that he had quit his job, and that he and Beverly had also gone back. The factory got a note

358

from him saying the same thing.'

'Did the girls have a mother?'

'No. She died. They just lived with him. When the police saw the letter and the note, they were satisfied and stopped the search.'

'How did you know about the letter?'

'I know lots of things, hombre,' Ashton said, winking.

'How long were they in Santa Alicia?'

'About four months.'

'You only knew Natalie for four months?'

'So?'

'Eighteen years later and you still remember the mole on her face?'

Ashton let out a breath that resembled a groan. 'We had a thing going, me and Natalie. She wouldn't have left like that without telling me about it. I went to the principal and demanded to see the letter. That bald-headed sonofabitch was always scared of me. He let me read it. It said that Natalie's father went back to Chicago, that he'd grown tired of Santa Alicia. I tried finding their number in Chicago. There was no listing. I even called the Chicago police, but they couldn't locate them. The dumb, fat-assed cops in Santa Alicia were no help, either. They wouldn't listen to me – I was only a punk kid to them. Something had happened to all of them – I just knew it. Years went by. Then I saw that model of her that you made, on television. Jesus, was that weird! It nearly blew me the fuck away, it was so real!'

Dutch's head was scrambled. None of this made any sense. Why had the father disappeared so abruptly? At least Dutch was lucky in one respect: the girls were in town long enough to get their pictures taken for the yearbook. 'Did you meet Stripling, the girls' father?'

'Yeah, I met him. Strait-laced. He didn't like me much. Said he hated bikes. He told me he didn't want me seeing Natalie.'

'Did he seem violent to you?'

'Hell, no. The guy was a wimp. A gust of wind would have sent him flyin' twenty feet in the air.' Then he understood what Dutch was hinting at. 'He was a scumbag, but he loved those girls. He would never hurt them.'

'Somebody did.'

'Whoever killed Natalie and her sister must have killed him too. I'd swear to it.'

His bones hadn't been found with the girls', but Dutch believed he was right. 'Do you remember any of the friends they made? Maybe Beverly had a boyfriend or something?'

Ashton shook his head. 'They weren't here long enough. Beverly and Natalie were very pretty, and the other girls in school didn't like them because of that. Beverly was different from Natalie. She was shy and she didn't take to boys much. She talked to me though. I guess you could say I was her only friend.'

'Do you remember when they disappeared?'

'Like it was yesterday,' the big man said, sighing. 'It was on a Wednesday. I was supposed to pick Natalie up at the schoolyard around seven o'clock. She was a cheerleader and was practising late for Saturday's game. When I got there, the yard was deserted. I went back to her house and talked to her sister who'd stayed home sick that day. She said she didn't know where Natalie was.'

'Where was the father?'

'Working late. He always worked late on Wednesdays.'

'Beverly hadn't disappeared yet, huh?'

'Right. But a couple of days after the police questioned me, I drove by the house and Beverly and her old man were gone. Totally disappeared!' He paused, thinking about that night, then said, 'I never saw them again.'

'All of them supposedly moved back to Chicago, including Natalie?'

Ashton nodded. 'You got it. Except I didn't buy it.'

'What about their furniture? Their clothing?'

'The house was rented. The furniture belonged to the owners. All the clothing was gone.'

Dutch leaned his head back and closed his eyes. The faces of the laughing blond girls floated through the corridors of his mind. He rubbed his eyes. 'The twins must have had lockers in this high school. What happened to the belongings inside them?'

Ashton grinned, then winked again. He stood up and went into his bedroom. A minute later he came out carrying a cardboard box. There was also a folded piece of paper in his hand. 'After I checked the house, I went back to the school and snuck down to the locker room. This is the stuff I took from their cubby.' He put the box on the floor.

Dutch knelt over it.

'You can look through the box. There ain't much in it.' Ashton said.

Dutch pulled out the twins' things: a sweater, school books, a couple of movie magazines, make-up, a school football jacket with leather sleeves. The jacket had a large eagle embroidered on the back, the same logo as the one on the yearbook cover.

'The jacket was Natalie's,' Ashton said, with a crack in his voice.

The Dutchman looked into the box to see what was left. A paperback copy of Miller's *Tropic of Cancer* and some ballpoint pens and pencils were on the bottom. He took out the book and thumbed through the pages. Several of them were dog-eared. Opening one up, he saw that it contained sexual passages, and that the sections were underlined in red ink. Probably Natalie's novel, he thought. She certainly wasn't a prude.

He put the book down, picked up the school jacket and went through the pockets: tissues, spearmint gum, a Trojan condom still in its packet, some nickels and quarters.

Ashton held out the yellowed piece of paper that was folded in half. 'I found this in the jacket pocket.' His voice was bitter as he stared at the prophylactic.

Dutch carefully opened it up and read the perfectly scripted words on it.

I watch you ride your bike every morning. Your golden hair sweeps the sky like an eagle in the wind. I love you, my little bird. Soon you will come to love me.
PS Get rid of the fat one.

There was no signature. But at the bottom of the note was a drawing of a centipede. Dutch didn't bother to count the legs.

'Do you know who wrote this?' Dutch asked, holding up the letter.

Ashton was fingering the condom. He looked disturbed. 'No. When I found the note, I began to think maybe there was someone else.' He tossed the prophylactic back into the box. 'We never used anything when we did it. What was she doing with this thing?'

Dutch delicately asked the next question. 'Do you know anyone she may have been seeing?'

Ashton's eyes grew cold and dark.

'Did she ever mention another guy's name?'

'Never,' he grunted.

Dutch put the letter close to Ashton's face. 'Whoever wrote this killed her. Think hard.'

Ashton took the letter and re-read it. 'I never could figure out who the fat one was,' he mumbled.

'I think you were, James.'

The half-filled beer can in Ashton's hand crumpled when he squeezed it, causing the brew to squirt out from the top like a geyser. His face turned red, and the scar on his cheek darkened to a deep purple. 'She was cheating on me. The dumb bitch was cheating on me! I thought we had something special.' He flung the crushed can across the room. It ricocheted off the wall and bounced on to the wooden floor, spraying the room with white foam. Ashton then clasped his hands over his face and rocked back and forth.

Dutch wiped some of the beer off his shirt, and waited patiently for the biker to calm down.

After a couple of minutes, Ashton lifted his head, pulled out a dirty handkerchief from his back pocket and blew his nose hard. 'Fucking women! They're all alike,' he muttered. He picked up the yearbook and flipped through the old, torn pages. Many of them were unreadable because of the beer stains. 'There was this one skinny jerk that used to follow her around. Natalie told me she wasn't interested in him when I asked her about the guy. I believed her. The kid was from a wealthy family.' He came to the page and dug his finger angrily into the photo.

Dutch moved over to get a better look. When he saw the picture of the boy and the name under it, his eyes widened.

'What is it?' Ashton asked, seeing the look on the Dutchman's face.

'This fellow came from here?' Dutch managed to get out, pointing to the picture.

'Yeah. His father owned that big chemical factory I told you about. It's been closed for years. That's where the girls' father worked.'

Dutch looked down at the photo again. The boy in the picture was a man now, but little else had changed. There were no heavy scars etched deeply into his cheeks when this photo was taken, but those feline eyes staring out from the page clearly showed someone with a vision.

'*Hellooo*, Jonathan,' Dutch whispered.

21

The middle-aged, conservatively dressed Beverly Hills real estate agent tapped her Mont Blanc fountain pen on her desk as she looked at the man sitting across from her who said his name was Harry Becker. He seemed relaxed, confident, successful. A New York producer moving to the west coast with a three-picture deal. She had worked with his type before. There could be a sale here, she thought.

The man, who wore expensive French jeans, light blue T-shirt and a navy double-breasted blazer, smiled at her. He crossed his Gucci loafer over one knee, put his hands up to his chin and shaped them into a pyramid. His black hair, with the small, dangling ponytail, was slicked back on his head.

'It's a beautiful house,' she said.

'Yes, I thought so, too. I was visiting a friend in Benedict Canyon and passed it.' He had a trace of a New York accent.

'Very traditional.'

'My taste exactly. How much are they asking?'

She opened up her book of listings and looked it up. 'One million two.' She glanced up to see if he flinched. He didn't. Yes, she just may have a live one. 'Is that within your price range?'

With his fingers still on his chin, he looked up at the ceiling. 'I was thinking more along one million flat.'

'There may be some play on the price,' she said quickly. 'The owners are serious about selling. They're building a house in Malibu.'

'Good. Is there anything wrong with the house?'

The agent laughed, causing her thick make-up to crack along the ridges of her mouth. 'Not at all. It's in immaculate condition. The owners are upstanding citizens in the community. Robin Diaz-Rampart is a criminal court judge. Her husband, Harris Rampart, is a Superior Court one.'

'My goodness. I'd hate to have to sue two judges.'

They both chuckled.

'Would you like to see the house?'

'When?'

'How about now?'

Hugo's basset eyes broke into a smile. 'I think that would be a lovely idea.'

'You know this jerk?' Ashton said, glancing over Dutch's shoulder at the picture of John Payne in the yearbook.

The Dutchman looked strangely at the big man. 'You telling me you don't?'

Ashton squinted his eyes, which wrinkled his sloped forehead, giving him the veneer of a Cro-Magnon. The big man moved in closer to get a better look at the photo. He slowly shook his head and scratched his cheek. 'He don't look familiar. Like I told you, bro, I saw him around the school. He was always staring at Natalie's tits. He came mighty close to being fitted with a new head by me a couple of times.' He glanced at Dutch. 'What do you mean, "Don't I know who he

366

is?'' Who is he? A movie star or something?'

'This guy eats movie stars for breakfast.' Dutch wondered what planet Ashton had been living on for the last twenty years.

'You think he had anything to do with Natalie and Beverly's death?'

'I don't know.' Payne was involved in some way, Dutch thought. Only a man with Payne's power could have influenced the police and the local government to obstruct the investigation of their death.

'How do I get to this chemical factory?' Dutch asked him.

'Why? What's there?'

'I don't know what's there.'

'Why are you so curious about it, then?'

Dutch went slow for him. He held up the yearbook so Ashton could look at the thin boy's picture. 'This is John Payne. The factory was owned by his father. You said that Payne followed Natalie around like a cat in heat. Suddenly she disappears. Then her father, who happened to work at the older Payne's chemical plant, quits his job. That same day he and the other daughter, Beverly, also vanish.'

A large *ahhhh* escaped from Ashton's lips as it dawned on him what Dutch was implying. 'You really think it was that skinny little jerk who did it?'

That skinny little jerk could have Ashton's head on a plate before he knew what was happening. His too, for that matter. 'It's a possibility,' Dutch said.

Again Ashton squinted his eyes, trying hard to comprehend everything Dutch was saying. 'You think that guy might have killed their father, too, then written the letters to the school and the factory to cover it all up?'

'I don't know too many fathers who would pack up and go back to Chicago when their daughter was missing.'

Ashton slowly scratched his beer belly, thinking. 'He could have walked if the price was right. The jerk's father owned the factory, remember? He had lots of money to buy Natalie's father off with.'

Dutch remained patient with him. 'You told me he loved those girls. I don't think there's enough money in the world to influence someone to do that.'

'I'd like to kill this fucker,' Ashton snarled through his teeth.

'We don't know if it was him.'

Ashton continued to rub his stomach, thinking about it. 'I think it was him.'

Dutch rolled his eyes. 'You going to show me where this factory is?'

'Yeah. It ain't far. I could show you.' He picked up his rifle, pushed open the door hanging from its one hinge and walked outside. Dutch followed.

The big man put the strap of the gun around his shoulder and began scaling the steep gorge behind his house. The Dutchman grabbed on to the boulders for support and lifted himself up the grade. They climbed about a quarter of a mile until they came to the crest of the mountain.

Dutch stood on the narrow rim and looked round. On one side he could see the vast blueness of the ocean and the town of Santa Alicia hundreds of feet below. In the other direction, he saw a deep valley. Except for several acres that were cut away, most of the land down below was covered with dense laurel and alder trees. But from this angle, Dutch could make out hundreds of marijuana plants growing in the exposed area. A camouflage net hung suspended over the crop so police helicopters scouring the area couldn't see it. Dutch now knew what Ashton did for a living. The gas station attendant and his drunken friends were lucky to make it out alive that night. He looked over at the big man, who had taken the rifle off his shoulder and was holding it firmly in his hands. Ashton, his head slanted suspiciously, was staring at the Dutchman. His jaw hung loose, and his eyes were set, as if he was contemplating what to do now.

Dutch quickly looked away from the marijuana fields.

'Nobody comes up here,' Ashton said, moving closer to Dutch, blocking his vision of the area.

'Pretty view,' Dutch said, his eyes fixed on the ocean. He could smell the big man's stale warm breath on his face.

'Very pretty,' Ashton muttered. After a pause, he suddenly said, 'Lots of Indian caves around here.'

Dutch turned to him. 'Caves?'

'Yeah, they're all over this fuckin' valley. Lots of weird shit painted in them.'

They had to be Chumash, Dutch thought. This used to be their territory. 'Any close by?'

'You want to see one?'

'I'd like to.'

Ashton thought about it for a moment, then turned down a gradient leading into the valley and towards the marijuana plants. Dutch trailed behind, staying a good distance from the biker in case he decided to turn round and level that big gun in his direction again.

As they made their way past the camouflage netting, the pungent aroma of the hallucinogenic vegetation filled Dutch's nostrils. They continued to climb down, holding on to trees and shrubbery for support. Halfway down the valley, Ashton stopped and pointed to something several feet from where they were standing. A gap could be seen in the side of the mountain. Most of the opening was obstructed by brush. Ashton went over to the cavity and tore away part of the foliage with his hands. 'I discovered this and a few other ones over the years,' he said.

Dutch went and looked into the grotto. It was pitch black inside. He had worked on anthropological digs before and he knew better than to rush in. Bending down, he gathered twigs and leaves and put them in a pile next to the mouth of the cave. Taking out the lighter from his pocket, he flicked the flame on and lit the dry material. It soon caught fire, filling the opening with smoke. Dutch quickly moved away from the hole and put his back against the rock wall. Within seconds, hundreds of bats flew out of the recess. Their high-pitched sounds echoed gratingly through the valley. Ashton screamed in terror as they swooped past him, brushing his face with their wings. He dropped his rifle and jumped in the air, slapping at his face. Confused, blinded by the sun, the bats circled once, trying to get back into the cave. Unable to penetrate the smoke, they flew off towards a dense patch of trees further down the slope.

Still clawing at his face, Ashton screamed furiously at the Dutchman. 'Goddamn it! You could have warned me!'

Dutch put out the small fire with his boot. Flicking on the lighter again, he knelt down and slowly made his way into the cave. He didn't have to go far before he saw the designs painted in the familiar Chumash colours of white, red and black.

The colours were much too bright for ancient paintings. He rubbed his hand on the wall as he had seen Smokey Pete do and licked his fingers. They tasted like animal fat, which meant they were painted in the not too distant past. And there was something different about these drawings compared to the ones in the Beverly Hills tunnel. Looking closer, Dutch saw what it was: the triangular and circular shapes were painted with a strange urgency. Little time had been taken with creating the forms; the colours were splotchy and uneven.

Further inside, Dutch found a drawing of the black centipede. Unlike the others, this painting was done with great care and detail. Again the arthropod had too many legs for a domestic species. However, it was the mouth that interested Dutch: sharp teeth protruded from its large jaws, and the bottom incisors overlapped the top ones. A strange feeling came over him when he realized that this was a human mouth implanted on the centipede. The eyes, angry and piercing, also resembled human ones. The legs were hands, with tiny claw-like fingers.

Dutch lifted the lighter. There were more drawings. Some of them resembled monsters of unimaginable horror: a face with pointed, blood-soaked teeth eating children; the silhouette of a deformed man putting terrified little boys into a sack; an old, hideous woman with the tail of a scorpion. Dutch was familiar with all of them. These were illustrations of the dark side of Chumash legends.

The further into the cave Dutch went, the more terrifying were the paintings. He felt he had entered the cavernous soul of someone who had descended deeper and deeper into madness. At the end of the

cave, there was a full-size drawing that took up most
of the wall. The depiction was blurry and smeared, as
if painted in great anger. It looked like the figure of a
man holding a little boy upside down by one leg over a
rectangular box. The man was painted red and the box
black.

Dutch walked out of the cave and into the bright
sunlight. Shading his eyes with his hand, he looked at
Ashton. The man was standing well away from the
opening. He was still slapping at his body, still
spooked from the bats.

'Do you know who painted the walls in that cave?'

Ashton had his mouth open in confusion. 'The
Indians. Who else?'

Dutch didn't pursue it. 'I'd like to see that factory
now,' he said.

Ashton nodded and walked past him, again
mumbling something about not warning him. He
continued up a small path heading north.

When they reached the crest, Ashton stopped and
pointed to a concrete building surrounded by a fence
and a barbed wire barricade overlooking the ocean.
'That's it,' he said. 'I brought you by a short cut.'

The building seemed deserted. The parking lot was
empty, and the concrete block walls needed painting.
The structure was still in good condition, and the land
it was built on was close to the ocean. The property
must be worth a fortune, Dutch thought. Why hadn't
the Payne family sold it after the factory closed down?

The two men made their way towards the linked
fence. They came to the back of the plant and saw the
loading area through the wire barrier. There was a
strange silence in the air as if nothing living had
touched this place in many years. They went round to

the front. The gates were chained and held together by a rusted padlock. Dutch looked up. The top of the fence was covered by barbed wire.

'Move back,' Ashton said, raising the muzzle of his rifle up to the lock.

Dutch took one look at what he was about to do and leaped out of the way. The sound of the blast was deafening, causing the Dutchman's ears to ring. He looked up at the gate. All that remained of the lock were steel shards dangling from the chain.

Ashton easily kicked the gate open with the heel of his heavy boot. Laughing, he turned to Dutch and patted the stock of his rifle.

Dutch moved his jaws up and down, trying to pop his ears. The citizens of Santa Alicia must have peed in their pants when they heard that, he thought.

As if reading his mind, Ashton said, 'The city council made them build this factory a long way from town in case there was an accident. A lot of dangerous chemicals were made in this place. I shot this gun around here many times when I hunted deer. Nobody ever came looking.'

'There couldn't have been much left of the deer after one of those cannonballs hit it.'

'Not much.' Ashton slung the rifle back over his shoulder. 'It saves me having to cut it up when I freeze it.'

They went up the factory steps and tried the steel door. It was locked. Over by the side wall, they saw a window coated with a wire screen. Several of the panes were broken.

Turning to Dutch, Ashton asked, 'Are we going in?'
'That's the idea.'
The big man grabbed the gun by the muzzle and

began to batter in the glass with the wooden stock. When there was a big enough hole to get through, he ripped away the screen with his hands. Ashton climbed in first, then Dutch.

Once inside, the Dutchman looked round. It was a large store-room consisting of several thousand square feet of empty space. Grey light barely made it through the other dirty plate-glass windows lining the wall.

As they walked along the floor, their feet sunk into the thick carpet of dust that covered it. Dutch realized it had to have been years since anyone was last in this building. Unused, flattened shipping boxes, covered with cobwebs and dirt, were strewn across the floor or leaning up against the walls. The Dutchman bent down and picked one up. Stencilled on two sides was the word XYLENE. He dropped the box back on to the stack, went over to a different section of the room and looked at another pack of cartons. He brushed the dust away from one of them. This one had TOLUENE printed on it. Dutch knew what that was from his college days at Indiana U. Toluene was used in the making of plastic cement. It was the chemical that got people high when they sniffed it. He straightened up and glanced through some of the other boxes that were leaning against the walls.

'What the hell you looking for?' Ashton asked, staring oddly at Dutch.

'I think this factory made chemicals that went into the manufacture of plastics.' He went through several more stacks. When he got to the far end of the room, he pulled one of the folded boxes out of the pile. There it was. TRIORTHOCRESYL PHOSPHATE.

Ashton, rubbing his beard in confusion, came over to Dutch. 'You find anything?'

Dutch held out the box, and pointed to the stencilled words. 'Triorthocresyl phosphate. That's the chemical that killed the twins. It's used in the production of plastics, like the other names on the cartons.'

'Payne!' Ashton growled. He squeezed the wooden stock of the rifle until his chunky fingers turned white. 'I'm going to kill that bastard!' He was staring at the broken window, his hand moving up the stock until it came to the trigger.

Did Payne kill those girls? Dutch wondered. He came from here. His father owned the factory that made the poison, and, according to Ashton, had followed one of the twins around for a period of time. Payne was also an expert in Indian lore and probably knew all about the Chumash cave paintings. He was certifiably strange; any psychiatrist would know that after being alone with him for five minutes.

None of these things, though, was enough to convict him of murder. There was nothing tangible linking him to the girls during the short time they lived in Santa Alicia. They went to the same school, that's all. Maybe the murders had to do with Natalie. According to Ashton, Payne liked her. She was a promiscuous girl. It was obvious that she was seeing someone else as well as the biker. Could it have been Payne? But what reason did he have for killing both of them, not to mention the man at the reservoir? Perhaps if Dutch knew the motive, he would find his proof.

Hugo went through the house slowly, lingering in each room. He nodded attentively as the agent talked, but wasn't listening. He was too busy looking for the reconstructed head. It wasn't in sight. Diaz must have hidden it, he thought. When the agent excused herself to go to the bathroom, he went over to the phone, found the number on the cradle and memorized it.

Driving back to Beverly Hills, the agent asked him what he thought of the house.

He shrugged, scrunching up his face. 'Too big. I'm a bachelor. Besides, the bathrooms are a bit too *fru fru* for me.'

Disappointed, she said, 'I have other listings in the area.'

'Good. Let me call you in a few days. I have to fly back to New York tonight.'

'Is there any place I can reach you, Mr Becker?'

'I'm in transit right now. I'll be staying at the Bel Air next week. We'll try again.'

That was two hours ago. He removed the wig, changed clothes in his car and drove to the desert. An explosion of fear began to rip through his body. He couldn't let the anthropologist find Steve's head. He hadn't destroyed it because of a vague sense of love for the man. That was a grave mistake, he now realized.

On the outskirts of Lancaster, Hugo turned off Highway 14 on to a dirt road heading into the desert. He drove several more miles until the gush of trailer homes and Winnebagos belonging to retired desert rats began to thin out. Eventually, only dry lake beds and sagebrush could be seen. Again he pulled off the road, driving over desert shrubbery and small cacti. When he felt sure that he was perfectly alone, he stopped the Jeep and got out.

It had been many years, but he remembered exactly where he had buried it.

He reached inside the passenger seat and took out an engineer's hammer. After walking a hundred yards over a dry gully, he began to climb down a steep hill.

When he reached the bottom, he immediately saw the two boulders jutting out from the mountainside. He went over and looked inside the gap that separated them.

It was there! After all these years it was still there!

Hugo reached in and pulled out the skull that was wedged inside. A small scorpion had its tail wrapped around the eye socket and was staring at him. Having no fear of insects, Hugo flicked it away like a piece of dirt.

He put the head on a flat slab of rock that protruded out of the desert sand and shattered it with the sharp edge of the hammer. When it was split into several sections, he turned the tool and began hitting the splintered bones with the flat part.

'Stay dead! Stay dead!' he screamed at the top of his lungs. The wind blew his voice out over the stark desert.

He hit the fragments again and again until there was nothing left but white powder that covered the boulder and his clothes.

Exhausted, he dropped to the ground. The sweat dripped freely down his chalky face and he gasped for breath.

That night up in the Encino hills eighteen years ago came rushing back, the memories stabbing at his body.

Visions of him and the wonderful man lying naked by the reservoir, their heads on the grass, their eyes focused on the few stars that had managed to get through the June clouds. The man with the slightly balding head was not like all the rest; he was gentle and kind, and his hands were soft and clean. He never asked him why he had no hair on his head or on his genitals. He never flinched at his deformed mouth.

The boy had met him on the Sunset Strip. At night the street filled with runaways just like him; boys begging for spare change or selling their bodies for twenty dollars.

After the girls died, he was afraid to go back to Santa Alicia. Not because of what he had done, but because of his father. The man frightened him. He always had. It had been that way all his life.

The authorities didn't concern him. He knew they wouldn't be looking for him or for anybody else in connection with the girls' disappearance. He had made sure of that.

Murdering the twins' father was easy. He knew the route the man took when he walked home from work. Hugo had followed him several times to make sure that he always kept to it. That night, Hugo waited for him behind a trash bin next to a deserted dry-cleaning store. It was right after Stripling had stopped at the police station to file missing person's reports on the girls. The man looked worried, preoccupied. He walked right past Hugo, not seeing him. Probably wondering about his daughters, Hugo remembered thinking, getting ready to bring the hammer across his chest. He buried the body not too far from the graves of the animals he had killed. Later that night, he broke into the factory and took the man's personal papers from his desk, plus his stationery. Assiduously copying his handwriting, Hugo wrote those letters that explained how he had found Natalie and was subsequently returning to Chicago with his other daughter, Beverly. Then he went back to their house, broke in, removed all their belongings and put them in his van. He brought them to LA and dropped them at the city dump, burying them under tons of garbage.

He stayed on in LA, living in his van. When the smell of the twins' decomposing flesh finally dissipated from the tunnels, he moved in.

After his money dried up, hunger drew him back out on to the streets. He knew he wasn't attractive because of his deformed mouth, but he had a lean, small, hard body, and he was adept at showing it off in tight jeans. Perhaps when it was late at night on the Strip, and all the pretty boys had already been taken, someone would pay for him.

Several men did.

Usually they were drunk, old or deformed. One was a paraplegic. Many of them were rough with him, demanding that he do degrading things. Once, in a hotel room in Hollywood, he slit open the belly of an oily-skinned truck driver with his Buck knife because he tried to whip him with his belt. Only one man had ever hit him like that: his father. It would never happen again!

It was a cool, overcast June night when Steve's red MG pulled up to him outside Tower Records. The driver smiled warmly at the boy, opened the passenger door of his car and asked him if he would like to go for a ride.

The boy was hesitant at first. The Strip was alive with street kids and pretty male hustlers. What could this faggot want with him? He could have anyone on the boulevard. Then he saw his arm. It was misshapen, the elbow protruding grotesquely away from his body.

Putting his hand in the pocket of his tight jeans, the boy began to finger the Buck knife for safety. He looked hard at the man's warm friendly face and bright grey eyes. Maybe he was for real. He took his hand away from the knife and got into the car.

They went to a small hotel in West Hollywood. The room was clean, not like the ones near Western Avenue where the other men took him. Steve was gentle with him and the boy liked that. No one had ever treated him that way before. Later, the man dropped him back on the Strip, gave him twenty-five dollars and asked if he could see him again. Hugo put his hand up to his mouth to hide its ugly shape, and nodded. He said he could be found on this corner every night around seven. This man could be his meal ticket, Hugo thought, watching Steve's car disappear down Sunset.

The boy stood outside Tower Records for several nights, refusing other men, hoping Steve would return. By the fourth night, he was cold and tired. He was just about to give up and go over to a waiting car with an old man inside, when Steve pulled over to the kerb in his MG. Smiling at the boy, he motioned for him to get in. He took him to a Polynesian restaurant on Pico Boulevard. They ordered a couple of Mai Tais and sweet and sour ribs. By the time the second drink came, Steve had told him that he was married with a three-year-old daughter, and that he worked as a CPA. He brought up his mutilated arm. He said he was born with the deformity.

The boy nodded, only half listening. With his big grinding teeth, he gnawed hungrily on the ribs, feverishly sucking out their marrow. He hadn't eaten anything but cold canned food for weeks.

Steve asked about him. The boy looked up from his food with wolfish, wary eyes. The man didn't seem to care that he was ugly and that he didn't have any hair. For the first time in his life the boy opened up to someone, told him about his alcoholic mother who had died of liver disease when he was young. Then he talked about his father and the terrible beatings he had received all his life. The only things he did not mention were the animals he had killed, the twins, and what his father had done to him when he was five years old.

Later that night, Steve said that maybe an arrangement could be made between them. He'd get the boy a place to live. Nothing fancy, mind you, just a small room, food and a little pocket money. He was married. Every time he hit the streets looking for men, he was playing with fire. Lots of diseases and crazies out there. His wife didn't know about his other desires.

The boy was elated. With his deformed jaw and the man's disfigured arm, they could almost be . . . twins.

Three days later, Steve found him a small one-room apartment off Highland and Franklin. They agreed to see each other twice a week. One of their favourite places was the Encino reservoir.

The boy now had a bed and could take hot showers whenever he wanted. All he had to do was fuck a tall, semi-bald man twice a week. He couldn't believe his luck. The *urge* was a thing of the past.

It came to an end thirteen days later.

He was lying in bed watching an episode of 'Bonanza' on a small black and white TV Steve had given him, when suddenly there was a loud banging on his door, quickly followed by several more thuds. The boy jumped up, went over to the door and looked through the peep-hole. His body began to tremble in fear when he saw who it was.

'Open the door!' his father screamed. 'I know you're in there! Open up!'

The boy quickly put on his jeans and grabbed his shirt from the edge of the chair.

The banging got louder, and the door began to splinter where the wooden groove of the jamb held the metal tongue of the lock. His father shouted again. 'You piece of shit! I'm going to kill you!'

Horror filled every inch of the boy. If his father got his hands on him, he would kill him. The door was ready to rupture. He looked frantically across the room for his shoes, but couldn't find them. They must be under the bed or under the couch. There was no time to search. He ran across the floor barefooted and tugged desperately at the window facing the fire escape, trying to get it open. It was stuck with paint. Panic-stricken, he kicked the plate of glass with the heel of his foot, shattering it. A sharp pain went through his calf. He pushed his body out of the cracked portal just as the door burst open. Looking up, he saw the large shadow of his father rushing towards him, his hands outstretched. In that split second, his father reminded the boy of the *haphap*, the evil sucking monster the Chumash feared in their legends. Hugo turned towards the fire escape as the older Frye's fingers grazed his shirt. Crazed with terror, he half-slid, half-raced down the iron rungs. When he touched down on the pavement, he ran past the seedy motels off the Highland and towards the neon lights of Hollywood Boulevard. Behind him he could hear his father's voice screaming out his name, calling him the worst things he had ever heard a father call a son. Tears stung his eyes.

When he reached the boulevard, he pulled a dime from his pocket and called Steve. The man had not given the boy his phone number. That was not part of

382

the arrangement. One night, when Steve had fallen asleep in his apartment, the boy had gone through his pockets and found his business cards in his wallet.

As the phone continued to ring, the boy looked nervously over his shoulder to see if his father was coming. How did he find me? he wondered. Bobby must have told him. I'll kill him! he thought. Answer the fucking phone! he silently screamed into the receiver.

Steve picked up. Hugo didn't let him say anything. He told him in a hardened voice that he needed to see him now, and to bring money and a set of clothes.

The man understood the implied threat and nervously said he would meet him. They agreed on the reservoir in a couple of hours.

When he hung up, he remembered that he had parked the blue van about a hundred feet from his apartment building. His father was roaming the streets around there. The boy went the long way round by circling the block, hoping to avoid him.

As he made his way towards the van, his leg began to feel warm and damp. He stood in the light of a lamp-post and looked down. The calf had been split open when he shattered the window. Blood flowed freely from the wound and ran down his leg. He looked up. Tourists, intermingled with the street people, had formed an arc around him and were staring, horrified.

Hugo had to keep moving. There were too many cops patrolling the streets. He wasn't eighteen yet. If they stopped him, they would take him in. He ran down a side street. Two more blocks and he saw the van. Limping badly now, he crossed the street and went over to it and opened the door. Just as he got in, he saw his father standing on the corner. His eyes were scanning the streets, looking for him. Hugo crouched down. He felt sick and weak. Turning on the ignition, he put the truck into first. With the headlights off, he drove slowly down Franklin Boulevard towards his father.

Then the *urge* rose up. It rushed over him like a powerful tidal wave, sweeping him into the bowels of hell once more. It was overwhelming this time. He clamped his jaw down hard, causing his huge protruding incisors to pierce his upper lip. The salty taste of his own blood stung his tongue. His eyes burned with hate. He quickly shifted into second and stepped down hard on the gas. The van picked up speed as it roared down the street.

He popped the gear into third. The speedometer needle was edging towards fifty miles an hour. Through tears of rage, he saw the figure of his father slowly turning his head in his direction.

He floored the gas pedal and jumped the kerb.

There was no time for his father to get out of the way or to scream. Just before the truck's bumper smashed into him, his face changed from fear to surprise when he saw his son behind the wheel. In the next instant, his body was lifted in the air by the impact, and his head crashed into the windshield, shattering the glass. Then he fell to the asphalt and was sucked under the wheels of the truck.

A hundred feet away, the boy stopped the van and looked out of the back window. The body was lying in a strange position. The axles under the chassis had ripped away the right arm and the bottom part of the left leg. Gunning the motor, the boy put the van in reverse, and ran over him again. He did that three more times before he finally sped off into the still night.

Even if anyone had witnessed the killing, it was too dark to see who was driving. He was in a maniacal mood. Sobbing one moment, laughing the next. The boy turned right and drove several miles on Cahuenga Boulevard. He then made a left and went up Laurel Canyon towards the hills. He tried to wash the blood off the windshield with the wipers, but the splintered glass made it impossible.

When he came to the secluded spot on Mulholland Drive, he parked the van. Steve's car wasn't there yet. Looking behind the seat, he found a soiled towel and wrapped it tightly around his leg like a tourniquet. He then lay down on the wet grass and waited for Steve. His body began to shiver from the cold night air and his lacerated leg started to throb.

Pleasure intermingled with the pain that raced through his body. He would never have to be afraid of that bastard again! He was free! Free like he never was before. But would he get away with it? Had his father told the neighbours in Santa Alicia where his son was living and that he was going to Los Angeles to find him? He doubted it. The man was too ashamed of him to say anything to anyone. It had to have been Bobby Santiago who told him where he was, he thought. The Indian was weak. He should have known better than to tell him anything.

He had killed his father across the street from where he lived. Would the police be able to put him and his father together at the same place? No. The apartment was leased in Steve's name, not his. In the two weeks he had lived there, nobody knew who he was.

He was home free.

No. Not true.

There was one person who could connect him to the man he had killed. The boy sighed. What a shame, he thought. If only Steve hadn't asked him about himself that night at the Polynesian restaurant. If only he hadn't opened up to him. From now on, he would never talk about his past life to anyone again, Hugo promised himself.

Ten minutes later, Steve came down the incline towards him. He was carrying a few pieces of clothing, as Hugo had asked him to do. The accountant looked disorganized and nervous. When he saw the condition of the boy lying by the water, he gasped. 'Are you all right?' He dropped the bundle, and bent down next to him, and saw the bloody towel wrapped around his leg. 'You need to go to hospital,' he said softly.

The boy shook his head no. Shivering from the cold, he picked up the sweater from the pile of clothes and put it on. Steve was big and the sweater hung on his thin frame like a shapeless sack.

Steve stroked Hugo's head. 'I'm sick of this lie. I don't care what anyone thinks any more. I'm taking you to a hospital.' His eyes began to cloud with tears.

Hugo nodded and touched his hand. Such a sweet, caring man, he thought. *Why him?* The Buck knife was in his pocket. He reached in and fingered the handle. 'Help me,' he said, with a trace of remorse in his voice.

Steve helped him up to his feet. Holding him around his waist for support, he led him towards the car. Hugo quietly took the knife out of his pocket and opened it behind his back with one hand. Clutching the bone handle, he thought again. *Why him?*

* * *

386

Now, Hugo stood alone in the desert, next to the pulverized skull. He had thought that it was an act of love back then to preserve Steve's head. He couldn't leave it with the rest of the body because it could be identified. Yet he couldn't destroy it. Looking back now, he knew it had been a mistake.

Stay dead this time, my friend! Please stay dead!

Hugo slowly laid his head against the side of the gully and began to wail − first like a human, then like his dream-helper, the coyote.

Please, dream-helper, come to me like in the past!

His cries rebounded back to him from the canyons.

Hugo cried uncontrollably for several minutes. When he was finally able to restrain himself, he wiped his eyes and nose on his sleeve and straightened.

His father was dead. He had killed him many years ago. There was nothing left of him. He couldn't hurt him any more.

A victim of a hit and run, the police said.

The boy returned to Santa Alicia with a well-rehearsed story about where he'd been for the last several weeks. He claimed he'd been living in the streets up in the Haight Ashbury district of San Francisco. After considerable questioning by the police, they began to believe his stories of escapades with drugs and women, and no one suspected that he had killed his father. They thought the boy had just run away, like so many teenagers in the early '70s. He used some of the money from his father's savings to stay at a boarding house until he finished high school. Since he no longer had a family, a social worker from the state was assigned to him and he had to report to her once a week until he turned eighteen. That would be in three months. He was gifted and his marks were always excellent. When he graduated from high school, he left Santa Alicia and never returned to that hateful small town again.

Today, he was a man with responsibilities. There could not be any mistakes. If he was found out, the humiliation of his childhood would be nothing compared to what it would be like now. He wiped the powdered bone from his face and clothes and walked swiftly back to his car.

Then he thought of the Dutchman, his twin. The *urge* inside him began to yelp with hunger, licking at his intestines. Having a twin meant not having to be alone. He had been alone for so long, since the day he killed Steve. Now, perhaps, it would be different again. Maybe one day he could share his story with Wilhelm Van Deer, and maybe he would understand. Especially when he saw how much they had in common.

22

'Now where are you going'?' Ashton asked, using the stock of his rifle as a walking stick. He was out of breath, attempting to keep up with the Dutchman's fast pace. They were heading back towards the path up on the crest. Directly below was the chemical factory.

Dutch turned around to look at the fat biker who was struggling to make it up the mountain. He waited for Ashton to reach him, then said, 'I need to find out more about Payne. He must have had a life in this town before he became a billionaire. If he did kill the twins, he may have committed other atrocities while growing up here. Maybe there were other similar murders in the vicinity. Maybe someone who lived here then remembers something, and with a little prodding might be convinced to talk about it.' The Dutchman began climbing again. Behind him he could hear Ashton gasping for air, trying to make his gelatinous body do things it wasn't used to doing.

When Dutch reached the summit of the mountain, he leaned over, gave the biker his hand and pulled him up to the top. Ashton was flushed and sweating.

'Does Santa Alicia have a newspaper?' Dutch asked him.

'Yeah,' the fat man said. He began to hack and cough. His face turned a deep red, and his lungs sounded like a radiator rattling on a cold night. When the fit subsided, he leaned over and put his stocky hands on his knees, trying to catch his breath. He then said, 'I should have shot you when I first saw you. If I did, I probably wouldn't be dying right now.'

'You'll live. Where's the news office?'

'On Main Street.' He leaned against a tree and wiped the sweat off his face with the front of his plaid shirt. His exposed white belly, the shape of a bloated pear, hung down over his jeans. 'It's a small newspaper, called the *Pacifico*. That's Spanish for Pacific.'

Dutch glared at him. 'You're a linguist. I'm impressed.'

'The paper comes out twice a week.'

'You actually read it?'

'Fuck no. I buy it to tear out the grocery coupons. You can save a lot of money doing that.'

Dutch thought he was joking; he wasn't. This Neanderthal would probably make someone a nice wife, he thought. He continued walking down the small path. When they got back to the cabin, Ashton said he wanted to go with him to the newspaper office.

The Dutchman, gritting his teeth, vehemently shook his head. He backed away towards the Bronco.

'Come on,' Ashton whined, following him. He grabbed the door of the four wheeler, preventing Dutch from opening it. 'Come on, man. I loved Natalie. I want to nail that bastard, just like you.'

Dutch scratched the stubble on his face and thought about it. This pot-dealer wasn't going to let him out of here until he agreed. 'OK,' he said finally. 'Meet me at the news office. But take your bike. I'm not coming back here.'

A smile broke out on Ashton's face. His eyes glowed, and he looked as if he was about to kiss the tall man on the lips. Dutch quickly jumped into the Bronco and sped off down the mountain before the biker could put his paws on him.

Dutch found the office easily. It was a small brick building located next to a barber shop with an old-fashioned red and white striped pole outside it. He hadn't seen one of those things since he was a boy. This town should be bronzed and put in the Smithsonian, he thought. He parked outside the news building and got out.

In the distance, he saw Ashton thundering down the street towards him on his big, shiny bike. A lazy dog lying in the road quickly scampered out of the way of the wheels, and a mother clutched her small open-mouthed son to her body as he roared past. He was wearing a black leather vest minus the T-shirt. Ashton pulled into a parking place next to the Bronco, sidled off the bike and strutted towards Dutch. Tattooed on his white hairless chest was the smiling figure of a robed Jesus looking like Dennis Hopper sitting on a chopper.

The Dutchman groaned to himself. This ageing biker was becoming a pain in the ass.

Behind Ashton, Dutch saw a large shape standing by the entrance to the hardware store across the street. As he started moving around the biker to get a better look, the shadow quickly darted inside the shop.

The Dutchman knew that physique well. 'Ciazo,' he said to himself.

'What?' Ashton asked, coming over to him.

So that's who's been following me, he thought. He had felt someone on his back during the drive here. What the hell does he want?

Ashton put his hand on the anthropologist's shoulder. His face was serious. 'Hey, bro, what's going on?'

'There's someone in that hardware store who's been trailing me from LA.'

Ashton turned in the direction of the shop. Cracking his knuckles, he said, 'You want me to talk to him?'

Dutch tilted his head and looked at the blubbery man standing next to him. 'He wouldn't hear you, trust me on that. This cop could cut your legs out from under you, and you wouldn't know they were gone until you tried putting on your pants in the morning.'

The biker's face turned pale. 'You didn't tell me about no cop.'

'Not a nice one. Stand out here and wait for me. If he heads this way, come inside and get me.'

Nervously stroking his bushy beard, Ashton nodded. 'Don't take all day, OK? I hate cops. If he fucks with me, he's dead meat.'

Dutch glared at him for a second, then went inside the newspaper office. The reception room was dishevelled, and like everything else in the town it had a post-Korean War look to it. Ageing Elks Club trophies and tarnished commemorative plaques hung on the faded green walls. Two old leather couches faced each other in the waiting room, and tattered *Life* and *Popular Mechanics* magazines were piled sloppily on the end tables.

The receptionist, a pretty Mexican girl, looked up and smiled at the Dutchman. Probably a high school student working part time, he thought. Somewhere in another room was the humming noise of the printing presses. Dutch asked her where the back issues were kept.

'I handle the back issues department,' a robotic male voice said from an office several feet down the hall.

Dutch looked over at the man. His frame was small and frail, and he looked to be in his early seventies. He was standing in the corridor, one hand in his pants pocket, and the other holding an electronic larynx up to his throat. A buzzing sound was coming from the contraption. The man must have had a laryngectomy, Dutch thought. His white shirt was stained with ink, and the sleeves were rolled up over his elbows. Paisley braces held up his wrinkled baggy pants, and wireless reading glasses hung on the bridge of his angled nose.

'What are you looking for?' the motorized voice asked.

Dutch smiled pleasantly at him. He wished he had dressed better for this. 'Anything you have on this town's most famous citizen.'

'And who'd that be?' The buzzing noise became louder as the man moved the machine closer to where his voice box used to be.

'Jonathan Payne.'

The old man frowned at the name. 'You a reporter?' he asked suddenly.

'No.'

'What are you, then?'

'Curious.'

'Don't lie to me. I know you're a reporter. You dress like one. In my day we wore suits and ties. What kind of writing do you do?'

'Dissertations.'

'You look too old to be in college.' He stared suspiciously at Dutch for a second, then gestured with his head for him to follow. 'Back issues are available to everyone. My name's Bloom,' he said as he opened a door to another room down the hall.

'Wilhelm Van Deer,' Dutch said. They shook hands.

Inside were shelves stacked with newspapers from floor to ceiling.

Bloom waved his hand over the contents of the room. 'The sum total of sixty years' worth of publishing.'

Dutch let out a deep breath. This could take weeks.

Bloom saw the frustration on his face. 'Why don't you tell me what you're looking for? Maybe I can help you.'

Dutch wished he could, but this man was basically a keeper of the past. He wouldn't know how to go about finding that flaw in Payne's personality that could link him to the twins. 'I don't know if you can,' he said.

'Along with my custodial duties, I'm also the editor and publisher of this paper. You saw our town. Its lifeline is down to a snail's crawl. Obviously, you can understand that I have a lot of time on my hands. Now, what is it you're looking for concerning Jonathan Payne?'

Dutch felt a burden being lifted off his shoulders. Maybe Bloom could be of help. 'Did you know Payne personally?'

Bloom grimaced. 'Slightly. I knew his father. He owned the chemical factory on the outskirts of town. The man also had a dog farm, bred them for profit. After Payne graduated from high school, he left Santa Alicia and joined the army. That's the last anyone around here saw of him. You know that man actually thought he looked like the actor John Payne.'

'You mean the guy who starred in *Miracle on 34th Street*?'

'That's the one. He didn't look anything like him. God, no! The actor was handsome. Payne was an ugly, skinny boy. He lived delusions of grandeur.'

'They're called visionaries.'

'Call him what you want. That visionary of yours never came back to Santa Alicia. With the fortune he made in his television stations and hotels, he could have revived this town. At one time Santa Alicia was a damn good place to live in. When he left, he took the heart and soul of this community with him.'

Dutch wondered what he meant. He glanced over the packed shelves. The room smelled of ageing paper. 'What happened to the factory? Why did it close down?'

'John's father, Henry Payne, disappeared. Nobody to this day knows what happened to him. The factory was his company and he ruled it with an iron hand. He also ran it like a Mom and Pop store. There was no one really capable of taking it over. John could have, but he chose to go to college after Vietnam instead.'

'He must have spent some time in the hospital first.'

'He did. Seven months in a VA hospital in Washington. His face was completely blown away. They had to reconstruct a new one.'

'Why didn't Jonathan take over the factory? He's a brilliant businessman. He could have hired someone to run it for him.'

'The boy hated the chemical factory with a passion.'

'I saw the plant. It was fairly big. Was it profitable?'

'Very. It also employed many people in the town. When the plant closed down, there was a lot of unemployment and hardship.'

'What happened to the dog farm?'

'That was sold.'

Dutch now understood what Bloom meant by Payne taking the heart and soul from this place. Without the factory there was nothing here for anyone. The town was now at its death rattle.

'I have it all on microfilm. Want to have a look?' He went over to a metal file cabinet, ran his finger down the dates of the contents and pulled out one of the films.

Dutch grabbed a wooden chair and brought it over to the viewing machine.

'It happened in '73. I remember the date because a few months later I went into hospital for surgery to remove a lump on my larynx and left there without a voice.' Bloom turned the knob on the viewing machine. The days and months sped by on the screen. He stopped when he came to August of '73.

The Dutchman looked up at him. There was anger in Bloom's face, something the mechanical voice could not express.

Dutch read about the plant and the affliction it caused when it was closed down. He continued to turn the dial upward, racing past earlier dates, stopping when he came to a front page article on the disappearance of the father, Henry Payne.

What happened to him? Dutch wondered. 'John Payne could have sold the factory and made a nice amount of money. Why didn't he?'

'Some things go beyond business.'

'Like what?'

'Hate,' Bloom said.

'His father?'

'Partially.'

'Who else?'

'The factory itself.'

'How could four walls inspire hate?'

'Henry Payne and the factory were one. You couldn't separate them. Any love that Henry was capable of, and trust me, it was very little, went into the business. The boy was denied his father's affection. Their relationship was strange, and often bitter. The father literally hated his son. He hated the boy because he was saddled with him after the mother died, and he hated him for being unconventional and a loner. John was an oddball, even in his youth. Except for one or two close friends, he usually stayed by himself. Sometimes he would go away for days at a time. When he came back, he'd look unkempt. His father would beat him to find out where he'd been, but he'd never tell him.'

'How do you know so much about him?' Dutch asked.

'We were neighbours. I could hear those beatings from my window. They were often quite brutal. The other things that he did to John, though, were probably worse than the beatings. Henry used to force his son to work in that factory every day after school. He was given odd and dangerous jobs that you wouldn't give the lowest paid servant. If there was a chemical or an acid spill, it was John who was told to clean it up. I remember seeing him several times with chemical burns on his hands. I heard one time he was forced to go up into the rafters to clean out a nest of dead rats that had eaten some of the chemicals. The

397

smell of the rotting carcasses was filtering down into the employees' work area, preventing them from doing their jobs. One of the workers who was there that day told me the boy was screaming and crying, begging his father not to send him up there. He said he was frightened of rats. Henry Payne grabbed his son, dragged him up the stairs and threw him into the room with the dead varmints. You couldn't really blame young John for hating that place.'

Dutch couldn't argue with him. 'When did he get hurt in 'Nam?'

'In '75. I think I have some coverage on that.' He went and got another spool of microfilm and popped it into the machine. Again the dates spun past. Bloom stopped turning when he came to the front page of November, 1975. The headline read: JOHN PAYNE BADLY HURT FROM FRIENDLY FIRE.

There was a photograph directly under the caption. Dutch zoomed in on it. A wounded 18-year-old John Payne, grimacing in agony, and holding a cloth up to what was left of his face, was being carried on a makeshift stretcher by four soldiers from his regiment. In the background, several transport helicopters were on fire. The Dutchman looked at the young stretcher bearers: two of them were staring down at Payne in horror. The other two had their heads turned away and were looking towards the burning aircraft. One of the soldiers with his face turned towards the camera caught his attention. He zoomed further in until that grainy black and white face filled the screen. Dutch put the eraser end of a pencil up to the monitor, tapped it and turned to Bloom. 'I think I know this one,' he said.

Bloom adjusted his reading glasses on his nose and

peered closer. 'He looks familiar. I may have seen him around town.'

'Around town? This kid came from Santa Alicia?'

'I think so.'

'I'd like a copy of this newspaper.'

Bloom went over to the bins, looked at the dates, then moved a wheeled ladder over to a section in the middle of the room. He climbed halfway up, retrieved the brittle, yellowed newspaper and handed it down to Dutch.

The Dutchman looked at the photo on the front page. It was clearer than the one on the microfilm. The anthropologist said, 'He's an Indian. His name is Bobby Santiago.' He was in his late teens then, around Payne's age, he thought. What really surprised Dutch was that they both may have come from the same town. In the photograph, Dutch could see the anxiety forged on Santiago's face as he stared down at the man on the stretcher. There was no doubt in his mind that Bobby and Payne knew each other. To encourage enlistment during that time, the armed services allowed friends who joined up together to be in the same unit. Were they friends in Santa Alicia?

He was getting close to connecting Payne with the girls. Dutch sat back down on the chair and smiled.

'You seem amused,' Bloom said, moving a chair over and sitting next to him.

'I'm thinking about sewers,' Dutch said.

'That sure as hell is different. You still haven't told me why you want this information on John Payne. You really a college student?'

Dutch ignored the question. 'You said that he went away sometimes, and when he came back he was dirty and unkempt.'

'That's true.'

'Did he ever show any interest in Chumash Indians? Did he ever mention painted caves to you or to anyone?'

Bloom looked up, thinking. 'Yes,' he said eventually. 'I remember his father complaining to me that all John cared about was Indian lore. Wait! Now I remember! The boy would go into the mountains around Santa Alicia to look for these painted caves. He did it with a friend of his.'

'The Indian?' Dutch asked, tapping his finger on the picture in the newspaper.

'I don't know. I heard Henry yelling at John about this friend that he supposedly hung around with all the time. He didn't want his son to see him any more. He beat the boy because he was starting to go to those caves more than he went to the factory.' Bloom got an introspective look in his eye. 'Drugs may have had something to do with it.'

'Payne took drugs?'

'His father thought so. I thought so, too. I remember John walking by my house once when I was mowing my lawn. He looked like he was in a trance, and he was stumbling, walking in a zigzag. He practically fell into the bushes. His eyes were red and droopy. I called out his name. He just kept going like he didn't hear me.'

Had it been Jimsonweed the boy was high on? Dutch wondered, remembering the roots that had been found in the sewers. The friend had to have been Bobby Santiago. He wondered if Santiago took Payne to the old sewers in Beverly Hills, smoked Jimsonweed with him and painted the Chumash symbols on the walls. Someone had lived in those caves eighteen years

400

ago. Why not Bobby and Payne? They were friends. Did they kill the girls together? If he could put Payne in those sewers at that time, then he would have enough circumstantial evidence to force an investigation. Dutch suddenly remembered the cave he had seen today near Ashton's property. Which one of them painted those gruesome drawings?

Dutch thought back to a couple of days ago when he, Bobby and Pete were talking on the breakwater. Santiago had looked scared. It wasn't over Ciazo. Was it Payne who frightened the Indian? That made sense. Bobby was the one man who could put Payne in the tunnels and, perhaps, even put him together with the twins. I'd be frightened for my life, too, if I were him, Dutch thought.

'Did Jonathan have any girlfriends?' the Dutchman asked.

'He never seemed interested in girls. He wasn't shy or anything. He just didn't see any place for them in his life.'

Carnal feelings were exceptionally strong in teenagers. If Payne didn't actively solicit girls when he was young, then he may have exorcised his sexual appetite in other ways.

'I would still like to know what you're looking for,' Bloom said, putting his face closer to Dutch's.

The Dutchman moved back. The sound from the larynx machine was hurting his ear drums. 'I think our friend may have killed two girls eighteen years ago, then buried their bodies in an old Indian graveyard.'

Bloom looked unnerved. 'Hey, wait a minute. I remember you. I saw you on television. You're the anthropologist who made those accusations at the

Indian grave-site in Beverly Hills. Why did you tell me you were a college student?'

'I didn't. You inferred it. I just teach at one.' His stomach was growling and he felt weak from not eating.

'You think Payne killed those girls? I wouldn't want to be the one who accused him.'

'I don't want to be the one either. I may not have a choice,' Dutch said, swallowing nervously. 'Did any other strange occurrences or crimes happen in this town while he lived here?'

'Depends on what you mean by strange.'

Dutch thought about it for a moment. He wasn't quite sure himself. 'The twins died from a form of asphyxiation. Were there any strangulations?'

Bloom shook his head. 'Not that I know of.'

'Any murders at all?'

'A couple of knifings during some bar-room brawls. That was it.' His eyes suddenly shifted. 'Do they have to be human beings that were suffocated?'

Dutch looked confused. 'What are you saying?'

'What about animals?'

Dutch began to understand. 'If I were this killer, that's what I would do. I'd practise on animals first until I got it right.'

Bloom's eyes focused on Dutch's forehead, then squinted as he tried to remember something that was lingering far back in his mind. 'I remember a story about pets disappearing in this town a number of years ago. Dead animals were dug up on a farm. They'd all been suffocated. I suppose I could go through the old files and find it.'

'Did they discover who did it?'

The publisher scratched his chin, thinking. 'I don't

402

think so.' He turned to the shelves containing the volumes of old newspapers. 'This may take a while.'

The door suddenly swung open and Ashton came into the room. His face was flushed with excitement.

'He's coming, and he don't look like he's in a good mood!' the biker said breathlessly.

'Damn,' Dutch muttered. He leaped up, pushing the chair away from under him. Pointing to the door across the room, he asked Bloom, 'Does that lead outside?'

'To the parking lot at the back. Why? What's going on?'

The sound of the front door in the reception area opening, then Ciazo's rough, threatening voice asking the receptionist where the Dutchman and the fat-bellied biker were.

Ashton's face started to turn pale as he listened to Ciazo's menacing tone. 'That guy could kill someone,' he said nervously, scratching his belly.

'He could and he has,' Dutch said, making his way quickly towards the back door.

The biker kicked a chair out of the way and also made for the back door. He and Dutch ran outside and around the back of the building. They inched their way along the red brick wall towards the street.

'What happened?' Dutch asked.

'The fucker came out of the hardware store and was staring at me,' Ashton said, his voice low and quivering.

'You do anything to make him come over?' He gripped the corner of the bricks and peered around the front. The streets were deserted. Ciazo was still inside.

'I don't like being stared at, man.'

Dutch turned to the sweating biker. 'Stared at is

better than dead. What the hell did you do?'

Ashton nervously furrowed his brow. 'Shit. I just grabbed my crotch, pointed to it, told him what he could do with it if he got on his knees.'

'Great move. If he had got his hands on your dick, he would have stuck it on his car antenna to get better reception. Dutch looked out at the street again. The Bronco was parked directly outside the news office but Ashton's bike was gone. He took the keys from his pocket. 'It was nice, Ashton, but I'm out of here.'

Dutch ran over to his vehicle, unlocked the door and got in. He tossed the newspapers in the back, started the engine and put the four wheeler into reverse. As he pulled out, a crunching, metallic noise came from under the chassis. The Bronco rose up over something, and thudded down on to the street again. Shifting into first, Dutch wondered what he had hit. Then he heard Ashton, who was standing on the pavement, let out a bloodcurdling scream. The Dutchman suddenly realized what he was yelling about. He looked in his rearview mirror and saw the biker's broken, twisted Shovelhead Harley lying in the parking space he just vacated. Ciazo must have put it behind his truck when they were inside.

He watched as Ashton rushed over to the broken remains, got down on his knees and lifted up the gnarled handlebars that were no longer attached to the frame. Clutching his head and rocking back and forth, he let out another wail. 'Motherfucker! Motherfucker! *Motherfucker!*' Spit ran down his beard.

People began to pile out of the stores on to the street to see what the commotion was all about. Ciazo

404

came out of the news office. He leaned against the window frame, folded his beefy arms and crossed his legs. A rare smile lifted the corners of his mouth.

23

When Hugo returned from the desert, he took Robin
Diaz's phone number from his wallet and dialled it.
Judges work from nine to five. He looked at his watch.
It was four o'clock.

A woman with a Guatemalan accent answered. The
housekeeper.

'Is Miss Diaz in, please? . . . No? I'm the clerk at
the Beverly Hills courthouse. I have a brief that she
wanted me to drop off. What time do you expect
her? . . . Six o'clock. That's too late for me. I was just
leaving. What about her husband? Is he in? . . . Out
of town, I see. Do you think I can just drop it off on
my way home? . . . Oh, you're terrific. Thanks a lot,
dear.' He hung up.

Once again he looked at his watch. He had two
hours. Not much time. The reconstructed skull had to
be somewhere in the house. The photograph of the
head on the news had been a bit blurry, and the
shadows harsh. A professional photographer would
have softened the features, making Natalie more
identifiable. With luck, that hadn't been done yet.

Hugo took a quick shower, washing the desert sand
and bone powder off his body. He then put on a low-
key sports jacket and tie. Opening the wardrobe, he

took out the blond toupee that was cut in the Waspish style of William Hurt. It gave him that fade-into-the-woodwork look he sometimes liked.

Hugo looked at himself in the mirror. Civil servant all the way, he thought, pulling the paisley tie up to the top of his ivy league, button-down shirt. He patted down the loose hairs on the wig, and left the house.

Just as he stepped outside, he had an idea. A brilliant one. He began to giggle, then rushed back into the house.

Hugo parked his Jeep in a public indoor garage in Beverly Hills, a block away from a Budget office. He rented a mid-sized, nondescript olive-grey Chevy, and drove it to where the Jeep was parked. He got out, opened the Cherokee's door and took a set of licence plates from the back seat. Making sure that no one was around, he quickly removed the old plates from the Chevy and attached the new ones. They were not listed with the DMV and could not be traced. He got back into the car and drove to Robin Diaz's house.

Since there were no pavements, Hugo parked the Chevy on the shoulder of the road a hundred feet down from the large home.

As he was about to get out, he spotted a TV cable truck in Robin's garage. *Damn it!* Again he checked his watch. He had a little over an hour before she came home. Hugo sat back and waited. How long would the cable guy be here? He'd give him fifteen minutes, then he would have to leave and try again tomorrow.

He thought about the housekeeper. Fortunately, she hadn't been there earlier so she wouldn't be able to recognize him now. The woman would probably know where the reconstructed head was. He would make her give it to him. Then what? Whatever happened afterwards would be in the hands of the *urge*. He would have nothing to do with it.

The *urge*. He could feel it inside him, waiting to be unleashed. It made him think of the twins, with their beautiful white skin and long blond hair.

The incident with the girls happened right after the beating from his father. The fierce anger inside him was overflowing like a volcano running amok. It had to be exorcised from his body.

If only that farmer hadn't bought that piece of land by the river and dug it up, the animals would never have been found. That's where he always buried the dogs and cats after he suffocated them. It was his cemetery. He alone created it and only he knew about it. He had been killing pets and wild animals and putting them there ever since he was five years old.

Taking his hate out on animals was the only relief he got from the terrible things his father did to him over the years. It was the only way he could appease the *urge*. When he was a teenager, he imagined that the painful *urges* were Chumash creatures from hell climbing up his intestines, clawing at his insides, trying to escape through his mouth. There were different kinds of creatures that made up the *urge*: there was the *haphap*, which was the sucking monster; then there was the ogre who stole children; and the old lady who threw burning trays at him. Bobby Santiago had told him a long time ago that these monsters were called *nunasis*, and that they came from the underworld to frighten children. Sometimes, when Hugo was in the depths of depression after a beating from his father, the monsters would become so real to him that he almost believed these Indian ogres existed.

The girls would still be alive if they had not found the animals, he thought.

The beating his father gave him. The shame!

He was awakened at six in the morning by his father's big hand snatching him by the arm and throwing him out of the bed. Hugo lay on the floor naked, looking up at the man's raging face.

'I'll kill you, you ugly little bastard!' his father roared at him. He grabbed the teenaged boy by his hair and slapped him sharply across the face. The impact of the blow shoved his razor-sharp teeth into the side of his cheek, splitting open his mouth. Warm blood gushed out and ran down his chin. Still holding him by the hair, his father dragged him outside the house and into the street. The pavement and the bushes ripped the skin from his legs and buttocks.

Though it was early in the morning, several of his neighbours were in the street. They wore their robes over their pyjamas, holding handkerchiefs to their faces and milling around the farmer's pickup truck. On the flatbed, over fifty decomposed carcasses and skeletons of animals were piled on top of one another.

'They found your name in a schoolbook that you left there!' his father screamed.

As the naked boy was pulled through the street, the small crowd watched in silence as Frye senior took off his belt and whipped him with the buckle end.

The pain! The humiliation!

The beating lasted for several minutes. It ended only when the bleeding boy slipped into unconsciousness and some of the neighbours grabbed the man and pulled him away.

His father had paid off the farmer, making him

swear that he wouldn't tell the police. The neighbours also promised not to discuss what happened. They saw no reason to see the man shamed in front of a courtroom for something his son had done. They liked Frye senior. He'd grown up in this town and was one of their own. Besides, the man had suffered enough from the loss of his wife.

It took several weeks for the wounds to heal. During that time Hugo was kept in his small room with no books, music or anything to write with. He was given one meal a day, consisting of stale, cold sandwiches. Light bulbs were taken out of the room, and thick cardboard was taped to the window on the outside to prevent daylight from seeping in.

Alone, the boy would close his eyes and pray for his lucky dream-helper to come to him in the shape of a coyote and take him away from here. Unfortunately, he had no Jimsonweed, and he could not see his supernatural guardian without it.

The nights were frightening. He hated the dark. The dark was filled with bad memories of what his father had done to him that horrible summer several years ago. Whenever he thought about that dreadful time, his breathing would become laboured, and the nightmares about the sucking monster would return to haunt him.

During that time in his room, he played with his toy soldiers and model aeroplanes, pretending that he was in Vietnam killing the enemy in black pyjamas. Most of the time, however, he stayed in bed, huddled up in the foetal position. With his arms wrapped around his legs, he spent his time thinking about his father and the different ways he'd like to kill him. The hate inside him was like a cancerous tumour that kept growing.

The insatiable *urge* that had been born during that long-ago summer, when he was a small boy, began to grow stronger during this time, nearly ripping his insides out.

He didn't want to kill the girls, not at first. But there was no choice. He could no longer kill animals. If he did, he would go to jail.

The boy first noticed them in the halls of his high school. They had just arrived from Chicago. He found them interesting. *Interesting* was the most he could feel for another human being. Each was the exact double of the other. The only difference was the mole on the face of one of the girls. Her name was Natalie. It amused him to watch her throw back her hair and sashay her hips every time she passed a group of male students.

At the beginning he desperately tried putting the *urge* out of his mind, but the hate for his father only got stronger. *Kill him, not the girl!* he cried out to himself. Once, he even went into his father's room late at night when he was asleep and held a butcher knife to his throat. He stood there for two hours staring down at the snoring man with the scent of gin on his breath. It would have been so easy. Instead, he lowered the knife and walked out of the bedroom. He couldn't kill him. Even in his sleep, that man held a terrifying power over him.

It had to be the girl! If he held off much longer, he would go mad.

If only they had left him his animals!

It took three weeks before he got up the nerve to make himself known. He drove by the school one evening and saw them practising cheerleading in the yard. His penis hardened and his mouth began to

412

water. He quickly scribbled the letter to Natalie. When the girls left the yard and went back into the school, he got out of the van, crawled through a slit in the chain-link fence and placed the note in Natalie's jacket. He quickly raced back to his van and sped away. For the next two weeks, he rode by the school at the same time and parked across the street. Natalie had noticed him watching her. She would smile and hold out her chest, making the pink knit sweater stretch tightly across her nipples. Sitting inside the van, he'd stroke his hard penis, eat dried mixed fruits and watch their supple bodies jumping up and down to the words of the school cheer.

The lights on the football field cast a pale glow on the muscles of their thighs. Natalie, as if sensing the exact moment he had an orgasm, would give him a knowing La Gioconda smile, then turn away.

That disgusting fat boy picked her up every day after practise. He'd wait outside the schoolyard and rev the engine of his Triumph, telling her to hurry up. Natalie would go over to him and straddle the back of the bike, lifting up her pleated cheerleader's skirt as she did it. Across the street, Hugo's large teeth would grind against one another as he looked at her solid rear end. When fat boy drove by his van, Natalie would turn and smile at him.

One day the fat boy didn't show up at the schoolyard. Beverly wasn't there, either. Natalie was alone practising with the other cheerleaders. Could he be this lucky?

He parked the vehicle and waited. When practise was over, he got out of the van, pumped up his nerve, and called quietly to Natalie through the wire fence. He stood in the shadows by a broken street lamp so the other girls couldn't see him.

Hearing her name, she turned around. When she saw who it was, she gave her aloof sexy smile and sauntered over to the fence. Unlike the other kids, she didn't seem to be frightened or repulsed by his protruding jaw and large overlapping bottom teeth. She pushed her compliant body through a hole in the gate and went over to him.

Smelling her sweat and perfume, the *urge* inside him began to surge through his veins like boiling lava. It had to be tonight! If he didn't have peace soon he would die!

'You've been hanging around every night. Who were you really staring at, me or my sister?' She had a smirk on her face.

He became less intimidated by her beauty. Suddenly he found her ordinary and dull, with nothing but boy things on her mind. Her thick Chicago accent was somewhat repulsive, and the sweet smell of the bubble gum she was chewing also disgusted him.

'I was looking just at you,' he said, putting his hand in front of his mouth to hide his ugliness. 'I was thinking maybe we could go out tonight?' He had never asked a girl on a date before.

She shrugged and blew a pink bubble. 'It was you who wrote me that note. Tell me I'm right.'

Hugo put his head down, smirking, pretending to be shy. He had seen Michael J. Pollard do this look in *Bonnie and Clyde*.

'I know it was you.' There was a sing-song quality to her voice, and her body swayed coyly back and forth. 'I've seen you around the halls. I've seen you watching me. Sitting in your truck all night . . . waiting. God! At first it scared me, then I started getting used to it.'

414

She let out a loud, nervous giggle. Then she squinted up her eyes, as if she were thinking hard. 'How can I say it? You know you're . . . you're like a little ol' teddy bear . . . it made me feel good, you watching me.'

A teddy bear! The moon behind the dark clouds blotted out the hate in his face. It will be tonight, he thought.

He spoke softly, pushing down the anger. 'Where is the guy with the motorcycle? I didn't see him tonight.'

'He busted up his bike, and had to get a part-time job stacking groceries at the supermarket to pay for it.'

'Where's your sister?'

She tilted her head to the side. 'Couldn't make practice. Girl stuff. That time of the month.' Natalie leaned tauntingly against the fence, chomping away on the gum. The top of her sweater hung loose, exposing the white flesh around her breasts where they disappeared into her bra.

The *urge* was like fire within him now, curling its fingers around his rib cage. 'Need a ride home?' he asked pleasantly.

She shrugged and cracked down on her gum. 'Sure.'

'Maybe you shouldn't tell your friends,' he said.

She cocked her head and looked at him strangely. Then she understood. 'You mean in case my boyfriend finds out . . .'

Hugo forced a smile. 'He's a big guy.'

'Isn't he though!' she said, laughing. 'Don't worry, I won't say anything.'

He drove around the corner, parked behind a large oak tree and waited for her to get her things. The other girls mustn't see him.

415

She met him at the van. He opened the door for her and she climbed in. When he suggested that they take a drive, maybe up in the mountains, she agreed.

All so easy.

He took her to a deserted place that he knew up in the Sierra Madres. After putting on the emergency brake, he turned to move closer to her and saw that she had her legs parted and skirt pulled up over her waist. Her panties were crumpled up, lying on the dashboard. Because of the darkness, he couldn't see much beyond her silhouette, and he clinically wondered whether the golden hairs between her legs were fine like angel hair or coarse and bushy.

She reached over and put her hand on his mouth and tried to stroke it. He roughly brushed her fingers away.

'I like your mouth,' she said heavily.

The rage! The urge! It started to swell up inside him.

'I thought I was a teddy bear.'

She giggled, then made popping noises with her gum once again. 'I like teddy bears. Especially when they have what you got.'

'What is it that I *got*?' he asked, looking away from her, biting down hard on his lip for control.

Again the chuckling and the infernal chomping of the gum. 'Don't you know what you can do with a mouth like that?'

He didn't understand.

She ran her hand up his thigh. 'The girls I know back in Chicago would give anything for what you got. Not my sister, though. Nobody can mess around in that royal crack of hers.' Natalie threw back her head and laughed at her own remark. When she finally managed to calm down, she said, 'James is the

416

worst when it comes to doing that.'

'James?'

'Yeah. The guy I date. His lips never get past my boobs. That and beer bottles are the only things he likes to suck on.'

She was talking about the fat one. Again the *urge* swooped up over his body. This girl was worse than commonplace; she was a nonentity. A fly to be squashed with a newspaper, then forgotten about. There would be no remorse in him for what he was about to do.

Natalie was now leaning against the door, her legs spread apart. One foot was up on the dashboard and the other on the seat. A pungent aroma emanated from her loins, filling the van. It made him light-headed.

'Now, baby, OK?' Her voice was thick. She lifted her body towards him, putting her hands around his head, trying to bring it down between her thighs.

The *urge* overwhelmed him, pulling and ripping at his organs. It became unbearable. It had to be now. *Now!*

So easy.

He quickly got on top of her. Holding one hand over her face so she couldn't scream, he turned her over on her stomach. He put his knee on her spine and grabbed her wrists, forcing them behind her back. Reaching into the glove compartment for the roll of industrial tape he had put there for this purpose, he wrapped the dark grey adhesive over her mouth, hands and legs. None of this was difficult: she was slight and small-boned, no match for his angular body.

He lifted her up, threw her in the back of the van and drove to the old sewer tunnels in Beverly Hills. It was after one in the morning when he got to the small street where the entrance was. He got out of the van, looked round to see if anyone was watching, then quickly pried the manhole cover away from the opening with a crowbar. After rolling the rounded steel plate over the kerb, he went back to the truck and opened the side doors. Covering the terrified girl with a tarp, he carried her on his back into the hole. He climbed down the rusted ladder, not caring that her head was knocking against the concrete walls. Dropping her like a sack of flour on the wet, slippery ground, he went back up and rolled the cover over the cavity. Climbing back down, he took her by the feet and dragged her through the tunnel. He left the tape over her mouth so he wouldn't have to hear her cry.

He lit a fire made of charcoal bricks. The smoke quickly vanished through the shafts that led out to the gutters of Beverly Hills. He took out the Jimsonweed from his pocket and began roasting it in the hot ashes. When the outside became crusty, he removed the root from the fire and ground it up against a rock. He then put the residue into a plastic cup and filled it part way with cold water. This was the dangerous part. Too little would have no effect; too much could kill him. Luckily, Bobby Santiago had shown him how much to use. After the mixture dissolved, he drank it down.

Closing his eyes, he leaned against the sewer wall and waited for his *atiswin*, the coyote, to come to him. He wanted the dream-helper to guide him in what he was about to do. In the past, the coyote always steered him in the right direction. As the hallucinations started, black, red and white shapes began to drift by his cavernous mind. A light appeared in the distance of his vision and started enlarging, covering his head in a field of white. His *atiswin* was coming, he thought happily. Soon he would see the coyote.

Instead, it was the dreadful *haphap* who came to him. The sucking monster that looked like his father. It was deformed, with sharp teeth and a mouth even bigger than his own. It had its jaws ajar and was sucking little children up into it. Just as it unclasped its gnarled hands to grab him, he forced open his eyes. Where was his *atiswin*?

Hugo was too terrified to drift off on the Jimson again because the *haphap* might come back. Instead, he stared for several hours at the terrified girl lying helplessly on the floor. Detached, he watched as exhaustion took over her body. The fear in her eyes and the muffled sounds coming from her taped mouth began to fade. When she fell into a deep sleep, he reached into his jacket pocket and took out the brown bottle containing the phosphate that he had stolen from the chemical factory. He went over to her limp body, ripped the tape from her mouth and quickly forced the thick liquid between her lips. She awoke and gagged, throwing up most of it. That was all right, he knew that small amounts of the poison would remain in her body. He forced the paralysing toxin down her throat several more times that night. By dawn, there was enough in her system to cause some muscular inactivity. He no longer needed to tie her up. She was helpless. The girl lay propped up against the painted wall, her mouth sagging open. Only her frightened eyes looked alive, watching his every move.

A thought occurred to him. Why not the other one, also? The other one was just as pretty. This way he would have two of them and the sucking monster would leave him alone.

So easy.

When it was dark, he left the immobilized girl lying in the tunnel and went out into the night through one of the shafts. He walked to his van and drove to the house where she and her sister lived. He knew the route by heart since he had followed both of them home many times. Luck was with him; he saw her twin sitting alone on the steps by the side of the house. She looked sad. Probably wondering what had happened to her sister, he thought. No one was around. He knew there wouldn't be. The coyote was watching out for him and would let nothing get in the way of what he was about to do.

He zipped his overly large navy sweatshirt up to his neck and pulled the hood over his head so she couldn't see his face. Only his beautiful, sad puffy eyes were exposed. Taking a Thomas Guide out of the glove compartment, he leaned over and rolled down the passenger window. He could see that her eyes were red from crying. He asked in a low, friendly tone about a fictitious address somewhere close by. At first she didn't seem to understand. Then he asked her again, this time with even more warmth in his voice. Her face brightened slightly. She inched her head in his direction.

Come to me. Hugo opened his eyes wide, letting her see how blue and innocent they were. He asked about the address again.

She stood up, went up over to him, thought about it for a moment, then stuck her head in the window to look at his map.

So easy.

It took them five weeks to die.

He fed them canned soup and water for three of

420

those weeks. When their oesophagus muscles eventually ceased to function, he stopped trying to give them food. He was happy about that, because without nutrients in their systems their excrement was less foul-smelling. Occasionally, he would use a funnel to force water into them. When he got tired of cleaning up their urine, he also stopped doing that.

During the first weeks of their captivity, he would drive in from Santa Alicia every night to be with them. After spending a few hours in the tunnel, he would make the three-hour drive back. The daily trip eventually became too much for him. His school work began to suffer. Hugo tapered off his visits. Seven days a week became five, then three.

When he came, he would sit for many hours cross-legged by the fire, high on *Datura*, talking to them, bragging, telling them about himself and all the things he'd done in his life, and all the things he still wanted to do. Sometimes he wouldn't say anything; he'd just drink more *Datura*, stare at the girls and listen to their guttural sounds as they fought for breath. Their faces contorted in pain with every cusp of air that managed to find its way down their frozen throats.

How strange they looked, he thought indifferently. They were propped up against supermarket cardboard boxes, their lifeless arms dangling across their limp legs. Their heads were angled upwards with their mouths stretched open, and they swayed slowly back and forth like hypnotized snakes. No, not snakes – centipedes.

He now understood why the creatures were sacred to the Chumash. The centipedes danced the dance of death for them.

Hugo also understood the horror the twins were

421

feeling now, and it excited him. He had felt the same thing, too, once. Sharing the same feeling made him part of them. He was no longer alone. They were his soulmates. It would sadden him when they died.

Natalie was the stronger and refused to give in. Her immobilized face somehow managed to convey the horror she felt as her sister fought for air, trying to inhale through paralysed lungs. Only when Beverly finally went into convulsions and stopped breathing, did Natalie give up hope. Her ocular muscles slowly became useless and her eyes closed. No sound, not even small groans, came out of her throat, because the laryngeal muscle was no longer functioning. Several hours later she also convulsed and died.

Their deaths saddened him. He was alone again.

He kept them with him for several more days after that. When he could no longer stand the smell, he dragged their bodies through the shaft to bury them next to the ancient remains that the Indian, Santiago, had shown him. Natalie's leg got stuck in a small crevice and he had to break it in order to get her into the smaller passageway.

The odour was so bad that he didn't go down into the tunnel again for several days.

Beautiful as the twins were, he never had any desire to have sex with them − alive or dead. The only times he saw them naked were when he took their clothes off to wipe the diarrhoea and urine from their bodies. When they died, he removed their garments once more. He took their sweaters, jeans and sneakers, and burned them in a trash can miles from the tunnel.

With the death of the twins and his father, the *urge* went away. The *haphap* was satisfied.

Until now.

Hugo stretched his arms in the Chevy, then looked at his watch. The fifteen minutes were up. He angrily turned the key in the ignition. Just as he was about to drive away, the cable man walked out of the front door carrying his tool kit and got into his truck. Hugo instinctively put his hand up to his face and looked in the other direction as the truck passed him.

The coyote was with him today. Grabbing an attaché case and the phony brief off the passenger seat, he stepped out of the car and walked diagonally across the street towards the colonial house. When he reached the door, he took a pair of surgical gloves from his pocket, put them on and rang the bell. A few seconds later, the peep-hole opened and a large brown eye peered out.

'Yes?' the voice said.

'I'm from the Beverly Hills courthouse. I called about an hour ago,' Hugo said blandly.

The door swung open a couple of feet, exposing a small, squat Spanish woman. She stuck out her hand for the manila envelope.

The door was opened just enough. He listened carefully for other voices inside. There weren't any. The housekeeper was alone. He put the attaché case down on the porch and handed her the envelope. Just as she took it, Hugo seized her wrist and pulled her towards him. Her body was hidden from view by the ficus trees on each side. Before she could scream, he had his other hand around her neck, cutting off her windpipe and voice. He let go of her wrist for a second, reached down and grabbed the attaché case. He then forced his way inside, closing the door with his foot.

Standing in the foyer with the frightened, speechless woman in his grasp, he quickly looked round. A large circular stairway wound itself up to the bedrooms on the next floor. Over to the right, the study. Past that, the living-room. The dining-room and the kitchen were to the left.

He opted for the study. Still holding the woman by the throat, he half dragged her into the room. It was filled with brass lamps, oak bookshelves and overstuffed couches.

Hugo threw her on top of one of the floral sofas. With his knee on her chest, he popped open the attaché case and took out a roll of industrial tape. He tore off a piece and placed the adhesive over her mouth, just as he had done to Natalie and Beverly eighteen years ago.

She looked up at him with terrified eyes. The passive expression on his face made the blood in her veins freeze.

With the quickness of a cat, he tore off another strip with his teeth and placed it over her nasal passages, preventing her from breathing. He then pinned her arms down on the couch with his hands.

She began to turn blue, her reflexes making her body jerk upward.

'The head,' he said quietly. 'Where is it?'

Her eyes widened and her frame continued to heave, trying to take in air.

'The head?' He could see her lids drooping. She was on the verge of passing out. Hugo lifted a corner of the tape, freeing her nasal passage for a moment and letting her suck in a small amount of air. A tinge of colour came back to her face. He then closed the tape back up again. 'Your employer has a model of a head. Where is it?'

The woman seemed to understand. Her head moved to her left. Hugo followed her eyes. There was a liquor cabinet and a cupboard. He smiled. Turning her over, he taped her hands up behind her, then removed the strip over her nose. She frantically began taking in air.

'Don't move. Don't scream. You know what I will do, don't you?' He stroked the back of her hair as if she was a little girl.

She nodded, trying to stifle a whimper that was escaping from her sealed mouth. Her body was shaking uncontrollably.

Hugo walked over to the cupboard and opened the door. It was filled with coats and jackets. He took an armful and dropped the garments on the carpet.

The large fire-proof safe was carved into the wall at the back. He tried the handle. It was locked. Hugo turned to the housekeeper, who was now crying. 'Do you know the combination?' His voice was low now and non-threatening.

She shook her head, her eyes bulging in her sockets.

Hugo let out a small sigh. 'Of course not,' he said. 'Why would you?' He sat down on the couch next to her and began to stroke her face, wiping the tears away from her eyes with his hand.

Hugo waited. It was not up to him to do what had to be done. He would take no responsibility in this. If the *haphap* came, then he would do it.

Holding her trembling head in his lap, he sat back in the fluffy down pillows and thought about what had happened to him when he was a child. It didn't take long. The *urge* began to awaken. It came over him like a gaseous explosion, jerking his body up from the couch.

He slid off the sofa. With his knees on the carpet,

looking down at her, he reached over and closed off her nasal passage, preventing her from breathing. Hugo stayed like that for a long time, watching with fascination as she struggled for breath. Her face turned from red to a deep blue. Just as she was about to pass out, he took his hand away from her nose so she could take one deep breath. When she had, he immediately squeezed the nostrils closed again. He did this for several minutes. The feeling of power and elation was strong within him, as it was when he had killed the twins.

All sense of time seemed to escape him. When he finally looked at his watch, he realized that he had stayed too long. Regretfully, he would have to end this. Robin could be coming home at any time. He kept his hands on the nose and mouth until the housekeeper went into a seizure and died.

He stared down at the dead woman. The *urge* had done this, not him. Too bad about the head. He would have to take his chances and hope that no one recognized the girl from the photographs.

Suddenly he remembered that he had a present for Robin. With luck, she would share her gift with the Dutchman. Hugo knew that he more than anyone would appreciate it. He reached into the attaché case and took out a small leather pouch, then left the study and went upstairs. When he came down several minutes later, an impish smile clung to his face.

He retrieved his case from the study and walked towards the front door. Just as he reached for the knob, he saw a female figure coming on to the porch. He glanced out of the small side window. A new black Mercedes was parked in the garage.

She was early, he thought, standing directly behind

the door with his back against the wall.

The sound of a key turning in the lock, then the door opening.

He quietly put the attaché case down on the granite floor. Death seems to always come in pairs, he thought, waiting.

24

Dutch got back from Santa Alicia just before nine at night and found Tara's Volkswagen parked behind his trailer. He edged the Bronco next to it. When he came round the front, he saw his assistant sitting on the cement steps leading up to the door. Bitch was lying next to her. Seeing Dutch, the dog wagged her tail and sidled over to him, her head hanging low to be petted.

Tara didn't look at him, her eyes set somewhere out in the black ocean. Her mouth was rigid and her hands were clasped over her knees.

The muscles in his stomach tightened. Something was wrong. He walked slowly over to her. 'Tara?'

She shifted her focus towards the silhouette of Catalina. 'Robin's dead,' she said impassively.

He stared at her blankly, refusing to believe he had heard her correctly.

She didn't bother to repeat herself. This time her eyes moved away from the water and down into the sand.

Dutch knelt next to her and grabbed her shoulders. He opened his mouth and tried to speak but no sound came out.

Her eyes moved up, clamping directly on to his.

'You heard me, Dutch. I thought it better coming from me than the police.'

His grip on her tightened. 'How?' It came out as a raspy whisper.

Tara wrung her fingers together, the skin turning white from the pressure. 'You don't want to know, Dutch.'

Detective Vincent Falcone sat on Dutch's couch, quietly staring at the anthropologist. There was no cagey smirk on his face today. A judge had been killed.

Dutch was straddled over a chair across the room from him, with his arms hugging the back. His eyelids were twitching involuntarily. He constantly rubbed them, but he couldn't stop their movement. A half-filled bottle of Stoly and an empty glass were on the coffee table.

'I know you had nothing to do with this, Dutch,' Falcone said. He scratched his head, not caring if his hair got mussed. 'We know you were in transit from Santa Alicia when she was killed. I'm here because her husband asked us to check up on you.' Embarrassed, he cleared his throat. 'He thought you were having an affair with her. You know how it is.'

Dutch glared at Falcone.

The detective held up a hand. 'The man's upset, Dutch. His wife has just been murdered.' He shook his head. 'I never saw anybody die like that before.'

Dutch closed his eyes tightly and clutched the slats on the back of the chair. 'I shouldn't have given her the skull,' he said.

'What skull?'

'The head of the twin. She was going to keep it in her safe.'

Falcone narrowed one eye, then nodded in understanding. 'The safe was open. There was no head inside. Lots of jewellery and bonds, but no head. We knew it wasn't robbery or the valuables would have been taken.'

'He just wanted the head,' Dutch said.

'Why did you give it to her?'

'Who was I going to give it to? You? Orville?' he spat out.

'What were you doing in Santa Alicia?'

'Doing your job. The twins came from there.'

Falcone leaned forward. 'You know who they were?'

'Do you care?'

'Don't be smart with me, Dutch. The man killed two women this afternoon.'

'Who found them?'

'Her husband. He just returned from San Francisco on a business trip. They'd been dead a few hours when he discovered them. The maid was killed first, also by suffocation. Judge Diaz's neck had multiple bruises. Looks like he spent more time with her.'

Dutch groaned, then slammed his fist on the chair back. 'That bastard! He probably wanted the combination to the safe. Knowing Robin, she wouldn't give it to him. She was from the barrio. She didn't scare easy.'

Concerned by her master's behaviour, Bitch touched his leg with her paw, but he didn't feel it.

'What did you find out in Santa Alicia?'

'That John Payne was born there. That he had to have known the twins. That they went to the same high

431

school together. Think you got all that, Vincent?'

Falcone exhaled deeply. 'Yeah. I just don't know what to do with all that.'

'I do.' Dutch's voice was cold.

'Her house was for sale. We checked with the real estate agent to see who she showed it to. She said she showed it to a movie producer this morning. He wouldn't give her his address. Said his name was Harry Becker. There's no one by that name in any of the theatrical guilds. She's working with our artist right now drawing a composite of the man.'

'What did he look like?'

'Typical for the movie business. Trendy clothes . . . a pony tail, black hair. She said he had sad eyes.'

That's the way the clerk at the police station described the man who paid for Bobby's bail, Dutch thought. Except he didn't have black hair then. 'Try the name Hugo Frye in your computer. See what you come up with.' He explained about a man using that name getting the Indian out of jail.

Falcone wrote it down on his pad. 'Look, if it's any consolation, I believe you were right. The sonofabitch who murdered the twins also murdered the judge and her maid. Unfortunately, not many people in my department share those feelings.'

Dutch let out a short, bitter laugh. 'Tell that to Robin Diaz and her Guatemalan housekeeper, Vince.'

Dutch sat in the back pew of the funeral home three days later, pulling at the knot of his knitted tie once again.

The pastor's voice echoed throughout the filled chapel. In the front pew, the husband sat with Robin's family. He was a good-looking man with grey hair.

432

His eyes were sunk deep into his skull from lack of sleep. A Latino woman, probably Robin's mother, sat next to him. She was bent over, her body shaking with grief. Another woman, pretty, with a lot of Robin's features, had her arm round the older one's shoulder, trying to comfort her. She was wearing a classy black dress with a matching veil. The sister, Dutch thought. Robin had told him about her. She was a literature professor at a university up in Oregon.

At the back of the room, two plainclothes policemen were stationed at each of the two exit doors, scanning the mourners, hoping the killer would have come to the funeral to see the results of his handiwork. It was a long shot. Sometimes it paid off.

He felt a deep sense of guilt over Robin. She died a horrible death for nothing. The skull was not important any more. He knew the names of the girls. But Robin and the killer didn't know that at the time.

The autopsy on her brain and neck showed that he had choked her nearly to the point of death a number of times. He eventually killed her by stuffing the sleeve of her sweater down her throat, blocking off her windpipe.

Bloom, the Santa Alicia newspaper publisher, had mentioned that there were stories of someone in that town years ago who asphyxiated animals. Was it Payne? When the funeral services were over, he would call the newspaper editor to find out whether he had uncovered anything more about it.

After the liturgy, he followed the small caravan of mourners to a cemetery in Westwood. Dutch stayed well back so Robin's husband and family wouldn't see him. He had already done enough to them.

During the service at the grave-site, Robin's mother

collapsed. Several mourners helped her up and sat her down on a chair. Dutch wanted to go to her, hold the old Mexican woman in his arms and say how sorry he was. But she wouldn't want that. Not from him.

When the funeral was over, he quietly left the cemetery and walked to the parking lot. Just as he was getting into the Bronco, he felt a hand touch his arm. The Dutchman turned round. It was the sister. Up close, she looked exactly like Robin.

'I know who you are,' she said. 'Robin used to tell me about you.'

His eyes welled up. 'I . . .' The words wouldn't come out.

She put her hand up to his mouth to silence him. 'You were her friend. Friends were important to Robin.'

The pain in her eyes was so potent that he was forced to look away. She reached over and put her cold fingers on his cheek, drawing his face back to hers. 'She wanted to help you. It was important to her.' Then her tears came. She put her arms around his neck and cried. The sobs erupting from her insides vibrated off his chest.

He folded his arms around her shoulders and held her tightly. He would find him, he told himself. He would find him and kill him with his own hands.

Stopping off at a gas station on Beverly Glen, Dutch went over to a pay phone and attempted to call Bloom to ask him about the dead animals. The old publisher wasn't in. He left a message with the secretary and hung up. Then he thought about Kevin Rousette, the helicopter pilot. The man wanted to talk to him about his employer. With Robin's death, he had forgotten all about him. He knew John Payne well. They had been together since Vietnam. Dutch had his number at home and would call him there.

Back in the car, he reached into the glove compartment, took out a bottle of Excedrin and popped three tablets into his mouth. His ear was throbbing again. One day he would find the time to have it properly taken care of.

Right now he wanted to see for himself where Robin was killed. Dutch drove into Beverly Hills. He also wanted to see if the killer had left his usual marking — the drawing of the centipede. When he came to her street off Benedict Canyon, he turned on to it, parking the Bronco in the same spot where Hugo Frye had parked. Dutch took off his tweed sports jacket, threw it over the back seat and got out.

Police tape surrounded the property. He ducked under the yellow strips and went up the front walkway leading to the door. A sign from the coroner's office stating that the house was off limits hung on the panel. Dutch ignored it. First he looked at the alarm light to see if it was activated. It wasn't. He then tried the door handle, rattled it. Locked.

He went round the back. The quiet was unnerving; the only sound was a mild wind blowing through the ficus trees. Dutch walked up the back porch steps and looked in the kitchen window.

He tried to lift the sash up, but it was also locked. Taking off his tie, he wrapped it around his hand and punched out one of the glass panes. He pushed his arm through and unlocked the window.

Dutch climbed inside on to the kitchen counter, then leaped down on the tile floor. A dripping tap and the steady hum of the refrigerator were the only sounds.

He left the kitchen and went into the hallway.

Dutch first looked in the dining-room and the living-room. Nothing seemed disturbed there. When he walked into the study, he saw the chalk silhouettes of the two women. One on the carpet, the other on the couch. He did not know which woman each belonged to. Dutch bent down and traced the marking on the floor with his fingers.

White fingerprint powder shrouded the furniture. Dutch looked up at the entrance way. He closed his eyes and tried to imagine what it must have been like.

Did you first walk into the study, Robin, and find the maid, or was the killer waiting for you in the hallway? Falcone said your purse was on the floor next to the front door, so I would have to go with the hallway. Then what? Did he drag you in here, and make you look at the housekeeper's grotesquely distorted face before he did those things to you? Did you fight him? The autopsy report said yes. Skin particles were found under your nails. The killer had B positive blood. I bet you went for his face and cut him bad. That way he would stand out. You knew that, too, didn't you? I will miss you, Robin.

Dutch moved slowly around the floor on his hands and knees and look around. He searched every inch of the area for the killer's insignia. It wasn't there. Getting up, he then went over to the walls and looked for the drawing. Nothing! This wasn't like him; the man needed to show that he'd been here.

Dutch walked into the hallway and went upstairs into the master bedroom. The blunt, naked feeling of being an intruder suddenly engulfed him as he looked down at the bed. It hadn't been made since the day she was killed. The floral sheets and the blanket were tangled up together. Did she and her husband make love here before he went off to San Francisco?

Mi morsa grande.

The police had left everything in this room the way they found it. Robin and the housekeeper had died downstairs, so there was no reason for forensics to examine the sheets.

Again Dutch searched the walls and carpeting for the drawing of the multiple-legged centipede. It wasn't here, either. Why not?

Dutch went into the oversized bathroom adjacent to the bedroom. There was a pleasant smell of lavender. He turned on the light by the wall.

Kneeling down, he searched the tile floor, then the walls. Again nothing. He looked under the sink. It was dark and wet here. He ran his hands along the upper back side of the porcelain basin. His fingers touched something hard and long, hidden away in one of the groves. It suddenly started to move. A strange sensation of slithering antennae touched his skin.

Then the pain . . . *Oh God, the pain!*

Screaming, Dutch pulled his hand away. Attached to it was a foot-long centipede. Its powerful mouth clamped on to the area between his thumb and index finger. The pain was like nothing Dutch had felt before. It was as if a hot piece of coal was welded between his fingers. Even in agony, Dutch knew he had to get the mouth open; the longer the arthropod held on to him, the more of its venom was seeping into his bloodstream. He swung his arm, slamming the centipede against the wall. The casing of the body cracked open and a trail of blood shot out and streaked down the flowered wallpaper. It still would not let go of him. Dutch smashed it against the wall

437

again and again. Parts of the shattered form broke off and fell to the floor, but even in death the iron jaws would not break loose.

God, the pain!

He was beginning to feel weak and light-headed. The Dutchman fell to one knee. Using all his strength, he grabbed the top part of the arthropod's mouth and pried the jaws open. When it was free from his hand, he flung the remains of the body across the bathroom.

Dutch tried to get up, but his legs were like elastic. Why was he feeling like this? *Oh, Jesus!* The creature's venom must be in his system. His hand was red and swollen, and he had to get to a hospital. Dutch wasn't sure how poisonous the insect was, but he couldn't take the chance. Then he remembered: *Centipedes paralyse their prey!* Could they also do that to a human being? *Oh, Jesus!* He had to get help! Holding on to the door jamb, he raised himself up. Slowly, he began to make his way down the steps towards the front door. His breathing was becoming heavy and laboured. He wanted to sit down on the couch and rest, but the thought of dying in the same way as the twins spurred him on. *Not that way! Not like that!*

Just a few more feet.

His eyelids began to droop and his vision was turning blurry.

Did the twins feel like this, too? he wondered.

As he reached for the handle of the door, it suddenly opened from the outside. Two human shadows stood at the entry way blocking out the sun. Dutch blinked his eyes several times, trying to get his vision back, but it was like seeing through vaseline-coated glass.

'You turn up in the wierdest places, Dutchman,' one of the shadows said.

438

It was a man's voice, and it was very familiar. Again he tried to see who was in front of him. He could only make out a bright blue coat. Next to him was another man, except this one was dressed in black. A police officer. When Dutch tried to open his mouth to speak, slurred, unintelligible words came out. His tongue had swelled to twice its size.

'I think he's drunk, sir,' the one in black said.

Dutch wanted to deny it. He had begun to do just that when he felt the ground sliding out from under his feet. As the floor began to shoot up before him, the hands from the bright blue jacket reached out and grabbed him under the arms, then gently eased him down on to the ground. Closing his eyes tightly, the Dutchman tried to block out the room that was now spinning faster and faster. Trying desperately to get air into his lungs, he began to smell the familiar sweet cologne coming from above him.

Falcone!

Breathing was harder now. The walls of his throat were beginning to close in. A strange, gasping rattle was coming from somewhere inside him. He could feel the detective unbuttoning his shirt, then smooth hands pushing down on his chest where his heart was.

This is too hard, Dutch thought. *Too hard*. The vision of Max laughing joyously, soaring in the air on his swing, came before him. Soon they would be together. The Dutchman relaxed, closed his eyes and waited.

'He's not breathing!' the officer yelled frantically.

'Aw, shit!' Falcone grabbed the Dutchman by his hair, putting his mouth next to his. 'Who do you love, baby? I hope it's me. Because I'm about to give you the best soul kiss you ever had in your whole fucking life.'

Falcone's words sounded like dim echoes to the Dutchman. The smell of cologne suddenly became more intense, and he felt lips on his own. Hot air began to race down his throat. The image of his laughing son with his arms out to him faded. Dutch opened his mouth and heard the rattle returning once more to his dry throat.

25

A man's high-pitched voice rang out somewhere above Dutch. 'Ah, we meet again.'

The Dutchman opened his eyes and looked up into the concerned blue ones of Dr Marshfield. The anthropologist automatically put his hand up to his head to feel for his ear.

'It's still there, Mr Van Deer. I had to redo the entire thing. Who sewed it on last? Salvador Dali?'

Dutch was disoriented and his left hand was throbbing. People in blue smocks swooped by, and the glaring light of an OR lamp hung over him. He was in the emergency room again, the one where he had had his ear sewn back on the first time. Dutch reached up and felt a plastic cup clamped over the bottom part of his face. When he tried to rip it off, Marshfield's hand shot out and stopped him.

'Oxygen. Mustn't touch, or you'll have a problem breathing again.' The doctor shook his head at him. 'One day your ear is gone, the next day a strange creature is nibbling away at your hand. I must say, you do keep my staff on their toes.'

Dutch looked down at his aching hand. It was discoloured and swollen. The V-shaped area between his thumb and index finger was wrapped in thick

441

gauze. Dutch tried to remove the mask again, and once more the doctor stopped him.

'You can take it off in a few minutes. First, let's get those lungs of yours working properly again. You're lucky to be alive. I gave you an antiserum to counteract the venom of that huge centipede. My goodness, but you do go in for the exotic. When the police brought the pieces of that thing in here, nobody had ever seen one as large as that. We called in an entomologist from UCLA to see if he knew the kind it was so we could determine which antiserum to give you. He said it was called a *Scolopendra gigantea*. He had no idea why its jaws were entrenched in your hand since its natural habitat is South America.'

Marshfield took a rectal thermometer from a tray and motioned with his finger for Dutch to turn over. 'We would be giving you an oral one if you didn't have the mask on. Please, Mr Van Deer.'

Dutch's eyes bulged at the thought of what was going to happen. Moaning, he clutched the steel corners of the gurney and turned himself over.

He was lying in that position when Falcone walked in.

The detective slid the palm of his hand lightly over the Dutchman's rear. 'Nice peach fuzz. I'm sure the residents at county jail are going to just love this tush when I book you for breaking and entering a house that was cordoned off by the police.'

Dutch tried to claw the mask away from his face again, but the doctor stopped him.

Falcone bent down next to the gurney and whispered into his ear. 'You and I were tonguing it for twenty minutes before the paramedics arrived.'

Dutch glared at the detective. 'Fuck you,' he

managed to mumble through the fog-coated mask.

The doctor pulled out the thermometer and read it. 'One hundred. Not too bad.' He moved around Dutch so he could see him. 'I want you to stay overnight where we can watch you. Turns out that it wasn't only the centipede's venom that almost did you in. The entomologist told us that the *Scolopendra gigantea*'s bite, although quite dangerous and painful, cannot usually kill a human being. We ran some tests on you. It seems that you're extremely allergic to its toxin.' He pointed to Falcone. 'Be grateful, Mr Van Deer. The detective here really pulled you through.'

Dutch turned over on his back. Falcone may have saved his life but he didn't need to have his ass exposed to him.

Marshfield began to undo the oxygen mask around Dutch's face. 'I think we're ready to breathe on our own now. How are we feeling?'

'*We're* feeling fine,' Dutch said, taking in several deep breaths. The muscles of his larynx hurt.

'We'll have someone wheel you up to your room in a little while.' Marshfield patted Dutch's arm. 'Just keep breathing.'

Dutch watched the doctor walk out of the room, then he turned to Falcone. 'Thanks,' he whispered. His throat was raspy and on fire.

'Don't mention it. Too many unexplained things have been happening lately.' He seemed nervous. 'That's why I went to the judge's house this afternoon. I wanted to look around for myself without a roomful of cops watching me. Lucky for you that I did, wasn't it?' He put one foot up on the brim of the gurney.

'I already thanked you, Vince.' Dutch cleared his throat, trying to get some of his voice back. 'Our boy is now leaving real centipedes when he kills instead of just their drawings. You guys can't be this dense. It *has* to be a cover-up.'

Falcone put his hands in his pockets, stared down at the floor and shook his head. He looked troubled. 'I don't know who's doing it or why. I just know it's happening, that's all. First, when I was told to give you a hard time at the Indian graveyard, I thought nothing of it. You and I aren't kissing cousins, you know. At least we weren't until this afternoon.'

'Who told you to give me a hard time?'

'Damn! I don't need this crap in my life.' He began to pace the OR floor and rub the back of his neck at the same time.

Dutch sat up. 'Who, Vince?'

'I don't want any part of this, Dutchman.'

'Then you should have let me die.'

He smiled bitterly. 'Maybe I should have. At first I thought it was just a joke played on you by the higher-ups. It came from the commander of my station.'

'I don't even know the guy. Why would he want to fuck with me?'

Frustrated, Falcone shook his head. 'I can't give you an answer to that. I just don't know. Ever since the earthquake, things have been different around the force.'

Dutch sat up on the gurney. 'How different?'

'The Beverly Hills station is where every cop dreams about working. Very few murders, no ducking bullets, drug deals are done discreetly in mansions and not in the streets. The only thing we do is give out some speeding tickets and occasionally drive a movie star who took a drug overdose to an upscale detox centre. Things started to change when you began clamouring about those goddamn bones of the murdered girls. The commander became edgy, snapping at everybody. This guy was an alcoholic with twenty years of sobriety under his belt. Right at this moment, he's at a bar somewhere getting drunk. Get the picture, Dutch? I could see the point of covering up all that Indian shit found under the streets. Beverly Hills would have taken a financial beating if the dig was allowed to continue. But not wanting to look into the murder of the girls. That's something else. What the hell gives?'

'Someone has to be leaning on him.' Dutch leaped off the table and went over to his clothes that were piled on a chair.

'Sure. But who? The police chief? The mayor? What difference does it make to anyone who those twins were?'

Dutch took off his robe and began to dress. 'Good question. They were your typical, basic teenage girls. One liked boys, the other was shy. There was nothing unusual about them. Unfortunately, someone living in their town took a fancy to Natalie.'

'Who?'

'John Payne, for one. He's the guy who's giving your commander a hard time.'

Falcone swallowed hard. 'You keep bringing his name up.'

'The man who killed the twins also killed Robin and her housekeeper. Even you admitted that.' Dutch sat on the chair and attempted to put on his cowboy boots. His sore hand was aching too badly to do it. He looked up at Falcone for assistance.

The detective bent down and helped him.

'Payne's father, a solid citizen of the town, went out one day and was never seen again,' Dutch said, staring at the top of Falcone's fashioned hair. 'The twins' father also disappeared around the same time the girls were killed. Then there's the bones we found next to the Encino reservoir. Our killer's been a busy boy.'

Falcone stood up and leaned against the gurney. He slowly shook his head. 'This is getting too big for me, man. *Jesus!* John Payne dines with presidents! I can't accuse him of these murders.'

'I didn't say he did them. You said it.'

'I know. It looks that way but I don't think he did. We showed the composite of the movie producer who was interested in the judge's house on TV. Good luck in finding him from that,' he said sarcastically. 'There were no distinguishable characteristics other than the pouched eyes. I don't believe Payne faked that with make-up.'

Dutch didn't either. Payne was too well known and the scars on his face were too deep to cover up. He took a good look at Falcone. The man knew more than he was letting on. 'You ready to be straight with me, Vince?'

The detective let out a small groan. 'Don't do this to me, Dutch.'

'Got to.'

Falcone pointed a manicured finger at Dutch. 'This goes no further, OK?'

Dutch nodded.

'Strands of coarse, grey-blond hair were found in the study and under Robin's nails.'

'Robin's husband has grey hair.'

'It wasn't his. We tested his. The man was cooperative.'

'It's also the same colour as Payne's,' Dutch said.

'This is the kicker. The hair was real, except there

446

were glue particles on the follicles,' Falcone said.

'A toupee? Does Payne wear one?'

'I don't know. I'm having it checked out . . . discreetly. The black hair with the pony tail could have also been a fake. There are thousands of people wearing wigs in this city alone, not to mention the rest of the country. The FBI and the local police are checking companies who manufacture these tops, getting the names of everyone who purchased ones with real hair. All this is going to take a while. When we get them, we'll throw all the names into the computer and see if it comes up with someone who likes to play with bugs. We came up with nothing on Hugo Frye.'

'I didn't think you would. What if our man, assuming it wasn't Payne, doesn't have a record.'

Falcone shrugged. 'It's the only thing we've got to go on right now. That and his blood type.'

Dutch also thought about the skin found under Robin's nails. 'Is Payne's blood type B positive?'

'Yes.'

Dutch let out a low whistle. 'Same as the killer. If he wears a wig, get a sample of it. Human hairs are unique.'

Falcone nodded, agreeing. 'This is where it really gets interesting. Wool fragments from a man's jacket were discovered on both female bodies.'

'What's so unusual about that?'

'It was of a Shetland variety. Get this one. Payne happens to own a large mill on the Scottish Islands and he has his suits and sports coats made there. I flew some of the samples out to Scotland Yard and they tactfully went through swatches from his factory. The fabric came from there all right.'

447

Dutch stood up and put on his blue broadcloth shirt. His mind was racing. He buttoned it up, then tucked the tails in his jeans. 'Where's Ciazo?'

Falcone's face turned to stone at the mention of the detective's name. 'Why?'

Dutch started to walk toward the door. 'Because I think he now works for Payne. He's looking for the Indian, Bobby Santiago. If he finds him, he's going to kill him.'

'Ciazo resigned from the Department two days ago. He cited personal reasons.'

'Right,' Dutch said.

'Where are you going?' Falcone asked. His voice was flimsy.

'To find Bobby. Want to come?'

Falcone shook his head slowly. 'Not if Jimmy Ciazo is looking for him.'

Dutch nodded in understanding. 'Where's my car?'

'In the parking lot. I drove it over. Maybe you'd better leave this one alone, Dutch. It has nothing to do with you,' Falcone said.

He wanted to explain to Vince that he had no choice; not after the twins had become flesh and blood. Instead, he just turned and walked out of the emergency room.

Dutch found his car and drove back home to change. When he got there, he thought about calling Therese. He stared at the phone for several seconds, debating. *What the hell!* He dialled her number. A young voice answered. It was the teenage daughter of Therese's next door neighbour. She usually stayed there and watched the house when she was out of town.

'Where is she?' he asked.

'Up north. She's going to meet with the governor and John Payne.' The girl's voice was tinged with awe.

Scone must be there, too, he thought. Damn it! He was still kicking dead horses.

Hanging up, he went into the kitchen and took several aspirins to numb the pain in his hand and ear. Dutch wanted to take something stronger but he needed a clear mind.

He collected a sack of dried dog food and took Bitch over to his neighbour, a widower and retired elementary school teacher. Dutch occasionally left his dog with him when he wasn't coming home. He told the old man that he'd pick her up later that night. Then he got into his Bronco and drove to the UCLA campus in Westwood.

Smokey Pete was an imposing figure, Dutch thought, staring at the Indian through the glass partition. He opened the classroom door and made his way to the back of the room and took a seat. Pete was standing in front of the packed amphitheatre lecturing his students on a Chumash narrative about the soul. The leather-faced old man didn't look up at the anthropologist once while he was talking, but Dutch knew he was aware of him in the room.

The students were entranced by what Smokey was saying. The man had charisma. He was theatrical in his gestures, like an actor playing to the last row in the house. His deep voice resonated throughout the big room.

Smokey was explaining that when a Chumash man died his soul went towards the west, following the sun. 'That's why the dead are buried with their heads facing in that direction,' he said. 'The sun lights the way for the dead souls. When they enter the light, their spirit becomes resurrected. The path to reincarnation was not a simple process. The Chumash's infrastructure was complex and their religious system quite diversified.'

Dutch laughed to himself listening to old Pete talk. In the classroom, the street lingo was dropped and the professional tone came out.

Twenty minutes later, the bell rang and the class emptied. Dutch sat at the back with his boots up on the chair in front of him. Pete was standing next to his desk, putting papers into his tattered leather briefcase. Long-forgotten Chumash words were written on the blackboard behind him. Without looking up, he said, 'What's happening, Dutchman?'

Dutch stood up and walked down the incline towards Pete. 'You had me captivated.'

'You don't have to stroke me, Dutch. What are you doing here?'

'I need to talk to Bobby. Time's running out.'

He snapped his case shut. 'Time for who?'

'For Bobby. Probably for me, too.'

'You saw him. He's in no condition . . .'

Dutch cut him off. 'Where the fuck is he, Pete? He can nail the killer!'

'You want to see Bobby? OK, I'll take you to see him. If you can make sense out of that crazed Indian, I'll make you an honorary member of the tribe. The man's popular. You're the third person to ask about him this week.'

'Who were the other two?'

'Ciazo was one. I told you about him. Yesterday, another guy came to see me. A big man. Red hair. Looked like he was strung out. Coke, maybe crack.'

450

'He have a diamond in his ear?'

Pete smiled. 'A big one. The Woolworth's variety.'

Dutch remembered him. 'What did you say?'

Pete walked towards the door. 'I told him Bobby was out of the country.'

'He bought it?' Dutch asked sceptically.

'The man was dumb, but not that dumb. I have another class to teach. You want to sit through it?'

'No. Just tell me where he is.'

Pete shook his head. 'He's scared. He sees you without me there, he'll go over the edge for sure.'

Dutch could understand that. 'After your class, meet me in the café outside.'

Pete agreed.

Dutch left the building and walked out into the hazy sunlight. Throngs of knapsack-toting students were trekking to their classes. He went over to the food stand across the quad, ordered a tuna sandwich and sat at a small outside table.

Why was he enmeshing himself in all this? he wondered. Everything in his life was falling apart: he no longer had a job, and the woman he still cared for was involved with another man. Yet he continued to remain obsessed with a killer whom nobody wanted to touch. Maybe he was finally becoming part of the human race again — a race he had dropped out of when Max died. To be part of something, one had to commit. Maybe that's what he was doing: starting his life all over again by committing himself to all the dead souls some madman had murdered.

Dutch sloped down in his chair, put the back of his head on the frame of the seat and lifted his face to the sun. It seeped through his bones, warming his soul. The sun was rebirth to the Chumash. It was becoming the same for him. He had been away too long.

Frank was sitting on the hardwood chair in the middle of Hugo's living-room. It was the same seat he had sat on the last time he was here. He stared at the sad-eyed, bald-headed man, who had deep scratches running down his arms. They were all red and swollen. Maybe they were infected, he thought. Some of the gouges cut right across the tattooed cobra. What the fuck had happened to him? If he had been in a fight, Frank hoped he had had the shit knocked out of him. Frank was holding a glass of that godawful iced tea. His clothing was soaked, partly from the humidity and partly from the drugs in his system. He was coming down from the crack, and his arms were twitching in all directions.

'You raise the heat in this place when you know I'm coming?' he asked.

Hugo sat back on the couch, holding a bowl of dried apricots in his lap, and smiled at Frank's irritability. The man looked bad, he thought. He needed the pipe, except he had no money to buy it with. That's why he was here. He held the bowl out to him. 'Care for one?'

Frank grimaced at the dull-coloured, sweaty fruit. The acrid odour in the house was making him queasy. Where had he smelled it before?

Hugo popped one in his mouth, taking his time with Frank, watching him grow more restless. The bald-headed man wasn't wearing a shirt or any shoes. Only running shorts. His hairless legs were curled up under him, like the arcing tail of a cat. Hugo's sinewy chest was so white, it was almost luminescent in the darkened room. 'Drink your tea,' he said quietly.

Frank stared for a long time at the slightly red

452

capillaries running through the droopy pouches under Hugo's eyes. They reminded him of rivers of blood. Fucker looks like a goddamn hound dog, he thought. He took a large swallow of the tea. It tasted bitter, like chemicals. 'What happened to your arms?' he asked.

'A cat.'

Frank glanced around. What cat? There were no cats in this house. The smell in here was getting to him. Why was it so familiar?

'What have you got for me?' Hugo asked.

Frank wiped his sweaty hands on his pants. 'I drew a blank, Mr Frye.'

The playful smile disappeared from Hugo's face. 'I gave you leads. Roberto Santiago is crazy. The man would stick out anywhere. I'm sure he wouldn't have been too hard to find.'

'Nobody wanted to give out any information on him. That old Indian, the one who teaches at UCLA, I think he knew where he was, but he wouldn't tell me anything.'

'You should have made him talk.'

'How? The guy's got some mileage on him but he's built like a brick shithouse. I came on hard, but the old fucker wouldn't move an inch.'

Frank turned his head towards the chest of drawers by the couch, the one Hugo had taken the money out of the last time he was here. It looked unlocked, but he couldn't be sure. Things were beginning to look blurry. Too damn dark in here. He rubbed his eyes. The next time Frye gets up to go into the kitchen, take what's in there and run, he thought. *Never should have come here to begin with.* Not after what he had begun to suspect. He read about the Dutchman and the bones in the newspaper. Frank wasn't stupid. He

453

could put two and two together, especially when he also read about the death of that judge who was friends with Van Deer. This hairless creep sure as hell must have had something to do with it. Maybe *everything*.

'What about his uncle? Didn't he know anything?' Hugo asked.

Frank quickly took another sip of tea. 'Nothing. He said he hadn't seen Bobby in weeks.' He gagged, thinking about the farmhouse in Riverside. 'What kind of place was that, anyway? It stunk of rotting meat.' Frank took another swallow, finishing off the glass. When he looked over at Hugo, he saw two of him. What the fuck's happening? Again he rubbed his eyes. The crack must be affecting my sight, he thought. *One more buy, then I'll wean myself off that shit. I mean it this time.*

'Let me get you some more tea, Frank.' Hugo stood up, took his glass from him and headed towards the kitchen.

When he disappeared into the other room, Frank got up from the chair. His legs felt strangely unsteady. He went over to the drawer, opened it and looked inside. It was empty. He searched through the other ones.

'There's no money in there, Frank.'

The red-headed man glanced up.

Hugo was standing next to the kitchen door, holding a refilled glass of tea in his hand and a package of cling film under his arm. Again that devilish grin was spread over his face. He squeezed the thick pocket of his shorts, letting Frank hear the sound of paper crunching inside it. 'This what you're looking for?'

A deep sense of dread came over Frank. As he began

to move away from the drawers, he suddenly fell to the floor. Something was wrong with his legs. He tried to get up but couldn't. *Something is wrong here!* Crawling back to the chair, he lifted himself up and sat down again. The seat was damp and smelled of urine. His? Frank's leg muscles began to quiver. When he touched them, he could barely feel anything. It was as if they belonged to someone else. He looked up at Hugo. He could hardly see him now. His sight was becoming more clouded. And that hissing noise! It was killing his eardrums.

Hugo put the box of transparent plastic wrapping on the couch and handed Frank the glass. 'You don't look well, Frank. Too hot in here? Drink up, then.'

Smokey walked across the quad and saw Dutch with his legs up on the chair and his face lifted to the sun. 'You ready to go, or you want to work on your suntan a little longer?'

Dutch moved his head away from the glare and looked up at the Indian. Pete's face was the colour of a worn copper penny. 'Where's Bobby?' he asked.

'Not at his uncle's. I just called there. Seems like this diamond-eared gent of yours also paid him a visit, trying to find out where Bobby was. He didn't tell him anything.'

'What kind of farm is it?' Dutch asked.

'A slaughterhouse for pigs. If the wind's wrong, the smell will knock you on your ass. The man is old. Sometimes he forgets to collect all the rotting carcasses.'

'That may be what Marsha Garowitz smelled when she was down in the tunnel.'

'More than likely. Bobby was staying with his uncle

around the time of the earthquake. That odour can get into your skin, it's that strong. He left there and came to Beverly Hills when he heard that they were digging up the street for the hotel.'

Dutch turned to the Indian. 'Where is he now?'

'The only place he has left,' Pete said.

Frank's eyelids were almost shut and his breathing was heavy and raspy. The glass was lying on the floor next to him where it had dropped from his quivering hand. A puddle of spilt tea was spreading around his feet. He tried to open his mouth to say something, but couldn't.

'Don't bother to talk, Frank. You'll only sound like a babbling fool,' Hugo said. 'Your iced tea was filled with succinylcholine chloride. I've been dying to try it ever since I borrowed it from an OR many years ago. It's a neuromuscular blocking agent used during surgical anaesthesia. The words too big for you, Frank? I'll simplify it for you. It's fatal when taken in overdose portions, and you have done just that. It also causes muscular paralysis, which you also now have. So don't think about trying to move. You'll just frustrate yourself.'

Frank tried. White spittle, generated by a minor convulsion in his body, dripped slowly down the corner of his sagging mouth.

'There is no known antidote and it is not a pleasant death. I'm going to do you a favour, because I don't have the time to watch you die. A pity. I would have liked that. You have narrowed down the options for me so I now have an idea where Bobby is.' He yanked out a large piece of cling film from the box and held it between them, making sure Frank got a good look at it through his swollen eyes. Then he continued to pull it out until it was all unwound. 'You like caterpillars, Frank? I do. They transform themselves into beautiful butterflies. They're the goddesses of the insect world. The metamorphosis takes place in a cocoon. Let's pretend you're a caterpillar, Frank. A nice big one with a diamond stud in its ear, and you're ready to make that change. Now all we need is a cocoon. What do you suppose we can use for one?' He pulled the plastic wrapping taut, causing a loud snapping noise.

Looking through the plastic, Frank saw Hugo's bulbous eyes. They seemed to be smiling now, not sad like all the other times. As the transparent film went round his face, clinging to his skin and blocking his breathing passages, Frank suddenly realized why the odour in here was so familiar. The reptile house at the LA zoo! His mother had taken him there to see the snakes when he was a boy. It had exactly the same smell.

Evening had given way to darkness by the time the Dutchman and Pete reached Santa Monica Boulevard and Crest Drive.

Dutch reached over to the back seat and picked up the newspaper clipping of John Payne being carried on a stretcher in Vietnam. He took the flashlight from the glove compartment and got out of the Bronco. A lot had changed since he was here last. Most of the streets had been repaved and the flow of traffic was back to normal again. There were no visible signs that an earthquake had taken place in this area only a couple of weeks ago. Beverly Hills had worked overtime in putting everything back to the way it was.

The air was heavy and lightning was beginning to crack open the night sky. Pete had his jacket off, and his shirt sleeves were rolled past his elbows. He pointed to the middle of the street on Crest Drive. 'Bobby used to get into the sewers by removing a manhole cover over there. Looks like the city took that away and covered up the entrance.'

'The city's very efficient at covering things up when it wants to be,' Dutch said unenthusiastically. 'Let's see how far Lenny and Marsha Garowitz got with their re-modelling.'

They turned on to the cul-de-sac and walked the short distance to the end of the block. Little had been done to the house. It was still split in half and unoccupied. The grounds around it were still broken open. Lenny probably didn't have the money or enough insurance to start rebuilding it, Dutch thought. He was glad of that now.

They climbed over broken fences and made their way into the backyard. Dutch shined his flashlight on the ground and moved the beam around until he came to the hole the police had dug to free Marsha. Fortunately, it hadn't rained and the sprinkler system didn't work so it wasn't glutted with water.

They slowly made their way down into the cavity. The walls of the tunnel felt damp. Dutch touched Pete's shoulder, telling him to stop. He listened for sounds. Everything seemed quiet. They continued to move, slouching down, until they came to the end of the fissure. The ceiling of the tunnel became smaller here and they had to get on their bellies and crawl. Dutch kept the beam in front of him. Bits of phalanges dangled from the tunnel. The pieces slid over the back of his shirt, feeling like a woman's fingers running down his spine. He cringed from the sensation.

Bad feelings began to fill his head. He shook them loose and turned his thoughts to Billie.

Cocoa-skinned Billie.

An old song of hers that he hadn't heard in years spun through his mind:

> *Blow, ill wind, blow away*
> *Let me rest today*
> *You're blowin' me no good*
> *No good*

It was his and Billie's song. Nothing that happened to either one of them had been any good.

Thirty feet in, Dutch saw the brief flicker of a light in front of him, then it went out. He's down here! he thought.

'Bobby!' Pete yelled. He had also seen the light. His voice was hollow in the tunnel. 'Bobby, goddamn it! I know it's you!'

The sound of movement where the light went out. Dutch pointed his flashlight in that direction. He could make out a foot with a torn sneaker disappearing into a smaller interlocking shaft. Slithering like a snake, Dutch quickly made his way through the sewer to the connecting tunnel.

When he saw the tiny size of the pipe, Dutch groaned. Every part of his being wanted him to turn round. He could barely get his large shoulders in through that opening. Forcing the feelings of fear away, he began to wriggle his body into the small shaft. There were only inches to spare around him.

'I feel like I'm a piece of pork wrapped in sausage skin,' he heard Pete say right behind him. He was also trying to fit his frame into the hole. The man was even bigger than Dutch.

Somewhere down the tunnel, the Dutchman could hear Bobby. The Indian was smaller boned than he or Pete, and he was getting further away from them. Suddenly, there was a dull banging noise, then cursing in Spanish.

I got him! Dutch thought, trying to move faster.

Several yards further in, Dutch knew he was right. The tiny shaft gave way to a ten-foot vertical round brick tunnel. It led up to the street on Crest Drive. It was the hole that the city had covered over. Bobby was trapped.

Dutch dropped down into the larger recess. It was big enough here for him to stand upright. He shone the flashlight on the iron ladder leading up to the street. Bobby was on the top rung banging furiously on the concrete slab where the manhole cover once was. When he heard Dutch behind him, he turned and glared at him like a trapped animal. His unwashed jeans clung to the lower part of his bony hips, and his tattered shirt was mostly torn away from his body.

'Bobby! Get the hell down from there!' Pete said, as he crawled through the shaft and also dropped the couple of feet into the tunnel.

The small Indian looked confused for a second as he recognized Pete, then the panic took over once more. He looked up and began clawing at the slab again.

'This dumb Indian is going to rip his fingers off,' Pete said in disgust.

Dutch reached up on to the ladder, grabbed Bobby by his foot and roughly pulled him down. The Indian broke away from him and scampered over the floor towards the shaft. Before he could get his body through it, Pete and Dutch each grabbed a leg. Together they dragged him back into the tunnel. The Indian kicked and threw punches, trying to break their grip. He slipped away and crouched down, staring at Smokey then at Dutch. There was nothing human about him. He was filthy, his long hair hung in his face, and his wild eyes seethed with hate and fear. Bobby looked more like a treed primate than a man. Letting out a yell, he charged the Dutchman. The anthropologist quickly moved out of the way, and Bobby hit the brick wall hard. He fell to the ground, then got up again. Once more he lowered his shoulders, getting ready to attack.

'Oh, hell, I don't have time for this shit!' Pete said. He grabbed Bobby by his dirty hair with one hand and punched him in the stomach with the other. The Indian sunk to his knees and rolled around the ground, holding his gut. Moans sputtered from his mouth.

'Give him a couple of minutes,' Pete said to Dutch. 'Let him catch his breath.'

Both men knelt next to the Indian with their backs up against the brick wall and waited. When Bobby finally managed to stop gasping, Pete grabbed him by his torn shirt with both hands, lifting his head off the ground. The Indian tried to get away, but Smokey held tight and began shaking him. Bobby's head bobbed up and down so hard it looked like it would snap off.

'Don't try it again,' Pete warned him. He pushed Bobby back down on the floor. 'Now, this man wants to talk to you. I want you to listen hard.' His voice turned gentle. 'I know you're scared, Bobby. I even know who's doing the scaring. Don't worry about it. We'll take care of you.'

Bobby's eyes turned dead from terror.

'It's OK, *compadre*. Nobody's going to hurt you,' Pete said. 'I promised you when you came back from Vietnam I'd look after you, didn't I? That's what I've been doing, right?'

The Indian managed a small nod.

'You're safe with us, Bobby. Your father's dead. He can't hurt you either, any more.'

At the mention of his father, the fear returned on Bobby's face.

'Me and Bobby go back a long time,' he said to Dutch.

'Hey, Bobby,' the Dutchman said, leaning over him. 'Remember that lady who fell into the tunnel? It happened during the earthquake. Remember?'

The Indian turned to Dutch.

'It was you who was inside with her, wasn't it?'

Pete looked strangely at him.

'Marsha Garowitz said that it smelled of dead flesh inside. You were staying at your uncle's farmhouse right before the quake, right? Then you came to Beverly Hills and the tunnels. It's the one safe place for you.'

Pete looked at the Indian. 'What were you going to do with the woman, Bobby?'

The Indian curled up his legs.

'Were you going to hurt her?' Dutch asked.

Bobby didn't respond.

'What then? Were you trying to help her?'

The Indian nodded, then tightly closed his eyes.

Pete looked at Dutch. 'He's going back to dreamland again.'

'You mentioned his father. What about him, Pete?'

'His father was a mean bastard. He tried to make an *'antap* out of Bobby. It wasn't in the boy's make-up.

462

Some people are made to be shamans, some are not. The man used to beat and terrorize him. He'd run away. Sometimes he'd stay at his uncle's, sometimes he'd come down here in the tunnels.'

'Where was his mother?'

'She took up with a truck driver and ran off. You couldn't blame the woman. He used to beat her too.'

'Where's Bobby's father now?'

'Dead. An accident. His father was a bus driver. The brakes failed one night on the Ventura Freeway. Slammed into the back of a semi. Lot of people hurt. He was killed. Happened right before Bobby went into the army.'

The Dutchman leaned back against the jagged brick wall. Bobby's story was similar to John Payne's, he thought. Both of them were abused by their fathers. Both had no mothers. They knew each other. Payne also stayed away at nights. Did he come to the tunnels with Bobby? Too much of a coincidence going on here. He reached into his back pocket and removed the crumpled newspaper with the photo of John Payne lying on the stretcher. A young, terrified Bobby Santiago was one of the bearers. He shook the Indian, but that made him move his body into the old man's arms. 'Get him up. I need to talk to him,' he said to Pete.

Smokey grabbed the Indian's chin in his hand and jiggled his head. Bobby opened his eyes for a brief second, then closed them again. Pete slapped him hard across the face. The Indian's eyes flew open.

Dutch held the newspaper to his face. 'See that picture, Bobby? That was you. That other guy on the stretcher, that's the one you're afraid of.'

The Indian's face lit up with terror when he saw the

463

photo. He tried to push Pete away but the old man held him in his arms with a vice-like grip. Bobby started pointing at the picture and shaking his head. Animal sounds were coming from his throat.

'I'll be damned!' Pete said in amazement. 'Look where he's pointing.'

Dutch angled his head to get a better look. Then he saw what Pete was talking about. Bobby's finger wasn't pointing to the young John Payne in the photo. It was pointing directly to another stretcher bearer whose face was turned away from the lens. The Dutchman took a good look at the figure. The man was wearing a combat helmet, but the sides and back of his head were hairless. When he first saw the grainy photo in Bloom's newspaper office, he hadn't noticed it because he was concentrating on John Payne's bloody face.

Dutch angrily slapped the ground with the newspaper and cursed himself. He had this thing back to front all the time. It wasn't John Payne. It was someone from their unit in Vietnam. Someone they both knew.

Up above them, a resounding crack of thunder, then the heavy sound of rain coming down hard.

Hugo Frye stood in the shadows of a tree across the street and watched Pete, Bobby and the Dutchman crawl out of the fissure. The three men were covered with mud. Water was quickly filling the hole up. He was too late. There was no way he could get to Bobby now. Anger raged through him. How much did that deranged Indian tell them?

The rain came down hard and poured off his bald scalp and into his eyes, blinding him. Maybe the

Indian was so out of it that he couldn't tell them anything. There was no way to know for certain now. The only positive thing was that even if Bobby had talked, they'd never find him.

Frank could, but he was no more.

Hugo didn't feel good about any of this. Bobby being alive was a loose end in his fastidious order of things. One day he would have to take care of that. There would be no sleep for him tonight. He could never sleep when he was upset. Jimsonweed would help, but he didn't have any. Hugo clicked his tongue.

If it's not one thing, it's another.

The scratches on his arm were pulsating from the infection. He thought of Robin and the fierce fight she had put up to live. Her nails had dug down almost to his bones. Damn her! He took a vial of antibiotic capsules from his pocket, popped one in his mouth and furiously chewed it.

26

The drive back to Malibu was treacherous. Heavy rains had chipped away further at the Santa Monica mountains, causing major mud slides to cascade down on to the PCH. Only one lane was open and traffic was bumper to bumper.

Pete had taken Bobby back to the safe house near the ballpark. The other Indians would watch over him.

Dutch was covered with mud from the tunnel and soaked to the skin. When he arrived back home, he showered and changed into dry clothes. Afterwards, he made a cheese sandwich with stale rye bread, washed it down with a beer, then looked up Kevin Rousette's phone number.

The pilot answered in three rings. 'I thought you'd forgotten about me.' His voice was upbeat.

'I've been busy.'

'Yes, I heard,' Kevin said, turning sombre.

'Oh, from who?'

'From Jonathan. He told me about the judge who was murdered and your relationship with her. Sorry about that.'

'The man seems to know everything about everybody.'

'That's why he is who he is.'

Dutch didn't argue with that. 'You said you met John in Vietnam.'

'Right.'

'You were in his platoon?'

'Yes.'

'See much combat?'

'Plenty. I was in a search and destroy unit. The kind you don't want to see your son going into. It's what war's all about. You search out the enemy and kill anything that moves. No prisoners. It secures the perimeter for the rest of your unit when they move in.'

'What was your job?'

'Flying a gunship. Them babies were something. Their guns could wipe out a whole division in minutes. When I wasn't flying those, I was in a Chinook, helicoptering those crazy bastards into the area.'

'Did you know Bobby Santiago?'

'Who?'

'He's an Indian.'

A pause, as if he was thinking. 'Oh, yeah. The Indian. Right. I remember him. I think he was captured. Spent some time at the Hanoi Hilton. That guy had no business being out there. The powers that be must have been crazy putting a gun in his hand.'

'Why?'

'The kid – at least he was a kid then – was a nutcase. His nerves were hanging by a thread. If a leaf moved, he'd shoot at it. Not the kind of buddy you'd want next to you when you're out on night reconnaissance.'

'Did he kill anyone?'

'Everyone killed in our unit. That's why you were there. It's something you volunteer for, nothing you're assigned to.'

'What about John Payne?'

'What about him?'

'Did he kill too?'

'I said, *everybody* killed. John was the smart one of the group. He made officer. A rarity if you hadn't been to college or weren't a lifer. He went on to Stanford after his tour was over.'

Dutch was thinking about the toupee particles found on Robin's body. 'Payne had his face blown away. What about his head?'

'Are you asking if it got blown away, too?' There was confusion in Kevin's voice. 'The guy's alive and thinks faster than a mainframe computer, Wilhelm.'

'That's not what I mean. I'm not talking about his brain. I'm talking just about the skin and bones. Did he need any plastic surgery on his head?'

'It's attached to the face, isn't it? Yes, he had surgery on his head.'

'Did his hair ever grow back?'

A long silence.

'You there?' Dutch asked.

'Yeah, I'm here,' he said. 'Sorry. I'm just not used to talking about the intimate details of John's life. I can get fired for this. No, not all of it grew back. Many of the hair roots were destroyed in the explosion.'

'Does he wear a piece?'

'Yes.'

'Why didn't he have a transplant done?'

'Too much tissue damage. The doctors didn't think it would be successful.'

'Did any of the men in your platoon shave their skulls?'

'You mean like a skinhead?'

'Yes.'

Laughter. 'Not in those days.'

'Was there a bald man in your platoon? I mean completely bald. With no hair, not even on the sides of his head.'

Another pause, more thinking. 'One,' he then said. 'They called him Happy. Ugliest guy you'd ever want to see. He had a mouth that looked like it belonged on a different species. Hell of a soldier, though. Had more nerve than anyone in the unit. I think he won a couple of medals.'

'What was his real name?'

'I don't remember because nobody used it. Right from the beginning everybody called him Happy.'

'I'd like to know what they called him *before* the beginning.'

'I don't know. All I know is that he didn't like being called Happy.'

'What happened when somebody did?'

'He didn't get crazy or anything. No, nothing like that. He didn't have a temper. I never even saw him raise his voice or get into a fight. There was just a thing about him, that's all. If you did something to him, he wouldn't forget. He'd be thinking about it all the time, plotting everything out in his mind until he got even. You had the feeling it could be ten years later, but he'd get even. Know the kind of guy I'm talking about?'

Dutch knew the kind. He stayed away from them. 'They called him Happy for a reason, Kevin. He didn't sound like the type of man that smiled a lot.'

'No, he didn't smile . . . except maybe when he was killing.'

Dutch switched gears. 'Did he ever play with the prisoners?'

470

'I told you, we didn't take prisoners.'

'I understand. But not all Charlies die after an assault. It's impossible. You must have come across some wounded VCs. What happened to them?'

'They died.'

'How?'

A pause, then . . . 'That was Happy's department.'

'What did he do to them?'

Silence on the other end.

'Did he play with their lungs or their windpipes, Kevin? Try to suffocate them? What did he do?'

'You sound like you already know him,' he said slowly.

'I'm beginning to.'

'This goes no further?'

'Trust me.'

'I don't want Amnesty International on my back after all these years.'

'I understand.'

'It wasn't me that did these things.'

'I told you, I understand. It was war.' Dutch tried to hide the barb in his voice but it came out anyway. 'Tell me about Happy.'

'They called him that because it was short for Hapsburg. One of the sarges in our platoon was a history buff. He pinned the name on him. It came from the house of Hapsburg. Know anything about them?'

'You talking about the Austrian dynasty?'

'Right. They were a royal line. All the descendants had large protruding jaws. So did this guy, but not like anything you've ever seen. He was a real freak.'

Dutch was beginning to get the picture. 'What happened to the sergeant who first called him that?'

471

Kevin sounded surprised. 'Why?'

'You told me Happy didn't forget wrongs. According to you, calling him Happy was a wrong.'

'The sergeant led a foot patrol across a delta one afternoon. There was an ambush. The sarge got it in the back. It would mean nothing except the ambush was a frontal assault. The only soldier directly behind him at the time was Happy. None of the bullets lodged in his body so they couldn't prove anything. After that, nobody called him Happy to his face.

'You said he was a good soldier.'

'The best. He loved to kill, like he was born for it. You got the feeling that he couldn't care less if they were wearing black pyjamas, GI fatigues or Santa Claus costumes. All human beings were the same to him – low on the totem pole. The men kept away from him, especially after the sarge died. They didn't want to chance provoking him. I mean, how'd you like to be walking point in a rice paddy with someone like that, knowing that he was pissed off at you? You'd get a stiff neck from looking behind you all the time. The man unsettled everyone. John was the only one who took a shine to him. They were pretty close. Nobody ever understood their relationship.'

Dutch gripped the phone tightly for the next question. 'You know what happened to Happy?'

'I asked John that a few years ago. He said the man died in a bar fight right after he was discharged.'

'Interesting,' Dutch said.

'Why?'

'I thought Happy never lost his temper. Never got into a fight.'

'Hmmm . . . Good point. Look, I got to go. I have to pick up Jonathan in a while. He's at his compound

472

in Big Sur. If you want, we can get together, talk some more.'

Therese was also at Jonathan's compound, Dutch thought. With Miles. 'I have to go up north, too. I'll call you when I get back.'

'What's up north?' Kevin asked.

'Maybe this guy that's from another species.'

'Jonathan said he was dead.'

'Visionaries have been known to lie sometimes, Kevin.'

After he hung up, Dutch took his father's old Colt .45 from his drawer, checked the clip and left the trailer.

During the trip north, Dutch stayed in the fast lane the whole time doing seventy miles an hour. Rain was a rarity for this time of the year in southern California. Roads were slick after being dry for so long, and vehicles skidded across the 101 Freeway like bumper cars in an amusement park.

The Dutchman's head was still throbbing from what Bobby had shown him: the Indian had pointed out another man. *Another man!* But that didn't clear Payne. He also wore a partial toupee, with the same coloured strands found on the bodies of Robin and the housekeeper. With luck, Falcone could get a sample of it. There were also the wool fragments from John Payne's mill in Scotland, and the B positive blood samples found under Robin's nails. It it wasn't Jonathan who killed the women, then it had to be his twin, Dutch thought.

But it was the other man who kept bombarding his thoughts. *What was your real name, Happy? Did you paint those deranged drawings in the caves up in Santa*

Alicia? Did you also come from there, the same as Payne? I think so. Enlist with your friends and fight together. Is that what you both did?

When he reached the town of Santa Alicia, the deserted main street was flooded like a rampaging river. Stalled cars were abandoned in the middle of the road and debris floated by his Bronco. Dutch drove around the refuse and stopped at the *Pacifico*. It was raining so hard that he was totally drenched the second he got out of his truck. His long matted hair clung to his back and against his cheeks. The water was over two feet high and swamped his cowboy boots.

He leaped over the rapids that were rushing headlong down the kerb and ran over to the newspaper office. A small light was on somewhere in the building. Dutch grabbed the door handle and rattled it. Locked. He banged loudly, hoping the sound would carry over the raging storm. Several seconds later, there was a snap of a latch opening.

Bloom, wearing a rumpled white shirt and the same braces dangling along the sides of his pants, poked his head out of the door. When he saw Dutch, he first looked surprised, then excited. He could use the company. Putting the voice machine up to his throat, he said, 'Get out of the rain. You look like a piece of seaweed standing there.'

Dutch came in and stood in the hallway. A large puddle formed around his boots.

'Take them off,' Bloom said. 'You're going to warp my floor.'

They went into the outer office. Dutch sat down on the chair and removed them. The aroma of something warm and nourishing was coming from the kitchen. 'I

474

tried calling you a couple of times. You're never in,' he said to the old man.

'That's because there's not much to come in for. I'm thinking about retiring next year. Close down the paper. The town's dying like a slow cancer.' Bloom walked out of the room holding a mug of soup and a spoon. He handed them to Dutch. 'My wife's formula. She was a wonderful cook. Thank God she wrote all her recipes down before she died. You like split pea? Great on a night like this.'

Dutch tried it. Bloom was right, it was good. He suddenly realised he was starving. The only thing he had to eat all day was the stale cheese sandwich he had made before he left.

'Come into my office,' Bloom said. Not waiting for a reply, he turned and walked into the room down the hall.

Dutch stood up, shook out the dampness in his jeans and followed him.

The office was small and crowded. Old black and white photographs of Santa Alicia, taken when it was a bustling town, hung on the walls. Bloom's desk was a roll-top, filled with stacks of newspapers and books. The publisher sat behind it in a swivel chair, putting his feet on top of the papers. He opened the bottom drawer and took out a bottle of Jim Beam and two paper cups.

'Ben Bradlee of the *Post* kept good bourbon in his desk, too. Who am I to argue with success?' he said, pouring a couple of fingers into each cup, then handing Dutch one. Bloom leaned back in his chair and sipped his.

Dutch finished his off in two quick swallows. He then picked up his soup mug and began to eat.

'Still interested in the fellow who suffocated those animals?' Bloom asked, raising one eyebrow.

Dutch looked up at Bloom, saw that he knew something and stopped eating.

'Before I owned a newspaper, I was an investigative reporter. It's like riding a bike. You don't forget.' Behind him, the rain was coming down in full force, and the cracks of lightning caused flickering shadows from the window blinds to roll down the old man's face. 'I did some research. I knew there weren't any newspaper articles written about the missing animals. Just rumours that persisted for years. Then after you left, I suddenly remembered the personal column of the paper. Maybe some of the owners bought space asking about the whereabouts of their pets. I did a cross-reference in my files during the period of the rumours. I hit pay dirt between 1960 and 1973. During that time there were twenty or more ads a year taken out inquiring about missing pets. Five times the usual amount for this town. After '73, the inquiries dropped back to four or five and stayed that way.'

Bloom may have one foot in the grave, but he was as sharp as a tack, Dutch thought, moving his body closer to the desk to hear better. The publisher's mechanical voice box was occasionally drowned out by the howling winds and the rattle of the rain against the building.

'I called up several of the old numbers in the personal inquiries. Most of the pet owners had either died or moved away. A few were still around. One of them happened to be a friend of mine. The man had a German Shepherd that disappeared in '62. I asked him if he knew anything about the rumours concerning the animals. He remembered them. He told me about a lettuce farmer he knew who claimed one night after he'd had a little too much to drink that he'd dug up a large grave on his property and found dozens of animal remains.'

'Was this before or after 1973?'

'It was in '73 exactly. This friend of mine was never the brightest man in the world. He never thought that maybe one of those carcasses could be his own pet.'

'Is the farmer still alive?'

'Barely. He's living at an old-age home in San Louis Obispo. I drove over to see him on Sunday. He's got a bad case of Alzheimer's, but I got lucky and found him in a rare state of cognizance. I asked him about the animals. He remembered. At first he was reluctant to talk about it, but I persisted and he eventually opened up. It was a boy who did the killing, he told me. The reason the farmer didn't want to talk about it was because the boy's father paid to keep his mouth shut. To him a deal was a deal. I had to explain that it happened twenty years ago and it didn't matter any more.'

'Did he remember the boy's name?'

'No. He said he never saw him or the father again. The man said that the father whipped the boy until he was unconscious.'

The hope that had risen up in Dutch suddenly sank back down in his stomach. 'Was there anything he remembered about him?'

'Yes. He said that the boy was strange-looking. Once you saw a face like that, it stayed in your dreams.'

Happy, Dutch thought. It was Happy! 'I heard about him. I was told that he had a mouth that was deformed by a sizeable jawbone. The bottom teeth must have overlapped the top ones. You've lived here all your life. Do you remember a boy fitting that description? He'd be hard to miss.'

Bloom thought about it, then shook his head. 'Santa Alicia is spread over a large area. Besides, I never spent much time with the children of this town. Maybe he moved away before he became an adult. Maybe he changed his looks. Plastic surgery can do wonders.'

Bloom was right. If the man still lived here and looked like that, he was sure to have been noticed. He suddenly remembered Ashton and his yearbook. Did the killer go to the same school as Payne? Somebody in this town must have known him.

Dutch got up and told Bloom he had to leave.

The man looked disappointed. 'You just got here. You want to go back into the storm?'

'That's the last thing I want to do.' Dutch shook the old man's hand and left.

Keeping the Bronco in four wheel drive, Dutch drove up the mud and rock-strewn mountain road to Ashton's cabin. With luck, Ciazo hadn't got to the fat drug-dealer, and he was still alive.

He was shivering from the rain, and wished he had brought a change of clothes with him.

The road was rough and dangerous, but the Dutchman finally made it to the cabin. Two motorcycles were under a tarpaulin by the door. He lifted up the plastic. One was Ashton's broken Harley. The other one was an old Triumph. Did Ashton have company tonight? Dutch glanced into the window. A dim red light flickered in the bedroom.

The rain was hitting the trees so hard that he doubted Ashton heard him drive up. Dutch took the

.45 out of the glove compartment and got out of the truck. He went over to the front door and listened. Over the beat of an old Led Zeppelin song, there were muffled, moaning noises coming from within. Dutch undid the safety on the gun and tried the door handle. It was open. He walked in. The front room was strewn with beer cans, bourbon bottles and fast food wrappers. Again he listened hard. Rhythmic groans were coming from the other room.

Holding the gun in front of him, he walked past the junk on the floor towards the bedroom. The door was closed. He leaned his back against the wall, turned the knob, flung the door open and looked in.

On a water bed with a mirrored headboard, Ashton was on top of a woman almost as big as he was. Both were naked. She had her heavy thighs wrapped around his and was pumping her body up and down to his movements. Their enormous bellies were pounding together, sounding like fly swatters striking a wall. The moans coming from their throats were almost in tune with the heavy metal music blaring out of the JBLs.

When the knob of the bedroom door struck the wall, Ashton turned around. 'What the fuck!' he roared. He got off the woman, grabbed a pillow and put it up to the front of his body.

Shivering from the wet and the cold, Dutch held the Colt up to him and moved closer. The elephant gun was against the wall and within Ashton's reach.

The woman got up on her knees when she saw him. Trembling from fright, she let out a wail as her body swayed on the water bed. Unlike Ashton, she didn't try to hide her nakedness.

'What are you doing here?' Ashton grumbled over the woman's screams.

Dutch pointed the gun in her direction. 'Tell your friend to shut up.'

Ashton looked at her. 'Shut up!' he snapped.

She didn't.

The biker slapped her on the side of the head and she quieted down. Then he glared at the Dutchman again. 'You got no business coming into my place like that.'

'You're so dumb, by rights you should be dead,' Dutch said to him. He looked at the woman again. She had more tattoos on her chest than Ashton had on his. Dutch walked over to the elephant gun next to the bong pipe, took it by the muzzle and shovelled it over to the other side of the room. 'Tell your lady friend to get dressed,' he said.

The fat on her body jiggled like a Jello mould as she quickly leaped out of the bed and began to pick up her clothes from the floor. Gathering them to her huge breasts, she ran to the bathroom and locked the door.

'I thought we were friends,' Ashton said. There was a whine in his voice. He continued to clutch the pillow to his body. 'You didn't have to break in here.'

Dutch put the safety back on the gun and stuck it in his belt. 'Actually, I thought I'd find you dead.'

Fear came over Ashton's face.

The room stunk of unwashed bodies, strong pot, stale beer and sex. Dutch couldn't take looking at Ashton's bloated white skin any longer. He leaned down, scooped up the biker's greasy jeans and plaid flannel shirt from the floor, and tossed them at him. Ashton stood up and got dressed. Dutch noticed that the fat hanging over his stomach completely covered his groin area like a loin cloth.

'Why am I supposed to be dead?' Ashton asked,

480

hopping up and down, trying to get one of his feet through a leg hole in the jeans.

'I thought Ciazo may have killed you. What happened after he put your bike under my wheels?'

'I don't know. I turned round and he was gone.'

'You were lucky.' Dutch closed his eyes. God, was he dumb! 'Don't you take precautions?'

'Huh?'

'I walked right into your house like it was a public rest room. You're a goddamn dope-dealer. Why the hell don't you lock your door?'

'Never had to,' he said. His ass came down hard on the bed, separating the water in the plastic mattress like a tidal wave. He was bobbing up and down, struggling with the pants, trying to push his other leg through.

The woman came out of the bathroom. She was wearing tight jeans, a black biker jacket, and steel-toed engineer boots. Pointing to Dutch, she asked, 'Who's this guy, Ash? One of your deals that went sour? I'm getting the hell out of here before I get my ass shot off.' She stomped towards the door.

'Hey, pumpkin, wait!' Ashton called after her, but she was out of the door before he could get to her. Furious, he turned to Dutch, 'Thanks, pal.'

Outside, the sound of a motorcycle engine kicking in, then the wheels cutting through mud as it made its way down the hill.

'Is she going to make it in this weather?' Dutch asked.

Ashton angrily kicked the bong, spewing hashish across the room. 'That woman could do fuckin' wheelies on George Washington's nose up on Mount Rushmore.'

481

Dutch sat down on a beanbag chair. He was soaked to the bone and a chill was eating its way inside him. 'Can I have a blanket?'

Ashton glared at him, then went over to his bed, pulled off the cover and flung it at him.

Dutch wrapped it round his shoulders. It smelled of sweat and semen. 'I want to see the yearbook again.'

'What for?'

'Just get it for me, OK? And if there's any more bourbon that you haven't already guzzled, get that for me too.' He took the ends of the blanket and rubbed the water out of his hair.

The biker tromped out of the bedroom and went into the living-room. He came back with a half-filled bottle and the yearbook.

The Dutchman took several long swallows until his insides felt warm, then turned the pages of the senior class book. He felt hungry. Bloom's soup hadn't done it for him. 'What do you have to eat?' he asked.

Ashton's face was turning scarlet. Putting his hands on his hips, he said, 'Do I look like your mother?'

Dutch didn't answer.

'I got canned stuff. Beef stew.'

'That'll be fine,' Dutch said, not looking up. He flipped through the pages.

The biker growled something unintelligible and went off into the kitchen.

Dutch continued to look through the book. He slowed down when he came to the graduating class. On top of the page was the school crest of the silhouetted eagle. He carefully studied the photographs of the seniors. Three columns down from Payne's photo, he came to the picture of a young Bobby Santiago. He had missed it the first time because he hadn't been looking for it. The Indian's face was sombre and there was a lost gaze in his eyes. So Payne and the Indian were in the same class together, Dutch thought. He was surprised that Bobby had actually graduated from high school. He looked at the other faces. The rest of the photos and the names under them were meaningless to him.

Dutch turned the page and looked at a collage of photographs of the senior class activities: the football and basketball teams, the drama club, wrestling, the debating team. Again he scanned the faces carefully with his finger. He stopped at the photo of the debating team. Payne was sitting at a table with three other teenagers: two girls and one other boy. Dutch looked closely; the other boy had no hair on his head, and his mandible protruded over the central and lateral incisors of his upper mouth. He had never seen a jawbone that big before on a human. The farmer Bloom talked to was right: once you see a face like that, it stays in your dreams.

So the great man and the killer did know each other.

The light in the room was too dim to read the names under the photos. That was because Ashton, in his attempt to create a romantic atmosphere, had draped his red bandana over the lamp shade. Dutch got up and removed it, then sat back down on the beanbag and glanced at the page once again.

He had no trouble finding the name. It was Hugo Frye. This was the man who had paid Bobby Santiago's bail. The clerk at the police station had said he was nondescript except for the eyes. He must have had plastic surgery done.

The photograph of two boys wrestling Greco-Roman style, with their arms locked around each other's heads, also caught Dutch's attention. The rest of the team was in the background looking on. Both boys were wearing head guards, but they were still recognizable. One was Payne, the other was the boy with the large jawbone. Although they were fighting, they were grinning at each other like old friends. Dutch turned back to the photos of the graduation class. The boy was not in any of the pictures, but his name, Hugo Frye, appeared in the absentee section. Perhaps, because of his face, he didn't want his photograph taken. The pictures of the debating and wrestling teams were candid shots, probably taken without his knowledge.

A few minutes later, Ashton came into the room carrying a metal pot of hot canned beef stew. He put it on the night-table. The biker took a spoon and two pieces of white bread from his back pocket and handed them to Dutch. 'Anything else?' He sneered.

The Dutchman's stomach turned, but he was too hungry not to eat. With the cover round his shoulders, Dutch went over and sat down on the bed, handed the yearbook to Ashton and began to eat. Wiping his mouth on the blanket, he said to the biker, 'Look at the two boys wrestling and the two on the debating team. One of them is Payne. Do you know the other one? It's the same kid in both pictures?'

Needing glasses, Ashton held the book three feet away from his face and up to the light. After a while, he nodded, then broke out laughing. 'Yeah. I remember him. Now that's an ugly sonofabitch. I busted his balls many times.' He laughed even louder, thinking about it.

'How about the other kids? They do the same thing to him?'

'Sure thing. They followed whatever I did.' Ashton was full of pride when he said that.

Dutch took a long, hard look at the biker's smirking face. He remembered what the pilot, Kevin Rousette, had said about the man known as Happy: he never forgot a wrong.

'He was smart, though,' Ashton said, still looking at the photograph. 'When you were taking a test, that's the guy you wanted to be sitting behind.'

'His name is Hugo Frye,' Dutch said softly, suppressing an urge to smack him.

'Really?' Ashton shook his head and shrugged. 'I don't remember his real name. We called him the barracuda because of the way his bottom teeth came out over his top ones. Barracudas have the same kind of mouth.' He made an attempt to show Dutch with his own teeth.

'I know what they look like,' Dutch said curtly. Nobody remembered Frye's name, but everybody remembered the nasty little titles they bestowed upon him. This man must have carried a lot of anger around.

Ashton continued. 'They weren't just your normal size teeth, either. They were gigantic. You wouldn't want to get your dick caught in there. He also had no hair. Scary motherfucker.'

Dutch tossed the book on the bed and continued to eat. 'Know what happened to him?'

Ashton sat down on the beanbag, his big ass sinking deep into the vinyl cover. 'No. I never paid any attention to what happened to any of these people after high school. Why?'

Dutch wanted to tell him what this kid had done then he thought better of it. Why do it to him? It wasn't worth it. Anyway, at this point, there was no proof that Frye was the one.

Dutch was cold, wet and tired. He stood up and went into the living-room. The rain hitting the corrugated roof sounded like a thousand tap dancers trying out for *Chorus Line*. Dutch pulled his boots off, then his clothes, wrapped the blanket around him and collapsed on the broken couch.

Ashton walked into the room and folded his arms. 'You ain't staying here, are you?'

'Believe it. Lock the door like a good fellow, will you?' Sleep was beginning to close in on the Dutchman. Frye's face, however, still remained in his head, refusing to go away. He began to wonder if that ugly boy, like Payne, had also had a father who hurt him. From what the farmer said, it sounded like it. He suddenly had a terrifying vision of those razor-sharp teeth of Hugo's coming his way.

At that same moment, Hugo Frye was standing out on the balcony holding his Buck knife. He had his hands and face up to the sky, letting the rampaging storm pour down over his small naked body. The cool rain soothed his fevered skin. It also helped tranquillize the *urge* that was now threatening to tear out his insides. Never before had the feeling been this strong. He waited for his mother's voice to come and soothe him, say sweet things to him as it had in the past, but only the sound of thunder rumbled through his head.

He could feel the Dutchman's presence, as if he were out here on the balcony with him. The anthropologist was coming for him. At the thought of that, he giggled into the rain-filled night.

A flash of lightning suddenly ripped open the sky

and Hugo bolted back. Was that his father's sneering face looking down at him from those clouds?

You're dead, Daddy! I killed you, remember?

Again the sky cracked open, and again he saw his father. His face was hard and pitiless, and his red, alcoholic's eyes cut deep into Hugo.

From the terror came the rage. 'Look what you did to me, Daddy! You did it! You're the one!'

Over his image, the memories of that summer came back to him with the velocity of the storm itself.

The living-room was filled with people laughing, eating and drinking. In the centre of the room was the casket of Hugo's mother. The boy was five years old at the time. He was so small that he remembered feeling closed in by a dense forest of nylon stockings and gaberdine pants. Hugo pushed through those legs to get to the casket. The boy put a chair next to it and climbed up. He looked down at his mother and the tears rushed freely from his eyes. She had been a drunk like his father but at least she cared about him. It didn't matter that when he was an infant his nappies were filled with faeces because she was too hung over to change him. It didn't even matter that he often went hungry because she sometimes forgot to feed him. Whenever he went into her bedroom when his father was at work, she would lift her aching head from the pillow and caress his face. Nothing mattered to him at that moment but her. His heart became filled with a love that threatened to explode within him.

Looking down at her now in the casket, he could see how bloated her face had become from the gin that eventually ate through her liver. At least the make-up covered her sickly yellow skin, he thought. She had an overlapping bite like his. It was her genes that gave him his cursed mouth. Her affliction, however, was nothing compared to Hugo's. The doctors called his an aberration. When he was four years old, Hugo ran and looked the word up in the dictionary. At that point in his young life, nobody knew he could read.

Over in the corner of the living-room, he saw his father laughing with several of his friends from the chemical plant where he worked. His father was tall and lean. He was semi-bald, with rough hair on the sides of his head that resembled toothbrush bristles. The men were drinking heavily. Watching them, the boy's stomach buckled with fear. He knew the rage in his father when he was drunk.

The adults suddenly grew quiet and turned their eyes towards the door. Hugo also looked to see what was happening. A man, accompanied by a boy his own age, had entered the living-room. The child was thin and awkward like him. His face was gaunt, and his eyes were big and hollow like a picture Hugo once saw of a concentration camp survivor. Their eyes met for a second, then both boys shyly looked away. The man wore an expensive dark blue suit. He went over to Hugo's father and said something to him. His father shook his hand, sighed deeply, and kept his head down, giving the image of a man in mourning. A glass and a Canadian Club whiskey bottle were quickly offered to him by someone next to his father. Hugo guessed he was a very powerful person by the way everyone was treating him.

Meanwhile, the other boy came over to the coffin, stood up on his toes, and stretched his neck to look inside. 'Is that your mother?' he said to Hugo.

Hugo nodded.

'She's very pretty.'

'Not really,' Hugo said, with a sorrow that ran deep within him. 'It's the make-up. That's not even her real colour. But she was very pretty at one time.'

The other boy put his hand on the mahogany rim of the coffin and got up on the chair with Hugo to get a better look. 'I never saw a dead person before.'

'Me neither,' Hugo said. For some unexplained reason, he felt close to the newcomer.

The boy ran his fingers along the smooth edge of the casket, his large eyes appearing deep in thought. Suddenly he thrust his hand into the box and touched the dead woman's face. He took it away quickly, as if he had touched a piece of hot coal. Gathering up his courage, he slowly put it back again. This time he ran it gently over her facial skin, tracing her nose, her lips, her cheekbones with his long fingers. His grey eyes were alive with excitement.

Hugo wasn't angry that this stranger was touching his mother. She was almost like a conduit, bringing them together. 'What's it like?' he asked curiously.

'Well . . . it's not warm, it's not cold,' he said. 'It feels like a rubber Halloween mask.' He looked at the boy with the big teeth. 'Try it.'

Hugo looked down at his mother. His heart was beating with dread. Though he was only five years old, death terrified him. It shouldn't matter if he touched her, he said to himself. She would like that. Besides, she would never hurt him, even in death. He put his hand inside the casket and stroked his mother's face. The new boy kept his hand there, too. Occasionally their warm fingers would brush up against each other's, then drift back again to the slightly cool skin of the dead woman. The temperature slip between life

489

and death was subtle, Hugo thought. The boy caressed his mother's skin for a long time, longer than he had ever done when she was alive. *Oh, how he had loved her!* He touched her hands that were clasped together, holding a rose between her breasts. His fingers then found one of her breasts and curled around it. He felt no pleasant sensation like he heard the older kids talking about. The tears welled up in his eyes. He looked up at the new boy. He saw that his face was filled with compassion. Perhaps out of his mother's death he had found a friend.

A searing pain suddenly shot through his head. He fell off the chair and on to the floor. His eyes were stinging, preventing him from seeing, and he groped blindly on his hands and knees. From above him, he heard a man's rough voice screaming. A calloused hand came down and slapped him hard across the face, sending him soaring against the table that held the coffin. Hugo wiped the tears away from his eyes and looked up. It was his father's raging face looking down at him. The man's cheeks were flushed and the veins bulged from his neck and temple. He grabbed the boy by his hair and lifted him up off the ground until their heads were inches apart. Hugo could smell the heavy alcohol on his breath.

'You touch your own dead mother like that!' He slapped his son across the face with every word he spit out.

The room was deathly quiet. Hugo's father took him by the back of his collar and dragged him up the steps and into his bedroom. He threw him on to the floor and kicked him several times in both legs. The boy scampered across the carpet and tried to crawl under the bed. His father clutched him by his pants, dragged him out, and kicked him some more. Hugo crawled over to the corner and huddled his upper body over his bruised knees, digging his chin into them for protection. He was shaking uncontrollably, and the tears flowed freely down his cheeks.

'You little bastard! Embarrassing me like that in front of my friends and boss! When they leave, I'll show you what's what! You should never have been born, you ugly bastard!' He started to walk out, changed his mind and came back to him. 'You know why God didn't give you hair on your body? That's the way he brands his mistakes so he can recognize them and not let them into heaven!' He kicked him one more time, then left the room and went downstairs.

Still trembling, the boy lifted himself up on the bed and curled up in the corner. At least Hugo knew his father had made that up about his hairless body being a mistake of God's. He had taken the Old and New Testaments from his mother's night-table and read them from cover to cover before he was five years old and there was nothing in them about that. Besides, Hugo didn't believe in God. What he had was a rare disorder known as *Alopecia universalis*. He had once heard the doctor talking to his mother about it when he was a toddler.

Hugo was frightened. What would his father do to him? His sore body was on fire. A few minutes later he heard some people leave. He sat up and looked out of the window. The boy with the man in the blue suit was getting into a car. As if an invisible hand pointed him in his direction, the boy with the gaunt face looked up at the window. He saw Hugo and smiled at him, then got into the front seat. Hugo watched the car until it disappeared out of view down the street. He didn't know his name, but he knew he wanted to be friends with him. He had never felt that way before. Then again, he had never had a friend before.

Within the next hour all the guests had left. The boy waited, his body twitching with fear at what his father was going to do to him. He always made good his threats. Downstairs, he could hear him putting ice into his glass and filling it up with whiskey. He was laughing and cursing, talking to his dead mother lying in the coffin. Soon, he knew, his father would no longer bother with ice, nor the glass; he would drink straight from the bottle.

Night came. His stomach growled with hunger, but he was too afraid to go downstairs and ask for something to eat. It had been silent in the house for a long time now. What was happening? Perhaps his father had passed out or had forgotten about him.

Then he heard his footsteps, and his stomach curdled. He was coming! *Oh, please, please, please don't let him . . .*

The door swung open. His father was standing by the entrance way, swaying from the alcohol. The stench of whiskey filled the room. An ugly smirk stretched across his face. His eyes were blood red, and the lids sagged halfway down them.

Terrified, the boy inched his way across the mattress until the bedboard prevented him from backing up any further. He picked up the blanket and held it up to his body like a protective shield.

The tall, bony man staggered over to him. His large frame cast a shadow over his son. 'So, you like touching your mamma, hey?' His voice was heavy and whiskey-coated. 'Did you touch her when she was alive, too? She let a lot of men touch her, you know. Not me, though. She wouldn't let me near her. You know how you were born?' He reached down, seized the boy's ankles and spread his legs open. He thrust his hips at him. 'Bang! Bang! Nine months later, a little monster named Hugo popped out.' He laughed, then his face turned into a glowing sneer. He grabbed Hugo by the arm and yanked him off the bed.

The boy yelled and squealed in pain as he was dragged out of the room and down the steps. He was taken into the living-room where the coffin was. The father picked the child up by his ankles and held him upside down over his dead mother.

'Take a look at her, you bastard! Take a good look. You like to diddle her? Well, I'm going to give you a whole night of it, and it's on the house.' He started to laugh again.

'Please, Daddy, please!' Hugo screamed.

The man lowered his son into the coffin. Holding his squirming body still with one hand, he dropped the lid over the top with the other. He then staggered upstairs, collapsed in his bed and passed out.

It was pitch black inside the coffin. Hugo was screaming in terror. He was lying on top of his mother's body, his face pushed up against hers. The lid of the coffin on his back prevented him from moving. In the darkness he could feel her stiff cheap dress cutting into his skin. Eventually, the boy's throat became sore and his yells turned into whimpers. He tried to move, but couldn't. Her cheek pressing against his felt lukewarm, like the belly of a snake. The acrid smell of formaldehyde singed his nostrils. There was also the smell of cheap, heavy perfume sprayed on her by the funeral home to block out the odour of death.

Hugo began to gag. He tried to breathe, but the air was almost nonexistent in the tight casket.

He had to get out! He had to breathe! What air there was came from a small crack in the lid which broke open when his father slammed it down on him.

Throughout the night, the boy emitted muffled moans. His lungs went into involuntary spasms as they attempted to fight for air. During one moment of clarity, he prayed to the God he didn't believe in to take him. Instead, the panicky feeling of suffocation returned again.

It was an altar boy who eventually found Hugo.

The coffin was brought to the empty church early the next morning and placed on the altar. Services were to begin in a couple of hours. The altar boy walked up to the platform and lit the candles next to the casket. As he was about to walk away, he thought he heard a dim sound coming from inside the coffin. Putting his ears to the polished wood, he waited patiently to see if he would hear it again. After a few seconds, he heard a slight moaning noise. He quickly crossed himself, then ran to the rectory next door and asked one of the senior fathers to come into the church. The old man, with the boy holding his hand, scurried down the aisle. Both of them placed their ears next to the coffin and waited. There it was again. With the altar boy's help, the priest lifted up the top. They found Hugo unconscious and near death.

That morning the police went to Hugo's house and awakened his father out of his drunken sleep. The man had no memory of what he had done the night before. With bloodshot eyes and fighting the worst hangover of his life, he told the authorities that the poor boy loved his mother so much that he must have climbed into the casket to be with her and pulled the lid down by accident.

No one questioned the father's story, and the boy knew that he wouldn't be believed if he told the truth. He spent a week in the hospital under observation, then was released in the care of his father once again.

That was many years ago, Hugo thought. The rain ran down his naked body and on to the balcony. That day, however, was a time of great moment for him. It was the day he met the boy with the big eyes who turned out to be Jonathan Payne. It was also the day the *urge* was born.

As the sky lit up with lightning and resounded with thunder, Hugo screamed out the words of Shylock that he had memorized as a boy: *'The villainy you teach me I will execute, and it shall go hard but I will better the instruction.*

'Didn't I better the instruction, Father?' he shouted to the black sky. 'You taught me what it was like to hate! I now hate better than you did when you lived your *damned* life! You showed me what it was like to slowly suffocate! I passed those instructions on to others!'

The clouds opened further, and the rain now came down in heavy sheets. He lifted his head up to it, letting the beads of water sting his face. His father's image was no longer there. Instead, he saw the Dutchman's angry eyes looking down at him, chiding him for the things he had done.

At first he felt shame, then raging anger. Enough punishment! *First my father, then you!*

'I have a surprise for you, my beautiful Wilhelm!' Hugo yelled into the storm. His voice was raw. 'It will be the ultimate gift one man can give to another!' As he said those words, he unconsciously began to carve another centipede on the wood railing with the Buck knife.

27

Dutch twisted and turned as he slept on Ashton's couch. Deep guttural sounds banged the walls of his throat. He was dreaming about that day again, when he was seven years old in Xenia. The visions hung down from the ceiling of his mind like old cobwebs that were too hard to reach.

'Read to me, Mommy', the Dutchboy says, climbing up on her bed with a Curious George *in his hand.*

His mamma smiling . . . the glow in her eyes . . . little purple flowers on her flannel nightgown. His head sinking into warm, goosedown pillows. The smell of her Shalimar perfume on the sheets. Her fingers stroking his fine, blond hair. Heat from the kerosene stove.

Suddenly a loud, deafening wind . . . the bed shaking . . . lamps falling off the night-tables.

The horrible look of fear in her eyes. 'Tornado!' she screams.

'Mamma! Mamma!' the Dutchboy cries, frightened, putting his arms around her neck.

Walls cracking open . . . the thunderous sound of the corrugated metal roof coming down on them.

The hands of his mother slipping away from him.

Trapped under debris. Hours turning into days. Blinding pain in his legs that thankfully gives way to numbness. Complete darkness. Hunger turning into ravenous thirst. Dust so thick, he chokes on every breath.

To breathe again . . . just to breathe.

And always that sweet, pungent odour that seems to be getting stronger every day.

When he can no longer stand the smell, he thrusts his face into the bed sheet next to him. The perfumed scent of his mother still imbues it. He can feel her presence and it eases the fear.

'Mamma!' he cries continuously, but there is never any answer. Finally, he manages to loosen his arm that is jammed under a concrete slab. Groping out in the darkness, he finds her flannel nightgown with the purple flowers and feels her soft, decaying body inside it.

'Mamma!' The scream from his parched throat stirs up the dust, causing him to cough.

He cries softly, not letting go of the nightgown. He knows his mother is dead and that the sweet odour is coming from her, but he needs to be near her flesh, no matter how rancid the smell. In his delirium, he feels the odour is part of her soul, and if it goes away so will she.

Then they come, softly at first, brushing their cold noses timidly up against his hands, his feet . . .

The Dutchman woke up. He always did when it came to this part. It was like the first reel of a film snagging in the projector and unable to go any further.

He closed his eyes again. The scent of Shalimar faded, and the old, familiar smells of his son took over: baby shampoo, freshly washed jeans, milk and oatmeal. It filled his senses.

The yearning for what used to be abruptly vanished when something cold touched the back of his neck.

Dutch opened his eyes in the darkness. The odour of Ashton's beer-stained, dirty pillows filled his nostrils. When he reached up to see what was pressing against his neck, a hand grabbed his arm, pushing it back down.

'Keep them where they are,' a heavy voice whispered in his ear. The man's hand went over to the front of Dutch's jeans and removed the Colt.

His face was so close to his that Dutch could smell the garlic on his breath. A coldness came over him when he suddenly realized that hard metal object against his neck was a gun.

'I want you to get up slowly,' the voice said.

'I don't have any clothes on,' Dutch whispered back.

'I'm not bashful.'

Dutch slowly got up off the couch, keeping the blanket wrapped around him. The room was dark, and the person stayed behind him, out of his field of sight. His eyes shifted to Ashton's bedroom. The door was open and he could see the fat form asleep in the bed. His high-pitched snore sounded like a tea kettle.

'Start moving towards the door,' the voice behind him said.

'My clothes,' Dutch said again.

The man jabbed the gun deeper into Dutch's neck. 'No clothes means you won't do anything stupid. Nobody likes to die with their dick waving in the air.'

Dutch recognized the voice and a fear cut into his loins. Jimmy Ciazo. He wasn't about to argue with him. He moved towards the door. Jimmy's thick hand

499

reached for the knob and opened it. A blast of cold, damp air hit Dutch in the face. The rain had stopped, but the ground was saturated with mud. Wrapping the blanket tighter around his body, he walked outside, sinking up to his ankles in it.

'Walk towards the road. There's a truck there,' Ciazo said.

Dutch hesitated, then tried to turn round.

The thick hand grabbed Dutch by the hair, keeping his face in front of him. 'Do what I tell you, or the fieldmice are going to be nibbling on your dead ass.'

Dutch believed him. He hobbled over rocks and fallen branches, banging his feet several times. The truck was parked by the crest of the mountain where the road ended.

Jimmy opened the door of the pickup and pushed Dutch inside. A second man was at the wheel, forcing the Dutchman to sit in the middle. Ciazo got in and sat next to him. The thighs of both men pressed up against his, preventing him from moving.

The night was dark and Dutch couldn't see the other man.

The engine started and they drove slowly down the dirt road that was covered with debris from the storm.

The headlights bouncing off the trees created a silhouette of the driver. Dutch could make out his slightly rounded head and high cheekbones.

When the light careened off a boulder in front of the truck, it briefly flashed on the man's face. It was the loan officer from Smokey Valley Savings and Loan. 'How's the banking business, Roberto?' he asked the Indian.

'Shut up, Dutchman,' Ciazo grumbled.

'Lending any more felons bail money?' Dutch

said to Roberto, ignoring Jimmy.

Ciazo poked him hard in the ribs with his elbow.

The anthropologist let out a grunt. Roberto smiled.

Dutch turned his head to look at Jimmy. The gun wasn't in his hand. It didn't have to be. He wasn't about to try and escape and Ciazo knew it. 'Nice to see that you guys are now brothers. Never thought you'd be hanging around with someone who's not white and Italian, Jimmy. Someone's got to be paying you well to do that.'

Ciazo made a motion with his elbow again and Dutch flinched.

'You work for John Payne now, Jimmy? He the guy that's paying you, huh?'

'Shut up, already.' He rubbed his jaw, beginning to look bored.

Dutch glanced out of the window, trying to get a sense of what time it was. The sky was black in the west, but a halo of light was just coming over the mountain from the east. That meant it must be around four-thirty in the morning. He wondered if they were taking him to see Payne. Dutch didn't think they'd hurt him, but he couldn't be sure, especially with Jimmy involved.

Roberto found a country music station on the radio and turned it up. Dutch unconsciously tapped his foot to the beat and leaned back in the seat, wondering what the crazy billionaire wanted from him.

Twenty-five minutes later the truck turned on to a private road that led up to a flat knoll. John Payne's helicopter was waiting for them. It was lighter now and Dutch could see Kevin in the pilot's seat. At least that made him feel better.

Ciazo got out of the truck first, then grabbed Dutch

by the arm and assisted him out. The wind was blowing hard up here, and he wrapped the blanket even tighter around his body. With Roberto and Ciazo holding him by the arms, Dutch limped across the rocky field towards the chopper. He could hear the squeaking of the bank officer's prosthesis as he walked. They assisted him into the aircraft. Once again, Jimmy and the Indian sat on each side of him.

Kevin was up front. He turned his helmeted head around and glanced over his shoulder at Dutch. The light from the small lamp inside the chopper glared off his military sunglasses. He nodded briefly at the anthropologist, as if to reassure him that everything was all right, then started up the engine. Dutch wanted to say something to him, but couldn't. Nobody knew they had talked.

Within thirty minutes, the helicopter was flying over large redwoods and madrones. Then the imposing jagged cliffs of Big Sur came into view. At the edge of one of the steep bluffs, a modern glass house jutted out over the Pacific. Dutch had read about this compound. It was Payne's retreat.

When the aircraft lit down, Roberto and Jimmy helped Dutch out of the chopper and took him into the house. Like Payne's other estate in Bell Canyon, this one was also expensively decorated with an eclectic assortment of art from all over the world. The rooms were filled with stuffed heads and bodies of carnivorous animals. Jackals, wolves, hyenas, weasels and mongooses were frozen in the attack position, their fangs and claws bared. The sight of those flesh eaters gave Dutch an uncomfortable feeling in his stomach. The men took him through the wood-panelled study filled with wall-to-wall books and out

502

to the pool area where the cabanas were.

'There's a shower in there. Use it,' Ciazo said. He pointed to the men's bathhouse.

Dutch looked down at his bare feet. They were caked with mud and covered with scratches. 'Where's Payne?' He tried to keep his voice steady, but the cold made it difficult.

Not answering, Jimmy and Roberto walked back towards the house.

Dutch went into the shower area. Past the lockers, there were several marbled stalls, a sauna and a steam room. Looking round, he realized the only door out was the one he came in at. He dropped Ashton's blanket on the cold tile floor, got into a stall and turned on the shower. The water felt good. He turned it up hot to get the dampness out of his body. Everything was there for him: soap, shampoo, toothbrush, paste, shaving equipment, and a dryer and brush over by the sinks. There were also new bandages for his ear and hand. Even a bottle of aspirins.

When he got out of the shower, he found a packet of new jockey briefs and black sweat pants with a matching sweatshirt draped across a chair. Next to it was a pair of white socks and tennis shoes. Everything was his size. Dutch wondered how they knew that. He got dressed, then brushed his hair and changed the bandages.

When Dutch emerged from the bathhouse, Jimmy was waiting. The Dutchman saw the dead look in Ciazo's face and knew it would be useless to talk to him. They walked in silence past the pool and tennis courts, and towards Payne's office overlooking the Pacific ocean. Jimmy opened the door and stepped aside so Dutch could go in.

Payne, wearing a blue striped business suit, was sitting by a large Louis XIV table at the end of the room. Several phones of different colours were within reach. A stuffed ferret with sharp, pointed teeth sat at the edge of the table, its brown marble eyes glaring threateningly at Dutch. Behind Payne, there was a huge window with a panoramic view of Big Sur. Dutch could see the black helicopter, like a giant locust, sitting on the landing pad by the cliff. Kevin was gassing up the tanks. Dutch turned and looked at the walls. Photos of Payne smiling with the President of the United States, world leaders, and sports figures slid by his sight.

The industrialist was drinking coffee and eating eggs and bacon. His eyes were scanning the front page of a *Wall Street Journal* folded next to him. 'You hungry?' he asked Dutch, not bothering to look up.

'No,' Dutch said. Actually he was. He hadn't eaten anything except for a little soup and Ashton's canned stew last night.

His eyes still on the newspaper, Payne said, 'Don't bullshit me, Van Deer. I know you haven't eaten. I told you before, I know everything about you. Even the size of your underpants.'

'I'm glad I help fill up your hours,' Dutch said. He sat down, poured coffee into a cup and took a few sips from it. The caffeine shot through his system. Looking at Payne, he asked, 'Why am I here?'

Payne pushed the newspaper away, leaned back and looked at him for the first time. 'You're becoming a wart on my ass. What gives you the right to run around Santa Alicia, poking into my life?'

'You woke me up at gunpoint to ask me that?'

'Damn right I did.'

'It's not your life I'm poking into, Jonathan. It's the twins' lives. The problem is every time I see them, I see you. Why is that?'

Payne didn't answer at first. He studied Dutch's face for a long time. Then, as he was about to say something, the helicopter engine starting up outside broke the silence.

'Where is the governor?' Dutch asked.

'He left last night.'

Dutch tried to steady his voice. 'I heard Therese was here, too. Where is she?'

Payne turned and looked out the bay window. 'There,' he said, pointing towards the helicopter.

Dutch walked round the desk and looked out. He could see Miles and Therese walking towards the pad. When they reached the edge of it, they stopped, put their arms around each other's waist and began to talk. Kevin was inside the helicopter, waiting. The blades began to spin. Dutch watched Miles and Therese hug for a long time. Then she let go of him and got into the aircraft. The 'copter lifted up and headed south towards Los Angeles. Miles, with his hands in his pockets, followed the machine with his eyes until it disappeared into the clouds. Then he turned round and slowly walked back into the house.

'They make a lovely couple, don't they?' Payne said, smiling.

Dutch glared at him. His insides felt like they were on fire. The man knew how to push buttons.

'She's an extremely bright woman, your wife. We had a very productive meeting.'

'Is that so?'

'She managed to convince me to keep the hotel site open for at least another month. By then, she should have some idea of what's down there.'

'Why did you need so much convincing? The twin girls were buried across the street.'

Payne chuckled. 'You get to the point right away. I like that. No, it's not the discovery of the girls that I was worried about.'

'It's certainly not the money you'd be losing if the construction was frozen.'

'Why not? I'm a businessman.'

'You're also a man with an inquisitive mind who funds archaeological digs. I would think you'd want to know what's down there.'

'Sometimes it's best to leave things buried. I hear you've been spreading rumours about me.'

'I have?' Dutch acted surprised.

'You told the police that I was the one who killed those twins.' The smile disappeared from Payne's lips.

Dutch walked away from the window and sat back down. He picked up his cup and took another sip of coffee. Clearing his throat, he said, 'That's the way it looked at the time.'

The skin around the scars on Payne's face reddened for a second, then returned to its natural pale colour. He tossed his napkin on his plate, turned back to the window and looked out at the steaming ocean. A mist was beginning to roll in, blocking out the horizon.

The cards were dealt. Both men knew that there was no going back from this point on.

'I didn't murder those girls,' Payne said quietly, still looking at the view. His tone was flat.

'I know that now,' Dutch said. The man dressed in the pinstriped suit seemed very different from the man he had met cutting up the coyote. One day he was a blood-covered huntsman, the next, an international banker. 'I just think you know who did do it.'

'How much do you really know about all this, Van Deer?' Payne's voice had a hint of annoyance in it. He clasped his hands behind his back and continued to stare out into the fog bank that had now moved closer to the jagged rocks below.

The moment of truth had arrived, Dutch thought. 'What are my chances of getting out of here alive?'

Payne shrugged. 'Does it really matter? You've been living on borrowed time ever since you survived the tornado as a child.' Turning round and seeing the surprise in Dutch's face, he added, 'I told you I know everything about you.'

The Dutchman got up from the table so their faces would be at the same level. He walked over to him. 'The name of the man who killed those twins is Hugo Frye.' Dutch looked for signs of flinching on Payne's part. There weren't any. 'He comes from Santa Alicia, the same as you.'

'Does he?' The man's face was like granite. Nothing showed in his cold, grey eyes.

'I can prove he's killed at least five people.'

'Who were they?' Payne asked calmly.

Was there movement just now in his eyes? Dutch thought there was. 'The twins, and an unknown man found at the Encino reservoir. Judge Robin Diaz and her housekeeper. I'm not counting an American army sergeant and God knows how many Viet Cong prisoners. Maybe there were others, too.'

Payne's jaws clenched tight. He was clearly upset.

'Why is Hugo Frye so important to you?'

There was a knock on the door, then it opened. Miles Scone peered in.

'Come in, Miles,' Payne said. 'You know Wilhelm Van Deer?'

'Of course,' Miles said. He came in and closed the door. A disturbed look seemed to cloud his face.

'Have some coffee, Miles. Finish yours, Van Deer. Sit down, both of you.'

Dutch sat down again. Miles poured a cup of coffee and went over to the couch.

'Miles and I have been close friends for years. There's nothing that needs to be hidden from him. So continue,' Payne said to Dutch.

'At the tunnel site, the murderer painted a Trinidadian centipede on the wall. At Robin Diaz's house, he actually left the real thing.' He held up his bandaged hand.

Payne's face began to redden again. 'I heard about that. I didn't know it was a Trinidadian variety.' He glanced quickly at Miles, then back again. 'How do you know this?'

'It was identified by an entomologist. Obviously, not everything has got back to you. What do you owe Frye that makes you cover up for him?'

'I don't cover up for anyone. But loyalty is important to me, Van Deer. I expect it from people and they expect it back from me.'

Dutch swallowed his anger. 'This sick bastard kills people.'

'I don't know that. It's only supposition.'

'Maybe about him, but not about you, Jonathan. The scale seems to be tipping in your direction. Even the police can't hide their heads on this one. A criminal court judge was killed. That makes it a whole new ball game.'

508

'They really think I did it?' Payne was sincerely surprised.

Dutch was amazed that this visionary didn't know anything about the physical evidence that had recently been uncovered. The police and Orville Priest were keeping information from him. This was his opening and it was time to move in. 'I know you wear a partial toupee. Hairs like yours were found on the bodies. Maybe the *same* ones.'

Payne now glared at him.

'You have B positive blood. Skin particles found under the nails of Robin, suggesting she fought with the killer, are from that grouping.' Dutch waited for that to sink in, then said, 'It gets better, Jonathan. Fragments of wool, the same kind that comes from your factory in the Shetlands, were also found on the victims. Either you're Hugo Frye or Frye thinks he's you.'

Payne slowly sat down and leaned into the Louis XIV table. He touched his hands together and put them up to his lips, forming a pyramid.

'The police can't sleep on this, not any more.' Dutch waited a beat, then said, 'Where is Hugo Frye?'

'There are things you don't understand, Van Deer.' Payne's voice was low, as if his mind was somewhere else.

'What is it that I don't understand?' Dutch also banked his body into the table. Their faces were only inches apart now.

'The sins of our fathers,' he mumbled.

Dutch waited for more, but Jonathan didn't continue. Was that fear in his eyes? he wondered. 'Whose father, Jonathan? Yours? I know what he did to you.'

Payne's eyes had a yellowish hue to them, the same colour as a jackal's. 'What the hell do you know about fathers, buddy boy! You didn't even know yours. You were lucky!'

'There's a pain that can come from that, too,' Dutch said.

'At least the pain wasn't physical, and it wasn't one of humiliation!' Payne snapped. 'You had no scars plastered across your body. Hugo and I, we had new ones every day.'

He's owning up to their connection. Good. 'Did Hugo's father abuse him too?' Dutch asked, controlling his excitement.

Payne dropped his hands to his sides, got up and slowly began to pace the floor. 'When we were kids, we used to meet secretly, take off our shirts and pants and show each other our bruises.' He went over to the wall with the photographs and plaques, and stared at them. 'Santa Alicia is a small town. I knew Hugo very well. He was a boy with a good mind. His father worked in my father's factory. We met the night before his mother's funeral. I also lost my mother. We became friends from the beginning. The world was a frightening and lonely place for both of us and we needed each other. We discovered we had many things in common: our mothers were dead, we were both abused by our fathers and we both had a mind. Sometimes we'd take long hikes up in the mountains and play an imaginary game to pass the time. A game of murder. Hugo would take on the role of the killer and tell me different ways he'd like to murder our fathers. I would play the devil's advocate. My job was to find his mistakes and catch him. My Holmes to his Moriarty. Eventually his plots became foolproof, without any snags. We were like Leopold and Loeb, creating the perfect murders together.'

'How did Bobby come into this?' Dutch asked.

'By accident. I'd seen him around school but I never paid any attention to him. On one of our hikes in the mountains we came upon an old Chumash painted cave. We found Bobby inside. The fool kid was drinking Jimsonweed, stoned out of his mind. He gave us some and we got high. When we came down, we talked. It seemed Bobby was hiding out in the cave from his father. Then he took his shirt off and showed us *his* scars. He said his father was a Greyhound bus driver, and that he was going to beat him again when he got back from his run. He became one of us. We'd meet after school every day in the cave and get high on Jimsonweed. Bobby would tell us all about the Chumash, especially about the spiritual side. He knew all about that because his father wanted him to be an 'antap. Bobby told us his father was crazy, and that 'antaps didn't exist any more.' Payne pronounced the word perfectly. 'He explained the paintings and what they meant. I was fascinated by all of it.'

'More so than Hugo?'

'Yes. Hugo was mostly interested in getting high. He loved the hallucinations that came from it. Sometimes he would go down to the cave alone and paint his wild fantasies on the walls.'

'Yes, I know,' Dutch said. 'I saw them. They were bloody frightening.'

'I wanted to learn more about the Indians. It was as if I had found something other than hate to stimulate me.'

'Something else besides Jimsonweed interested Hugo. He was mesmerized by centipedes.'

'Was he?' Payne had a leery look in his eyes.

'I think you know that. Centipedes symbolized death to the ancient Chumash. Death was also something that interested Hugo.' Dutch caught a glimpse of Miles in the corner. He was looking deeply disturbed by the conversation. 'Hugo was absorbed by the act of asphyxiation. How did you find the tunnels? From Bobby?'

Payne nodded. 'One day, Bobby took us down into the deserted sewer pipes in Beverly Hills. He said that's where he came when the screaming and the beatings got too severe at home. Bobby told us that the grounds were holy because of the graveyard. Some of the older Chumash knew about it and the old sewers running through it. He showed us the paintings he'd done on the walls of the pipes. The boy wasn't too bright but he was a damn good artist. Sometimes all of us would spend days in the sewers, talking, drinking Jimsonweed, pretending we were free from our fathers. Once, right before graduation, Bobby met us down in the sewers. He was walking slow and in agony, holding his rib cage. His father had beaten him with the handle of a broom. That's when the conversation came up again about killing them.'

'Did anything ever come of that?'

Payne vehemently shook his head. 'It was just a game, that's all.' His voice was threatening.

Dutch knew better than to pursue it. 'When did Frye's father die?'

'Right after Hugo ran off to Los Angeles.'

'How did he live?'

'I believe he may have been hustling.'

'I saw his picture. He was not good-looking.'

'No, he wasn't. Hugo's father cornered Bobby one

day and forced him to tell him where his son was hiding out. He went to Los Angeles to find him and was killed by a hit-and-run driver. The police never found out who did it.' Payne paused, then said, 'I never knew until recently about the man found at the reservoir. I don't know what, if anything, Hugo had to do with that.'

He was still evasive, Dutch thought. He was still protecting him. 'When did *your* father disappear, Jonathan?'

'Right after Hugo returned to Santa Alicia.'

'What do you think happened to him?'

Miles stood up. 'Jonathan, as your lawyer, I'm advising you not to continue this.'

Payne waved Miles back down with his hand. 'I know what I'm doing,' he said. His eyes danced as his mind retraced the road back to his past. 'I never knew for sure what happened to my father. Never really cared.'

'Didn't you have any ideas?'

Payne looked quizzically at him. 'You mean that he may have been dead? Sure. You want to know how I felt? Elated! Like a terrible weight had been lifted off my shoulders. I didn't care if he was dead or alive as long as he never hurt me again. When I came of age, I closed down that factory, along with the memories.' Payne took a long cigar out of a humidor on the table, tore the tip off with his teeth and lit it. He moved towards the picture window, put his hand in his pocket and looked outside again. The fog bank now covered the entire view of the cliffs and ocean.

'You and Frye played perfect murder games. You must have suspected what might have happened?' Dutch asked.

'Oh, I suspected all right.'

'Maybe more than suspected?'

'Jonathan, stop this now,' Scone said, putting his cup down.

'Shut up, Miles,' Payne said irritably.

'What was the perfect murder that you and Frye concocted?' Dutch asked.

'Hugo's version of the perfect murder was to hit the person hard with a blunt weapon in the chest, smashing the breastplate which in turn would pierce the heart. It works fast, and there's no blood because it's all internal.'

'What about the body? How would you get rid of it?'

'My father was part owner of a Rottweiler breeding farm about three miles south of Santa Alicia. Those dogs are ornery creatures. They'd eat anything when they're hungry.'

Dutch choked back the bile that was coming up from his stomach. 'There were still the remains,' he managed to say. Was that a smile on Payne's face?

'And remains is your line, right, bone man? Hugo also had the answer to that one. The bones would be pulverized and scattered over the mountains. Nothing would remain. Without a body, it's almost impossible to get a conviction. That is *if* a murder was committed, which it wasn't.' His eyes burned through Dutch, daring him to contradict that.

Dutch didn't. Something else was coming into his head. 'And Bobby's father?'

'What about him?'

'He also died.'

'An accident. His bus went out of control. It happened right after all of us joined the army together.'

'Who's all?' Dutch asked, unsure of how many he was talking about.

'Four of us. Bobby, Hugo, Roberto and myself.'

That's right, Dutch thought. Peter had told him that Roberto was in the same regiment as Bobby. He had forgotten about that. 'Where was Hugo when you went into the army?'

'In Santa Alicia. He got pneumonia and didn't join us at Fort Bragg until a month later.' Again his eyes jumped as he began to understand what Dutch was indicating. 'There's no proof that he killed Bobby's father when we were away,' he said sternly.

Still protecting this guy, aren't you? Dutch thought. *Why? OK, let's probe.* 'What happened in Vietnam, Jonathan?'

'What?'

'You got hurt. Friendly fire.'

'In Mai Loc. I was on patrol.'

'Frye with you?'

'Yes.'

'I saw the UPI photo. He was one of the stretcher bearers.'

Payne stared at Dutch with a look of admiration. 'You don't miss much, do you? The man saved my life that day.'

'How?'

'We were deep in enemy territory when our Phantoms dropped napalm on us. Not only did those idiots wipe out half my platoon, they blew up our medical supplies and transport helicopters as well. I had lost a lot of blood and was barely alive. Without a chopper, the only way back to the hospital behind the lines was by foot. There was no time for that. I needed an immediate transfusion. The problem was that my blood type was a bit rare.'

Dutch understood. 'You had B positive blood. So did Hugo.'

'He was the only one left alive in our platoon who had it. While waiting for another transport to arrive and fly us out, a medic gave us the transfusion. It was done right in the middle of a fire fight. How many friends do you have who would do that for you? Hugo not only carried me out of the jungle, he willingly gave me his blood, almost at the cost of his own life.'

'How did you know the twins, Jonathan?'

Payne took a long puff on the cigar and slowly let out the smoke. 'I used to sleep with one of them,' he said finally. 'Natalie, I think her name was. It was a casual thing. Just a passage into manhood. The girl slept with a lot of the boys from school. After a couple of weeks, we stopped seeing each other.'

'Was Hugo jealous? Did he also want her?'

'You put too much importance on base emotions, Van Deer. Sexual desires had little to do with Hugo's make-up.'

'Yet he wrote Natalie a love note.'

'Hugo?' He looked sceptically at Dutch.

'Yes, Hugo.'

'I told you, he wasn't interested in emotional or physical ties with women. Why would he write her a love letter? If he did, he would have told me.'

'Maybe Hugo didn't have those feeling for her. Maybe he wrote the note to get her attention. Did he tell you everything he did?'

'Absolutely,' Payne said flippantly.

The man was arrogant, Dutch thought. He would be easy for someone like Hugo to fool. 'Their father was supposed to have gone back to Chicago. He never made it.'

Payne shrugged, letting out more cigar smoke. 'I know nothing about that.'

'Frye may have killed him.'

Payne let out a short snicker. 'Poor Hugo. You have him knocking people over like flies.' He continued to appear amused, but his nervous, flickering eyes betrayed his real feelings.

'You said you and Natalie were no big deal. If you weren't afraid of everyone finding out about your involvement with her, then why did you want to close down the hotel dig?'

Jonathan laughed. 'I get you here to ask you questions, and you're the one who winds up asking me them.'

'Why?' Dutch repeated.

'I told you, business reasons.'

Dutch shook his head. 'I don't think so, Jonathan. You have more money than God. I was wrong before. It never had anything to do with the twins. It was something else you didn't want anyone finding out.'

'What the hell are you talking about? My past life is an open book. Read *Time* magazine.'

'I did. The article said that your father disappeared.'

'Lots of fathers disappear. Look at yours.'

'Mine wasn't eaten by Rottweilers.'

Payne started moving towards him.

'Your father was murdered, Jonathan. That's what you didn't want anyone finding out. Focusing in on the twins meant focusing in on Santa Alicia, the place where you grew up. I think deep down you always knew that Frye killed the girls. Once the police found out that Frye did it and you knew him, they would start to think about your father again. If Frye confessed, it would ruin your chances of becoming governor. Maybe worse. It could make you an accessary. Except I don't think it happened that way. I doubt if he even consulted you before he did it. I doubt if he even consulted Bobby before he did away with *his* father. It was a game to you, Jonathan. It wasn't one to him.'

Payne's face was turning red once again.

'Maybe you were grateful to Hugo for more than saving your life in 'Nam. Maybe your gratefulness had to do with him killing your father.'

'That's enough!' Miles stood up and went over to the anthropologist.

Dutch ignored him. 'Where is Hugo Frye now?' he said to Payne.

'Dead!' he snapped.

'Wrong, Jonathan. Hugo Frye paid Bobby Santiago's bail. He gave the police department his real name. I've seen Bobby since then. The man's scared. He believes Frye wants to kill him. Why do you think that is? Because that Indian could finger him, that's why. It started out as a make-believe game about murdering fathers. Nothing wrong with that. Angry children do it all the time. Except Hugo took it a step further. It takes a special breed to do that. The earthquake not only uncovered an Indian graveyard, it also uncovered a series of grisly murders. The man desperately tried to cover it all back up, even by committing murder again. I think you're beginning to see that. Now where is he?'

'Not your concern, Van Deer.'

Dutch looked confused. 'What am I missing here?

Aren't you taking loyalty too far? I really don't need you for this. The money that was used to pay Bobby's bail was drawn from a bank that you own. Frye had an account there. It shouldn't be too hard to get a subpoena to have the account expropriated and find out where he lives.'

'The bank doesn't know where he lives. That's the way he wanted it. It's my bank and I honoured his request. The money came from a private savings account,' Payne said. He reached for the red phone on his table.

'What about his mail, credit cards, a goddamn social security number?'

'There's nothing on him. His savings account has several hundred thousand dollars in it. The money was put under his real name by me many years ago. That's it.'

'In gratitude?'

'Yes. After the army, Hugo Frye, as every one knew him, vanished. That account is the only proof that he ever existed.'

'John, you've done enough for him. You don't owe him any more. He's going to bring us all down,' Miles broke in.

Payne held his hand up, stopping him, then spoke into the phone. 'Tell Jimmy I'll be ready to go in half an hour,' he said to someone on the other end. After putting the receiver back into the cradle, he looked at the Dutchman. 'I have an appointment. Stay here with Miles. Jimmy will come and get you.' He buttoned his double-breasted jacket and gathered up his leather attaché case from the antique table.

'John . . .' Miles said. He was clearly upset.

'It will be taken care of, Miles. I promise.' Without

519

saying goodbye, Payne walked out of the door.

In his own way, this man was just as crazy as Hugo Frye, Dutch thought. He glanced over to Miles. The lawyer looked frightened and lost. 'How is he going to take care of it?' Dutch asked him.

'I don't know,' Miles replied.

'He won't turn him in. Will he kill him?'

Scone just shook his head, as if in a daze.

'Christ, to think Therese loves someone like you,' Dutch said, angered by the man's fear.

Miles shook his head. 'She doesn't love me. She told me that this morning.'

Dutch stared at him, stunned. 'I saw you holding each other at the helicopter pad.'

He sighed deeply. 'We were saying goodbye.'

No wonder the man had looked upset when he came in. Dutch wanted to ask him more but there wasn't time for that. 'Where is Hugo Frye, Miles?'

Miles stared mutely at the closed door, continuing to shake his head. 'Why won't he understand?' he said. 'I knew Hugo was insane from some of the things Jonathan told me. I had no idea, until now, the magnitude of it. Frye has to be stopped. It can't go on.'

Dutch grabbed him by the lapel. 'Where the fuck is he?'

He turned and faced Dutch, then his frightened eyes slowly went up to the ceiling.

Dutch followed his gaze. After a couple of seconds, he began to understand. Still clutching Miles's jacket, he shook him harder than before. 'You telling me he's been here all the time?'

'He stays here,' Miles said, barely audible. 'In the room above the office. John told me that. I hear him sometimes, but I've never met him.'

'Show me where!' Dutch hissed. 'Show me where the fucker stays!'

They went upstairs. There were two doors, both closed.

'In there,' Miles said, pointing to the room on the right. 'That's his room. Nobody, including the help, goes in there. John's orders.'

Dutch grabbed the handle, turned it and flung open the door.

It was a small room, sparse, with a twin-sized bed, a night stand next to it and a lamp on top of that. That was all. It was as impersonal as a motel room. There was nothing in here that had a human stamp on it. No books, no pictures on the wall, not even a scrap of paper.

Dutch pulled the covers off the bed. The sheets were fresh. No one had slept in here last night. He looked questioningly at Miles.

'He was here, all right,' Miles said. 'I heard him screaming something from Shakespeare out on the balcony during the night. John was clearly disturbed about it this morning. I tried telling him to get rid of him but he wouldn't listen.'

Over by the wall was a set of French doors leading out to a balcony. Dutch opened them and went outside. He immediately saw the carved centipedes on the railing and on the columns. There were hundreds of them covering the wooden supports.

Miles looked at them. 'Oh, God!' he moaned. 'I didn't know the extent of it.'

'He stays here. Why haven't you met him?'

'I rarely come to the compound. Nobody does. It's John's retreat. I don't think even Hugo comes here

521

that often. I asked John about him, but he got evasive every time I did, refused to talk about him.'

Dutch came back inside and opened the wardrobe door. It was empty. He went into the bathroom. The floor, toilet and sink were spotless, as if a sanitation crew had scoured every inch of it. Didn't the sonofabitch ever piss? He wondered. There was a wrapped bar of soap in the shower stall.

Disgusted, Dutch flung open the medicine cabinet. Nothing but empty glass shelves. He was about to walk out when his eyes caught something small and cylindrical in the corner behind the door. He stooped down and picked it up.

A plastic pill vial. He turned it over until the label faced him.

'What is it?' Miles asked.

'A prescription for Augmentin, an antibiotic. Our boy has an infection.' Dutch's temple was pounding now. He must have lost or forgotten about it. *The man had finally fucked up*.

The sound of footsteps coming down the hallway towards them.

'There's no name on the vial,' Dutch said. 'Our boy has always been a careful guy. He must have ripped it off, just in case someone found it. There's a partial logo of a drug store − looks like Save-on. There's also the last three digits of a prescription number.'

The large frame of Jimmy Ciazo walked into the bedroom.

Dutch glanced over at him. 'I know you're in private practice now, Jimmy, but do you still remember how to act like a cop?'

His dead eyes moved in Dutch's direction.

He held out the vial to the Italian. 'I need a patient's

name from these numbers. Someone lost his medicine and I want to return it.'

Ciazo turned his gaze slowly towards Miles for instructions.

'Get it,' the lawyer said, nodding that it was OK.

'Mr Payne won't like it,' Jimmy said quietly.

'It will be all right. Just get it,' Miles said again, his voice shaking.

Jimmy called the main office of the drugstore chain where the database of customers was kept. He told the woman who answered the phone that he was a police officer and gave her his old ID number. He then told her that he needed the name of a patient and gave her the three legible digits left on the vial. She didn't bother to check Jimmy's ID. Even if she did, it was too early for his resignation papers to be completely processed.

The ex-detective stood in the same position for three minutes without moving a muscle and waited for the drug store employee to scan her computer. When she finally got back to him, he took out his old, frayed PD notepad and ballpoint pen from his side pocket and wrote something down. He then hung up without saying thank you. Looking down at the pad, he turned to Miles and said, 'The prescription was filled out at a drug store in Santa Monica. They only have a PO box on this guy. I can always check that out if you need it.'

'I need it,' Dutch said.

'I wasn't talking to you,' Ciazo said to Dutch. He was looking at Miles, waiting for an answer.

'Get it,' Miles responded.

'Did you get a name?' Dutch asked, his fingers turning white from squeezing them against the palms of his hands.

523

Ciazo glared at Dutch, curling his lip. 'Of course I got a name. You think I'm stupid.'

Dutch took the notepad from Jimmy and looked at the writing on it. He had no trouble deciphering the name. Ciazo's clean handwriting would make any elementary school teacher proud. 'Oh, Christ, so that's who Hugo Frye is now,' he said, stunned. Then a cold fear came over him when he realized who was with him. 'Oh, Christ!' he said again, this time screaming out the words.

28

Therese looked out of the helicopter's portal and saw Topanga Canyon and the multi-million-dollar homes of Malibu hanging over the ocean on wooden pillars. We should be heading inland soon, she thought. That raised her spirits. The air-conditioning was off and the craft was stuffy inside. She had asked Kevin to turn it on but he said it wasn't working properly. Her clothes were damp with perspiration and she removed her jacket. Kevin had taken his off twenty minutes ago. His khaki shirt was darkened with sweat, yet he didn't seem bothered by the heat.

She sat back and thought about Miles. He had come into her life after she had been living alone with her grief for two years. At first it was fun feeling alive again. Lately, however, she had been thinking more and more about Dutch. The confusion was cluttering up her life. She needed to step back, see where she wanted to go.

A few minutes later, she felt a slight vibration. Glancing out of the window, she saw that the ship was descending. The Santa Monica pier was off to her right and a gutted amusement park was directly below her. Why hadn't they turned east, towards John Payne's office? 'Why are we going down, Kevin?' she asked.

Kevin looked over to her and smiled reassuringly. 'Feel that shaking just now? A slight problem with the rotor tail. Nothing to worry about. I need to take a look at it. There's a deserted area down below. Fortunately, my house is right there, too. I can land this baby in my own backyard so you don't have to sit outside in the heat. We should be back up again in a jiffy. Your seat belt fastened?'

Therese checked the strap around her shoulders. It was. 'I need to call the girl staying at my house and tell her I'll be late,' she said.

'No problem.' Kevin removed the cellular phone from the cradle and handed it to her.

As she took it from him, she caught a glimpse of a cobra curving its tail around the inside of his arm.

'If it's not one thing, it's another,' he said, shaking his head and clucking his tongue.

Ciazo didn't have an easy time getting the address. The clerk at the Santa Monica post office wouldn't give information like that over the phone, police or no police. Jimmy had to call a homicide detective he knew at the Santa Monica station and ask him to go next door to the post office to talk to the clerk. Five minutes later the detective called back with the address and Jimmy wrote it down. He seemed a little surprised. 'I didn't think anyone lived there anymore, not after the fire,' he said to Miles, looking at his notepad. 'It's in a vacant three-block area about half a mile from the pier.'

Dutch took the paper from him, then went over to the phone and picked up the receiver.

Jimmy put his large hand on the cradle, killing the dial tone. 'Who you calling, Dutchman?'

'The police.'

Ciazo slowly shook his head. 'Not today.'

Confused, Dutch looked at the Italian. 'I just got through telling you. Rousette is the killer.'

'No police. John Payne's orders. I've already gone too far with this shit.' His expression remained rigid, like an android's.

'Therese is with him, Jimmy.' Dutch's voice shook.

'We don't know that,' Jimmy said.

Miles broke in. 'Maybe she's not with him. Perhaps she's already home by now.' His tone was wooden, having a hard time believing his own words. He called her number. The house sitter answered and said Therese had phoned a few minutes ago from the helicopter and told her that she would be a little late. Miles hung up. He took out a small address book from his breast pocket and nervously thumbed through the pages. Finding what he wanted, he began dialing. 'It's the number in the helicopter,' he said. He waited for the ringing to start at the other end. There was only dead silence. He tried again. The same thing. 'There must be a problem with the phone,' he said to Dutch and Jimmy.

Looking pensive, Ciazo bit down on his bottom lip. It was one of the rare instances when anyone had ever seen the Italian look unsettled. 'Time you left us, Dutch,' he said finally. He took a set of keys from his pocket and handed it to him. 'These are yours. I had someone drive your truck up here after I picked you up.'

Puzzled, Dutch took them. 'You telling me I'm free to go?'

Jimmy unfurled his eyes. 'You always did look a gift horse in the mouth, didn't you? Let's go.' Leaving

Miles in the room, he took Dutch by the arm and half-walked, half-shoved him outside.

They stopped by the Bronco parked next to the front door.

He knew it was pushing it, but Dutch had to ask him anyway. 'Why were you trying to find Bobby Santiago?'

'To make sure nobody else found him first. I was trying to keep him alive. That's what Mr Payne wanted.'

He had misread this man. 'You were trying to keep him safe from Kevin Rousette, whose real name is Hugo Frye. Payne must have suspected him all along. I need help on this one, Jimmy.'

Ciazo's jaw tightened. He was torn. 'I want to but I can't. I work for John Payne now. In a couple of minutes I have to take him to his appointment. I suggest you go on home. Take up a hobby like stamp collecting and leave this shit alone. Forcing this issue will only incriminate Mr Payne further in this mess and he's not going to like it. Forget about this, Dutchman. Rousette will be taken care of in time.'

'I can't wait for that time, Jimmy. He killed a friend of mine. Therese may still be with him.'

Ciazo's face hardened. 'Forget about it, Dutch, I mean it.' He pulled out the Colt semi-automatic and bullet clip, one from each of his back pockets, and handed them to Dutch. 'These are yours. Try not to shoot yourself in the leg.'

Kevin landed the helicopter in the deserted, pot-holed street next to his house. He helped Therese out of the craft, then went back in and turned off the power to the radio attached to the control panel. Picking up the microphone, he held it next to the window so she could see what he was doing and flicked the button on and off a couple of times. He shook his head, tsk-tsked, and put it back in its holder. 'The thing's dead,' he said to her, feigning puzzlement. Then he took the receiver from the cellular phone and held it up to her ear. No dial tone. He had disengaged the cord from the battery while they were still in the air. Kevin pushed some of the buttons a couple of times, just to make it look good, then shrugged. 'It's got to be the electrical system. That's a little unnerving. I'm glad we were on the ground when we found out.' Again he gave her that reassuring smile as he stepped out of the craft. 'Let's go inside and I'll call for help.' He suddenly stopped, leaned into the chopper and took out a roll of industrial tape and a wrench from a pocket under the console. The adhesive stripping was the one he had used to tie up Robin and her maid. Putting the centre of it through his index finger, twirling it around, he said, 'Hot day. I could use some iced tea. How about you?'

The road signs posted next to the treacherous curves on Highway One read fifteen miles an hour. Dutch took them at forty, the wheels of the Bronco nipping the edge of the cliffs at every hairpin turn.

Holding one hand on the wheel, he reached into the glove compartment and took out the UPI photograph of John Payne being carried off by the soldiers. He put it up on the console so he could glance at it while driving. Hugo was the stretcher bearer in the top left-hand corner staring at the burning helicopters. Probably one of his choppers that had been blown up. He was a helicopter pilot in Payne's unit, not an

529

infantryman. Rousette had lied to him about that yesterday when they were on the phone. Talking about Hugo Frye as if he were another person, Rousette had made himself out to be a paranoid loner who took pleasure in killing. Dutch believed that to be true. The other part, about him winning medals, was probably fabricated for the Dutchman's benefit. Delusions of grandeur. Other things that may also have been true were the stories about the murder of his sergeant, the torturing of the prisoners and that Hugo never forgot a wrong.

Then he thought about Frye's extended jaw. He had never got a chance to see Rousette's face clearly because he had always worn a helmet when Dutch was around him. An abnormality like that, however, would have stood out. Sometime after the war he must have had plastic surgery. Payne said there was no ID in the name of Hugo Frye other than the savings account. That meant that the persona of Kevin Rousette had been created after Jonathan put several hundred thousand dollars in his bank for Frye.

A couple of hours later, the mountainous road gave way to a straight ribbon of blacktop. He stopped off in the town of Cambria and tried Therese's number again. The sitter, a little irked, said she still hadn't returned. Her parents were expecting her for dinner and she had to leave soon. Did he know what had happened to her? Dutch said he didn't, then hung up.

Therese should have been back way before now, he thought. His muscles tightened at the thought of her still being with Frye. He got back into the truck. Within seconds, the speedometer was up to eighty-five and climbing.

* * *

A blanket of darkness lifted and Therese opened her eyes. Everything was muddy, like a lens out of focus. Her head felt as if it was on fire. Tears ran down her face from the pain. Therese wanted to moan but something was pressing against her mouth, preventing her from doing so. She tried to move her hands, which were behind her back, but couldn't. When she inhaled, the smell of wet carpet filled her nostrils. Then there was that strange hissing noise.

Where am I?

Her senses slowly began to return. The last thing she remembered was refusing the iced tea that Kevin brought to her on his porch, then turning away to look at the burned-out amusement park. That's it.

Her sight began to come back. *A room . . . very little light.*

There was a carpet under her, damp and acrid smelling. Once again she tried to move her hands, but they held fast behind her back. She was tied up, she suddenly realized. On the floor, next to her, was a pile of clothes. Her own.

My God, I'm naked! Her skin shrivelled with terror.

Therese heard footsteps behind her.

She turned on to her back so she could see. The pain in her head roared when she moved, forcing her to close her eyes. When she opened them again, she saw Kevin squatting down next to her, his thin lips stretched into a smile. He was wearing shorts, no shirt. His milky skin was covered with a sheen of perspiration.

'I hit you on the head with a wrench so you wouldn't fight me. Sorry about that,' he said. 'A pity you didn't want anything to drink. Would you like me to remove the tape from your mouth?'

She nodded. The back of her head felt as if there

was an ice pick jabbing at it.

'Don't scream,' he warned her. 'Not that it would matter. Nobody could hear. I just hate the sound of screaming, that's all.'

Again she nodded.

Kevin roughly ripped the tape from her mouth. His hand felt like wet rubber on her face.

'Why?' was all she could blurt out.

He didn't answer her.

She looked into his eyes. What she saw there caused a trickle of fear to run down her spine. Kevin's eyes were slits that seemed to be laughing at something deep and private inside himself. His jaw began to move up and down as if he was chewing on something tough and sinewy. 'You'll be a gift for Wilhelm,' he said finally.

Her voice was husky with dread, 'Kevin . . .'

He put his finger on her lips, silencing her. The *urge* suddenly rose up within him, clamping down on his organs, squeezing his life's blood out of him. 'Would you like to see something beautiful?' he asked, the smile remaining fixed on his face.

Be calm. Don't provoke him. 'See what?' she asked, trying to control her fear.

'Something I've never shown to anyone.' The smile was broader now, and he had a guileful look about him. His expression suddenly softened. 'It's time,' he whispered. He brushed his hand against her cheek.

The terror had taken over her entire body now. 'It's time for what, Kevin?'

'For purity.' He moved closer to her, reached out and took her by the arm. 'Come. You can never love them, they won't let you. But at least you can get to know them.'

He began to pull her by one arm across the carpet.

'Kevin, please, you're hurting me!' she screamed.

'It's time for pureness. Oh yes. Oh yes.' He went over to the desk next to the couch, opened the top drawer with his free hand and took out a brass key ring. 'Oh yes. Oh yes. Oh yes.' Then he dragged her out of the living-room.

'Kevin, stop it!' Therese screamed. She was kicking wildly at the carpet with her bare legs.

'*Yesyesyesyesyesyes*.' He yanked her into the hallway, unlocked a door leading to the basement, and pulled her down the staircase. '*Yesyesyesyesyes*.'

Therese's arm felt as if it was being jerked out of its socket. Her body ached horribly. There was no carpet to soften the hard stairs, and her ribs felt ready to crack.

When he reached the basement at the bottom, he pulled a chain, turning on a dim overhead light. The heat down here was almost unbearable. He carted her over the damp cement floor with its deep musty smell, past the old, no longer used boiler room. Therese managed to push herself up on her feet. Her legs were covered with bruises and cuts. She tried to jerk herself free, but he was too strong. His hand enveloping her upper arm was like a steel clamp cutting off her circulation.

'Now I'll know,' he said, nodding emphatically.

'What will you know? Kevin, please stop this. You're hurting me!'

'You'll see. You'll see,' he said. He stopped at the closed door at the end of the corridor and unlocked it with one of the keys on the brass ring. When the latch clicked, he pushed the door open. It was dark and moist inside. There was also a powerful gamy odour, like the interior of a rain forest. The source of the steady hissing was in this room. Here the noise was deafening. Turning to her, he said in a loud voice so he could be heard, 'We'll only keep the light on for a little while. Light disturbs them.'

Disturbs who? She opened her mouth to say something, but he put his finger to her lips once again to quiet her. Smiling to reassure her, he said, 'It will be pure. I need to know.' He reached up, grabbed the light chain and turned it on.

What Therese saw made her cry out in horror. Most of the large room was converted into a tropical jungle enclosed by fine wire mesh. The floor outside the enormous cage was an industrial metal grating used to drain off water. Behind the netting were hundreds of enormous centipedes crawling over the foliage, trying to escape the light. Some of them were babies. Thousands of eggs lay under the leaves waiting to be hatched. A myriad of skeletal remains, mostly mice, littered the wet ground. The hissing noise was coming from an enormous humidifier over in the corner. It filled the room with moist, hot air. Next to it was a curled-up rubber water hose used for washing down the floor.

Hugo closed the door behind him. He walked over to Therese. She backed away from him in horror. The floor grating hurt her feet.

'What is this place?' she muttered, too frightened to cry out.

'They're beautiful, don't you think? Priceless, actually.' She tried to slip past him, but he caught her arm and flung her backwards. Her body hit the netting, knocking several of the large arthropods off the wire mesh. He went over and opened the screen

534

door to the cage. 'This will be pure,' he said to her.

Therese ran over to the old oak door but it was closed and her hands were still taped behind her, preventing her from opening it. Pressing her back against it, she turned to face him. 'Let me out!' she demanded.

Hugo just smiled. He went over to her and stroked her face. Looking at her lovely, frightened mouth, he felt a twinge of *something* pass through his body. It was the same *something* he had felt for the twins, he thought. Perhaps it was love. He could never completely identify it. Hugo then picked her up in his strong arms and carried her over to the door in the netting. Dropping her on to the wet earth inside the cage, he quickly closed the door, snapping the clasp. She raised herself up off the mossy ground, crawled over to the mesh, banged her body against it and yelled, 'Kevin, please! For God's sake!'

'Goodbye, Therese,' he said softly, walking to the door. Just before he went out into the hallway, he turned off the light. *My darlings need the darkness.* Her screams turned to silence as soon as he shut the thick door.

'Pure,' he whispered. He went back up the stairs to his bedroom.

The 'wet room', as he liked to call the one in the basement, had been renovated slowly. He had drawn up the specifications himself after studying the giant centipedes' natural habitat. It had taken six different contractors who didn't know each other four years to do the work. Each one was hired to do a specific task. This way, no one person would ever know why the room was being built.

The *Scolopendra gigantea* was the perfect species to

work with; they were big, strong and dangerous. He had learned years ago, after he was bitten, that just one of those large arthropods could not produce enough venom to disable a human being. But it had put a thought in his head. How many, he wondered, would it actually take? A hundred? A thousand? Now he would know. If he found out, then Therese's death would be pure. The triorthocresyl phosphate he had used on the twins was only a poor substitute, a rehearsal for this day. The real thing was the toxin from the beautiful centipedes. Nature in the raw! No laboratory could duplicate that.

In the recesses of his mind, he had toyed with this idea for a long time. Now Therese would be the one to give him the answers he longed to know.

His babies hadn't eaten in a couple of days. They must be very hungry by now, he thought.

Hugo went into his bedroom, removed his false eyebrows and lashes, then his expensive toupee. He laid the piece carefully over a mannequin's head on his dresser.

Looking in the mirror, he saw the slight scars next to his jaw where a large section of mandible bone had been removed by a plastic surgeon in Washington many years ago. In fact, it was the same doctor who had reconstructed Jonathan's face. Without the overbite, Hugo's features were now lustreless, almost as if his identifiable characteristics were also severed during the operation. He liked looking anonymous. It gave him the freedom to be anybody he chose to be. With the new face came a new identity. Rousette was his mother's maiden name. Part of her now lived on in him.

Hugo never knew exactly how much Payne had paid

for his operation and for the dental surgeon. The industrialist would never tell him. Well, he had earned it, hadn't he? 'What are friends for?' he murmured.

He had thought about and planned for this time ever since they were kids concocting plots to kill their fathers. When he lived in Santa Alicia, Hugo was sure about two things regarding Jonathan: first, that he would become very wealthy in his own right; second, that Jonathan could be very generous when he felt he owed someone something. And he owed Hugo plenty! He had made sure of that. After all, it was Hugo who had killed his father and saved his life in 'Nam. Over the years, Payne had given him a lot of money because of that. It was invested wisely, leaving him, if not wealthy, at least financially independent.

He had paid his dues for that money. More than paid them. For years he had allowed himself to be under the thumb of that egotistical bastard, flying him around like a servant, doing everything he asked him to do. John insisted that he use the same toupee-maker he used, and wear jackets and suits from his factory in Scotland. The man was repressing. Well, now things were going to be different. Hugo didn't need him any longer. He had enough money. It was time to free himself from Payne's grip. The moment he had waited for had come.

He could feel his own power flooding through his veins now. Bobby Santiago, Payne and that gimp, Roberto Gomez, were the only people who could connect him to his past. If they were dead, then the past would no longer exist. All his unearthings would finally be buried for good. He would then be free to travel the world as a veiled stranger, detached from everyone. Hugo smiled at that. He smiled because he now had the power to carry it out.

Suddenly his thoughts turned to Therese. The idea of going downstairs again and watching her slowly expire from asphyxiation began to cause a sense of extreme happiness within him.

Only her bones would be left.

Oh, so pure!

These thoughts began to be overpowered by the dull throbbing in his infected arm. He went over to the bed and unzipped the overnight bag he had brought with him from Payne's house. Hugo took out his Dopp case and groped around inside it for the vial of antibiotics. It wasn't there. First he dumped the shaving kit on to the bed, then the overnight bag. Not there. He methodically searched through the pockets of his clothing. Nothing.

His face turned grave. He must have left it at Payne's house.

A mistake, he thought. The first one he had made. Not good. Not good at all.

29

Total blackness. They were all around her now, slithering over and under the foliage, their *whooshing*, fluttering noises increasing with their excitement.

Therese felt one of them brush across her leg. She let out a stifled scream and backed away before it could clamp its jaws down.

She desperately wanted to reach out and feel for the cage, but her hands were taped behind her. Inching forward, she eventually touched the wire mesh with her leg. She banged her body hard against it several times, hoping the cage would break apart. That only dislodged the arthropods from the top section of the screen. Several of them fell on to her shoulders and head. Therese screamed frantically as she shook them off. Her body began to tremble with terror and she started to weep.

Get control! Think, Therese, think!

The cage door! She remembered seeing Kevin opening it. The door was held in place by a small clasp.

She moved her body towards where she thought the cage entrance was, using her shoulder to feel for it. Her feet brushed past more arthropods. There was a sickening crunching noise as her bare foot came down on one in her path.

Where was the goddamn door!

Suddenly there was a surging pain in her ankle as a centipede sunk the tip of its jaw into her. She cried out in agony. Never had she experienced pain like this! Again she desperately felt for the wire opening.

Another bite . . . then another. Her arms and legs were on fire. She could feel their antennae tickling her skin as they reached out for her.

Where was the door?

There was no longer a rational part left in her mind. She had to get out. *The pain! Oh, dear God!*

They were crawling up her body, piercing her flesh with their hungry, sharp jaws. Through the torturous agony, she could feel their venom entering her bloodstream. Her legs were beginning to tremble with weakness.

WHERE WAS THE FUCKING DOOR!

Then she felt its tubular frame. She catapulted her shoulder into it. The thin metal clasp snapped in half and the door flung open. Therese fell on to the steel floor, hitting it hard with her right shoulder. She moaned in pain. The cage door dropped next to her, its casing resonating loudly on the grating. Therese shook off one of the centipedes that was clamped to her leg. Her strength was ebbing from her and breathing was becoming difficult. *Jesus, what was happening?*

Holding the broken screen door up with her knees, she slid her body under it, using it as a shield. She dragged herself and the section of mesh along the grating towards the wall. When she felt the wet stone surface, she edged her body towards the door. Eventually she found the wood panelling and attempted to stand up, propping her back against the wall for support, trying to find the handle with her bound hands. Her legs would no longer support her weight and she dropped back to the ground. Parts of her body were cramping up. She was beginning to salivate abnormally and her tongue was thickening. Nausea pains flared through her stomach. Therese huddled against the wall, snuggling under the pliable segment of mesh.

The centipedes had found the opening in the cage and were crawling out of it and inching themselves along the grating. When they reached Therese, they began to creep up the mesh. Therese grabbed the netting with her teeth and shook it with her body. Most of the insects fell to the floor, then began to climb all over again. There was not much strength left in her now and she found that it was becoming more and more difficult to dislodge them from the screen. Soon she'd be totally paralysed, and would only be able to watch in helpless horror as they made their way over the top of the netting to clasp on to her body.

Her mouth sagged open and her swollen tongue stuck out between her lips. Tears began to run down her immobile face. She didn't want to die like this. *Not like this!*

The Dutchman turned off the PCH and found the deserted, gutted area where the amusement park had once stood. Two blocks in, he saw the black helicopter sitting on the tar street.

She's with him. There was no doubt in his mind now. Had he hurt her? The thought of what Frye had done to Robin caused a terror to flare up within him.

He looked around. Both sides of the street contained rows of abandoned tract homes. Glancing down at the address on the paper, he realized that

Frye's house was directly in front of the chopper.

Turning off the motor, Dutch took the Colt from the glove compartment, snapped the clip into the handle and got out of the truck.

Upstairs in his bedroom, Hugo peered out of a crack in the shutters and saw the Dutchman running towards his house. He sighed deeply. Yes, he had made a careless mistake, and because of it his twin had come for him. As if against his will, a fervour, like the feeling a roller-coaster rider gets on the downward trajectory, raced through his stomach. How beautiful he is, Hugo thought. He wanted to cry out to this blond man who was his soulmate, take him in his arms and embrace him. No one could ever understand the horrors they shared. No one? Wilhelm didn't know it yet, but they only had each other in this brutal world. Then the feeling of elation suddenly faded like bites of cotton candy when he realized that the anthropologist would also have to be added to the list of former friends. In order to be free, there had to be no one. *A pity*. His mind began to work as he closed the slat of the shutter. Who knows Wilhelm better than me, he thought as he quickly went down the stairs, two at a time. *It will be done with love, just like it was with Steve at the reservoir so many years ago.*

Dutch undid the safety of the gun and pulled the nickel-plated slide towards him, skating the bullet up into the chamber. When he got to the door, he pushed hard against the knob. It was locked. He went through the dead hedges surrounding the house and looked in the window covered with steel bars. A closed shutter jutting up against the glass panes blocked his view.

542

There was no light coming from inside. The house appeared deserted. Was Frye in there? Dutch believed he was. If so, then Therese had to be in there too.

Down in the basement, Hugo held up a torch and looked at the heat level on the humidifier. It was accurate. It had to be for his little darlings. The needle was set at eighty-seven degrees with ninety-three percent humidity. He turned the knob, stopping at the 110-degree mark. The noise grew louder. Hugo smiled. Yes, he knew his Dutchman, all right. He turned off the torch and left the basement to await his guest.

Dutch went back to the Bronco and took out a lug nut wrench from the tool compartment. When he returned to the window, he stuck the angled instrument between the cross bar section and the stucco wall. Using his body for leverage, he leaned on it with all his weight. The bolts holding the steel bars easily tore out of the mildewed plaster. Dutch tossed the tool on the ground. Holding the gun by the barrel, he broke the window pane. Finding the latch on top, he slid the sash up. The shutters on the inside were locked. He kicked them hard in the middle, shattering the clasp.

The heat and humidity hit him as soon as he climbed into the darkened room. *Christ, it was like a boiler room in here*. The smell was wretched, and the hissing sound was hurting his ears.

He went over to the end table and turned on the lamp. The furniture was old and damp, with a green mould covering most of it. A photograph over the fireplace caught his eye. Walking over to the mantel, he picked up a framed 8 by 11 photograph. It was the picture of four unwashed, unshaven soldiers holding M-16s and posing for the camera. They were obviously out in the bush when this was taken. There was Payne, Santiago and the bank officer, Roberto Gomez. The one at the end, with the big jaw, was Hugo Frye. A helicopter with a snake painted on its bow loomed in the background. Dutch knew about those crafts. It was a Cobra, one of the most deadly of all gunships. He had a feeling that this one was flown by Frye.

Holding the .45 in both hands, he went out into the hallway. He tried the basement door. Locked. Putting his ear against it, he could hear that the loud sizzling noise was coming from somewhere inside.

He turned and walked up the narrow groaning staircase, listening for any sounds of movement. Every time his boots came down on the carpet, the old oak floor underneath creaked. He tried to breathe, but the air around him was thick and heavy. *Deep, slow breaths*, he said to himself. Billie was not here to help him now.

Dutch crept along the hallway, then pushed the door of the bedroom open. Looking in all directions, he carefully went inside. Finding the light switch by the wall, he turned it on. The room was like the one Hugo had occupied when he stayed at Payne's house in Big Sur. Clean, neat, and devoid of life.

Almost.

On top of the dresser, Dutch saw Frye's hairpiece hanging neatly on the mannequin's head.

He was somewhere inside this house, Dutch knew it. The thought of being in the same quarters with that man made his body ripple with dread. Again he fought for air. There wasn't much of it. He wiped the sweat

544

from his eyes with his sleeve. *Damn! He needed to breathe!*

He pushed open the cupboard door and saw Hugo's different toupees lined up on the shelves inside the glass protector. Several garment bags hung on the pole that stretched across the cupboard. Dutch opened two. Both contained Shetland wool jackets.

He listened again for noises, but he heard nothing. Walking out on the landing, he saw a closed door at the end of the hall. He hesitated. His instincts said something living was in there. Dutch bit down on his lip. His heart was beating so fast he thought his arteries would explode from the pressure. *Please, Therese, be alive!*

Then he heard Hugo's pleasant voice coming from behind the door: 'You may come in, my friend.'

The decision had been made for him.

Holding the slippery gun tightly in his sweaty palm and standing with his back against the wall, Dutch pushed the door open with his foot. The room was in near darkness. Out of the corner of his eye, he saw the silhouette of Hugo standing by the window with his hands folded behind his back. A sliver of sun broke through the split in the shutter, emitting a halo of light around his bald head. He was still wearing gym shorts and nothing else.

Hugo turned round and faced Dutch. His lips broke into a smile and his eyes filled with affection. 'I'm glad you came,' he whispered.

Dutch had to blink several times, clearing his eyes of the perspiration that was dripping down into them. He could not see the man's face in the darkness.

'I always knew this day would come. Would you like to sit down?' Hugo arched his hand over towards a wooden chair in the corner, the only piece of furniture in the room.

A splinter of sunlight touched his arm and Dutch saw the tattoo of the cobra. With its fangs and outstretched tongue, it looked fearsome, poised to strike. The tattoo was the same as the one on the gunship in the photograph downstairs.

'No? Perhaps a drink then?' Hugo said.

'Where's Therese?' Dutch said threateningly.

'She took a taxi back to her house.'

'You're lying.' Sneering, Dutch cocked the hammer on the .45.

'Why would I do that? She left. Feel free to call the cab company. They'll tell you.' Then the smile faded from Hugo's face and he looked sad. 'I believe you're not going to give me much time, are you? Let's get down to it, then. There are things I need to know. Tell me, did your lungs ache when you tried to get air into them?'

Dutch stared at him, not understanding. 'What are you talking about!'

'Oh, I know about it, believe me. What about your rib cage? Remember how it felt, as if it were going to explode inside your body? I used to think it would rip my intestines apart.'

Yes, Dutch remembered that feeling. So along ago . . . under the collapsed house.

The smell of Shalimar and flesh.

He could feel his throat constricting. The panic was beginning to rise within him. Dutch clenched down on his teeth, trying to force it back down.

'Did you try digging to get out?' Hugo asked, his eyes alive with curiosity.

Dutch remembered that too.

My fingers . . . how they sting . . . all bloody and sticky. Nails all gone. Let me die. Please God, let me die!

How would he know? Dutch thought. His mouth was open now, trying to grasp at particles of air that floated in front of him.

'I was there, too,' he said. 'I felt what you felt. I *feel* what you *feel* now. That's why I talked to you on the phone and answered your questions. You wanted to talk about Jonathan, I wanted to talk about us. Now we can do just that.' The flicker of sun moved down over Hugo's shoulder like an eclipse, throwing his face into total darkness. 'We are the same, you and I. You know that, don't you? We could have been friends.'

'Where's Therese?' Dutch said again, fighting for air. His voice was guttural and his face had begun to redden.

'I know you so well, Van Deer. What did it feel like when they came for her?' His voice was trembling with passion now.

Think of Billie. 'What the hell are you talking about?'

'So pure,' Hugo said, barely audible.

The man's crazy, Dutch thought.

'They did their job. What nature intended them to do. I wish I could have been privileged like you to witness it.'

Then Dutch understood.

The aroma of rotting flesh. The whiskers of the rats almost sensuously touching his face as they passed by him going towards her.

Hugo moved closer to him. 'Could you see what was happening?'

Sobbing . . . listening helplessly to the wet rubbery

sounds of their voracious hunger.

'What was it like?' Hugo's eyes were fiery coals now, piercing the darkness.

'Mamma!' he wailed, trapped under the debris. 'MAMMA!!' *The suctional noises continued for hours and he could feel her spirit slipping away from him.*

'How I wish I had been you!' Hugo said fiercely.

Trying desperately to smell her one more time but her soul was already gone.

Don't let him do it to you. *Think of Billie!* 'Where is she?' Dutch put the barrel of the gun up to Hugo's head.

Hugo sighed. 'Back to that again. Does it matter? She has nothing to do with what we shared together. You and I have so much to talk about and so little time to do it in.' His face seemed to glow like a wild animal's through the obscure light. He put his palms together in the form of a pyramid, a habit he'd copied from Jonathan. He looked like a child praying at his bedside. 'Did your mother's dead skin feel a bit cool, like the early morning air, when you touched it?' Hugo rubbed his hands slowly together, as if reliving the sensation in his head.

That sonofabitch knew! How? Dutch almost passed out from the heat and lack of oxygen, but the anger that pierced through him was keeping him alert and saving him from that terrible panic. This man − this *thing* − that was in front of him seemed to thrive on no air.

'Of course I never got the chance to find out what mine really smelled like. Not like you. You were a lucky man. I only smelled the embalming fluid and the cheap Five and Dime perfume the funeral home sprayed on her. You were buried with your mother for so much longer than I was. I've heard it's supposed to be like rotten cabbage. Is that true?'

Hot, uncontrollable rage blurred the Dutchman's vision. He wanted to pull the trigger and kill him.

Hugo didn't flinch or look away. Instead, he winked. 'They were wrong about it being like rotten cabbage, weren't they? The twins didn't smell like that, either. But we both know that, don't we?' Again he winked.

Air! He needed to breathe! Dutch grabbed Hugo by his sweaty throat, forcing him back against the shuttered window, and smashed his head against it. The slats splintered and the daylight swarmed inside the room. Dutch continued to whip Hugo's bald head against the window until the glass broke. Air rushed into the house. He took deep swallows, pushing down the terror of suffocation that was threatening to drown him. 'Where the fuck is she?' he managed to blurt out.

Blood ran down Hugo's head. His bulging eyes sagged downwards in despair. 'I give you my soul to forge with yours and all you want is that bitch.'

Dutch closed his fist and punched him on the side of the head. Hugo's head snapped back, but his lithe body stayed where it was. He looked at Dutch with mild surprise, then lifted his fingers to his mouth. Blood began to trickle from his lips and drip down on to his white, naked chest. He dabbed his mouth with the palm of his hand.

'I thought we could have talked for a while,' Hugo said. 'About things only we know about.'

Dutch clenched his fist again.

Again the bald-headed man didn't blanch. 'We can't be together for long, mind you. Soon we'll say goodbye. You have to understand, I've been alone for so many years with these feelings. I need to talk with someone who sees things like I do.'

The hate was so strong for this man, Dutch didn't know if he could control the finger that was tightening on the trigger. He forced the rage down. 'She's in this house, isn't she?'

Hugo shrugged.

Dutch punched him again.

This time Frye's feet gave way and he clutched the wooden chair for support. Blood spurted from his nose and splattered across the floor. 'You're being violent, Dutchman. That's not characteristic of you.'

'Where the hell is she?' Dutch yelled at him.

'She's now pure.' A knowing smirk came over his bloody mouth. 'I suppose it's time,' he said. Hugo removed the key ring from his pocket and held it up. 'Come. I'll take you to her. I had hoped we could have talked a little longer.' He walked past Dutch and out of the door.

Keeping the gun pressed to the back of Hugo's neck, Dutch followed him down the steps and into the hallway. Every breath he took now was painful, as it was when he was a boy trapped under the debris. The only thing that kept him from running out of the house was the knowledge that Therese was somewhere inside.

Using one of the keys, Hugo opened the door to the basement. It was black and dank-smelling down there, and the heat was almost unendurable. Dutch grabbed Hugo by his wet, slippery shoulder. 'There's got to be a light switch.'

Hugo reached up and pulled the chain above him, turning on the light.

Dutch pushed him forward, making Frye walk faster down the stairs. At the end of the basement, with its sweaty walls and cobwebs, Hugo stopped at the closed door and turned to Dutch. He waved the key tauntingly in front of the anthropologist's face, as if asking permission to open it.

'Is she alive?' Dutch's voice quivered. He put the barrel of the Colt up to Hugo's mouth.

'I told you. She's now pure. In God's eyes that makes her alive.'

Therese, over the staccato gurgling in her trachea, could hear noises coming from the other side of the door. She wanted to scream out for help, but her vocal chords were too swollen to emit sounds. Dozens of centipedes were climbing over the mesh screen that covered her body. She could feel their touch on her face as their legs slipped through the minute gaps in the netting. Not too long ago, the arthropods had begun to climb up the stone wall that she was leaning against. To get away from them, she had painfully crawled to the middle of the room.

The voices were coming from the corridor again. One of them she recognized as belonging to Frye. But the other voice?

Dutch . . . it was Dutch!

She tried to scream but only a gargled sound came out of her paralysed throat. Then one of the creatures reached through a small hole in the screen and lightly stroked her bloated tongue with its tail.

'Open it!' Dutch growled. His eyes stung from perspiration. He held the side of Hugo's head against the door with the muzzle of the gun pressed forcibly into his jaw.

'Anything for a soulmate,' Frye said, the smile

remaining clamped on his face. 'How is your breathing, Wilhelm? Are you sure you want to stay here?'

'Open it,' Dutch screamed. His eyes were straining from his sockets. He was now fighting the panic with every ounce of his strength.

'Of course,' Hugo said. He leaned over, unlocked the door and threw it open.

It was dark inside. The corrosive smell of earth and insects unleashed from the room forced Dutch to put his hand up to his mouth. *That deafening hissing noise!* And the other sound. What was it? Like thousands of thin legs crawling along metal. It reminded him of heavy rain hitting the tin roof of the Ohio house when he was a boy. Over that din, there was the slight prattle of something resembling a running brook. No, not a brook. What? It was like someone desperately gasping for air. 'Put the light on!' Dutch yelled. He turned but Hugo was not there. His eyes scanned the basement for him but he was gone.

Putting his hand on the wall inside, he searched for the light switch. He immediately pulled away when he felt the familiar writhing body of a large centipede crawling along it. *Oh, Christ!* Then Dutch remembered that Hugo had used a chain, not a switch, to turn on the light in the basement. Was that put in as a precaution so he wouldn't run his hands against the wall as Dutch just did? If so, then the chain had to be in an easy place to find. He reached up, swooped his hand around in the darkness, and found it at once.

The naked bulb on the ceiling illuminated the room in a blast of burning light. Not prepared for what was inside, Dutch's body immediately jerked back against the damp brick wall of the basement. He stayed frozen like that for several seconds, unable to move.

Inside, the floor seemed to be swaying back and forth under a mass of slinking blackness. In the middle of the room, a mound of skulking centipedes were climbing over each other, trying to get to something underneath them.

The insects by now had begun to make their way towards the open door, spilling out into the basement. Dutch quickly moved out of their way and climbed up on to a stack of boxes next to the wall. In the other room, Dutch could see Frank's skeletal remains in the cage. His red hair was still attached to the skull and the fake diamond stud was in his ear canal.

The black floor seemed to move like a tidal wave towards him, unmasking the grating, exposing Therese's body. The fine netting covered her figure like a veil. Dozens of the centipedes still clung to the mesh, trying to get to her.

Run! Run! his aching lungs screamed at him. Instead, he leaped off the boxes and rushed into the room towards Therese. His boot heels came down on the insects in his path, crushing them.

Be alive! Please be alive!

Sensing the presence of new blood, the arthropods clinging to the mesh turned their open jaws in his direction. Dutch grabbed an end section of the screen and flung it across the room. He looked down at Therese's still body. Her skin, once the colour of cream, was now a deep blue. There was no movement in her limbs and her glassy eyes stared silently up at him.

Be alive!

Reaching down, he touched her hand. It was warm!

As his fingers closed around hers, he could feel there was still life inside her. Over the noise of the centipedes and the humidifier, he heard the slight rasping sound coming from the inside of her chest.

He grabbed her in his arms and carried her out of the room, racing towards the stairs, swerving to avoid the centipedes that were crawling on the ceiling and walls. Dutch became oblivious of their mouths sliding toward him. All he understood was that he had to get Therese out of here.

The steps leading out of the basement were narrow and he had to carry her sideways, with his shoulders brushing up against the wall. He hoped that none of them were up in the darkened stairwell. Dutch knew that he was allergic to their bite, but even that didn't matter right now.

Goddamn it, Therese, breathe!

Time and space had no meaning for him. He felt no pain, no hate, no other human emotions. Nothing cluttered his head except the hunger to keep her alive.

Halfway up the steps, he suddenly realized something: why was the light in the stairwell out? He had made Hugo turn it on before they came down here.

Hugo leaned up against the door in the darkness and looked down at the silhouette of the Dutchman carrying Therese. *Just a few more feet, my twin.* He was holding a rusty coal shovel over his head – one that he had placed next to the old, unused boiler when he first came downstairs to turn up the humidity. He had planned this entire game while Wilhelm was breaking into the house. So far, it had worked perfectly. When the Dutchman got a little closer, he would swing the spade, aiming it at his breastbone. He had killed the father of the twins and Jonathan's old man in the same way. Later, he would get his little pets back into the other room, using Dutch's body as a lure. They would find him delicious. But right now . . .

Wait a minute. Why has he stopped climbing? *Come to me, my soulmate.*

Dutch peered up into the darkness. *You're there, aren't you?* He stood perfectly still, trying to see or hear something over his own forced breathing. Somewhere upstairs, he thought he heard the squeaking of the oak floors under the carpet. Footsteps. Someone else was in the house! The sound was getting louder now, heading towards the basement. Yes, they *were* footsteps! Just as he heard the latch lifting and the door opening, he saw the rusty flat end of the shovel coming down on him like an axeman's blade. He moved his body, but not fast enough. The end nipped him in the forehead.

Still holding Therese, he found himself falling backward, hitting his head and his bandaged ear against the concrete steps as he slid down the stairs. He could feel the hard shells of the centipedes cracking under him.

With Therese on top of him, he hit the bottom of the stairwell. He opened his eyes. There was no real pain at first, just a dull ache and a wetness on the side of his face next to his ear. His mind wanted to close up like a steel curtain and rest but he forced himself to remain conscious. He had to get up! He couldn't lie here. Not with those creatures around. *Move! Stay here and you'll die! Therese will die!*

Then he heard a shout coming from upstairs.

Sitting up, Dutch lifted Therese on his shoulders and slowly raised himself off the floor.

The light in the stairwell went on. Dutch looked up and saw Frye, still grasping the shovel, backing down the steps. Out of the darkness came Ciazo. He was holding his Beretta in front of him.

Frye walked past Dutch, then stopped and looked at him. His lips cracked into a smile. He flicked his eyes back and forth, from the Dutchman to Ciazo, then back again, as if he were thinking. Then his jaw muscles began to relax, as if a decision in his head had been reached. Nodding at Dutch, he whispered, 'Better this way, soulmate. We really are the same, you know.'

Dutch looked up at Jimmy standing on the steps. The Italian cocked the hammer of the gun, aimed and fired. A shot rang out, echoing loudly throughout the basement.

Hugo hit the concrete floor hard, part of his head blown away.

The shell from Ciazo's gun bounced down the steps. Jimmy went after it, picked it up and stuck it in his pocket. He then went over to Hugo's body and poked his fingers into the open head wound, looking for the bullet fragment. He was working fast, trying to find it before the centipedes converged on him. He discovered the lead piece protruding out of the left cerebal hemisphere and popped it out with his thumbs. He then stood up and turned to Dutch. Irritated, he said, 'I told you it would be taken care of. Now get the hell out of here.' A centipede crawled on Jimmy's shoulder and he casually brushed it off like a flake of dandruff.

Forcing his weakened legs to move, the Dutchman raced up the steps past Jimmy. When he reached the landing, he turned and briefly glanced into the basement. Hugo had now disappeared under a film of arthropods. From the top of the steps, they looked like one giant centipede taking on the shape of Hugo's frame. It was as if he had metamorphosed into the only thing he loved.

Gulping air into his scalding lungs, Dutch left the basement and ran down the hallway towards the front door. Flinging it open, he went out on to the lawn and put Therese gently down on the grass. Ciazo's car was next to his truck. He caught a brief glimpse of a tight-mouthed John Payne sitting in the passenger seat.

Dutch turned Therese's face towards his. Her half-open eyes were empty pieces of onyx, but she was still alive. The Dutchman put his lips down on hers and blew what little breath he had in his lungs into her mouth. Somewhere behind him he could sense Ciazo coming out of the house. The Italian picked up two five gallon gas cans next to the door, then went back inside.

Dutch blew again and again into her mouth. As he did, the words of Billie stung his brain like a blistering hailstorm.

Let me rest today
You're blowin' me no good, no good

This time he prayed it would not be an ill wind that he was passing on to her, like the one he had passed on to Max.

He felt the heat of the fire roaring behind him, heard the sound of wood crackling and things exploding. In his head, he also thought he heard the silent screams of centipedes as their bodies shrivelled up in the flames.

Nothing mattered. He only sensed a primeval craving to keep his mate alive. Pressing his hand over Therese's warm fingers, he continued to blow his life into her. Suddenly he felt one of her fingers curl slightly around his own.

Drops of tears ran down his cheeks and fell on to her face.

Was that a trace of a smile forming around her mouth? Max and Therese, he had made both of them smile. He was truly the magic man again.

Epilogue

It was the coldest December ever recorded in Beverly Hills. Palm trees turned brown and died. Sprinkler pipes ruptured under the lawns of mansions, flooding Santa Monica Boulevard, turning it into a river of ice. Rapturous children skidded over it on garbage can covers. Half a block away, frost, like spun silk, covered the grass around the excavation area.

A cab drove up to the site and stopped. Dutch and Tara were inside. Packed duffel bags were jammed in the back seat with them.

'We got a plane to catch in an hour,' Tara said, glancing at her watch.

'I'll only be a minute. Try not to leave without me,' he said, winking. He got out of the taxi and walked across the street, trying not to slip on the ice. A sign with the logo of PAYNE ENTERPRISES hung next to the site.

He looked up at it. 'The sonofabitch knows how to keep his word,' Dutch said out loud to himself.

A couple of days after Hugo was killed, Jonathan phoned Dutch and asked him to meet him at the bar at the Peninsula Hotel. He said they needed to talk. Dutch agreed. When he got there, he found a CLOSED placard on the door of the wood-panelled saloon.

559

Dutch tried the handle. It was open. Payne was sitting alone at a table near the grand piano, drinking a martini. There was no bartender or anyone else in the place. Dutch walked round the bar, took a Corona from the refrigerator behind the counter, opened it, then went over to Payne's table and sat down.

'I'd like to thank you for not reporting the way Hugo Frye was killed.' Payne said, clearing his throat.

Dutch shrugged. He had done the forensics on the charred remains and declared death was by fire. 'That's the way I saw it. There was no bullet found in the body.'

Payne nervously tapped his fingers on the table. 'I'd also like you to forget my involvement with Hugo in Santa Alicia and that I was there the day he was killed. The police don't know anything about that.'

'I guess it wouldn't look good, you running for governor and all,' Dutch said, turning the beer bottle slowly in his hand, studying it.

'You seem to understand the situation.'

'Except, Jonathan, the police already know he worked for you and that he killed Robin and her housekeeper. I told them that. They also found the charred bones of another man in the rubble of Frye's house. Dental records identified him as Frank Barney, a known street hustler. Traces of a neuromuscular blocking agent were found in his remains. Hugo sure as hell loved his little experiments, didn't he?'

Payne waved his hand as if to say all that's taken care of. 'My records will show that I fired Frye a day before the fire. The district attorney is meeting with me in a couple of hours. I'll explain to him that the man was acting strange. I had to get rid of him. He was a loner . . . someone I knew from my home town.

560

He saved my life in Vietnam. I felt sorry for him and gave him a job as my helicopter chauffeur. He'll believe that.'

That story was OK with Dutch. As long as Hugo was dead, it didn't matter how he died or what his real connection was with Payne. Therese was out of intensive care and was expected to live, that was the important thing.

The police blamed the fire on a broken gas main. Ciazo had worked on it, making sure it was faulty before he torched the place. Hugo's death was officially listed as an accident.

'It's forgotten about,' the Dutchman finally said.

Payne did something out of character: he let out a long sigh.

'One thing. Did you know that he killed your father back then? Not suspected, but actually *know*?'

Payne's eyes furled, and a bitter smile swept across his lips. 'That you will never know.'

Dutch nodded. The man had a right to keep that part to himself. He fingered the Corona for a couple more seconds, thinking, then leaned into the table and asked him if the job to head the dig in Tanzania was still open.

'It's filled. But it can always become unfilled,' he said, realizing there was going to be a price for Dutch's silence.

'Unfill it.' Then he asked him if he would help clear some of the obstacles for Therese on her dig.

'How?'

'Enlarge the site. Therese thinks there's something down there. She needs more room to explore.'

'That may cause problems with the city.'

'Problems have never stopped you.'

Again Payne agreed. 'Anything else?'

'No, that's about it.' Dutch got up from the chair. 'Enjoy running California, Mr Governor.' He grinned at the industrialist.

Payne smiled back. They shook hands. An understanding had been reached.

That was three months ago.

As Dutch headed towards the dig now, he turned up the collar on his Navy coat and tucked his hands deep into its pockets to ward off the cold. White streams of air floated out of his mouth.

When he reached the edge of the quarry, he looked down and saw Therese with at least two dozen helpers painstakingly sifting through the dirt with colanders and brushes.

Dutch stood on top of the mound and watched them work. In the three short months since the dig began, Therese had unearthed what might be one of the biggest finds in California. Originally, the artifacts that were uncovered pointed to only a Chumash village. Then Lenny Garowitz began selling Spanish coins to collectors, using the money to rebuild his house. When the authorities questioned him, he told them that he had discovered the pieces on his property, not too far from the hotel site. Therese began to suspect that there might be more than an Indian village there. With John Payne's help, she persuaded the city of Beverly Hills to give her permission to enlarge the excavation site out towards the Garowitzs' property line. So far, over a dozen chests of Spanish jewellery and gold, intermixed with Indian relics, had been taken out of the new quarry. The day before, the workers had dug deeper and found the remnants of a wall which might have been part of an old bastion that pre-dated the Spaniards' arrival in the new land. The archaeological community was euphoric. Who built it? Would part of California's history have to be rewritten?

This was going to be an endless job, Dutch thought. After shaving away the layers of that settlement, they would then have to dig through one hundred centuries of Indian history that was also down there. What would there be after that? The site was an endless pit of evolution. John Payne might never see his beloved hotel built on that ground.

The ancient bones found in the graveyard across the street were now reburied in the Santa Monica Mountains, at a secret spot known only to the Indians and to him. Smokey Pete woke him up at four in the morning one day and drove him and Bobby Santiago, sobered for the occasion, up to the remote area. Dutch watched in silence, along with fifty Indians, as the bones were placed in the graves with the skulls once again pointing towards the west.

The Dutchman wrapped the big collar of his coat further around his neck and walked down into the quarry.

Therese, wearing a hooded sweatshirt, old jeans and rubber boots, was squatting on the dirt floor, digging around a three-foot section of the stone wall. When she saw Dutch, she stood up, brushed herself off and went over to him. Knowing he was leaving for Tanzania today, she forced a tight smile and said indignantly, 'The damn plane's on time. I checked.'

Dutch put his hands up to her face and looked at her. Therese's cheeks were red from the cold and her glasses were covered with dust. She looked tired. Hell, she had almost died three months ago, now she was working fifteen-hour days! He said, 'Why don't you come with me? The plane's empty. I can still get you a ticket. It'll be like it used to be, like the time we found Maybellene together.'

Her eyes turned sad. 'I can't. This is my dig, Dutch. I belong here. Besides, you found the old girl, not me.'

He nodded and let her go. 'You and I, we spend too much time probing the goddamn past. Sometimes I think we need to live in the present too, like we did when Max was alive. I miss it.'

'So do I.' She nestled her head into his chest and held him tightly, warming her body with his. 'How long will you be gone?'

Dutch shook his head. 'Depends on what we find. The human race has been fornicating for millions of years. Lots of bones out there for me to go through.'

She understood. Neither one could easily give up the search for the past. They both understood that somewhere back there was the key to their existence. Biting her lip, trying to suck in her tears, she said, 'Watch that ear, OK?'

Dutch put his hand up to his lobe. Other than a thin scar cutting across it, the ear was entirely healed.

Dutch climbed back up to the street and got into the cab.

'You really up for this?' Tara asked him, seeing the bleak look on his face.

'Yes, I'm up for it,' he said dourly. 'This is what I do for a living, isn't it?' The taxi made a U-turn and passed by the mouth of the quarry going towards the freeway. He sat back and closed his eyes, suppressing the desire to stop the cab and run back to Therese.

Tara also sat back, withholding the news she had heard that morning until they reached the airport's off ramp. Turning and looking at Dutch's sullen face, she said, 'I hear the crew found part of a thoracic vertebrae in Tanzania yesterday that's over three and a half million years old. The rest of the remains can't be too far away.' She waited for his reaction.

Bones older than Maybellene. *Oh, Jesus!* Dutch suddenly smiled. Tara could lift his spirits more than anyone else. His wistful thoughts about Therese took a back seat as he began to think of what the body of this ancient *A. afarensis* might look like.

More Thrilling Fiction from Headline:

—— JONELLEN HECKLER ——
CIRCUMSTANCES UNKNOWN

SHE'S ALREADY LOST HER HUSBAND.
NOW HER CHILD IS AT RISK...

It was supposed to be the perfect family holiday: Tim and Deena Reuschel in a magical cottage up in the mountains with their five-year-old son Jon. But the idyll ends in nightmare when Tim's body is found washed up on the river bank. Despite the circumstances, Deena refuses to accept that the tragedy was an accident and when her suspicions are casually dismissed by the police, she begins her own exploration of Tim's past, searching for connections to her husband's death.

But someone else is taking a close interest in Deena's investigation. Someone whose twisted obsessions are focussed on the young woman and her precious son. And with every clue she manages to uncover, Deena brings herself and Jon closer and closer to mortal danger...

'A superb mystery thriller' *Woman and Home*

'A suspense tale that draws the reader in from the first line' Mary Higgins Clark

'Chilling suspense as the killer's psychotic personality steadily deteriorates' *Publishers Weekly*

FICTION/THRILLER   0 7472 4133 3

PHILIP CAVENEY
SPEAK NO EVIL

THE LATE-NIGHT WHISPER
FROM HELL...

Radio presenter Tom Prince hosts the graveyard slot: the after-midnight phone-in programme for Manchester's *Metrosound*. Despite a broken marriage, he now finds personal happiness with a caring girlfriend and his seven-year-old son Danny. Otherwise Tom is stuck in a rut...and about to be hurtled out of it with terrifying momentum.

It begins with just another late-night call, from a man who talks in a strange whisper. But this one claims he has committed a murder, and is standing over his victim's corpse.

Thus begins a chilling nightly dialogue between Tom and 'the Whisperer'. Badgered by police intent on tracing the killer, Tom reluctantly keeps the line open, while the gruesome deaths continue. And as his audience constantly grows, he suddenly finds himself a celebrity.

Though Tom himself is the focus of this terrifying bloodlust, his child and his girlfriend are soon exposed to extreme danger – never knowing from which dark shadow the next surprise blow will fall.

And as he begins to understand the full horror of the Whisperer's psychosis, Tom realises that his success may cost them all too high a price.

FICTION/THRILLER   0 7472 4045 0

A selection of bestsellers from Headline

GONE	Kit Craig	£4.99 ☐
QUILLER SOLITAIRE	Adam Hall	£4.99 ☐
NOTHING BUT THE TRUTH	Robert Hillstrom	£4.99 ☐
FALSE PROPHET	Faye Kellerman	£4.99 ☐
THE DOOR TO DECEMBER	Dean Koontz	£5.99 ☐
BRING ME CHILDREN	David Martin	£4.99 ☐
COMPELLING EVIDENCE	Steve Martini	£5.99 ☐
SLEEPING DOGS	Thomas Perry	£4.99 ☐
CHILDREN OF THE NIGHT	Dan Simmons	£4.99 ☐
CAPITAL CRIMES	Richard Smitten	£4.99 ☐
JUDGEMENT CALL	Suzy Wetlaufer	£5.99 ☐

All Headline books are available at your local bookshop or newsagent, or can be ordered direct from the publisher. Just tick the titles you want and fill in the form below. Prices and availability subject to change without notice.

Headline Book Publishing PLC, Cash Sales Department, Bookpoint, 39 Milton Park, Abingdon, OXON, OX14 4TD, UK. If you have a credit card you may order by telephone — 0235 831700.

Please enclose a cheque or postal order made payable to Bookpoint Ltd to the value of the cover price and allow the following for postage and packing:
UK & BFPO: £1.00 for the first book, 50p for the second book and 30p for each additional book ordered up to a maximum charge of £3.00.
OVERSEAS & EIRE: £2.00 for the first book, £1.00 for the second book and 50p for each additional book.

Name ....

Address ....

....

....

If you would prefer to pay by credit card, please complete:
Please debit my Visa/Access/Diner's Card/American Express (delete as applicable) card no:

Signature ....Expiry Date ....